Spirits & Shards
FALLING

A J Hawkins

Christine,
Enjoy!
Ade Hawkins

Copyright © Adrian Hawkins 2014
Cover art by Cristian Popa
All rights reserved.

The right of Adrian Hawkins to be identified as the author of this work has been asserted by him in accordance with
Copyright, Designs and Patents Act 1988.

Published by Zengoth Publishing,
An imprint of GMTA Publishing
First published in 2012
This edition 2014

ISBN-13 9780957324299

No part of this book may be reproduced in any form without the author's express consent.
This book is a work of fiction and any similarities to actual persons and/or places are purely coincidental.

GMTA Publishing
http://www.gmtapublishing.com
www.zenpub.org

My sincerest thanks go out to all those whose belief in me never faltered, especially my ever-supportive wife, BJ. Without her, you would not be reading this now.
You kept me going when the dark doubts crept in.
An extra special thanks goes out to all those who, in one way or another, helped me improve this novel more than I thought possible.

-Notes-

Welcome to Silandrius.

There are many tales to be told in this world, some large and epic, some small and personal. This is one of the latter.

Although there are many similarities to our world, there are many notable differences too.

For example, time here is decimalised: there are ten hours in a day, one hundred minutes in an hour, and one hundred seconds in a minute. There are ten days in a week, five weeks in a month, and ten months in a year.

Days of the week are referenced by number, from one-day to ten-day.

Silandrian numerals are also quite unique, as you will see by the chapter numbering.

There are many other differences, but I'll leave the joy of discovering those to you.

Enjoy.

-Timeline-

As the series progresses, a timeline will slowly be revealed to help keep track of the myriad events that have occurred throughout Silandrian history.

The date at the beginning of this tale is 28/07/25032.

"It's astonishing sometimes just how quickly everything can change. Thing stays the same for years, then out of nowhere comes one big rush… after that, people move on, and it's nothing more than a memory. An ever-dulling echo we fear to forget, lest we lose sight of ourselves."

-Kol Solborn

-Prologue-

Horran Venura seated himself in one of the black lunim and darkwood chairs inside the cavernous conference room, apprehensively wondering why Vincenul Miriandus had called him into Corp HQ. A private meeting with a member of the board was never a good omen, and Vince in particular had a notorious reputation for putting people in unenviable positions.

"Morning, Horran," the parasitic rapid-climber greeted upon entering the room, his cocked head wearing that malevolent-looking oleaginous smile. The air of cocksure smugness he wore fit him even better than his exorbitantly expensive impeccably-tailored all-black Vahirinese-style suit. The only flash of colour in his entire getup was provided by a douchebag razor-thin red tie. Vince was an abhorrent man, having facilitated some of the greatest atrocities of recent times, all in the name of progress. His greatest achievement was that the vast majority of the good people of Darina City didn't know about it. "How are you this fine morning?"

"I'm a busy man, Vince. Get to the point."

"Straight to business," Vince noted as he sat next to Horran, ignoring the other twenty-two vacant seats lining each side of the long, gently convex-sided table. "That's what I've always liked about you." Every word was laced with sweet poison, but Horran was certain Vince knew nothing of his work. But then, megalomaniacs knew how to get what they wanted. "But there's no need to rush. I know so little about you. Tell me about yourself. What have you been up to lately?"

Horran glared at his considerably younger 'boss' impatiently. When the silence persisted, he braced his palms on the table's shiny waxed surface and scraped his chair back as he rose. "I don't have time for this." Few others could get away with such insolence.

"Okay, cool your jets," Vince soothed amiably, "no need to be so impatient." Despite there being no one else and no recording equipment in the room, Vince spoke in little more than a whisper. "I've got a new toy hot from the lab, real miraculous breakthrough stuff, and I need a top neurologist to give it a whirl. I'm told you fit that bill."

Horran relaxed back into his seat, regarding Vince dubiously over the top of his spectacles. It bothered him that there were developments happening in his specific field of expertise that were being kept from him, but he tried not to let his frustration be known by either his facial expression or his tone of voice. He was also far too sagacious to be won over by a little ego-massaging. "And what exactly is it you want me to 'give a whirl'?"

Vince slipped a half-inch-wide, inch-long flat metal tin from his suit jacket's inside pocket and passed it to Horran. "This new wonder-drug, the fabled key to cognitive rejuvenation."

Horran was stunned silent for a few moments. He took the tin, but daren't open it. "You mean... someone actually cracked it? At long last..." How many lives had been ruined in the pursuit of this one formula, this fabled elixir? Maybe at long last it would all be worth it, as long as they could save more minds than they'd already lost.

"It took more man years than I can count. The simulations have been incredibly positive. Instantly beneficial. This is from batch PSI six-two-six."

"Catchy," Horran mocked as he studied the silvery tin in awe. As much as he hated to admit it, even to himself, his curiosity *was* piqued. He even knew precisely the right person to test this on. He just sincerely hoped it lived up to such lofty promises. "Anyone could do this. What's so special about me? There's something you're not telling me. This does something else, doesn't it? Yet you'll keep me in the dark because knowing would pervert the results."

"Precisely. You're a very astute man, Horran Venura." As if having somehow heard his earlier thought, Vince added, "Listen, I heard you worked wonders with a patient who survived exposure to OX-double-one-seven a few years ago."

Horran flashed an expression of indignation. That case was supposed to be confidential. "What of it?" Who blabbed? Who couldn't he trust?

"Hey, relax, we're all friends here. It was a risky procedure, one that worked wonders despite the odds. Few others could have pulled it off. It proves that you're the perfect neurologist with access to the perfect candidate. Send a remote pulse to that little implant of his, give him a little headache. Do what you have to do to bring him to you. Give him those, keep a close eye on him, and feed me the results. You know how important this is."

Horran sat in silent contemplation for a moment. If he said no, Vince would pick someone else, probably someone who lacked the expertise he possessed.

Vince leaned so close their shoulders almost touched, speaking even softer. "Come on, Horran. I know you want to test these."

Horran stared at Vince mistrustfully. He'd rather try them on himself, but he still had far too much to do to risk his own life just yet. "These drugs will help him?"

"And then some!" Vince laughed in that overly-genial manner Horran truly detested. "The lab results were *very* positive. *Amazingly* positive. We just need to perform a little field test, take it to the next level."

"And they won't cause him any harm, will they?"

"I wouldn't ask you to do this if they weren't safe." Vince held his hands up, palms forwards. "What do you take me for?"

That's what I'm afraid of.

What choice did he have? "Alright. But on one condition, and I want your word on this — if *anything* goes wrong, you'll put it right, no matter the cost." Horran held his hand out.

Vince grinned widely, baring his pearly whites. He shook Horran's hand firmly. "Absolutely."

I
-Half-Life-

Having survived yet another week stewing in the bowels of hell he called work, Jerin Endersul finally arrived home, of light mind, heavy body and weary soul. He dismounted his heavily rust-speckled bicycle, lolled his head back and let out a long sigh of pure relief. At least the sensation of sickness had passed now. His thoughts were dominated by one gratifying thought: *Three nights off...* it had been a long arduous week, but at least it was behind him now.

Who knew, he might even get to spend some time with his increasingly phantasmagoric partner. *Yeah right, that'll be the day.*

Right now, only one obstacle stood between him and respite: that damned door.

He put his bicycle behind the warped gate and unlocked the door easily enough, but when he tried to open it, the damned handle wouldn't budge, as ever.

He tried Juli's advice of lifting it then trying again, but to no avail. He just didn't speak the esoteric language of doors. He was going to have to resort to the only method left to him: brute force.

He backed up against the mesh fence only about a metre opposite, summoned what dregs of energy remained, braced his right shoulder and charged. The momentary clamour as the door flew open and rebounded off the hallway wall was obstreperous on that otherwise perfectly silent early weekend morning. Jerin might have felt bad about it had the only person liable to be woken by the ruckus not been the one responsible. He doubted it would motivate the lazy self-serving swine upstairs to fix it though.

Physically and mentally depleted, the last of the steam he'd been running on now well and truly gone, he stepped into the not-very-warm flat, flicked the light switch, hung his keys on the wall-mounted hook, and waited for the light to rise from a dim filament glow to something he could barely see by.

He wearily drooped his right shoulder, his tattered backpack dropping to the floor with an empty thud. He swayed, bracing his left arm against the peeling-papered cold wall to wait out the ephemeral loss of balance and vision. Working while all the sensible people slept was something he never had gotten used to, but he hadn't felt this bad since first trying to acclimate nearly three years ago. Why was it suddenly getting so hard again? Why couldn't life just leave him alone?

When the fuzziness passed, he slipped his coat off and lifted it towards its hook, his arm growing heavier with every passing second. He thrust the coat forwards and it lopsidedly came to rest. *Close enough.*

He stepped into the front room, activating the battery-powered lamps, one sat atop each of the three bookcases spaced around the room. He threw a brief, contemptuous glance at the shelf that bowed beneath her myriad folders heaving with corporate crap. He couldn't remember the last time he'd come home to her since she'd decided it was time to start 'climbing' that seemingly endless corporate ladder, constantly assuring him that all these early starts and late finishes would be worth it in the end. It was a wonder she wasn't more tired than he, and he certainly wouldn't stay on for so much as an extra minute beyond the end of his shift, not for free. What was the point? He only worked to earn a wage, and a year on, Juli still had nothing to show for her 'investment' but her continual absence. If he recalled correctly, her dubious-sounding 'provisional promotional assessment' was today. What did that even mean? It would be a miracle if it actually amounted to anything.

He rubbed his right temple absently as the persistent dull throb sharpened, piercing the shroud of fatigue, his last painkiller a distant memory. He headed to the kitchen for a swig of faux-milk straight from the bottle, spotting a bright green post-it note stuck lopsidedly to the fridge door, the black felt-tip scribblings barely legible: 'Sorry if it's a little dry. X'

Good ole Juli. He'd be emaciated if not for her, too tired to fix himself something when he wasn't too tired to feel hunger.

As he wondered what tasty treat might lie within, his stomach gurgled vacuously and he began to salivate, but his stomach churned and he recoiled as his nostrils were met by a mildly putrid stench. He saw what looked like a lump of rock in a puddle of mud. No, worse, it looked like a pile of faeces. He quickly took it out and closed the fridge before he let too much cold out.

Nostalgia brought a slight smile to his face when he realised it was a whole breast of phesan marinated in teriyaki sauce. They hadn't made that in years. The sauce was to mask the faintly rotten tang of the cheap meat they bought, this particular breast having sat in the freezer for at least a month, the fluctuating power insufficient to maintain a consistent temperature in the fridge-freezer, causing it to slowly soften before refreezing each week, giving him cause to wonder whether Juli had got it hot enough to kill all of those unseen germs.

If it *was* crawling with salmonella or who-knows-what, at least it would score him a few extra nights off, though he wouldn't be able to enjoy them knowing he couldn't afford it. He would soon discover he needn't have worried: it was so overcooked he doubted the meat's entire moisture content amounted to as much as a single drop.

Now that the worst of the smell had passed and he had actual food before him, he realised just how famished he was, and any deity you could care to mention knew they couldn't afford to waste it. He unenthusiastically studied the slightly crystallised sauce.

Since the cold might mute the soured flavour, he decided against reheating it. He took a knife and fork from the drawer and attempted to cut into it, but the dark outer shell was as hard as plastarch. He stabbed the fork hard into the top, lifting the plate with it. It would have been funny if it wasn't so disgusting. He put it back down and slowly forced the knife between plate and food, twisting it and freeing his dubious prize with a loud *snap* before lifting it towards his mouth, retching as its vile aroma hit the back of his throat anew. He held his breath and went for it.

His teeth fought heavy resistance to rip a thick strip free. It tasted bitterly rotten and became repulsively slimy as the sauce rehydrated upon mixing with his saliva. Shrapnel-like fragments broke free, scraping his oesophagus when he swallowed. He choked, fumbling for the nearest countertop drink, swigging straight from the bottle. The flavour combination was sickening. In his blind haste he'd grabbed cheap store-brand 'cola', more akin to sugared shit.

Though he was loathe to waste such a rare and costly treat, he couldn't stomach another bite. Despite all meat being lab-grown, he couldn't shake the mysteriously pervasive mental image of a just-dead bird lying on the side of the road with a tread-mark over its head, the culprit scraping it from the asphalt with a blood-and-rust-speckled shovel before selling it from the back of that same archaic van.

Much as it pained him to do so, he dropped the virtually inedible lump into the bin and decided to call it a day, deactivating the lamps as he headed towards bed via the bathroom, where he zealously scrubbed his teeth and tongue in a desperate bid to remove all traces of the repugnant aftertaste, gargling mouthwash strong enough to strip paint for a full minute, somehow only making it worse.

He sat on the side of the bed, the head-throb building to a crescendo. If he could get some sleep, even just a little, he might be able to stop it from becoming a full-blown migraine. He slipped his woefully outdated compu-phone from his right-front trouser pocket, setting an alarm for that afternoon. If the capricious, bug-ridden thing failed to go off today, he would likely smash it in a frustrated rage; he couldn't afford to miss this appointment. Since making it two months ago, the pain level had increased exponentially. Though there were other neurological consultants, none understood Jerin's condition like Mr Venura, and he was a difficult man to pin down.

At least in Juli's absence he didn't have to hide the pain, wincing and groaning as his mind and body once more became dissonant as he clumsily tried to fumble into his pyjamas, fatigue-numbed limbs stubbornly refusing to comply. He gave up, throwing his bedclothes aside, rolling under the duvet onto the stone-cold mattress in his boxers and t-shirt, raising his knees to his chest for warmth.

He was already dreaming before he was asleep, visions of last night's little furore seeping back into his mind, and he was far too exhausted to rebel.

*

"What's your problem?" Marv asked in his most pompous managerial tone, leaning forwards with his elbows propped on his desk's edge, hands clasped, face wearing that annoyingly smarmy grin.

Jerin said nothing, his gaze fixed on the bare red-brick wall opposite. There was no point; Marv was completely impervious to logic and reason, and incapable of empathy.

"Wren says you nearly smashed a mug then remarked that it was better than smashing someone's face. Was that a threat?"

No, it was a simple fact, you fuckwit! But aside from a nasal sigh, he remained silent.

Marv sighed impatiently. "Would you care to enlighten me as to what prompted this outburst?"

What had happened was very simple: Marv had once again ignored Jerin's pleas, and the wenches had been their typically loud and obnoxious selves, inevitably building to the point where Jerin could no longer physically bear it, causing him to explode in a fit of rage. Trying to warn Marv that he wasn't feeling especially great was always fruitless; Marv never listened, and he never learned.

Jerin had still said nothing. There was no point; he knew exactly where that avenue of conversation led.

Marv slouched into his dull grey high-backed office chair. "I took the liberty of reviewing your performance over the past few weeks, and I've noticed that you've been getting progressively slower."

Jerin hated that smarmy persona, but he knew exactly how to test it. "Am I really? That's weird, because I thought I was working with the pace of the conveyor belt. You can't actually go any quicker than that, so I fail to see how that makes me 'slow'. In fact, the last time I checked, I was the only one capable of doing the job to a standard I would personally consider acceptable."

"Jerin, has anyone ever told you that you can be a touch arrogant?"

"Only arrogant idiots who feel the need to project their insecurities onto someone else to make themselves feel better. There's quite a difference between that and frustration, but I wouldn't want to mess with your warped, narrow world view."

Marv bristled, grinning through clenched teeth, but didn't rise to it. "It's been noted that you have a habit of frequently stopping the belt and disappearing from your station."

"Has it, now? Could that possibly be because Falz is incapable of clearing the stacks of filled trays, so I have to stop the belt and do it for him? Tell me, when you were reviewing these files, what exactly did they say about Fabulous Falz?"

"He's being dealt with," Marv replied with a listless sigh.

I've yet to see any evidence to support that theory. "I mean, does he do *anything*?"

"He's being dealt with," through gritted teeth. Jerin had expected Marv to snap; he hated hearing Jerin moan about Falz as much as Jerin hated the very idiot in question.

But, of course, *Falz* was Sundrosian, *he* could get away with anything. As could those way past their prime, such as Gan, who held everything dangerously close to his face yet insisted he didn't need his sight corrected. Or Fran, whose tongue permanently protruded from the corner of her mouth. And what about Hinges, Motormouth and Shit-For-Brains, the trio of Moronic Wenches who were always so busy yakking and cackling shrilly at ear-splitting volume that they missed components which then had to be collected and sent round again? What excuse did they have? But whenever he mentioned anyone else, all he got in reply was, "Other people have it worse than you." *Yeah, that's just what I need to hear when I'm in pain; that someone else's problems are more valid than mine. Thank you very much.* Jerin was the only one who never seemed to catch a break.

Case in point were the number of times Marv had pulled Jerin aside for not being cleanly shaved. Jerin replied that it didn't exactly matter and that the floor manager Kaxan had a beard, but Marv simply stated that a full beard wasn't the same as the "designer stubble" he accused Jerin of having, when it was simply a matter of Jerin being too exhausted to stand before the mirror to perform the pointless, monotonous task.

Jerin needed to get away from this circus. Marv was a keen advocate of the ancient management maxim: *Never back down, never admit your mistakes*.

What did he have against Jerin? This wasn't about his work ethic, this was personal. Marv had a grudge against him, just because he refused to agree when Marv called a spade a broom.

"I'd like Roz to sit in," Jerin stated.

"That isn't necessary," Marv replied. "This isn't an official meeting."

"I insist. It's my right as a member of the union."

Marv made no secret of the fact that he hated the union. If you were a member, you were against the company, and thus nothing more than an ungrateful heathen.

"Well Roz isn't here tonight, so let's settle this trifling little matter between us, shall we?"

"If she isn't here then we'll have to adjourn."

Marv's patience was waning. "Just tell me what the problem is."

"What's the point? You never listen to a word I say."

"Then why don't you enlighten me?"

Jerin sighed. "You know how irritable I can get. I can't help it. If you'd just let me take my breaks at different times..."

"You know what I think about that. It fractures the team into little cliques."

It was too late for that in the wenches' case, but Jerin knew he was going to have to make it even simpler for Marv to get it. The problem was he knew exactly how Marv would respond. "At the very least, I just need to get away from the noise of the canteen." *The people in the canteen* was more accurate.

"Do you now?" Marv asked, leaning forwards in fevered anticipation, that smarmy grin spreading across his face again. "And why is that?"

"Don't be an arse, Marv. You *know* my medical history. You *know* I have a problem with the low frequencies when you pump that shitty excuse for music into a microphone and out through those tinny speakers. It makes my head hurt, and it makes me nauseous." It was impossible to explain pain to someone who had never experienced it. In an effort to reach Marv, Jerin asked, "Have you ever suffered from travel sickness?"

"I can't say that I have."

Like you'd admit it if you had.

"Lucky you. Well, it's much like that. After a while it becomes so debilitating that I struggle to maintain my balance, and every iota of energy disappears, so *of course* I get grouchy and slow." He was sick of the repetition; it really was like talking to an exceptionally slow child. *No, Johnny, don't put your hand on the hot stove top.*

Marv donned his pompous cap and predictably replied, "If your headaches are returning, we'll have to assess whether it's suitable for you to continue working here," missing the point so spectacularly he should have been a banker. The biggest problem Jerin had when dealing with Marv was that the self-important tosser always acted as though he was the smartest person in the room. In the case of most of his colleagues that was probably true, but that hardly made it acceptable behaviour.

Jerin's hands flew up in exasperation. *Moron!* It was as though Marv's very soul had slowly been expunged from his rear end after so many years of filling up on dry, insipid corporate cake.

What Terrengus Corp idiot ever saw fit to instate a mindless drone like *this* as a manager? Marv was so naïve and brain-washed that Jerin could picture him taking his horrendously unflattering coveralls home if it was allowed, eating in them, sleeping in them... even making love in them, were there women of low enough self esteem to be with such a prig. As far as Jerin could tell, becoming a manager was less about actual ability and more about how much one could suck the corporate cock without choking.

Jerin struggled to contain his gradually-building temper. "See, this is what I mean when I say you don't listen."

"But you just said..."

"That the music was the root cause of the problem."

Marv was clearly confused. "But in the canteen...?"

"I wouldn't even have had a headache if not for the noise you insist on making."

A look of contempt slowly narrowed Marv's eyes. "But people enjoy the music. Is it fair to them if I turn it off for *you?*"

Jerin snorted a derisive laugh.

"Did I say something funny?"

"Hilarious."

"Perhaps you could enlighten me." *That* word again, the staple of his false benevolence routine.

"Skipping the part where you clearly think it's fair to make me suffer, I suggest you hold a vote to see how many people even *want* that shitty short playlist repeated over and over, night after night. I've never heard *anyone* utter a single word of appreciation when you put it on, but I hear a lot of weary groans."

"This isn't a democracy. This is *my* shift."

Ooh, get you! I am manager, hear me roar!

Jerin knew better than to try appealing to Marv's humanity. If he had so much as a semblance of it, it was buried too deep to ever be found. He asked earnestly, "Marv, my head hurts and I feel sick, could you *please* just turn it off just for tonight?"

Marv sighed, a sign that he was finally ready to come to a compromise. "I trust you'll be seeing the doctor on one of your days off," not even trying to make it sound like a question.

"No, I just thought I'd carry on feeling ill, actually. I just love having a constant headache so much. I'd suggest you give it a try, but maybe you have one too, maybe that's why you're such an insufferable dolt all the time." Marv glared at him. In a serious-yet-impatient tone, Jerin explained, "I made an appointment a couple of months ago, which I did tell you at the time, not that you care enough to even try remembering. That appointment happens to be later today, actually."

"Good. Then I'll be expecting you to be more compliant upon your return."

"Does that mean you'll actually turn the music off then?"

Marv took a moment to consider this. "Alright. Fine. But just for tonight. But I expect to see an improvement in your working speed when you return. And if a *single person* complains that it's too quiet, the music's going back on."

Hardly the definition of 'fair'.

Jerin rolled over in bed, trying to swat the dream from his mind, to no avail. He saw Marv's perturbed visage with enhanced lucidity.

"Who are you to tell me how fast to work? You can't even *do* my job, so shut up until you know what you're on about!" Jerin shouted at Marv, taking control of the dream.

There was a series of mechanical clicks and hisses. After a moment, Marv answered in a monotone voice, "It is my job to tell you how to do your job, nothing more."

"Bingo!" Jerin smiled. "By definition, you're a waste of space!"

"We aren't here to talk about me."

"No, we're here so that you can tell me that I should be able to do something you can't. Why don't you go fuck yourself?"

Marv's face was stricken by a 'this-does-not-compute' wide-eyed slack-jawed expression as he struggled to find a suitable reply within his corporate lexicon. Steam began bellowing from his ears and his jaw dropped off of some unseen hinges, revealing broken coils of spring. Then his eyeballs ejected from their sockets.

Jerin rose from his seat and turned away from this bizarre effigy, lucid enough to know that none of this was real. He reached for the door's polished metal handle, casting a perfect reflection of his approaching hand, when he heard a klaxon blaring behind him. He turned back as Marv's entire head slowly began rotating counter-clockwise, accelerating until it became a whirring blur that slowly turned grey. It stopped abruptly, its face now covered with crudely-riveted overlapping squares of metal plating, complete with glowing red eyes, a speaker box for a mouth, and pincers for hands.

Marv-o-tron took a sheet of paper from the desk in its

right pincer then telescopically extended his arm across the room until the sheet was hanging before Jerin's face, shaking it for dramatic effect. "This piece of paper says you should be faster!" The metal face began to glow red hot as steam once more bellowed from those now-unseen ears. "So go faster!"

Jerin struggled to restrain an amused smile. "Oh, okay. If a piece of paper says it, then it must be true. Tell the piece of paper that it can have a go at doing my job if it thinks it can do better. You're an idiot and a waste of space, Marv. So long."

Jerin opened the door and stepped through. As the darkness beyond engulfed him, he thought, *One day, I'll tell the real thing what I think of him.*

*

Jerin woke abruptly a full hour before his alarm was due to go off, still exhausted after just seventy-five minutes but frustratedly aware that he wouldn't be able to fall asleep again if he tried. The fading echo of a nightmare clung to the edge of his mind briefly, the booming words *I will reclaim you* quickly evaporating entirely.

Hazy beams of dim light fanned above the sagging blackout curtains, affording him just enough light to see his lamp switch. He flicked it and recoiled from the comparatively harsh light.

Though it was cold enough to see his breath, both quilt and mattress were sodden with the same sweat that stuck his t-shirt to his skin. He shivered as he reluctantly uncovered himself, immediately succumbing to a sneezing fit, each nasal eruption more violent than the last, amplifying the lingering echo of his headache greatly. He grabbed a tissue from the open box atop his bedside drawer and blew. He felt lousy.

Whatever sleep he managed to snatch on his nights off was never enough to catch up from the lack of it over the week before, causing a permanent fatigue-malaise which made him feel like he was twenty-seven going on sixty. He shuddered; if he felt this bad now, how the hell would he cope when he reached that age? As it was he seemed to pick up virtually every cough and sniffle doing the rounds, his immune system well and truly shot to bits. He'd quickly discovered sleeping tablets didn't help either, only offering a short, dreamless chemical coma that had seen him snooze through his alarm more than once.

Not that most would even be aware just how tired he typically was. He'd become annoyingly accustomed to it, though it became increasingly agitating when his memory went on holiday, his coordination pulled a vanishing act, and his motor skills took their leave, leading to him dropping everything he touched and often losing his balance.

As his feet landed heavily on the faded, flattened sickly-green carpet, he felt the slosh of fluid inside his skull cavity. He *hated* that sensation; it often followed a particularly harsh headache. He hoped it would pass quickly; it usually did, but occasionally it lingered for a few days.

He donned his heavily bobbled navy blue fleece from atop his dusty old easel in the corner by the window, managing only a languid shuffle to the toilet, sure his sweat was freezing rather than evaporating. He'd be shivering all day as the prevalent cold of those dark days worked its way deep into his muscles, all the way down to the bone. Even if their heaters had been man enough to stave it off, their selfish landlord siphoned most of the power for himself, necessitating the conservation of what little power they had to keep the food frozen by sitting in the dark by the dim light of those lamps, which he activated on his way to the kitchen to boil some water for tea now and cold drinks later. He and Juli couldn't reason with their landlord without him bringing up the issue of owed rent, so they'd given up trying.

Jerin sat on the sofa, expanding his phone to tablet size, always amazed by its transmogrification from five- to ten-inch display. In a bid to distract himself from ruminating over the issues at work, he opened the sketching app and tried to remember some of the transient ideas that flowed through his head during the tedium of his mindless job, frustrated that he so often forgot them before he had a chance to note them down. All of those ideas still eluded him now. Worse, that damned infuriating meeting with Marv kept replaying over and over in his mind until he became so agitated he shouted, "Enough!"

He massaged his right temple and tried to recall something more recent. When nothing came to him, he cast his mind back to the single recurring idea that yearned to find its way onto the screen, but he just couldn't envision it as vividly as he once had. He cursed his mind's inability to guide his clumsy hands as he made one mistake after another, forcing him to draw in short, staggered lines. After several minutes, all he saw was a sketchy, indistinct mess, further compounding his already dire state of mind.

Perhaps it would be better to consume rather than create for the time being. He remembered an artists' group Riccardo had told him about via *BestBuddies.com* a few days ago, hoping that a quick glance might offer some inspiration. Juli didn't 'get' art, his or anyone else's, citing contemporary art as "pretentious rubbish," a point which he largely conceded, admitting that many of her examples could indeed have been painted by a supposedly autistic child. He later discovered that some of them *were*, while others were painted by the shameless parents of similarly-afflicted children.

He felt a rush of excitement upon seeing he had a message from his recently-added artist friend, Jezebel. He opened it eagerly; she had attached a non-watermarked rough sketch of a Vahirinese behemoth dwarfed by the mountaintops it stood amongst. Though it was only a conceptual piece, it left him feeling paradoxically both inspired yet inadequate.

He typed a congratulatory message, expressing his regrets over not living in such a culturally-rich area from which to draw inspiration, lamenting the limitations of life within the city in a bubble. He wanted to say more, but fatigue had once more shut the mental door marked 'vocabulary', leaving him fumbling for words that were on the edge of his mind.

He checked his neglected email inbox, overflowing with the usual dross, many of which were the now-ignored daily messages from a job website he signed up to about a year ago. Since he hadn't read any for a while, he opened the latest, not expecting much. He wasn't disappointed: *cleaner, accounts manager, marketing director, cleaning assistant...* the dichotomy of them might have been hilarious had it not been so galling. He remembered now why he'd stopped opening those emails in the first place. Even if he could find something suitable that miraculously paid enough, fitting an interview around working nights presented its own logistical nightmare. One woman even assumed he didn't need sleep, erroneously stating that he had "all day" to attend one.

Who am I kidding, who would hire a brain-dead moron anyway?

He hastily deleted the messages and put his phone away with a sigh. Just thinking about money and the future made him feel physically sick. If only he could endure the sleep-deprivation-born muscle fatigue and the ennui of his crappy job until their financial situation stabilised... but depression was a bitch, and her claws dug deep, right down to the bone. No, deeper than that — into the very soul. He had to purge every thought of work from his mind. If he even thought about the drudgery of the coming working week, he would lose the will to live.

Sometimes, all he knew were the energy-sapping twins, desolation and despair. He'd contemplated suicide more than once. All he had to do was get a sharp knife from the kitchen and make one quick, deep slash across his left wrist, and it would quickly all be over. But knowing his luck, the blade would be blunt, he'd fail, and people would mistake it as a cry for help. That fear of failure was almost as paralysing as the affliction itself. But even contemplating ending it felt like cheating, like skipping to the last page of a mystery novel. The destination was the same, but you missed the entire journey; that sense of awe in discovering something unexpected and good. But those moments were very far and few between in his life right now.

Besides, that was the coward's way out, wasn't it? Everyone said it was selfish. He guessed maybe it was. And in his heart, he knew he couldn't do it to Juli. He sometimes imagined how he'd feel if he came home to find she'd taken her own life without so much as talking to him first.

He wanted to talk to her about it, he really did, but how could he possibly broach a subject like that? *Hi, dear, I love you and all, but sometimes I just want to kill myself.* If not for her, he wondered how long ago he would have given in to the dark thoughts, the inability to think beyond today, the chilling dread of setting foot inside that depressing building yet again. He'd long ago lost count of just how many times he'd wanted to walk out. Too many, that was for sure. What was even the point of living when he had next to no joy left?

He tried to push those thoughts from his mind and convince himself that it wasn't all bad. They paid the bills on time, even had enough spare to go out on occasion, but he felt like he was living to work rather than working to live. No, scratch that; what he was doing could hardly be called living. All he was succeeding in doing was surviving. It was just a shame that existing and occupying space weren't marketable skills; they were pretty much the only things he was good at. Thank goodness Juli was able to pull him from his predominantly dour mood every now and then, typically with a quick romp beneath the sheets that made him forget the world for just a short while, but thanks to his recent recurrence of headaches it had been a while since they'd last done that, and he had to be so careful not to get her pregnant. This wasn't the right environment in which to raise a child, no matter how much she wanted one. He didn't want to bring another mouth into this world knowing they'd struggle to feed it. People who did that made him sick. And besides, what kind of a father would he make, anyway? *Not a good one, that's for sure.* He just didn't have the patience for children.

He closed his eyes, his mind drifting once more to the sheer futility of human endeavour and the freedom and serenity granted by death. He could only imagine the peace that he had never known his whole life, which had always felt like some kind of waking dream. His old friend Kol had said something similar one night, after one too many bottles of drascas, but the subject had never come up again. Perhaps they were both too worried about sounding stupid.

Jerin was lacking for money and the knowledge and confidence to do anything about it, but one thing he certainly wasn't lacking was regret. He had an abundance of that, and more to spare. All those years he wasted… he could have done something, gone down a better path… what, he didn't know, but something. *Anything.* He could have. He *should* have.

If I could start over, I'd do it all differently. But it was so easy to say in hindsight.

He reminded himself that, eventually, all he knew, all *anyone* knew, would be gone, and the experiences of all people will have been for nothing. Everything would disappear back into the aether from whence it came, and perhaps the universe would start over. In the end, no one was any more than mere flesh and blood. Death was the great equaliser of all.

Right now, that was a strangely comforting thought.

He glanced at his watch, and guessed he should probably start heading to the clinic. He wrapped up and set out.

*

After a long lethargic walk, Jerin finally reached his destination, the cold of the air having made his sniffle considerably worse along the way.

At least he didn't have to sit in the waiting room for long, having arrived just in time. His name flashed up on the board, and he quickly paced to room six, the one at the end of the beige door-lined corridor, ever the one that was farthest away.

"Ah, Mr Endersul, please take a seat," Mr Venura invited warmly, gesturing to the empty faded grey plastarch bucket-style seat beside his corner desk, regarding Jerin over the top of his chrome-rimmed spectacles. Jerin hadn't seen him for a couple of years, but the man so highly qualified that his title had ironically reverted from 'Dr' back to 'Mr' hadn't changed: he still used paper and ink (from the same pen!), had the same haircut, though it was a paler shade of grey now, and still refused to undergo corneal regeneration. It made Jerin smile to see the distinctive titanium ring with its shiny middle band between two duller ones still on his right ring finger.

"And what can I help you with today?" Mr Venura asked amiably.

"My headaches are back," Jerin replied, "and they're bringing their friends nausea, lethargy and dizziness along for the ride." He didn't need to state the fact that the painkillers did very little to help: Mr Venura was well aware. Jerin remembered one other thing. "Oh, and the low-frequency noise sickness is back too."

"Hmm. And what of the bouts of delirium? Have they subsided?"

"They're less frequent and intense now, but I still get them on occasion. I've learned to recognise them though."

"Well, that's good, but you really should be fully healed by now," Mr Venura said concernedly, as though thinking aloud. "How frequent are these headaches?"

"Very." Jerin sneezed, grabbing a tissue from the pack in his pocket to blow his nose. "Sorry. There's a constant dull throb which turns into a migraine at least once a week." He voiced his deepest fear, unspoken even to Juli:

"I haven't felt this bad since before the op."

Mr Venura's eyes widened. "None of your scans following the op show any sign of recurrence. I wouldn't have signed you off if there was any chance of that."

Jerin trusted Mr Venura, and the absolute certainty in his voice did much to assuage his concerns, but some small doubt still niggled at the back of his mind.

"Are you sleeping well? Have you had any dreams that you remember in the past year or so?"

"My sleep is snatched and bitty, but I have a lot on my mind. The only times I remember dreaming are when I get a headache, like today."

Mr Venura exhaled a long "hmmmm" as he slumped back in his swivel chair, clasping his hands, resting his elbows on the armrests. "Your inability to remember your dreams is a touch concerning... as for the headaches, sleep deprivation would only exacerbate the underlying problem. You still seem to have your faculties though, so perhaps there is something we could try. I've recently procured a small consignment of a new wonder-drug fresh from the Terrengus Corp labs. It boosts synaptic rhythm, so it could help enhance the synergy with your implant. This new substance is also designed to induce a deeper, more convalescent sleep. Given your unique situation, I think it's just the thing you need."

Jerin was in too much pain to consider how suspiciously perfect it sounded, but was still concerned there may be a sting in the tail. "Are there any known side effects?"

"Well, your dreams may be a touch more vivid than usual, and there's a good chance you'll start remembering them."

Jerin smiled in response to Mr Venura's light-hearted remark, but had one more query: "And how long will I have to take these pills?"

In a serious tone, Mr Venura replied, "In a worst-case scenario, you might need to take them for a solid week once every few months. I'll book you in for a diagnostic scan to ensure that chip of yours is functioning correctly, just to be on the safe side, but these capsules should do the trick."

Mr Venura turned to his computer screen, quickly typing before turning back to Jerin. "The pharmacist will be expecting you. Take a white capsule at bedtime. It'll knock you out pretty quickly. Though they're safe to touch, they are mildly radioactive. The black capsules contain a formula that will break down the errant radioactive particles in your system. They'll then pass safely through your urine. They're best taken on a full stomach, although most people don't like to eat that close to bedtime, so it's up to you. But the important thing you absolutely *must* remember is that you *must* take a black capsule first thing the morning after taking a white capsule. *Never* take two whites or two blacks in a row. Do you understand?"

Jerin nodded.

"Good. I'm giving you a week's supply, and I'll book you in for this time next week to check your progress. Is that alright with you?"

"Yes, that's fine. Thank you so much," he said with relief as he slowly rose to his feet, still feeling a tad unsteady, proffering his hand. As Mr Venura shook it, Jerin noticed there was something strange about his smile, a kind of unease. Jerin paid it no mind, making a note of the appointment on his phone as he headed down to the dispensary, where he collected a small silvery flat metal tin. He pocketed it and stepped out of the warm light into the thick freezing fog that dampened and numbed his face on contact. *Damn, that came down fast.* Freezing puddles were already forming, making for a treacherous walk home. He blew his running nose again before pulling his scarf over his mouth and donning his thick gloves and woollen hat. With every inward breath he could feel his nose hair freezing.

Even with the hat, about a third of the way home he could feel the two-inch scar that curved around the back of his right ear becoming tight and tender. After another ten minutes, he could feel the cold seeping into his head, like a ghostly hand slowly wrapping itself around his brain. It was too much to bear.

He stopped and removed his right glove, undid his coat's top button, and slipped the tin from his pocket, trying to still his shivering hands as he opened it. It was eerie: one side was bathed in a white glow while the other was pitch black, a hinged metal plate separating them. He carefully took out one of the tiny white ovoid capsules and swallowed it dry before resuming his journey.

After just a few minutes his head began to swim with the familiar sensation of intoxication of severe exhaustion, but this was somehow *heavier*, as though fatigue had crept from behind, tapped him on the shoulder and sucker-punched him in the face.

The cold seemed to recede as all sensation vanished. He needed to sit down before he tripped over his own rapidly-numbing feet, spotting a concrete bench beneath a rare working streetlight ahead, barely visible through the fog. It was so close, yet just out of reach. He hobbled towards it with all the determination of a thirst-quenched man chasing mirages in the desert.

He touched it to ensure it was real before falling heavily and clumsily onto it, then blacked out.

*

Juli paced down one corridor after another, past dozens of closed doors, her peripheral vision awash in a sea of dull grey as she directed her gaze towards the not-quite navy blue carpet with yellow flecks, causing a sensation of motion sickness that didn't help right now. In her single-minded determination, she almost collided with the tea boy, Doon, as she turned a corner, narrowly side-stepping him and his trolley at the last second. The toilet door was finally in sight.

She locked herself in a cubicle and breathed slowly. *Relax. You're fine. Everything's...* her pitiful excuse for a lunch came back up, but at least it was over quickly, her pristine silver-grey skirt suit escaping unscathed. She washed up, catching her own ashen reflection beneath the dim glow of the subtly flickering battery-operated lights. She reached into her purse for her near-depleted, rarely-used lipstick, but the vibrant red only made her skin comparatively paler.

It would have been silent if not for the distant echo filtering through the ceiling vents. It sounded like all the noises from the far corners of the building were funnelling through, and it made her paranoid. If she could hear them, could they hear her? She hoped not, she hated when people made a fuss over a little bit of anxiety-vomit.

She returned to her office with a very milky coffee to extinguish the fire in her throat. She studied her computer screen with dubious pride, admiring her previously-neglected, now-clear in-folder, indicative of someone in desperate need of busy work to take their mind off the time. Then again, busy work was all her job seemed to consist of these days. She hated clearing her virtual in-tray entirely; if you worked too hard, the company expected that and more next time. It had taken her weeks to get the pace right. It meant reading every question properly, even if it became glaringly obvious what it was going to be after just the first few words. The files she couldn't understand or couldn't be bothered with had 'accidentally' been deleted. Rosie had to be aware of that, but no one ever mentioned it. Maybe it was a test to see whether people would waste company time doing things that weren't meant to make sense. That wouldn't surprise her in the least.

5:52. She had to stop looking at that damned clock in the corner of the screen.

The empty folder icon changed to one containing sheets of paper, heralding the arrival of a new file from Rosie, the company's omniscient simulated intelligence. Juli promptly opened the new file, which she typically made a habit of never doing lest she break the 'always busy' illusion. Her mind switched to autopilot as she absently read and typed, somewhat disgusted at herself when she realised just how fluent she had become in company jargon. She resolved to shoot herself if she ever caught herself speaking this shit.

She rolled her eyes as she came across the same questions time and again, subtly reworded, copying her previous answers almost word-for-word, wondering whether she could get away with writing, 'see answer in box number x'. No doubt it was some crappy corp method of testing who was and wasn't paying attention.

When it was done, she uploaded the file back to Rosie, taking a generous mouthful of coffee from the massive mug.

That must have killed a few minutes.

She allowed herself a glance at the screen-clock: 5:57.

Damn it!

She absently ran her fingernails (which she kept short since the time she drew blood after becoming a little over-enthusiastic in bed with Jerin) over the edge of the desk, *tap tap tapping* away as she tried to think of something else that would kill a few more minutes. *Anything* else. Filling in forms day in and out was by far the most boring job she'd ever had in this place, but if she wanted to get any further up that damnable 'ladder', she had to do and understand every job, even the most mundane. With Rosie having highly sensitive microphones in virtually every room and control over the data flow of the entire building, it occurred to Juli that this job probably wasn't necessary at all, but she considered that the corporate overlords would likely be sadistic enough to subject its candidates to such a form of mental hazing. She was well aware it was nothing to do with preserving the 'human touch'.

Tap tap tap.

"Juli, do you *have* to?" Not a question, more an exclamation to *quit it*.

She looked up, meeting Mila's gaze across the corridor. They both kept their office doors open; neither of them enjoyed being shut away, feeling all alone in these glorified closets.

"Sorry, I'm a bit nervous." *And bored.*

"Oh yeah, your assessment's today, isn't it?"

"Yeah." In a building containing over two hundred and fifty drones, Mila was one of a very small handful that Juli knew and actually liked. Talking to her was the only thing that kept Juli sane some days.

"Good luck," Mila said in that 'rather you than me' tone.

"Thanks. I just wish I had something to take my mind off it. I don't know why they don't do these things first thing in the morning. The wait is torture!"

"Pity you've already had lunch. Whenever I'm nervous, a visit to Nature Valley Park always works for me. It's spring at the moment and they've got baby quollings!" she *squee'd.*

"Nature Valley Park? I've never heard of it. Where is it?"

Mila scoffed in disbelief. "Are you serious? How long have you worked in this city?"

Juli fell silent, too embarrassed to explain that she only travelled here for work.

Mila sighed. "It's on the corner of Glerin Vine."

"Oh yeah, I know where you mean. So what is it?"

"Nuh-uh," Mila said in a schoolmarm-like manner, waving an index finger, "you'll have to see for yourself. Unless you know where it is, you could walk right past it without ever knowing it was there. Find the big metal roller door with the faded painting of a red rose on it beside a windowed booth and you're there. It's only two silvan. Trust me, you'll love it. I usually go there every one-d'y to take my mind off the week ahead after another weekend has zoomed by in a blur."

Juli ignored the shortened pronunciation of 'one-day' that made her cringe and considered that two silvan was two more than she could justify frittering away this side of payday, at least on her own. "Perhaps next time I take a day off I'll take Jerin along, make a bit of a day of it."

"Sounds fun! Let me know what you think," Mila beamed.

Juli wondered what it was like to have a whole weekend off every single week. All she could afford was the odd nine-day off, and that was at her boss's insistence.

She silently cursed herself as her eyes were once more drawn back to her screen's damned clock. Another distraction was sorely needed.

It occurred to her then that she had some 'important' module-related form from a while back that she had stored in another folder because it reminded her of Jerin. She knew it was rather sad, but they were forbidden from having any personal items in the office or storing any personal data on the company server, so it was the best she could get away with.

She opened it and was greeted by a technical drawing of a module surrounded by esoteric descriptive terminology, reminding her why she'd put it off in the first place. She didn't understand it anymore now than she had then.

She let out a listless sigh and began reading, failing to comprehend any of it, absently eating from a small packet of biscuits she took from her bag to stave off the shakes.

*

Jerin muttered Juli's name as an unusually vivid dream ran through his mind, but it faded the instant he was jolted awake by a shake of his shoulder sso violent it rocked his entire body.

He struggled to sit upright, groggily asking "Huh?" Had someone spoken to him? Come to think of it, where was he? He was sitting on something cold... a bench. He glanced around, but couldn't see anyone through the fog, made opaque by the streetlight. It was quite apt, considering how thick with disorienting fog his head was.

He lifted heavy hands to rub heavier eyes, realising his skin was damp. *How long was I out? I need to get home...* he shivered violently. He tried to stand, but it felt like someone had buried an axe in his stomach, causing him to fall back onto the bench. He felt under his coat for blood and inspected his fingers: nothing. He felt a firm shove against his right shoulder again, swatting it away absently, distracted by the pain in his gut.

"I'm fine, I just need to get home," he mumbled, wondering whether there was anyone there or whether he was just talking to himself. Every word produced a fresh cloud of warm breath that hung in the still air.

"I don' care how fine ya'are," a gruff, ineloquent male voice barked so loudly it made Jerin jump. His heart was racing as he looked around frantically. "I jus' wancha to ge'off me bench!"

Suddenly a long-grey-bearded heavily weathered face broke through the mist as though lunging at him. Jerin pushed it away, the foul stench of stale urine and mature body odour making him dry-retch. The face disappeared back into the darkness beyond the illuminated fog. Was it real, or some kind of hallucination? Who would really lunge at a person then disappear again?

And yet Jerin heard a brief scuffing of shoes on the pavement before the eerie silence resumed. The adrenaline coursing through Jerin's veins muted the pain in his gut enough for him to try standing again. He planted his feet firmly on the ground and grasped for the support of the back of the bench with his left hand. His muscles were so weak that even just standing was difficult. Walking was worse; he swayed drunkenly with every step, struggling to put one foot in front of the other while avoiding the slick patches of ice.

After a short time lumbering forwards like this, he glanced back over his shoulder at the person who had been tormenting him: a homeless man, adorned in a heavily mottled grey coat, bedding down on the bench. That man was true to his word: he really didn't care about Jerin. He guessed the homeless had to be selfish to survive, so long as the cold didn't kill them.

Streets came and went in a dark, misty haze until he came upon what looked like a pile of discarded rags spilling from the mouth of a driveway. As he stepped around them, he realised it was actually an elderly woman who had slipped, presumably on the frozen trail of water leaking from the overflow pipe of the abandoned house this driveway belonged to. He tried to call to her but his throat was too dry for him to make an audible sound. He tried his best to salivate and swallow so he could speak as he crouched beside her.

"Are you okay?" he croaked.

She groaned painfully as she rolled onto her back, rising to a sitting position. Her face was a patchwork of islands of skin outlined by deep, dark crevices. He tried to take her hand but she withdrew it.

"Let me help you up," he insisted.

"I don' nee' yer help!" she barked. She tried to stand, placing her palms on the cold concrete, her left foot slipping as soon as she put weight on it. She fell onto her rear again with a soft *whump* and a weary groan.

"The ice is slick," he said softly. "It's hard to get traction. Let me help you."

As her face caught a distant dim light, he realised that what he had mistaken for a tuft of fringe was actually blood trickling from a small graze on her forehead. She blindly took his hand with a defeated sigh of "Fine". He stepped beyond the ice and bent his knees, anchoring himself as he gently pulled her up, her joints cracking audibly as she rose with a pained yelp. After a moment she was back on her feet but visibly shaking, her pride likely more damaged than her body.

"Where do you live?" he asked.

"Jus' up there," she said, pointing to a bungalow a short distance ahead, lit by a tiny lamp by the front door. "I can make it jus' fine."

"I'm going that way anyway, I'll walk with you. It'll be nice to have some company for a short while."

"Suit yerself," she shrugged.

He walked beside her, looking straight ahead, watching in his peripheral vision as she hobbled in obvious pain, wondering what fate might have befallen her had he not come along. He pictured the hobo selfishly stepping over her to get to *his* bench.

"I'm not used to kindness," she smiled through crooked dentures. "Yer don' see tha' much these days."

"What was I going to do, leave you to freeze?"

"Uvvers woohd. Tha' or rob me."

She shuffled along arthritically. "Do you have a husband?" he asked, hoping there would be someone home to keep an eye on her.

"Passed 'way few year' back, bless 'im," she sighed. She smiled wanly. "Don' worry yerself, I can manage. I'll be jus' fine."

"You should see a doctor, just to be safe."

"Oh, I'm use' to thuh odd bump."

"I wish I was closer to home. I could use a nice hot cup of tea," he suggested, wondering whether she might invite him in. Somehow he doubted it.

"I har'ly know yer!" she barked, stepping to the side, putting a little distance between them.

"Sorry. I know. Can't be too careful these days," he added, admiring her wary sagacity. "Lots of people posing as kind folk, waiting for the right chance to present itself…"

She eyed him warily. "Aye. Can't be too careful."

They reached her driveway, and he held the loose gate open as she stepped through. "Here," she said as she rummaged in her handbag, dropping a sweet into his open palm. "T'ain't much, jus' suffin' fer yer trubbles." He thanked her and stood watch as she made her way to the front door. She turned to face him. "Thank you, young man."

He was genuinely touched, even a little choked up. He bowed theatrically. "Any time, my good lady."

She cawed a laugh as she fumbled with her keys. "Nah ge' yerself home to thuh wahm!" she yelled.

"Alright, alright," he acceded. "Good night," he waved, closing the gate.

He admired her tenacity, and though he wondered whether she might be better off in a nursing home, he could relate to the reluctance to admit to defeat.

He resumed the now-short journey home.

*

6:95. *At last!* Juli finished the last page of the latest report, sent it on its way and got a move on; she didn't want to be tardy.

She hurried to the stairwell and quickly ascended the two floors two steps at a time, no mean feat in these semi-high heels, proceeding down several nondescript corridors. She sat on the soft-top bench-like seat beside a fake pot plant in the recessed waiting area to catch her breath, silently cursing herself for lapsing on her exercises, all too easy with no time or money for the gym. She hunched forwards, forearms crossing her thighs, hands dangling loosely between her bare knees, watching the rhythmic sway of her hands as she bounced her heels impatiently. Her stomach was churning at the peak of anxiety now.

She looked at the clock opposite: 6:96:97... 98... 99... *Just three more minutes... three hundred itty-bitty little seconds.* She watched in fevered anticipation as each second quickly ticked by. *Two hundred and eighty-nine... eighty-eight... eighty-seven...* it was maddening, even more so than the rest of the day, but there was no other focal point on that bare wall to distract her. She became aware of the cacophony of chatter spilling out from the nearby refectory and tried to pick out individual words, but it was an indecipherable babble that seemed to grow louder the longer she waited.

Just a few more seconds... please be on time... slightly early would be even better...

Her heart was pounding like it was trying to break free. *Keep it together.* She was no good under pressure. She remembered some relaxation exercises she'd found online, inhaling deeply, holding it briefly, then exhaling slowly. She did this a few times and was astonished to find that it actually helped. She was more nervous about finally meeting the boss she'd only ever heard from via email. It would be nice to finally put a face to the name.

She watched as the clock counted the last few seconds: *three... two... one...*

As if by clockwork, the door swung open dead on 7:00:00.

"Miss Tenzalin?" the well-groomed dark grey-suited man asked in a perfectly clear, well-spoken voice.

She smiled and nodded.

"I'm the ever-elusive Mr Manrose," he smiled. "May I call you Julianos?"

Juli smiled at this simple courtesy. In a rather formal manner, she replied, "You may, but I prefer Juli."

"Okay. Juli, please come in."

She rose with a stumble, her legs having gone numb from the pressure of her leaning on her thighs. As she passed her assessor, she couldn't help notice that the ring finger of his right hand was adorned with an interesting silvery band that had a shiny middle strip between two duller ones; an alternative wedding ring perhaps, though it wasn't worn on the traditional left hand. She wished she had such a trinket to display to the world. *Maybe one day.*

As he closed the door behind her, the noise of the building fell away to complete silence. "Peace and quiet," Mr Manrose sighed. "It's so hard to get around here."

Juli's first impression of Mr Manrose was exactly what she had expected: he was the grey. Of all the company bigwigs she had seen, he had the most conspicuously generic look by far, as though he made a concerted effort to blend in, ironically making him stand out. His obviously dyed black hair was short and neatly trimmed. He looked as though he ate Corporate Flakes for breakfast and looked over the company's stock before driving to the office in his zealously-polished company car. She imagined his wife dressed up all prim and proper with nowhere to go, their home sterile right down to the last hair on the family dog, their impeccably-groomed privately educated kids reciting passages of Strausenhein's ancient doomsday transcripts from memory each morning before school.

"It's good to finally meet you, Juli. Please, take a seat," he said with an inviting gesture of the right hand, a tablet computer now in his left.

In the centre of the massive, largely empty office that could easily accommodate twenty the size of her own sat two lost-looking darkwood chairs facing one another. They were zealously varnished and adorned with luxuriously soft maroon lunim seats that caressed her bottom. She placed her left leg atop the right in as ladylike a manner as she could, wrapping her hands around her raised knee, waiting patiently, trying not to grimace as pins and needles made her feet tingle.

Against the far wall of the office sat a tiny desk, with not a piece of clutter atop it, not even a family photo. A likely rarely-used filing cabinet stood in the left corner, and another of those ghastly fake plants in the right.

She guessed Mr Manrose didn't spend much time in here. Doing so could drain anyone's soul.

Mr Manrose cleared his throat as he took his seat, his gaze meeting hers.

Juli was well aware she could turn a few heads, especially in this rear-hugging skirt, yet he didn't steal so much as a single glance, eyes fixed firmly on hers, almost hypnotically. She couldn't help but wonder whether Mrs Manrose saw much action in the bedroom. Somehow she couldn't imagine this man instigating that kind of thing, but she could picture him arriving home with the occasional customary bunch of flowers and box of chocolates. Unless, of course, he was either gay, a eunuch, or an expert in monk-like self-control.

"I'm ashamed to admit that the company doesn't afford me the time to meet my staff personally," Mr Manrose explained in a surprisingly affable manner, "so I'm sorry to say I don't know a thing about you, but I'm sure we can fix that little issue quickly enough."

She returned his smile, but said nothing.

"This assessment is designed to assess your suitability for provisional promotion, but to be frank it's a load of shit," he said, almost making Juli choke with unexpected laughter. "Most of what the company wants me to ask you is an insult to both your intelligence and mine."

Juli was well and truly disarmed. She was glad to find that her preconceptions of Mr Manrose had been so wide of the mark, but she hadn't been expecting *this*.

"I have to keep up so many pretences for the company, as I'm sure do you, but in here I prefer to be *me*, and I'd like you to be *you*. There are no cameras, no audio recorders. Rosie has no presence here. So tell me, how do *you* feel about the manner in which this company currently operates?"

Juli was unsure how to answer this question. "Honestly?" she asked tentatively.

"Please. Be as blunt as you like."

She decided *what the hell?* "I think it started as a genuinely altruistic company under Lazarus Terrengus, but under Reginald it's lost its way and become a profit-seeking farce." How long had she had to pretend to be someone else just to try and get ahead in this place? She'd never before articulated such thoughts inside these walls; to speak so freely was incredibly liberating. "It's not even a shadow of its former self. It's like I'm watching it collapse around me."

Mr Manrose smiled, his smooth face creasing, making him look older. "I'm so very glad to finally meet someone else who has the spine to say so."

"The things they do are so *stupid*," she continued, myriad thoughts simultaneously vying for attention. "The financial wing wonders why they keep losing money when they insist on lending to people who can't afford the repayments; every area of the company seems to be run by a clueless kid who's never worked in that area before being promoted to manager of it, and the only reason they got the job is because they used the heads of those around them as stepping stones, while people like myself with years of experience and knowledge of virtually every facet of the business continue to be ignored; the feedback team takes no notice of the online forums detailing problems with their mobile software updates, and they can't be bothered to release any at all for older handsets that are still in wide usage, not even to fix simple things like the alarm function…" she trailed off, breathless with exasperation, realising she had been emphasising her points with wildly animated hand gestures.

Mr Manrose chuckled heartily. "I appreciate your passionate candour. I couldn't agree more. This company was salvaged by those who dared to think differently. If it continues to promote only toadying sycophants, we'll regress back to the dark ages of the riots. I need people like you to get this company back on the right track. How would you feel about being a part of a new-age management team?"

There were still dozens, perhaps even *hundreds* of issues Juli wanted to raise, all filed away at the back of her mind, but she knew that the time for those would come later. She was sure this company harboured many dark secrets, and if Mr Manrose was true to his word, perhaps he was her way of getting to the root of the problem. She doubted she could kill that root, but she would deal with that when the time came.

"I'd feel great about it," she enthused. "It'll be so nice not to have to talk nonsense just to make the bigwigs think I know what I'm doing."

"I have to say, I like you, Juli. You're exactly the sort of person I'd hoped to find." He proffered her his right hand. "Congratulations. You're in."

"That's it?"

"That's it. I'm afraid you'll have to endure a few tedious weekend workshops starting the day after tomorrow. It's just a load of nonsense designed to extirpate anyone who doesn't fit the company mould, so turn up, keep quiet when you can, and try not to die of sensory deprivation. I'll make sure you pass. I'll even see if I can wrangle you some pay... the company seems to love the idea of people doing these things out of the kindness of their hearts, but I have a different philosophy, especially considering the low pass rate. Oh, and please don't mention a word of this meeting to anyone else. Secrecy is our best friend for the time being."

She mimed zipping her mouth closed, somewhat embarrassed at the childish gesture afterwards.

"Oh, on a side note, I see you've been working rather hard recently, putting in the overtime."

"Yeah, I kind of need the extra cash at the moment."

"I can understand that. Were you planning on coming in tomorrow?"

"I was... is that okay?"

"It's absolutely fine, but please, take the day off, with full pay. I like my staff to have a little rest every now and then. I find it makes people more productive, and it's great for morale."

Juli was stunned. She gasped, "Really?"

"Really. No strings."

She leapt up and wrapped her arms around him, a rather clumsy gesture as he still sat in his chair, her chest just inches from his face. She quickly jumped back. "Oh, er... sorry about that."

"Not at all." Was he blushing?

"It's just... no one around here does things like that, not for people like me."

"Glad to be of service."

At least that would cheer Jerin up.

"I have a feeling you'll go far," Mr Manrose smiled. "It may take a few months to push through your pay rise, but bear with me, you *will* get it. " He handed her his business card. "Here's my personal number, in case you have any issues you need to talk to me about. Always in confidence, of course."

"Thank you," she said. As she left, a smile slowly spread across her face. After all this time, all the struggling, scrimping and saving, fighting over money, early starts and late finishes, there was light at the end of the long, dark tunnel. She couldn't wait to tell Jerin.

U
-Passing Ships-

Jerin was rudely jerked from his slumber by loud voices engaged in a heated debate at the front door. Though the bedroom door was closed, the front door was right outside it, a design flaw so ludicrously illogical that only someone with a degree could pull it off.

"You'll get it next week," Juli said sternly.

"Good girl," a familiarly condescending voice chimed. *Nate*. After several silent seconds, he heard Juli sigh as she struggled to close that damned door, *clunk, clunk, SLAM*. The whole flat seemed to shake.

Since the only time they ever heard from that fugada was when the rent was late, Jerin guessed Juli had messed up yet again. He was annoyed, but not the least bit surprised.

Jerin sat up. Head still foggy with residual sleep, he spotted the wrapper from the sweet given to him by the old lady sitting atop the rubbish mound in his wire-mesh bin, thinking nothing of it, only to look closer and realise it wasn't a sweet wrapper at all. He picked it up and threw it back down in disgust; it was nothing more than a dirt-filthied piece of white waxed paper. *Did I eat something out of that?* He couldn't remember at all. *What the hell did that old lady give me?* Another part of his mind asked, *What old lady?* and that ephemeral dizziness returned.

He opened the top drawer of his bedside cabinet and took a black capsule, hastily closing the drawer as Juli opened the bedroom door. She was smiling diffidently, bringing him back to the moment.

"Hey, honey," she soothed. "Sorry if I woke you. Go back to sleep."

"I'm up," he croaked, throat bone dry, and no wonder: a glance as he donned his watch revealed it was three o'clock. He was astonished; he couldn't remember the last time he'd slept so well. He hadn't even noticed her slip into bed beside him or get up to answer the door. "Who was that?" he asked disingenuously.

"Nothing important, just someone selling insurance."

Though part of him wanted to confront her over this blatant lie (*who the hell would even bother trying to hawk insurance in a largely unpopulated area?*), it wasn't worth the grief. She would counteract with something like "why didn't you do the dishes/vacuuming/tidy the flat," and he would reply, "I was exhausted and went straight to bed, awoke after just a couple of hours still exhausted," she would remark "typical," and so it would go on, until one of them (usually him) stormed out in a huff. He just hoped she didn't ask him how dinner was.

Aware that he had been silent for a little too long, he derailed that destructive train of thought by asking, "You got your provisional promotion, then?"

She couldn't contain her glee, jumping in jubilation, declaring, "I did! How did you know?"

"I could tell by your smile," he lied. Now that he thought about it, he was unsure how he knew. Could it be…? Was his mind finally back after such a long hiatus?

"Aren't you happy for me?" she frowned.

"I will be, when it finally means something more than never seeing you. You so rarely take your days off…" She didn't respond. He had an inkling there was something she wasn't telling him, causing him to wonder what secrets lurked behind those beautiful grey eyes, but since he was keeping one of his own he decided not to press it. "Speaking of which, shouldn't you be at work already?"

"They gave me a paid day off."

He was skeptical. "What's the catch?"

"There isn't one."

"Hang on… so they give you all this grief for months on end, then they just give you a promotion and a paid day off? Who do you have dirt on?"

"Good things do happen occasionally, you know. And just think, in a few months…"

"That's what you've been saying for the past two years!" he interjected, sick of this too-oft-heard remark. Her expression became forlorn. "I'm sorry, that wasn't me," he lied. He didn't want their fleeting time together to be tainted by this.

"It's different this time, honestly. It's just a few tedious workshops then I'll finally get a proper promotion!" She motioned to applaud herself again, but when he glared at her skeptically, she dropped her hands to her sides and swung them back and forth.

"So you have to do these workshops in work time and not your own time, right?"

"Well, most of them will be on weekends…"

"And they'll be paying you?"

"Hopefully they should be for *some* of it…"

He threw his hands up, a gesture that had become second nature whenever they spoke about her damned job. "They're taking the piss, Ju. Last time I checked, that was called 'slave labour'. You do all the overtime they send you, and what do you have to show for it? You lose so much on tax it isn't even worth the price of fuel… and, more importantly, it's keeping you from me."

"You have to invest in yourself if you want to get anywhere in this world!"

"You really will swallow any garbage they feed you, won't you?"

She couldn't think of a reply, staring down at her bare feet in shame. She suddenly looked at him with an unexpected smile. "I'll make it up to you," she beamed, her lilac robe dropping to the floor, crumpling around her ankles.

The sight of her naked body still filled him with lust, his eyes flicking up and down her slender frame. Despite it all, he still loved and fancied her like crazy. He tried to push all concerns aside. Maybe she was right… it had been too long since anything good had happened to them, and he didn't know how to react any other way.

"Trust me," she said. "Things are going to be better

from now on."

"Well then," he said, taking her petite hands in his, drawing her in, "maybe we should celebrate." She played along, falling onto the bed beside him. He motioned to give her a kiss then stopped, looking her in the eye. "I'd kiss you, but I've got breath that could slay a dragoth!"

"Mmm, sexy," she said sarcastically, pushing his left hand away as it cupped her right breast. "Go brush your teeth first!"

"Hey, you're the one who stripped off. You know I can't be held responsible for my actions now." He wrapped himself around her.

"Ew! I just showered and you're all sticky," she protested.

He grabbed her, spun her around and pinned her to the bed. "You'll need another shower in a minute…"

"Hey! I can't remember the last time you were this amorous. Are you feeling alright?"

"Better than ever," he beamed in exhilaration. He meant it; he honestly couldn't remember the last time he'd felt this good. Even his sniffle had vanished without a trace.

She stroked his chest with her left hand, looking him in the eyes. "Well then, perhaps you'll have to show me just how good a mood you're in!"

"I'll do more than just show you," he teased. He instinctively motioned to kiss her, then stopped. "Maybe you're right, maybe I should brush my teeth first."

Juli sighed with theatrical exaggeration. "Trust you to start the engine then get out. Fine. Go. Brush. But be quick! And don't forget the mouthwash! And lots of it! Like, a gallon!"

"I love you too," Jerin mocked, doing as bade, stopping for a piss first, not having realised just how full his bladder was after such a long sleep. He lolled his head back, smiling as he realised how refreshed and alert he felt for the first time in far too long.

Thank Terrengus for those damned fine capsules. How

did I ever cope without them?

He reached for the flush, not noticing the slight glow of his urine.

Their surprisingly energetic romp reminded Jerin just how much he loved the sound of Juli's delighted screams. *Hear that, Nate? You'll never make a woman as happy as that!* Man, did it ever feel good... she'd asked him to go inside sans-condom, and he'd been tempted, but he'd known there would be no way he could have pulled out in time.

Afterwards, Jerin decided he needed a shower, letting the water run for a few seconds to get lukewarm before he stepped in.

As he sparingly lathered his body, he realised he could actually *smell* the mild sweetness of the soap. Even the sensation of the streams of water softly cascading onto his skin felt more sensual than before.

He stepped out of the shower, head completely enveloped by the massive towel, and could see Juli in his mind. She was wearing a small pink vest top that barely contained her ample breasts and a long diaphanous white skirt over skin-tone tights, the kind of resplendent gear she wore to announce her desire to go out. Without removing the towel he said, "Isn't it a touch cold out for that?"

"How did you know what I was wearing?" she asked.

"You know my mind does weird things," he reminded her.

"I don't think that was ESP as much as you taking a sneaky peek!"

He didn't correct her, finally removing the towel to see she was indeed wearing what he'd pictured. He hadn't had such a clear vision for years, since before the op. He took a moment to admire her alluring beauty. She was trying to look good for him, and succeeding.

"Well, what do you think?" she asked with a twirl.

He smiled, still stupidly euphoric from their romp, all concerns pushed to the back of his mind. He wished he could lock them away for good.

"You look gorgeous, but as I was saying, isn't it a touch brisk for an outfit like that?"

"Hence the tights," she winked. He decided not to ask how they'd keep her arms and shoulders warm. "A friend told me about this park, and I thought you might want to check it out," she explained with innocent, school-girl-like glee, even placing the toes of her left foot on the ground while her raised heel swung side to side, hands tucked behind her back, head cocked to the right.

"Why not?" he shrugged.

She smiled, swivelling her hips and waving her arms in the air in the familiar-but-long-unseen display he called her 'happy dance'. She gave him a quick kiss before running her fingers against the grain of the stubble on his left cheek. "You need a shave, mister!"

He rolled his eyes. "I suppose I can endure it for you. Is this park far?"

"No, just on the outskirts of the city. What are you going to wear?"

"Under my thick winter coat? I guess… jeans and a t-shirt?" He wasn't exactly a fashion aficionado, sticking to what he liked. *Sand-blasted, torn jeans hanging below the arse? I don't think so!*

"You can wear your smart jeans if you like."

"I have 'smart' jeans? How can you tell the difference?"

"You just get dried and shaved, I'll dig them out for you," said as if she intended to grab a shovel to turf up some long-buried chest. Given the state of his clothes drawers, that wasn't far wrong.

Emerging from the bathroom with a smooth chin, he found a pair of pretty faded black jeans and his slightly uncomfortably tight white t-shirt laid out on the bed; not what he would have chosen, but since she had taken the time to pick them out he thought it rude not to humour her. Besides, she'd told him before that she liked how he looked in that top, though personally he found it rather unflattering, making him incredibly self-conscious.

Once suitably attired he went into the front room where Juli was putting in her earrings. "Are you ready?" he asked.

"Yup yup!" she smiled widely, springing to her feet. "Let's go!"

*

The short walk from their tiny one bedroom flat to the car took them past many abandoned houses and flats, reminding them just how lonely they were out here, but at least they could enjoy the peace and quiet afforded by the absence of squabbling kids, scolding parents, barking pets and inconsiderate neighbours playing loud music at all hours.

It was just a shame Nate wouldn't go too, preferably leaving them the flat.

With his newly-sharpened olfactory senses, Jerin could smell the faintly fungal aroma in the cold air, bringing a sensation of nostalgia from when they first moved here, back when it had been the somewhat dubious smell of home.

He and Juli scraped thin layers of droplet-laden ice from the car's windows and windscreen before hopping inside, which was even colder than out, Jerin shivering as it quickly worked its way through his thick coat. He had no idea how Juli could stand it; she wasn't even wearing a coat, though he noticed her shoulders were trembling slightly as she pressed the ignition button.

The car's engine struggled and spluttered to violent life, leaving a thick cloud of choking carbon fumes hanging in the air as they pulled away.

As they reached the mouth of the small cul-de-sac, he noticed two men, one older, one younger, father and son perhaps, carrying brown unmarked boxes into the back of a big black van. *More people moving on.* He couldn't blame him. Given the chance, he would do the same.

After just a few corners, thousands of incongruous pinprick-lights appeared on the horizon, marking the skyline of that big, cold city which seemed to glower down on this now-swept-under-the-rug suzerainty. Those distant lights were far brighter than any closer to them, the few working street lamps so dim they did little to illuminate the streets.

Juli took Jerin on what he assumed was her usual work route, around fairly complicated turns and bends he would struggle to memorise in a single journey. On one corner she turned right, left at the end, left again then right, tracing a box-shaped route, causing him to wonder why she hadn't just gone straight at that initial right turn, but a cursory glance down the dark road as they passed its top end revealed that it was blocked by several large metal dumpsters, their contents spilling across to the buildings opposite, the source of the dim light revealed as an open fire in a metal dustbin surrounded by basking homeless people.

Lost in thought for much of the journey, contemplating what fates might befall the hobo and the old woman he'd encountered on his way home from the clinic, he was surprised by how soon they reached their destination, the car coming to a halt on the side of a very nondescript street. He hadn't even realised they were just inside the actual city, its outskirts almost as squalid and derelict as much of Sendura. How had he not noticed the trip over the bridge? Had he really been *that* out of it?

"Is this it?" he asked.

"Not quite, but there tend to be less vagrants around here."

This didn't exactly leave him brimming with confidence. Still, if someone wrecked or stole their car, they'd be doing them a favour. It was insured for far more than it was worth, which was less than its scrap value.

Jerin looked over at the empty darkness on the horizon that was Sendura as Juli led him by the hand down several streets, the unmistakable whiff of urine hanging in the air. *Delightful.*

She took him down an alley, stopping near a heavy

metal roller door with a faded reddish rose painted on it. Beside it was a filthy bulletproof-windowed booth, inside which stood a fairly young smooth-faced, smartly-dressed, black-capped male attendant.

"Is this the Nature Valley Park?" she asked apprehensively.

"Sure is," the attendant confirmed. "You'll be amazed by the full seasonal spectrum and the ten-hour day-to-night cycle, just as nature intended!" he beamed proudly, his wide smile revealing his braces. "It's a lovely, temperate spring day inside."

If the attendant's boasts weren't unfounded, Jerin would be glad he brought his phone along to take some pictures.

"Two please," Juli said as she placed a five silvan note on the booth's metal counter before taking her change.

The attendant nodded enthusiastically and opened the door, which slowly rolled up, revealing a long stairwell that descended into darkness. "Enjoy!"

Their footsteps echoed as they apprehensively descended twenty, thirty, forty, and finally fifty stairs, eventually spotting a beam of bright light shining through the tiny window in a blue-painted metal door, which Juli opened. They stepped through onto a short balcony complete with stonework handrails, gazing in awe at the sight stretching before them. It must have been about a hectare wide and three or four long; it was *huge*.

Beneath brightly humming overhead strip-lights was a verdant valley filled with sights the likes of which neither of them had ever before seen: well-trimmed rolling grass hills with trees sprouting here and there; baby quollings pecking their tiny adolescent beaks at tufts of grass for unseen bugs; there was even a sparklingly clear, deceptively deep lake with an island in the middle, several older people standing on the two bridges, admiring the wildlife. Groups of teenagers were dotted here and there, sprawled out on picnic blankets, chattering away in warm-day getup, their cold-day garments laying beside them.

"Whoa," they gasped in unison at the sight and sound of all this flora and fauna.

"Could it be anymore secluded?" Jerin rhetoricked.

"Why would anyone want to hide something like this?" Juli pondered.

Jerin took his coat off, folding it over his left arm. "I don't think I'll need this for a while."

They descended each of the four sets of ten concrete steps, performing a u-turn at the bottom, walking the lower parallel path to the next set, until they reached the park proper, where they crossed the surprisingly springy green grass hand in hand. It was like being in another world.

The air was warm and sweetly clean, filled with chatter, chirruping and the soft sough of the artificial wind through the trees' bountiful foliage. With Jerin's newly sharpened senses, it was the most exquisite sensory overload.

Juli released his hand and performed an exuberant twirl, stopping to face him, rising onto her tiptoes, bringing her lips to his, stealing a kiss which he quickly stole back as she dropped onto her heels.

Moments like this made life worth living. If this could last, perhaps the next few years wouldn't be such a toil after all.

They carefully stepped around dozens of near-camouflaged gilatoads, crossing to a bench sitting beside the surprisingly large elliptical lake, sitting in the shade of a tree. They watched a group of recently-hatched quollings dive into the water behind their cawing mother, stopping briefly on their way to search for food in longer tufts of grass by the water's edge.

Jerin's eyes met Juli's, and they smiled lovingly at one another. She took his hands in hers, palms towards one another, fingers interlocked, and began swaying his hands rhythmically to a song playing in her head.

"Must you?" he sighed facetiously.

She stopped swaying, offering a playful frown.

Suddenly her smile reappeared as she spotted something behind him. "Hey, do you want an ice cream?" She opened her purse and scraped a few lonely coins from the bottom, jingling them in her cupped palm.

"They have *ice cream* here?" he asked, glancing over his shoulder at the kiosk a short walk away.

"Evidently!"

"Well in that case, yes please, with a flake."

He followed her to the kiosk, taking his phone out to snap a few pictures along the way. They found another nearby bench on which to rest as they greedily devoured their sweetly dripping creamy snacks. He took a bite of the flake that was colder than he had anticipated and grimaced.

Juli laughed, slapping her thigh as she did. He'd forgotten how he enjoyed the sound of her laughter.

"Are you taking the piss?" he asked, trying not to spit chocolate flecks at her.

"Of course," she laughed.

"Charming!" He leaned close to her ear, and before she could pull away, perhaps fearing a playful reprisal, he whispered: "Empty sugar bowls and candy wrappers blowing in the wind," gesturing with his hand something fluttering on the breeze.

She scrunched her face as he sat back, as if to say "*What!?*"

"I always wanted to whisper sweet nothings in your ear."

She laughed so hard she nearly spat ice cream all over him. "Stupid boy!"

"Guilty," he smiled.

Jerin took pictures of her as she tried to catch melting streams of ice cream running down the cone, holding his phone in his right hand, trying to stabilise it against the heel of his left palm without dribbling ice cream all over it. When she realised he was snapping her, she hid behind her cone, laughing like a loon at his faux-pouty expression of frustration.

When the laughter had faded, he saw an unmistakable bushy tail. "Is that a skwarril?" They watched the purple-furred diminutive rodent clamber carefully down the tree's trunk before leaping the last few feet to the ground. The surprises just kept on coming.

They threw it pieces of their cones as it cautiously approached, smiling as it sniffed at the ground excitedly, watching in hushed awe as it sat up and greedily devoured each one in turn, holding them between its forepaws. It stopped its scavenging once to ward off a greedy pyjahn, sending plumes of feathers in all directions with a humorous jump-kick which Jerin caught on camera, eliciting much rapturous laughter. He'd be remiss not to upload that to *BestBuddies* later.

With their snacks consumed, they resumed exploring the park, determined to get their four silvans' worth, ascending the wooden steps of one of the bridges crossing the water, resting their forearms on the railing, leaning forwards, watching about twenty adult quollings and a few short trails of youngsters of various sizes mingle about on the water's surface, while tadpeas and various types of fish swam below.

Jerin elbowed Juli gently in the side, looking away childishly when she looked at him. She looked back at the water and he did it again.

"What?" she barked impatiently.

"Nothing..." he teased, elbowing her again the moment she looked down at the water.

She slapped him playfully on the arm, connecting harder than intended. "Tell me!"

Mock shock spread across his face as he clutched his arm. "Ow! Clumsy wench! Why would I tell you after that?" He crossed his arms and turned away, adding a playful "Harrumph!"

"Why were you elbowing me, mister?" She was trying not to laugh.

"I was only going to say I love you, but I don't now!" He *harrumphed* again.

"Oh, you're playing that game, are you? Fine, I don't love you either." She crossed her arms and turned away, adding her own flippant "Harrumph."

They glanced over their shoulders at one another and erupted into fits of laughter, attracting bemused glances from the myriad bystanders, neither of them caring.

He took his phone out again and tried to snap her, but she covered her face with both hands.

"Oh, come on!" he protested. "Just one?"

"No!" she giggled, peering at him between fanned fingers. He took the picture anyway, dropping his phone hand from her sight. She dropped her guard and he quickly took a candid shot of her, causing her to yell, "Oi!"

He couldn't remember the last time he'd laughed until his face ached. Had he remembered the ring buried at the back of the top drawer in his bedside cabinet before they'd left, he might have brought it along and finally given it to her... had he been able to work up the nerve. The moment felt right, but he'd had it so long he was almost embarrassed to give it to her now, though he was facing the increasing inevitability that the right moment might never come. It wasn't like they could afford to actually get married for another decade at least, anyhow. Maybe, if she got this promotion, it could be sooner...

Truth be told, Jerin wasn't much for marriage. To him, it was a waste of a whole lot of money just to have a digital document that told them what they already knew stored on a database somewhere along with a handful of memories, but he knew Juli wanted it, and he loved her enough to grant her this wish.

She'd been keen on the idea after seeing photos posted by supposed 'friends' on BestBuddies revealing the needless extravagance of their own weddings that they hadn't seen fit to invite her to. She preferred the idea of a small, tasteful ceremony which she had no intention of inviting those particular people to, intending to post the pictures so she could snub them right back.

He was snapped from his daydreaming when he saw her turn to face him, smiling. "Thanks for this," she said softly.

He leaned over and kissed her repeatedly, revelling in the joyous touch of her silky soft lips against his. All this attention was slowly arousing him again, which was rather painful in these jeans, reminding him why he'd stopped wearing them when he went out with her when she was adorned in her sexier garments.

He said nothing, but considered, *If only every day could be like this. If only you hadn't messed everything up.* Damn those dark thoughts… they just wouldn't stay away.

*

On the journey home after an hour in that glorious park, they spoke of their disbelief of the experience.

"I haven't seen animals since my dad took me to an indoor zoo as a kid, and I've never seen plants like those," Jerin remarked.

"I've never seen anything like it at all," Juli replied. "We'll have to go there again."

"Definitely," Jerin agreed as they arrived home. Looking around now, he was suddenly so much more aware of the lack of plant- and wildlife. It was like death had cut a swathe through the land itself.

As they exited the warm car and walked back round to the flat, the cold air made the scar behind Jerin's ear throb slightly. He raised a hand to it instinctively.

"Your head again?" Juli asked with genuine concern.

"Not my head, the scar," he replied. "My stomach feels a little odd too." He met her concerned gaze. "I'll be fine once we're inside," he assured.

Juli's phone-specs buzzed excitedly in her handbag, playing their annoyingly chirpy text alert. She quickly pulled them out and put them on, reading the message that hung before her eyes.

"Who's that?"

"Alezi. I promised we'd meet up for tea once she was back. Do you mind?"

"No, go, catch up. I'm sure she'll have many more ridiculous stories to tell."

"Her stories aren't always..." Juli trailed off as she considered this.

"Like the one about the valley where time stands still?"

"That *is* a contentious story..."

"Oh, come on. It's a crazy conspiracy theory and a myth. She'll believe anything. Remember the one about the marauding beasts of Vahiras island?"

"Okay, okay, I give. She talks nonsense, granted. But at least she's entertaining! And she is a good friend."

"I know, I'm just playing. Go see your crazy friend."

"You're sure you won't get bored?"

"I have one or two things to keep me occupied. I'll be fine."

She gave him a quick peck on the lips, to which he added his customary two. She motioned as if to return to the car, making an "eh-hh-hhhh" noise as she shivered.

"Perhaps you should change into something warmer first," he suggested.

"Good idea!"

She crossed her arms tightly over her chest and they headed for the relative warmth of the flat, where Juli changed into some of the clothes she reserved exclusively for meeting Alezi while Jerin sat on the sofa and switched on the holovision, the two vertical tubes illuminating slowly. Now that he was sitting down, he realised his head did feel a little fuzzy.

When Juli was ready, she headed back into the front room. "You're sure you'll be okay?"

"I'll be fine," he assured. "Go. Have fun."

She leaned towards him and gave him another quick kiss. "Love you. See you soon."

"Love you too."

And she was gone again. As he flicked through HV channels to find anything worth watching, his tired eyes were bombarded by fast-moving colourful adverts for kids' toys, cruelly enticing youngsters by placing virtual versions of them within their reach. He reduced the image's depth to just a third, closing his eyes and muting the sound until this sensual assault had passed.

*

Juli loved Alezi dearly, but the girl's fashion sense had become ridiculously pretentious — less diplomatic people might call it snooty — over the last few years. It wasn't that she followed the trends — Alezi was her own strange creature — but she often referred to Juli's everyday tops and bottoms as "peasant clothes."

Juli didn't have the cash to frivolously fritter away at upmarket boutiques, but she did have a few treasured 'posh' outfits she'd accrued over the years that she now reserved for meeting her old friend, since she and Jerin couldn't afford to go anywhere ostentatious enough to warrant wearing them otherwise.

She chose the semi-casual maroon faux-soft-lunim waistcoat, beneath which she wore a classic just-pink shirt. She completed the look with a pair of dark brown bellbottom jeans she later discovered were a counterfeit designer pair — a cheap pair would have been less mortifying, but she liked them all the same. This was the look Alezi told her was called 'autumnal', though neither of them knew what that meant.

She even applied a conservative touch of makeup before wrapping herself in her favourite beige trench coat, making sure the belt was tight to keep out the cold. She grabbed her favourite golden brown faux-lunim handbag on her way out.

Alezi had invited her to the *Gluttonous Gastropod Bistro*, an expectedly affluent café situated in one of Darina's more upmarket districts. It was so typical of Alezi to meet for an early afternoon drink in a place so ostentatious it sold the most expensive coffee in the city. Juli set its location on her phone-glasses and set off, following the roads highlighted by her high-tech specs.

After paying the extortionate parking fee, she spotted

a small corner shop and bought a cheap sandwich so she had an excuse for not ordering the overpriced food. She spotted the bistro up the street ahead of her by the radiant light spilling down, a beacon which illuminated everything around it, screaming *notice me!* As she crested the slope, she was greeted by a building as shamelessly opulent as she'd expected: marble pillars with gold floral-style decorative touches surrounding a giant glass box. Everything about it screamed *Alezi*. A quick glance at their animated specials board revealed that even a small pot of tea was going to cost her more than she liked.

She spotted her friend waiting behind the spotlessly clean glass, looking effortlessly glamorous as she clutched a gorgeous golden-hued genuine lunim bag, its oversized designer logo clearly visible, wearing a long maroon skirt and brown blouse, both decorated with intricate floral patterns. Their outfits were strikingly — almost shamefully, to Juli — similar, though Juli's was older, what Alezi liked to call "retro-chic." Even Alezi's dark brown deep-heeled shoes looked too expensive for Juli's purse.

Juli didn't consider herself a failure as such — she knew of many far worse off than she — but she always felt so inadequate and outclassed in Alezi's presence. But Juli could hardly blame her friend for playing up to the successes of her glamorous job, and she was sure Alezi never meant to lord it over her.

"Good day, ma'am," a posh waitress in an impeccably neat indigo-and-white maid-like uniform greeted as Juli reached the entrance.

"Uh, hello. I'm here to meet…" she saw Alezi gliding towards her as if floating on air, her immaculate blonde locks flowing behind her.

"Juli, hi," Alezi greeted with a wide smile, kissing her friend on the cheeks. "It's so *good* to finally see you again."

Juli had to ignore the pretentious persona and posh accent that drove her mad. At least Alezi wasn't wearing sunglasses on a dark day, but if she said anything as clichéd as "dahling," she was going to piss herself laughing. Her skin looked paler than Juli remembered, but maybe it was just the exaggerated contrast of her dark clothing.

"Alezi, it's been too long." Juli had to concentrate to maintain her normal accent; such proper-sounding ones had a way of pulling her in, and it sometimes took her a while to realise she was mimicking them. "I didn't realise upmarket places like this still existed," she said, admiring the opulent interior's cream carpet and blonde beechwood furniture.

"There'll always be people with more money than sense," Alezi replied.

"What, like you?" Juli smiled.

"Oh, how very droll," Alezi deadpanned.

They made their way over to the table adorned with frilly doilies atop an indigo tablecloth, draped over the edges at a forty-five degree angle. As they settled down Alezi looked up, smiling at someone Juli couldn't see.

"What can I get for you ladies?" the waitress from the door asked politely.

Juli grimaced as she glanced over the open tabletop digital drinks menu, ordering just the tea until she caved in to temptation when Alezi insisted the glerin scones were "to die for."

The waitress departed with a courteous bow and a smile. Juli certainly couldn't fault the service, but they were the only customers.

"I *love* your outfit!" Alezi beamed. "As you can see, I'm also into the whole retro-chic thing at the moment. It's not often I get to forage through my wardrobe for an old favourite. I wish I could stick with the same look for longer, really get to enjoy it."

"I don't have much choice, I'm too poor for such wasteful living."

"Relax, Juli, I didn't mean anything by it. I just envy that care-free lifestyle. I have to think about every little thing. My diary is full of so much nonsense. I constantly have to make notes on what I can wear, and where I can get away with it."

Juli couldn't work out whether this was a thinly-veiled insult or not: she was never quite sure how to take Alezi. More than a pinch of salt was typically required.

"Some days I forget where I am and what I'm doing. It can take a lot to stay grounded. That's part of why I *need* friends like you, someone who won't reprimand me for dropping the persona. But enough about me; how are things with you and Jerin?"

"I don't know..." Juli was staring down at a doily, absently fiddling with its edge. "We had a great time today, before I came here, but that's because Jerin's having a rare lapse in pain. Since the whole financial mess we hardly see each other, and when we do he's typically so introverted and distant. Since he started nights he doesn't talk about work anymore, which can't be a good sign."

"Bummer. So how much do you still owe?" Alezi's forced accent was slowly melting away.

"About twelve grand. The bank takes its share before I even see it. It's taken us nearly two years to repay just a fifth of the legal costs. I can't carry on repaying them for another eight! The worst part is that I need another hundred and fifty to make up this month's rent, but if I withdraw that, I won't have enough left in my account to pay the bank, then they'll hit me with escalating charges..." she placed her hands over her face for a moment. "I do all the overtime I can get, but it's never enough, and that's on the rare occasion the corp decides they can afford to pay me. Between upkeep, fuel and carbon condensers, my car eats up all my spare cash. I wish I could just get rid of that scrapheap, but I need it for work now that no trams run from Sendura... oh, it's all such a mess!" She ran her fingers through her hair in frustration. "I don't think Nate will dare evict us, but I wish he'd back off. The way he leers at me makes my skin crawl, he's so damned *pervy*. The dictionary definition of fugada."

"Juli..." Alezi said dolorously.

"I haven't told Jerin I haven't got enough for the rent this month yet. I don't think I can. He doesn't trust me as it is."

"Can you blame him?"

Juli's sullen expression was that of an innocent puppy intentionally kicked.

"Sorry, sorry," Alezi soothed, raising her hands. "Sometimes the bitch just walks out of the cage. Do you need me to help you out?"

"I couldn't ask that of you. If I borrow it from you I'm still in debt. I need to break the cycle... I just need a way of making a little extra, just as a one-off."

"You know what I love about you, Juli? You're like a cat; no matter how big the fall, you always land on your feet. You'll find a way. You always do."

"Thanks, but throw a cat from just the right height and it dies on impact," Juli replied morosely. "Up to five stories, it lives; above seven, it walks away without a scratch. But that weird area in the middle? Fatal, because it can't judge it right. That's where I think I am."

The waitress reappeared with a pot of tea, two mugs and a plate with two buttered scones atop it. Juli closed her eyes as she inhaled the deliciously spicy aroma. She motioned to pour the tea, but Alezi reached out a hand to stop her.

"Give it a minute to brew."

"Well, sorrr-ry! I'm not familiar with Vahirinese cuisine protocol. What about my scone, can I eat that yet?"

Alezi shrugged. "If you like, but the spiciness of the tea is really brought out by the sweetness of the scones."

"Fine, I'll wait then!"

"Now, where were we? Oh yes. If you need fast money, you know there's always Sirens."

Though the very mention of that place brought

innumerable memories and emotions flooding back, many of which she'd much rather forget, she couldn't mask her unexpectedly pleasant surprise. After all, she'd had many good times there too, and the thought of it disappearing altogether made her a little sad. "Fox and Vix managed to keep it going?" She hadn't visited that area of town once since she'd stopped working there.

"They sure did. You know how tenacious those two are."

"Yeah, but Sendura's so desolate these days... I thought they'd go bust for sure."

"There will always be lonely men with money," Alezi shrugged.

"But surely there are better places in the city? Besides, with HV, those so inclined can have a naked girl practically dancing in their lap."

"*Practically* being the operative word. It isn't the same. But yes, there were difficult times, but the girls hung in there. Vix's solution was a little *drastic* for my taste, but it did the trick. They were also quick to capitalise on the fact that you can't *touch* an HV projection."

The fact that things had changed made it an even less appealing prospect. Juli squirmed at the very notion of strange men groping her arse, but remained silent.

"Besides, there are plenty of crims in Sendura who like to have somewhere out of the city they can hide when the psi-cops go on their dark night witch-hunts."

"Psi-cops?" Juli asked skeptically. "You mean those 'mental reprogrammers'? Isn't that just some paranoid rumour started by the cops to keep the people in line?"

"Nope. Believe me, they're real."

Juli wasn't convinced. "How can you be sure? Have you ever actually seen one?"

Diffidently, Alezi answered, "Well, not actually, but I've heard enough stories..."

Juli rolled her eyes. "You really will believe any old shit people tell you, won't you?"

"Well, whatever. The bikers run that area of Sendura now, enforcing their own law. They call themselves the 'Misfits'."

Juli's eyes widened with incredulity. "Isn't that dangerous?"

"Nah," Alezi dismissed. "Most of them behave well enough, as long as you don't pry into their business, and they're a damn sight more civilised than any cop that ever had the balls to go in there, and it's been a long time since that happened. The girls haven't had a serious incident since they made a deal with the bikers; protection for a share of the profits, though most of the money comes from the bikers themselves."

"It still sounds rather hazardous for my liking."

Alezi shrugged. "Suit yourself, if you want to pass up some easy cash."

Juli stared absently through her own reflection in the window as she considered this. How else could she make money at short notice?

"I gave up doing that sort of thing years ago," Juli said quietly, remembering that last night. It had been awful enough before the incident. "I didn't like the kind of person it turned me into."

"Ah, I'm sure most paying men expect that kind of thing," Alezi dismissed. Another thought occurred to her: "Or did Jerin ask you to stop?"

Juli was astonished; did Alezi really not remember? *She always was a bit of a scatterbrain*, she considered. "In a way I wish he had, but he accepted me for who I was. I forget the exact words, but he basically said it was my life to live. But the one night I performed after we got together just felt wrong." It wasn't a lie as such, it just omitted a rather sizeable chunk of the truth. Juli was sure she would never forget that last night, likely twisted far beyond the reality by the tricks the mind often played. After all, if Alezi had forgotten all about it, how bad could it really have been? "Once we got together, his were the only eyes I wanted to see me undressed."

Alezi motioned sticking her fingers down her throat over this sentiment, which Juli responded to with her patented *whatever* sneer.

"The only other choice is prostitution," Alezi shrugged. "You look a damn sight better than most girls who stand on street corners. Many men would pay a small fortune to tap you," she winked.

Juli's face twisted in mock disgust. She knew Alezi was joking, but annoyingly she was right; the bar was the only real solution for a stubborn woman who refused to accept the offer of help from a friend. And what were the chances of something like *that* ever happening again? *Slim to none. Besides, Alezi says they have bouncers now.*

"Trust you to tell me all of this *after* we order scones!"

"Ah, one won't hurt," Alezi insisted.

"I haven't even had the time to work out for about four months, if not longer."

"You still look gorgeous to me!" Alezi said as she finally poured the tea. "Just remember not to push yourself too hard or you'll be sore in the morning!"

"Er, thanks…" the compliment made her feel a little uneasy. Juli wasn't entirely convinced Alezi wasn't queer; it *had* been a long time since she'd seen a man on her arm. She took a sip of the dark red tea. "*That* is sublime!"

"Made with the finest Vahirinese leaves, *don't you know*," said in that faux-posh accent again. "Try the scones."

Juli did; they were warm, buttery and moist, the glerin sweet and succulent.

"It's like an orgasm in my mouth!" Juli spluttered, trying not to spit out precious crumbs.

"Aren't they delectable with the spices of the tea? I know this place is a little pricy, but it's so worth it." She paused, then added, "We can swing by the bar once we're done here, if you like."

"Yeah, okay," Juli replied uncertainly. She wanted to spend a little more time with her friend anyway.

Alezi gasped with sudden excitement. "You should dance in your office gear! Men *love* a sexy secretary! You could really clean up!"

"No thanks!"

Alezi was baffled. "Why not?"

"Listen, I'm not exactly looking forwards to dancing at the bar again as it is. I'd certainly rather not associate it with the day job!"

"Hmm, I guess I see your point."

Once they were finished, the waitress returned to collect the used crockery and deliver the bill. Juli reached for her purse.

"I'll get this," Alezi insisted.

"I have enough."

"Juli, it's fine, really. It was my choice of venue, it's only fair."

Juli wasn't going to argue. Alezi's purse was a white lunim diamond-spangled number with gold trim, a close match to the building's exterior. Juli glanced at the time.

"Shit, we better get moving; my parking ticket runs out in five minutes."

"Okay," Alezi replied, donning her coat and scooping up her handbag.

"After the bar, can we go to your place?" Juli asked. "I don't want to disturb Jerin if he's fallen asleep. He never seems to get enough rest these days."

"Okay, sure," Alezi said hesitantly.

Their shoes clip-clopped as they made their way down the hard cobbles. Juli grimaced as she realised Alezi would see her embarrassing car.

"Please don't hate my car too much."

"Why? What's wrong with it?"

"You'll see. Just don't be *too* cruel."

"Hey, I got here on a tram, so what can I say?"

"You still live in the city then?"

"Kind of. I rent a little house in a cul-de-sac just on the outskirts up north in Materia, in part of the old town that never got renovated. It isn't as flashy as my old place, but it's considerably cheaper, and it has more character and charm." Juli glared at her. "What?"

"Who are you, and what have you done with Alezi?" Juli asked facetiously. "You only went away for six weeks, and now you're like a whole different person!"

"We all have to grow up eventually, right?"

Juli smiled. "I never thought I'd see this day."

"Besides, I figured, why waste the cash on some needlessly affluent studio apartment when I'm hardly ever there?"

"Good point. How's the power up there? Do they ever change the local module?"

"Occasionally, I think, but power deficits have been ever more common recently. I don't buy much chilled or frozen food since I had to bin a load a few weeks back."

"That's a pain. Half of what Jerin and I eat has to be overcooked to ensure it's safe."

They rounded the corner into the cul-de-sac of crowding office buildings, Juli stopping before her rust-speckled dark blue car in all its displendour.

"It's so retro!" Alezi cooed overenthusiastically.

"It's a rust bucket!" Juli admitted.

"Well, granted, there's some rust, but it's *cute*! And it even has tyres! I haven't seen those in an age!"

"They're a pain, too. Only one place I know can replace them, and they're never cheap. I wish I could afford to replace the whole damned thing."

"You can't get rid of it. You have to retire something like this, give it pride of place."

"Perhaps I should just sell it to you!"

Alezi's eyes widened excitedly. "Would you really? I might have to take you up on that!"

As they squeezed inside, Juli could hear Alezi stifling pained moans, struggling to manoeuvre herself within the tiny space.

"Sorry, it's a little small," Juli apologised. "Jerin calls it 'the Midget'."

"It's not that bad, it's cosy…" Alezi insisted, right

before banging her elbow on the edge of the door grip with a yelp. "Well, maybe it is a *tad* small."

*

Juli shuddered with nostalgic embarrassment and remorse as she parked in one of Sendura's least lively sectors. Once upon a time, this place had been the centre of her universe. How times — and people — changed, she reflected. The last time she'd seen 'Foxy' and 'Vixen', she'd been saying goodbye for the very last time. She was moving on with her life.

And yet, nearly seven years later, here she was.

She was horrified at how dilapidated the building was, as though the decay of the surrounding area was somehow contagious. The air was exceptionally stale here. The neon Siren's Song sign hung askew, giving off an audible buzz. Most of the letters were perpetually dark, the few that worked blinking pathetically as if in their death throes. The mermaid's once bright green tail was conspicuously dark, yet the yellow outline that marked her skin still glowed faintly. The long red-orange curl representing her hair seemed as bright as ever.

Alezi led the way up the concrete steps, opening the heavy peeling-red-painted riveted-steel door.

As they walked down the short half-plastarch-panelled red-walled corridor, Juli could almost hear the incessant thump-thump-thump of the bass over the eerily prevalent silence. The vile cacophony of stale beer and debauchery made her gag as it hit the back of her throat. After her emergency shift, she'd be smelling it for days.

They reached the office and Alezi pushed the door open, cheering, "Foxy!" throwing her arms high and wide.

"Lady! It's been too long!" Fox replied. They gave one another an exuberant hug, Alezi lifting Fox off her feet momentarily, then they simultaneously gave one another a friendly kiss on the left cheek.

Tamila 'Tammy' Greshen looked almost as youthful as Juli remembered. She'd always envied her ever-flat stomach in spite of her penchant for shovelling 'fish' and chips down her gullet, but given the slightly more modest skirt, she guessed those unhealthy dinners had finally caught up with her. Juli suddenly remembered Alezi mentioning Tammy giving birth a few years ago. She looked good for it, but Juli worried about the fate of a child raised by a lone parent who worked in such a lascivious environment.

The bitch inside Juli emerged on cue, making her wonder whether Fox's perfectly jet-black hair was dyed; she had begun noticing the odd grey strand in her own barnet. She locked the bitch back in her cage, wishing she could throw away the key, but she had her uses.

Fox looked at Juli with a friendly smile. "Crystal!"

Juli once thought she'd never hear her old stage name ever again. "Hey, Fox."

Tamila quickly looked Juli up and down. "You look good, girl!"

"Thanks. You too. I've never seen someone in such great shape after having a kid!"

"Plural! I stopped at two, though. Believe me, it took a hell of a lot of work to get back to this, but we've got to work hard to keep the lonely men happy, don't we? So what brings you back to our neck of the woods after such a long sabbatical? If I recall, you settled down… which I still find hilarious, by the way."

"Thanks," Juli replied sardonically. "I know it's a pain, but is there any chance I can do a shift tonight, please?"

"Wow!" Fox yelled in surprise. "You don't visit, you don't call, but when you need something…"

"I made a mistake," Juli admitted, averting her gaze to hide the tears welling in her eyes. "Let's just leave it at that, okay? Doing a night here is fitting punishment enough."

Fox raised her hands, palms forwards. "Hey, who am I to judge? I'm just glad to see you."

"Thanks."

"Where's Vix?" Alezi asked.

"Resting. She's got a bit of a belly ache."

"I'm not surprised!" Alezi choked.

Juli looked at Alezi, more confused than ever. "First you make a passing comment about Vix's 'solution' being drastic, now this. What *is* this all about?"

"You'll see soon enough," Alezi said.

"It's better to see it than hear about it," Fox added. "You'll understand when you see the reaction it draws from the crowd. Word soon gets around. Many come in the hope of seeing her not-so-little routine now, and she does so hate to let down her fans." She hunched and brought up the ancient desktop computer's calendar, studying it intently. "Hmm... I'm sorry to say tonight's booked solid, but we have an opening tomorrow, if that's good for you?"

Juli mulled it over, chewing her lips. Could she muster the required energy and enthusiasm after a mind-numbing day at the office? What choice did she have? "Tomorrow night's good, I guess, but... I still don't know..."

"Hey, I'm not busy, can I come along too?" Alezi asked.

"Sure thing," Fox replied cheerfully.

"Great!" Alezi clapped, clearly not deterred by the lecherous crowd of dangerous men that reputedly awaited them, which was all Juli could think of. But Alezi certainly wasn't shy about taking her clothes off for a bunch of fugadas; it was how she made a living, after all.

"Then I guess I'll see you both tomorrow night," Fox beamed.

"Great," Juli said nervously, glancing down at the once-varnished, now-blotchy, concrete floor.

"Are you okay?" Fox asked. "You look like you're about to hurl."

"Juli's worried about upsetting her boyfriend," Alezi answered for her.

"Ah," Fox said.

"Invite him down, he'll have the time of his life!" Alezi suggested.

"That's easy for you to say. Have you ever even had an actual boyfriend?"

"Hey! I'm offended! I've had relationships! Well, one... I think. Did I ever tell him that he was my boyfriend? Come to think of it, I kind of just followed him around for a while... is that bad?"

They both chose to ignore Alezi's rambling.

"My man thinks it's hot," Fox shrugged. "He loves the idea of me making other men hot under the collar when he's the only one who gets to touch me where it counts. But if your man's not into it, what he doesn't know won't kill him, right?"

"I guess..."

"Juli, it's just a bit of skin," Alezi said in dismay, "what's the big deal?"

"I can't believe you're the same girl who used to dance on tabletops pouring vodka down her chest!" Fox remarked.

"People change," Juli replied. "I'm more responsible now... or at least I try to be. There's just never enough cash to go around."

"Look, earning money is hard," Fox said. "Looking like we do is a gift, one that doesn't last forever. Why not earn a few easy bucks while you can? What's any job but selling your soul for a few silvan a day?"

Juli sighed, "Yeah, I guess you have a point. I'd just really hoped these days were behind me. I hope my old outfit still fits."

"You still have it?" Alezi asked in disbelief. "After the supposed finality of your farewell, I figured you'd burn it!"

"I thought about it, but I wanted to model it for Jerin, but I never get the chance before he gets hold of me!"

Alezi whispered, "Oh, barf" and Fox smiled, squealing with typically girlie joy. "I can't wait! It'll be just like old times!"

As they departed, Juli wasn't sure she'd ever felt so ambivalent about anything before. She just hoped Jerin would understand if he found out.

*

Jerin awoke in a stupor as he heard Juli entering the flat, noticing the HV was still on with the sound off. He hadn't felt *that* tired... weird. He vaguely remembered having a strange dream. He didn't remember much about it, but could still hear the echo of a voice telling him, *You should not be, I will reclaim you.* What the heck did that mean? Most of the inspiration for his art came from dreams; perhaps there was something interesting to be mined from that. Mr Venura hadn't been kidding about his dreams being more vivid, that was for sure.

He greeted Juli when she entered the front room. "Hey, honey," he croaked, adding a yawn. Now that he saw her, he recalled a dream about her and Alezi talking in a flashy bistro before meeting some old friends at a bar. He tried to cast the thought from his mind, but the unusual clarity of the vision made it impossible to shift. "Did you have fun?"

"Yeah, thanks."

"So is Alezi as up-herself as ever?" he asked cynically, rubbing the crust from the corners of his eyes.

"A little, but she means well."

He stood up and stretched gratifyingly. "I'm going to make myself a cuppa. D'you want one?"

"No thanks. Listen, Alezi's invited me out to a club tomorrow night, her treat. Do you mind?"

He shrugged, the lingering dream giving a weird sense of déjà vu. "Not at all. You two should have some fun while you can."

She smiled. "Thanks. You're so cool. I'll make it up to you." She kissed him, then gave him a hug. "I'm going to bed," she yawned. "Early start."

"Okay."

As Juli tucked herself beneath the covers, Jerin sat sipping hot tea before the HV, still too drained to do anything productive.

When his empty belly inevitably gave a hollow

gurgle, he cooked himself a frozen pizza, the sparse sprinkling of cheese combined with the cheap tomato sauce doing little for his palate, but at least it filled a hole. After that he frittered away most of the evening talking to his *BestBuddies* friends — mostly Jezebel — about nothing in particular, laughing as they sparked up a four-way conversation with two people he didn't know, all reminiscing over and posting links to videos of commercials from their respective childhoods. The trouble with dark days was just how slow the internet became, the servers struggling under the heavy demand caused by the many at home with nowhere to go and nothing to do. Jerin wondered how many of those were simply too lazy to go and do something; he'd have swapped places with them in a heartbeat.

When social networking lost its appeal, he decided to kill some time pursuing that tricky purple cosmic star in *Super Mario Universe*, amazed that the spatial controller still held a charge after not being used in so long. He swore profusely as he died twenty times in a row at the same damned hurdle. Before the expensive controller took a short flight into the nearest wall, he decided to call it a day. Though he didn't yet feel quite tired enough to sleep he had nothing better to do, so he decided to take another of those glorious white capsules before slipping into bed. He welcomed the drug-induced euphoria, allowing it to carry him away to the place where he could be free, if only for a little while. He revelled in the warm touch of Juli's skin as he cuddled up to her, quickly joining her in the land of nod.

UI
-Rose-Tinted Memories-

02:10. She'd been trying for half an hour, but there was no way she was getting back to sleep before her alarm went off. She'd been tossing and turning all night, but miraculously hadn't woken Jerin. He didn't even stir; he was dead to the world. If the dizzying sensation of fatigue she was currently experiencing was how he usually felt, she could suddenly sympathise. Perhaps she could even forgive him the odd missed chore.

Her short sleep had been filled with a very vivid dream of that much-ruminated last night at the bar, leaving her hoping it wouldn't once again become a recurring nightmare. She cursed herself for making such a simple slip-up that had left her no choice but to go back to that dreaded place tonight. She had no doubt that the trepidation over that was what had kept her from getting back to sleep.

It's only one night, she reminded herself. She could get through it. She was so very close now to finally getting the promotion she'd been chasing for so very, very long, and this was the beginning of the final stretch. But even knowing that was enough to get the anxiety flowing again. Why did she have to be so bad with stress?

She had a quick shower followed by a strong coffee in the hope of waking her sleep-deprived brain, once more skipping breakfast.

Since she was up and had nothing better to do she decided to set off early, holding her breath before trying to start the car. It was another potential obstacle just waiting to fall in her path.

"Come on, Midget," she said softly as she pressed the ignition button, hearing the familiar stuttering strain of the engine, which was quickly followed by the entire vehicle shaking even more wildly than usual, causing her right elbow to *thump* against the door handle, right on the funny bone.

She swore under her breath, then spotted that fugada Nate peering at her through his back window, the position of his second floor flat giving him a clear view over the heavily warped wooden fence. He didn't even look away when she met his freaky gaze.

She cast him and money matters from her mind. She still had plenty of time — *no need to panic* — but still struggled to calm her turbulent stomach as she set off.

Her car pitched and yawed violently over the cracked, broken asphalt that was left in such a state of disrepair since uneven roads were no issue for modern hover cars. More than once she'd had to take the car to a garage due to damage caused by potholes, but she had become familiar with the zig-zag route she needed to take down the thankfully deserted streets to avoid the worst of them — at least until another bad one opened up, which would no doubt render her financially destitute once again.

After the dark and empty streets of Sendura, the bright headlights of the innumerable cars in the city were dazzling. The traffic on the city roads was particularly horrendous this morning. The ring-road around the business district was gridlocked. She kept glancing at the clock, watching it go from 02:89 to 02:95 in very little distance. She didn't actually need to be in the office until 03:75; *loads of time.* Her fingers drummed the steering wheel impatiently as one selfish bastard after another refused to let her out, all inconsiderately gliding past in their gleaming modern machines.

She eventually squeezed through a small opening as the flow slowed, driving the short jaunt to her exit, stopping before the first junction to allow another car to go first. The driver took the invitation, surely raising a hand in gratitude behind those dazzling reflections, but another selfish driver forced their way out as the lights turned red, stopping on the wrong side of the road to avoid a collision, causing another jam. Juli sighed listlessly; morons like this were the reason she abhorred driving.

She was becoming hot and exasperated now, lowering the window a little to avoid sweating up a stink. She began to hum agitatedly as another full nine minutes passed at this particular junction. Some moron beeped their horn as if that was going to help.

She was amongst the first to arrive at the office, allowing her to park closer to the mammoth building than usual. No doubt someone would be moaning later about how someone had stolen 'their' space, though the chance of her bumping into that specific person in a building this expansive was next to none.

She took a short, casual stroll across the ground-strip-lit path, taking a moment to glance around. It was strange to think that all the different-style buildings surrounding what had become the central 'core' had once been businesses completely independent from the corporation. But that was a different time. Now, those had all been shut down, gutted, and appropriated, connected to the corporate building by enclosed walkways at many different levels to save time. This was the march of progress, and she would have reflected on how untidy and ugly it looked, had it not been so familiar to her. She didn't even pause to think what might happen if all the corporate buildings around the city were ever connected in such a manner. There would be no need for anyone to ever go outside.

The glass entrance doors of the most affluent building rolled back smoothly as she approached, the lobby's overhead spotlights basking her in their bright white glow, so very harsh on her still-weary eyes.

"Morning, Rosie," she addressed the automated receptionist, which quick as a whistle replied, "Morning, Miss Tenzalin," with very human inflections, its silicone lips moving in precise sync. She still found its realistic human visage somewhat unnerving. What was so wrong with one of those retro-style metal-faced automatons?

'She' even had purely decorative legs, and once a week someone changed 'her' outfit for a clean one, even styling 'her' hair differently now and then. More than once she'd heard people talk about Rosie as if it was a living person.

Juli took the stairs, promising herself she'd avoid the lift from now on to get herself in better shape, hoping that climbing the ten half-floor flights would soon become easier, arriving on her level out of breath.

As she opened the door from the stairwell to the open-plan lobby, she saw a familiar face hovering over a steaming mug of coffee. "Hey, Keresay." She remembered she hated being called *Kerry*.

"Hey, Ju."

Juli was about to reply when her brain caught up. "Hang on, what are you doing here on a ten-day?"

"I get bored sitting at home with nothing to do, so I figured I might as well make a good impression..."

"Are you hoping for a promotion?"

"I don't know. I mean, I was... but I'm not so sure it's for me..." she sounded and looked troubled.

"Why? What's up?"

Keresay averted her gaze. "Ah, it's nothing. Probably just me being stupid."

"Hey, if something's bothering you, you know you can tell me."

"I know, but since there's nothing you can do about it, there's no point. I just need to forget about it."

"It'll eat you up if you don't tell someone. I might have a little pull now that I'm in the club, so to speak."

Keresay's eyes lit up. "Juli, that's great! Congratulations! It's about time this company promoted someone who isn't a useless dolt!"

"Thanks. So out with it, girl. What's up?"

"Well, back when I started, there were no positions in software coding, so Lazarus offered me a position in testing, promising to move me when a vacancy came up."

"Ah, I see."

"I'm fully qualified and very capable, but the coders

hate me. I don't think they take kindly to criticism."

"It was the constructive kind, yes?"

"Well... mostly..."

Juli shook her head disapprovingly. "Keresay, I know you mean well, but perhaps it would be better if you kept your opinions to yourself."

"I know, it's just that I want the job so badly. But those stubborn middle-aged men... I've never played the sexism card before..."

"Then don't start now," Juli interjected. "Trust me, it won't get you anywhere around here."

"A position was listed this morning, and I don't want to miss out. I just want a chance to prove myself."

"I understand," Juli replied. She wished she could assure the young girl that the company was more professional than that, but they both knew it was a lie. "When I get the chance, I'll have a quiet word with Mr Manrose."

"Thanks, Ju," Keresay smiled, standing on her tiptoes to give her a quick hug. "You're a star."

Juli glanced at the clock on the wall behind Keresay. "Crap, I better get going. No doubt my brain will be a steaming pile of mush by the end of the day."

"Good luck," Keresay beamed before disappearing towards her own closet-sized office.

Juli decided to stop by own her office to get directions. Keresay was about the age Juli was when she met Jerin and decided to put more effort into developing a 'respectable' career. She just hoped Keresay was more sensible than her.

Rosie had informed Juli that the training workshop room was located on the ninth floor of the little-used south-east building, but the nearest crossing was on the floor below the one her office was on, a floor she didn't know too well, and though she did her best to memorise the route displayed on her office computer screen, she quickly got lost and confused, unable to find anyone to ask for directions. She spotted the crossing through a window, but getting to it was a whole other matter. The nearest door was locked. She backtracked, looking for another way. Once she realised she had to pass through a disused office to reach it, she was rather less than eager to cross the ill-maintained walkway, which had cracks running along every surface, even the metal-plate floor. She glanced at her watch; she hadn't the time to go all the way down to the ground floor and find its main entrance, assuming it was open, which she didn't imagine it would be.

She had to cross. She drew a deep breath and dashed, squealing with fear as she heard a slight *creak*. A little breathless but safely on the other side, she looked around and found the lift, only to find an 'out of order' sign upon it. She sighed at the prospect of having to climb five floors. *At least it's good exercise*, she thought, heading up at a brisk but not too energetic pace.

She opened the first wooden door at the top to find a distinctly classroom-like setup, about twenty people all sitting at tiny desks facing a large wall-mounted-screen, and guessed she was in the right place.

As she walked in, she heard someone remark, "Just in time." The comment came from a young man with slicked-back hair, who didn't even look at her, too busy playing with his phone. His red-and-black striped tie was undone, each end drooping over his shoulders.

What a douche, Juli thought. "No one told me how to get here. That walkway doesn't look very safe," she replied.

He rolled his eyes. "You cross on the tenth floor. There's a new walkway up there." His cocky attitude made her sick; this was the kind of idiot who rose despite his brazen disdain.

"Thanks." He offered no further reply.

She headed towards the front, finding a free seat in the middle. She sat down with a weary sigh, anticipating the day's events the way she would a fresh slice of shit cake. She had a pretty good idea she knew how this was going to play out, and as soon as the ditzy course leader arrived, her suspicions were confirmed.

Like everyone else in the room she was considerably younger than Juli, her auburn hair pulled back into a bun so tightly it stretched her forehead. She was wearing a designer suit no one but a brown-nose could get away with at work. It wasn't indecent as such, but it left very little to the imagination. She regarded them all over the top of her red-framed phone-specs.

"Good morning class," she joked pathetically. The boot-lickers who wished they were standing where she was had to keep their sides from splitting, in fits of obviously forced laughter.

That greeting set the tone; it was exactly like being back at school, though Juli doubted she could get away with spending the day writing various versions of 'Juli heart Jerin' all over her notebook. For one, they didn't have notebooks anymore.

She spent most of the morning struggling to stay awake, using her still-on phone-specs to browse *BestBuddies* for anything of interest while the instructor blathered on about profit forecasts, or some such nonsense. She really didn't care. She wanted to go to the toilet and never come back. But she had to attend. Mr Manrose would take care of the rest, she didn't doubt that. He'd certainly been right about the tedium.

Her mind wandered and wondered in equal measure, and so it inevitably found itself turning to the thorny subject of what was to come that night. Right now, that night felt like it was a million years away.

Was it really ten years since she and Alezi had gone out virtually every night, drinking and dancing into the early hours? Alezi had always been the confident one, though Juli often joined in the laughter as she delivered yet another cruel put-down to any amorous man who dared request a dance with a lame chat-up line. The best of the worst made it into Alezi's digital diary. Juli smiled to herself. She *knew* Alezi still had that file.

Juli sighed, considering Alezi's glamorous life. She always seemed to be away on a photo-shoot in the city's glitzy eastern-most district, Solaria, where all the movie stars lived. Juli couldn't even imagine what it must be like to actually be there... pictures were incapable of capturing the buzzing atmosphere she imagined. What did Alezi know of hard times? Juli caught her own reflection in one of the darkness-backed windows. Was Alezi really that much more attractive than her? Or did she simply know how to 'work it' better? Maybe Alezi was smarter than Juli gave her credit for.

As her focus passed through the window to the perfect darkness beyond, she wondered what Jerin was up to right now. She hoped he was doing something worthwhile, and not just vegetating. She was so glad to see him in higher spirits. Maybe it was a good omen, a sign that they would make it through this yet. She actually believed it this time.

"Julianos, what do you think?" came an unwelcome outside voice, rudely jolting her back to reality.

Her attention was quickly diverted back to the instructor, and Juli suddenly became aware she was propping her head up with her hand, elbow resting atop the desk.

She ignored the snide sniggering from the woman on her left, noticing that the wall-screen read 'improving productivity'.

She hoped she could bluff her way through it, quickly thinking of one of Jerin's most common lamentations from back when he would occasionally talk about work.

"I think we need to better understand the job we're advising people on," she replied, hoping she was in the right ballpark.

"Oh, really?" the woman replied in clear surprise, likely not used to hearing from someone who dares challenge the oft-misjudged ideas of the board. "Why so?"

She had to project confidence now, or her point would lose its impact. "Well, I recently filled in a form about production line efficiency, and realised that I have no idea what those people do. I sit in an office all day; I have no idea how long it *actually* takes to repair a module, so what right do I have to tell them to work faster?"

"Good point," the woman conceded. "Any thoughts?" she asked the room.

The nameless woman to her left snorted, "Lucky."

"This company is all about profit," a young male voice said from the back of the room. Juli looked around to find the source of the remark: the cocky young idiot who had greeted her. His arms were crossed, and he was leaning his chair against the wall and resting his feet on the desk. "Surely that begins with looking at where we can save money?"

"No, it doesn't," Juli replied reactively. *Drat, I'll have to elaborate now.* "If all you ever do is worry about cutting costs, you eventually reach the point where you're actively *losing* money because you don't have enough people to do all the jobs. When did people become so stupid that they forgot that old phrase, you have to spend money to make money?" Juli wasn't sure she had articulated her reply very well, but was confident her point was clear.

The woman leading the group nodded. "Another good point. Does anyone else have an opinion they'd like to share?"

No one said anything, all staring directly ahead, either too incompetent to understand or to formulate the words to counter this undeniably valid point.

"Well, Julianos has given us much to think about," the woman said. "Thank you for your contribution," she said directly to Juli, who offered no reply, resisting the urge to shrink back into her seat.

Why had she said anything? Mr Manrose had told her to keep her head down... she should have kept her stupid mouth shut; everyone would start calling her a 'free radical' now. She hoped it was nothing Mr Manrose couldn't take care of. *Oh well,* she thought, *at least it's better than being called a brown-nose.*

*

Jerin awoke to a loud door slam in a timeless darkness. *Nate, you inconsiderate bastard.* He wanted more sleep, but was awake now. Everything Nate did generated noise, even making a cup of tea. He could hear the spoon hitting the sides of the mug. Even when there was no actual sound, the air had the buzz of restless activity.

He clicked his lamp on, rising with neither a wobble nor a hobble, unaware of the time but aware Juli had already departed for work, sitting in that room full of corporate idiots. His dreams about her were getting ever more vivid, but what was really strange was their mundanity, like he was seeing snapshots of her everyday life. He felt like some kind of spectral stalker, as though he was somehow tethered to her. Were these dreams some weird side-effect of the capsules? He took a black one and the residual fog of fatigue lifted immediately, restoring his mental acuity. He was surprised by how well they worked, and so very glad they weren't the mind-killers he'd anticipated, but there were downsides to having honed senses.

One was the cold. He shivered as he got out of bed, the air considerably colder than yesterday. He quickly climbed into an even colder pair of jeans; he would normally wear joggers, but this was his way of promising himself he *wasn't* going to just sit around the flat all day. He did a few star-jumps to get the blood pumping in an effort to warm himself up, but he was so unfit he had to stop after just a few, his breathing quickly heavy and laboured, sweat dappling his brow. He tugged at his t-shirt to let a little heat out.

His hearing was considerably sharper now too, which might have been good if it didn't make the noise from upstairs even more annoying, especially that of Nate's HV, the muffled bass notes of which sounded like someone trying to talk with their mouth closed.

But the upside was totally worth it.

He sat on the sofa and set his obsolete compu-phone

to tablet mode, opening the *BestBuddies* app, promising himself to procrastinate for no longer than quarter of an hour. He quickly spotted the thumbnail photo of Jezebel in the corner of the screen that heralded a message from her (*not a bad-looking girl for a mechanic*, he thought upon first seeing her picture, admiring the contentment etched into every pixel. That she bore something of a resemblance to Juli may explain why he was drawn to her). He opened the message eagerly.

He smiled at the attached photo of her latest sculpture: a massive face constructed from various mechanical odds-and-sods. He doubted any of her reputedly non-artistic co-workers would see the funny side. He clicked the link in Jezebel's message marked 'inspiration', opening a page overflowing with Vahirinese myths and legends that had inspired artists for generations; too well-mined a source for his liking.

He wasn't surprised to find that many of the historic images had religious connotations. Before he could pass comment on their grandiose pretentiousness, he saw Jezebel had already posted a few biting words of her own, all of which he found hilarious, quickly throwing his own two cents in for good measure, his articulation fully restored. He typed, *Didn't people have the sagacity to question the absence of these so-called 'Gods' back then?* He wondered whether the people in question really had been as gullible as many seemed to believe now. After all, how much of the recorded history was truly accurate?

It never failed to amaze him that a couple of computers could unite people living on opposite sides of the world. He had made and lost many friends online over the years, but none had struck a chord as quickly as Jezebel. They were like kindred spirits half a world apart. She boosted his confidence in a way only another creative could. As much as he appreciated Juli's opinions, only so much encouragement could be wrought from the occasional well-meant but ignorant "that's good". In his secret heart, Jerin had often wondered whether he would have been naïve and reckless enough to go through the rigmarole of migrating to Vahiras back when he was young, dumb and single, had he befriended her early enough.

Sufficiently motivated, he decided it was time to finish a piece of his own to contribute to the online community, casting aside the often-disheartening idea that everything he did had been done better by someone else.

He closed his web browser, took out his purpose-bought stylus (for extra precision) and opened the sketching app, deleting his last pathetic attempt and starting afresh. All the old ideas came back to him, the flood gates well and truly open. The trouble now was picking just one, but that one persistent idea was vying for attention more than any other. He saw that image in his mind's eye much more clearly now.

Many of his favourite artists had been inspired by the pain and misery of their own existences, but none had suffered the precise cruel twist of fate that had befallen him. After the op, he'd looked back on his previous work with the aching sense of loss an avid cycler might feel when they looked at their precious bike after losing a leg, so he'd stopped looking before he became despondent enough to stop creating altogether.

Despite his rapport with Jezebel, he hadn't burdened her with the story of his op. If she were to critique his work, he would have it judged on its own merits. Kind words born of sympathy weren't conducive to honing his skills.

The image from his dreams was so vivid now: the city in the sky falling towards a mountain range. He had no idea what that dream meant, but he loved the macabre details it inspired. He patiently drew every lick of flame bursting from the holes in the inverted domes that his mind told him kept this imaginary city afloat.

His hands flowed in a rapid series of fluid strokes and arcs. After a while he held the image back and smiled, the elation bringing tears to his eyes: it was actually good. No longer did he feel like a false artist, no better than a poor man gatecrashing a cocktail party in a stolen suit. It brought an unexpected sense of nostalgia that reminded him of his late beloved companion, Nibbler. Before he'd been killed, the amiable black-and-white cat had been glued to Jerin's side, often nudging his elbow as he drew a crucial line before jumping onto his lap, using his compuphone's enlarged screen as a pillow as he purred and plonked on Jerin's lap emphatically.

It made him feel so alone. Talking to Jezebel helped, but words on a screen were no match for physical company and the passion of animated conversation. He couldn't remember the last time he'd seen *any* of his friends; they'd grown so used to his constant declining of invitations for one reason or another that no one bothered asking him anymore. Even if he had tried to adjust his sleep pattern so he could attend a get-together, fate often conspired against him, ensuring he would awaken at stupid-o-clock, leaving him long exhausted when the time to meet rolled around.

And who could say how long these wondrous capsules would work? To be so lucid at such a civilised hour was an opportunity he was loathe to waste. He was isolated by circumstance enough without choosing to make himself a recluse. He didn't want to become like the hermit upstairs, twitching the curtains, watching the world pass by. Jerin so often yearned to meet up with his old friends. Right now he'd settle for getting away from the muffles and bangs of *him* upstairs for a while. Now it sounded like he was in the bathroom forcing up phlegm. *Lovely*.

Too self-conscious in the prevalent silence to dictate a generic message (and paranoid that Nate would eavesdrop on his business), he quickly typed one, sending it to whoever might be free — a somewhat deflating eleven in all. His phone being as it was, it would be miraculous if the message reached its many intended recipients. He didn't hold up much hope; the last time he'd been free, no one else had. In that case, he resolved to still go *somewhere* to avoid feeling trapped in that tiny flat; not that there was anywhere in Sendura worth going.

If not for his poverty-stricken status and the lack of trams running from Sendura, he could have gone into the city to visit a gallery and feed his mind, though he was always the first to admit he didn't understand much 'real' art, preferring recognisable images over indistinct blobs and shapes. Amongst the images that had stuck with him from his only previous visit many years ago were those of an anguished woman being comforted by family; a lone suited man walking through the debris of a fallen office block; an animal cradling its sleeping child with unmistakable love in its gold-ringed eyes. He yearned to convey such emotion, to tell a whole story in one image.

He had found a few online galleries, but all the professional ones demanded hefty fees to view works at a decent resolution without a watermark. The amateur galleries were so over-saturated with crap that it took longer than it was worth to trawl through it all to find the few gems.

He looked back at his own image, admiring it proudly. It would be a good image to transfer to canvas. He'd barely touched the paints, brushes and mini-canvases Juli bought him years ago; they were far too valuable to waste. His mostly-empty sketchbook was worth a small fortune now, since art-grade paper was becoming ever harder to source.

In the prevalent silence, the obstreperous sound of a reply arriving on his phone made him jolt with enough shock to make him drop the stylus. The momentary excitement quickly passed when he read the deflating words: *sorry, who is this?* from Purvil, someone he'd once considered a good friend. He told himself to stop being so pessimistic. Perhaps Purvil had lost his contacts somehow and was too embarrassed or just plain forgot to ask Jerin for his number again via *BestBuddies*.

Jerin patiently replied, but no reply from Purvil followed.

He resumed sketching, but the device's text alert soon abruptly blurted again, flashing a notification on the screen. He was pleasantly surprised to see the sender was one Kol Solborn. His old friend from those bygone cinema days was notoriously lazy, and slow at rising. His rare replies were typically dense, and this was no different, Jerin's eyes eagerly taking in every word.

Kol now lived and worked on the far side of Darina, but was in Sendura for the day to see family, and happy to take time out of his schedule to meet up for a drink. Jerin just wished the stubborn bugger would create a *BestBuddies* profile so they could talk more often.

Jerin smiled to himself; he enjoyed reminiscing with Kol, recounting many hilarious moments, such as the time the security cameras caught Patras slipping over in the sweet shop, landing heavily on her arse after spraying too much air freshener which had condensed into puddles on the polished faux-wood floor. Kol and Jerin had never had anything remotely close to an argument. Jerin had conceded the validity of Kol's disparaging lamentations about certain colleagues Jerin got on reasonably well with. They certainly agreed on the issue of Purvil's capricious nature.

Kol ended his message: 'Where shall we meet?'

Jerin replied: 'It has to be the Jester.'

'See you at six?'

'See you there.'

'One more thing, any chance I can borrow your copy of X Hunters?'

Jerin snorted a laugh, *typical Kol*. He briefly considered this. He hated lending things out; they never came back in the same condition. But Kol was a good friend, and Jerin trusted him far more than anyone else (even Juli), so he replied: 'You can, but when will I see you to get it back?'

Too soon to be a reply, Kol sent: 'I'll post it back if I have to,' clearly a preemptive after-thought.

Jerin typed: 'Fair enough,' quickly finding and

throwing the movie into his going-out messenger bag while he remembered.

He was looking forwards to seeing Kol again. It had been far, far too long.

*

When the time to go meet his friend finally arrived, Jerin eagerly wrapped himself up in his scarf, gloves and thick coat, and set out. His route to meet Kol would be longer than it could, but he was fiercely determined he absolutely *would not* go down Ferrelus Road; some memories were just too damned painful.

The lonely rattle of the film in Jerin's surprisingly spacious bag was all that accompanied him on the long walk. It was so incredibly dark now. The relentless gloom obscured all: pursed concrete lips spitting tufts of long-dead grass; discarded shopping trolleys; numerous knee-high concrete lumps and other detritus that had fallen from long-neglected buildings not designed to withstand the consistent fluctuations of the barrier's warming and cooling cycles. He swore as his shin connected with something hard and jagged, continuing with a hobble.

Jerin reminisced over how he and Kol had once whiled away many a lunch break and an evening in the Jester, situated virtually opposite Hit Flix, discussing their woes over a plate of mashed potato and pie (of questionable meat content but drowned in undeniably divine gravy) and a glass of sweet drascas.

When Jerin and Kol first started at the cinema, the Jester had been *Jovial*, and after the death of Tyrus's wife, Isabella, he had renamed it the *Morose Jester*, changing the smile on the iconic sign to a frown and adding a lone tear.

In the years since leaving the cinema, Jerin had only ventured this way with Juli on the rare occasion to see his old friends and a free film by the grace of Desra, the kinder of his former two bosses, until it inevitably closed its doors for good almost two years ago, becoming just another boarded-up building in the sector many called 'the boardwalk', largely abandoned during the riots of his youth.

Tyrus had boarded up the Jester's windows, yet to this day stubbornly remained open for business. There was no one to demand rent and the old codger could still procure the odd keg of ale, even if he did drink most of it himself. According to Kol, the reason Tyrus never took the boards down was because he was concerned that some roving vagabond might put a brick through his expensive stained-glass windows.

Jerin rounded the last corner and saw the ever-slender silhouette of Kol Solborn leaning casually against the wall of a ruined bank, head tilted back as he poured a generous sprinkling of gunpowder from a white unmarked sachet onto his protruding grey-stained tongue. An acrid plume of smoke rose from his mouth as the dry powder reacted with his saliva.

The top of Kol's ancient long grey duster-like coat of myriad pockets was open despite the cold, giving him easy access to the inside pocket, into which he placed the packet as he spotted Jerin.

"Jerry!" Kol chimed, wispy black tendrils expelling from his nose and mouth.

"Kolly!" Jerin replied. Kol deplored his affectionate nickname as much as Jerin did his own, but it had become their friendly greeting years ago after a typo on Jerin's ticket for a group holiday booking. They firmly took one another's right hand and leaned into a manly embrace, wrapping their left arms around one another's shoulders.

When they parted, Jerin wafted away the unseen cloud of stink with one hand, trying not to gag as it burned the back of his throat. He wished he could voluntarily close his nasal passages.

"Sorry," Kol said, "I forgot how sensitive your nose is to that stuff."

"I don't know how you put up with the vile stuff."

"I don't know how you don't," Kol shrugged.

"Typical addict, addicted to an addictive substance,"

Jerin faux-reprimanded. "It's a terrible sign of weakness, you know."

"A lot of sanctimonious so-and-sos tell me that," Kol replied.

"Maybe they're right," Jerin deadpanned.

"Maybe *they* should try some, maybe it would lighten them up a bit."

"Maybe *they* would rather gargle dirty toilet water."

Another shrug. "That can be arranged."

After a few seconds' failure to keep a straight face they both started laughing like a pair of naughty schoolboys.

"It's so good to see you again," Kol said once he was able to.

"You too. It's been way too long."

Jerin couldn't remember precisely how long it had been since he'd last seen Kol — maybe a year, if not longer — but it was as though they'd met just yesterday, only with far more to catch up on.

"Life goes on," Jerin lamented. "Does anyone even still live in this dump?"

"There's a small community in the north-west. It's better maintained than most of this." Kol ran his fingers through his mid-length dark brown mane, which looked to have been combed back but wasn't gelled.

"That's right, the so-called 'Free Radicals'... you have to admire their courage, I guess."

"Yeah, I suppose."

"Maybe Juli and I should join that little community of theirs... but I don't think she'd take to that kind of lifestyle."

"One thing's for sure, it isn't for everybody. It's harder work that most realise." Kol checked the time on his phone, which he'd bought from Jerin as a favour, insisting he didn't need anything flashy. "We've still got a few minutes 'til Tyrus opens up."

"I'm sure they'll fly by," Jerin smiled.

They slowly made their way towards the pub, walking

on the opposite side of the street to the old cinema, stopping to admire it in all its boarded-up, dilapidated displendour. Without maintenance, the barrier's cycles had warped its metal panels, some worse than others. To top it off, some moron had scaled the building to spray a massive dried-dripping red 'S' directly in front of the missing Hit Flix lettering, visible only as a stencil formed from many years' accumulated dirt.

"What a waste," Kol lamented.

"A lifetime of memories happened in that place," Jerin sighed.

"Yeah," Kol agreed with a sigh. "Gone but never forgotten. Not yet, at least."

"To be honest, I can't believe how long it held out after everything else went. At least it had a good run. I just still can't believe how quickly it happened. One minute it was here, the next…"

"It's astonishing sometimes just how quickly everything can change. Thing stays the same for years, then out of nowhere comes one big rush… after that, people move on, and it's nothing more than a memory. An ever-dulling echo we fear to forget, lest we lose sight of ourselves."

"Deep," Jerin admired.

"I've been reading Strausenhein. It's funny how it works its way into your brain. It changes the way you think."

Jerin wrinkled his face in disbelief and disapproval. "Why? Every time I had to read that shit at school I just wished I was anywhere else. I always found it so… impenetrable."

"Me too. But in recent years I've begun to understand it. You should give it another go. It's public domain, so you can just get it on the 'net."

"Maybe I'll look into it, if by some miracle I'm ever simultaneously awake and bored enough."

They both looked in the direction of the Jester as Tyrus slid the lock mechanism back with a heavy *clunk*.

Without a word, they both slowly strode in that direction, the razor-thin shafts of light peeking between the window boards caressing their clothing as they passed.

Kol pulled the stiff-hinged metal door open with a grunt, holding it for Jerin, who entered with a courteous nod.

Jerin was overwhelmed by nostalgia as he inhaled the unmistakable cacophony of aromas that were so uniquely the Jester: the must of slowly rotting wood and stale alcohol with a hint of urine, the hot metal after-stench of diffused gunpowder particles, and something else he could never quite place.

Save for the thicker layers of dust, the Jester was exactly as Jerin remembered it, each piece of furniture and every dirt-speckled glass wearing its age with pride. It was comforting somehow, like arriving home after a very long journey.

They approached the bar, on which Tyrus was leaning heavily, wearily lifting his head and furrowing his brow as he tore his gaze from whatever he was watching on the ill-defined flickering monovision in the far corner opposite the bar, plugged into an old-fashioned wall socket via a fibre optic lead. Tyrus looked *old*, like he was defying death. His bushy beard looked to be about two or three years old. He smelled like he hadn't bathed in almost as long. His left hand listlessly swirled a filthy rag over the same spot on the counter, creating a clean island amidst a sea of grime.

Jerin shivered, deciding to keep his coat on; it wasn't much warmer inside than out, yet Tyrus seemed comfortable in just a creased shirt beneath a heavy-weave faux-woollen jumper. The old barkeep grunted and swayed slightly as he stood upright, the smell of alcohol thick on his breath. At least he was an agreeable drunk.

"Hey, Tyrus," Kol said with a polite nod. Tyrus's tired eyes regarded him, but he uttered not a word. "Two bottles of drascas, please."

"Four," Tyrus replied gruffly, coughing and swaying

uneasily on his journey to the counter-top fridge at the far end of the bar. He duly returned with two bottles, prying the caps off with a *fizt* on the edge of the pumps before placing them on the counter.

"First round's on me," Jerin insisted, laying his last fiver on the counter. "Keep the change."

"Cheers, mate," Kol said as he picked up one of the quietly fizzing bottles.

Tyrus gave a courteous nod and a grunt Jerin assumed meant "thanks."

They took their drinks to a table by the front-left window, lit by the dim conical glow of a bulb beneath a dust-opaqued red, blue and purple lampshade patterned to match the windows, which themselves were lightly speckled with condensation. The ancient varnished darkwood chairs creaked as they sat, placing their drinks atop faded beermats. Jerin's seat was a little wonky, so he placed his bag on it and moved to a marginally less wonky one.

They both slouched, comfortable in one another's company. Kol glanced around, lost in thought, admiring the thick black wooden beams that ran along the ceiling. Particles of dust hung lazily in the air. "I can't believe how little this place has changed. I mean, look at the alcohol residue on this table! I bet you could get drunk just by sucking on the wood!"

"I may be skint, but even I'm not that desperate!" Jerin laughed. In his distracted state, Kol's stare lingered on the darkwood table for a while.

Jerin took a hearty swig of his drink, savouring the complex flavours of the slightly translucent dark brown fluid: fruity with a touch of aniseed, so sweet and refreshing, the taste of a misspent youth. He just hoped it didn't react with his new medication.

"So, how's life in the big city treating you?" Jerin asked.

"It's fine once you get used to all the people. Nobody has time for anyone, they're always in a rush."

"I'm not sure I could live somewhere that busy. Too much congestion. I imagine it must feel pretty claustrophobic."

"The area I live in isn't too heavily populated, but there are some rather brutish people about. Some drunken idiot tried to steal my phone the other week."

"Really? What did you do?"

"Punched him in the nose and ran!" Kol laughed. "I probably should have given it to him. It wasn't until I started legging it that I realised he might pull a gun on me, but I had a couple of drinks in me and obviously wasn't thinking clearly!"

Jerin shook his head in mock disapproval, taking another sip of drink. "I forgot how much I love drascas." He let the bubbles dance on his tongue momentarily before swallowing. That stuff held a fizz like nothing else he knew. "I can't remember the last time I had one."

"They're a little pricey, but they're well worth it. I think I'd go insane if I couldn't mull over the day's little annoyances with one of these in my hand."

"That'd be the addict talking again!" Jerin laughed. "Maybe that's where I'm going wrong. I just can't afford it these days. All my spare cash goes on headache pills."

Kol looked concerned. "You still get those, huh?"

"From time to time. Being tired or stressed makes them worse, and I'm always tired and usually stressed. The tedium of being alone at work doesn't help. I can feel every minute ticking by. Every hour feels like a whole night, and every night feels like a week. When I get a headache, all my fatuous dolt of a boss says is that they'll have to reevaluate whether it's suitable for me to keep doing the job. Considering it's the plant's fault I get the headaches at all, it's just more salt in the wound."

"What an arse," Kol noted.

"You said it. Marv has it in for me because he thinks Falz is the dog's bollocks and I'm the only one with the balls to call him useless. That brainless prick can't even tie his own shoelaces. We're supposed to do an hour's work between quarter-hour breaks, but I'm sure Falz does the opposite. But I have to watch everything I say about the idiot because he's Sundrosian. Ever since Marv started chatting up that Sundrosian girl he acts like he's a member of their secret little club and won't hear a word against them. If I dare criticise Falz, I'm accused of racism. I don't care where someone's from, an idiot's an idiot."

"Idiocy is indiscriminate, I don't get why some people fail to see that. I know plenty of Silandrian idiots, far more than I do of any other race." Kol shuddered. "Though I must admit, I've never understood what attracts some people to Sundrosians."

"I know, right? That sloping forehead you could ski down, the jutting lower jaw... could you imagine oral sex with one?" Jerin jutted his bottom jaw out and said "Come get sexy time" in a typically Sundrosian-like dim-witted tone.

Kol was reclining, sipping from his bottle as Jerin did this, quickly jerking forwards, almost spraying drink everywhere. "You bastard!" he laughed, leaning over the table, sticky drascas running down the back of the right hand he'd raised to his mouth.

For the second time in as many days, Jerin laughed until his face ached.

Kol fell silent, wistfully adding, "I miss this."

"But wait, it gets better," Jerin teased. "To top it all off, Falz outranks me because he has... drum roll, please..." he drummed his fingers along the edge of the table "...a degree! And as we all know, that trumps everything!"

"Ah," Kol nodded eminently. "Of course. As long as they have one of those it doesn't matter if they're about as productive as a brick."

"At least a brick has a use," Jerin added. "I don't get why anyone would waste years studying just to end up in a place like that. Then again, it was probably Falz's only chance of getting a job, given his obvious mental deficiency. Some idiot didn't even see the harm in teaching him to drive... I can't even afford to take lessons, and the state just hands him a license and a car. From what I've overheard, he's already had at least three accidents. Thank goodness for sticky shields, eh?"

Kol was shaking his head in agreed dismay. "I've seen idiots like him handed everything on a plate too many times. Because political correctness has gone insane, it's actually *easier* to pass tests and courses if you're handicapped. It's positive discrimination. The state assigns them a personal tutor, and they get whatever they want."

Jerin lamented, "I'm not saying they shouldn't have jobs, I just think they should be offered something better suited to their limited abilities. The intrinsically incompetent just shouldn't be allowed to have positions of power where one mistake can cost lives. Screw it, maybe I should play dumb, see if it gets me out of my mess! Maybe I could score myself a hover-car, lessons and a license, even a nice home in the city."

Kol laughed. "Just do your Sundrosian impression and I'm sure you'll do fine!"

"Hell, Purvil used to do creature makeup, maybe he can do me a facial prosthetic!" When the laughter had died down, Jerin added, "If I was in charge, I'd have the balls to do things differently."

"That's the problem, though. People who dare to challenge convention never get anywhere. I'm pretty sure the corporate bigwigs are afraid of independent thinkers showing them up, so they promote idiots to play it safe, ensuring the same old problems just continue until people give up and accept them. They're too apathetic to realise just how complacent they've become."

"That sounds like the corporation I know!" Jerin agreed.

Kol made an "mmm" sound, raising his empty bottle in one hand and two fingers with the other to signal Tyrus to bring them two more, which he promptly did. Kol handed over a five silvan note with a quiet "Keep the change," the barkeep offering a grateful grunt in return before vanishing with the empties.

Jerin thanked Kol and they both took a long, reflective swig.

"Idiots like your boss piss me off so much that sometimes I swear I want to *kill* them," Kol said, his intense gaze piercing the table.

"I could easily throttle both of those idiots," Jerin added, feeling the alcohol's influence swimming in his mind, bringing forth his innermost dark desires. "If I could get away with it. I recently calculated that I need to stay on nights working with those arseholes for at least another two years before our finances finally level out. I'm not even sure if I can do it... just the idea of it makes me feel ill. The last three years have been far beyond your average endurance test... I'm not sure I can last *that* much longer without killing someone." *Or myself,* he didn't add. "I feel trapped. The crap we have to endure just to live honest lives... I swear, I can understand why people become thieves now. All these fancy gadgets and gizmos that will supposedly enhance our lives are being dangled just beyond the reach of the common person... it's like entrapment, drawing out their inner thieves. The number of times I've been in a position where I could easily swipe something, knowing I could have gotten away with it, yet I never gave in... is it honesty or stupidity?" He decided not to mention Kol's infamous father, feeling somewhat embarrassed at the unintended implication. "But we're not supposed to talk about such things, are we? We all have to be good little boys and girls. If not, there's always prison." Jerin finally stopped, feeling no better, failing to get it off his mind, where it continued to gnaw away, slowly making him ever more bitter.

Kol gazed into the mid-distance somewhat introspectively as he replied, "I wish I could help, I really do. I hate to see people like you having their souls crushed in places like that." His gaze turned from the far wall to Jerin. "Is there no one there to fight your corner?"

"Roz, the union rep. She can be a bit condescending at times, but she means well, and she knows her stuff. If not for her, I'd probably be out of a job." Jerin found himself staring fixedly into the stained surface of the darkwood table in deep contemplation now. "I don't even know what it takes to be a manager in a place like the plant. It's like you have to be completely brain-dead to ignore the inherent insanity of all the company bullshit..." he gesticulated wildly as he launched into a frustrated tirade: "Hey, these here instructions say we should stack the most fragile components on the top shelves, ensuring they'll explode into their component atoms if they get knocked down, but hey, even if it doesn't make a lick of sense, it's an order, so let's blindly do as we're told!"

Kol's brow wrinkled with incredulity. "You're kidding, right? Why would any idiot put fragile stuff on the top shelf? That's just asking for trouble!"

"You think that's dumb? I swapped them over once and got hauled into the office for a good old finger-wagging. I can't believe I ever wanted to advance in that place..."

"You're obviously too smart for the job!" Kol laughed. "It sounds an awful lot like you'd need to undergo a frontal lobotomy first!"

"Oh, it gets worse too. Since Reginald took over the company, he's been cutting the plant's hours back, so now we can only get about half the modules repaired each week. Yet when it was Reginald's birthday, he couldn't hold off his celebrations until the reactor came back up, so we were forced to do overtime so there were enough working modules to prevent him from bleeding the city dark!"

Kol shook his head in disbelief. "If only Lazarus knew..."

"The module near our flat is long past the point of needing to be replaced, but even if there were enough modules to go around, who would bother just for us? If I knew how I'd do it myself, but no doubt I'd be sacked for 'stealing company property' and daring to use my initiative. I can't stand 'Reggie'," Jerin derided. "He's done no good for anyone since he took over. He just fritters away daddy's hard-earned fortune while the good people suffer…"

"He's the bane of the city," Kol agreed.

"I hate that damned photonic reactor, but at least its power fluctuations are predictable. And without it, I guess I'd be out of a job. Those glorified batteries are clearly deteriorating though, they can't hold anywhere near the charge they used to. Despite the scouring of Sendura, high-quality replacement parts are becoming harder to find, and no one seems to realise where that's going to end…"

"People prefer to bury their heads in the sand than admit to what is essentially a very inconvenient truth. No one wants to admit liability, least of all 'Reggie'."

Jerin took a mouthful of drink in agreeable silence before reverting to his original subject. "All jokes aside, I'm stuck in such a deep rut. I *need* another job… right now I'd take just about anything, but I just can't find a feasible way to do it. I'm not sure I'd trust myself to cycle the busy streets of Darina, and it would take over an hour each way to walk it every day, which I could just about cope with if not for the insurmountable wage decrease of working during the day. Everything in the city that pays enough requires either a degree or experience. How do you get experience if no bugger will give you a job?"

Kol shook his head. "It's so short-sighted… any idiot can have a degree, it's no proof of ability. Just because some teacher threw shit at a wall, it doesn't prove any of it stuck."

"My feelings exactly. I was so inspired when I read that several big names disagree with degrees, pointing out that they wouldn't have got their jobs if they'd needed them, that I applied for a job in a Vahirinese kitchen about a year ago. I just lied on my CV. I actually did better than several other candidates, but as soon as the boss discovered my lack of a degree, he showed me the door. In my book, ability trumps all."

"Witless pricks," Kol remarked. "Have you spoken to Juli about all of this?"

"I can't, she'll just feel guilty again. Which is right, since most of our debt was caused by her reckless spending in the first place. Not to mention the fact that she's somehow fallen behind on the rent yet again. Every single time I dare think we might finally be getting our finances back on track..." he tugged at his hair and quietly grunted in frustration. "I've lost track of how many times she's done that now. How many times can one person make the same mistake without ever learning anything? Is that even possible?"

Ignoring the rhetoric, Kol replied, "Shit. If I were you, I think I would have run out of patience by now."

"I'm close. I can feel the anger bubbling away inside, but it usually gives way to numb acceptance. It's probably just as well... what good can come from me losing my temper? She'll just cry again, making me feel like the arsehole." Jerin shook his head. "I just wish I could get through to her. We had car troubles earlier in the year, so she borrowed a little cash from her mum, only to pay it back as soon as she had it, leaving us short in the face of another financial emergency. I just wish I could make her see that we have to watch our own backs. I'm tempted to tell her to get her wages paid into my account so I can handle it all, but I shouldn't have to. I just wish I knew whether there was anything I could have done to avoid it."

"It's no good blaming yourself, mate, it's not your fault."

"I don't know. I mean, I know she makes these mistakes... I never should have relaxed and taken my eye off the proverbial ball. I just hate it when she does this... I just can't get past this feeling of sheer annoyance, and it means that during what little time we get together I struggle to be push it from my mind and enjoy her company, which makes me feel even more terrible because between her doing all the overtime she can get and me working nights I hardly see her as it is."

"They do say absence makes the heart grow fonder," Kol mused.

"That's a bad joke for us. When I'm on my own, all I think about is what we've lost. I wish I could just hack this damn mind chip and forget about it. I do love Juli, but after all she's put us through, sometimes I can't help but wonder if I'd have been better off if we'd never met." He'd never expressed this dark thought aloud before, and actually felt worse for saying it.

"I know it's an old cliché, but it really is true that we never know what we have until it's gone. You and Juli might have rough patches, but that's part of being in a relationship... you have no idea what I'd give to have that, even if just for a while, bad parts and all. It's got to be better than being alone."

"What are you talking about? You've been with loads of girls."

"Yeah, but it never lasts beyond a one-night stand and maybe an awkward breakfast the next morning. To connect with someone on an emotional level... I have no idea what that's like. I don't think I've ever been in love."

Jerin took his phone from his right trouser pocket. "Hang on."

"What are you doing?"

"You want a chance to put up with all that relationship stuff, be my guest... I'm sending you the address of the dating site where I met Juli."

"How much is membership?"

"This one's free."

"Really? Thanks," Kol smiled. Then the smile turned sour. "Hang on, wait a sec... isn't this the same site where you also met the aloof bitch?"

"You said 'bad parts and all'... well, she was a very bad part. But hey, we all make mistakes, right? Mine was being impatient enough to ask out the one who replied first."

Kol's phone buzzed, heralding the message's arrival. "I'll check it out later. Thanks."

"No worries. Best of luck. After all the girls who've messed you around, you deserve someone who appreciates you."

Kol put his phone away. "Listen, don't let money come between you and Juli. It's an evil commodity that divides society enough as it is. It doesn't even have any intrinsic value. Money's just... a bitch."

"Yep," Jerin said, *popping* the *p*. "It is when you don't have it. And yet it makes the world go round... I wish I'd never opened that damned credit account, then I wouldn't have kept piling on the debt to keep myself entertained in Juli's absence. I'm my own worst enemy... we've trimmed so much fat from our monthly budget that we're practically down to the bone. I sold everything that was worth anything ages ago, not that I'd be able to find any shops to buy anything from me now if I had anything left to sell. And woe betide should I ever get sick."

"You don't get sick pay?" Kol spat incredulously.

"Not for the first two nights, then that's my spare cash gone for the month."

"Harsh."

"Tell me about it." He sighed listlessly. "After almost dying, I promised myself I wouldn't waste my second chance," Jerin threw his hands up; *you know the rest*. His eyes fell to the table, unable to meet Kol's as he added: "Maybe it would have been better if I'd died."

"Don't joke about shit like that," Kol scolded. "That was scary."

Jerin's gaze remained downcast in that introspective fashion. "I know. I hate saying it, but I can't help it. If I'd died and the corp had admitted liability, Juli would have inherited a small fortune... but because I survived, we didn't get a penny. It's disgusting to think that I'm worth more dead than I am alive. Juli might not know it, but she'd be better off without me. Any time I mention our debt, she reminds me that she racked it up when I fell ill."

Kol quietly replied, "I know things are tough, but look at what you do have, not what you don't. You're still here, and you still have a job. That's something to be grateful for."

Jerin nodded numbly. "But is that really living? Sometimes I wonder. I mean, the news is forever raising the issue of over-population, then they contradict themselves by rambling on about how people with terminal diseases need medication to draw out their pain-ridden lives when it would be kinder to let them slip away. It makes me think that modern medicine has gone too far. Perhaps I was *supposed* to die. I'm sorry, I don't mean to bring the mood down, it's just… you're the only one I can talk to about all this."

"I know how you feel," Kol said seriously. "I still get depressed from time to time too."

"How do you cope?"

"A little yellow grass in a rollie works wonders for me," Kol shrugged.

Jerin had no issues with drugs — they were necessary to his wellbeing, after all — but he was concerned about the side effects. "Isn't this stuff bad for your mental health?"

"Hey, I've been tempted to end it all more than once, and that stuff has stopped me every time. As long as I stay away from *red* grass, I'll be fine. Besides, bad mental health is better than dead, right? I know you can't take the smoke, but you're welcome to have some to bake into some brownies if you like?"

"I appreciate the offer, but I'd better not. I really shouldn't mix anything with the new drugs the doc gave me. I probably shouldn't even be drinking, but to hell with it. Most drugs don't react with alcohol anyway, that's just a myth."

"I hope the new pills do the trick," Kol said, finishing his second and last drink.

"They seem to be working so far," Jerin said, keeping the details of his recent dreams to himself. "I just hope they keep it up." Jerin's gaze rose, drifting towards a spike atop the disused black wrought-iron fireplace guard behind Kol. "But enough of this depressing shit, how's life with you? Is the world of automotive sports photography still treating you well?"

"Some days are more tedious than you'd imagine, but it could be worse. Though there are changes afoot I'm not exactly happy about."

"Like what?"

"The company's restructuring, amalgamating the auto-sports and general sports, so I might have to cover tedious shit like graftball," he shuddered. "I'd rather shoot myself."

Jerin shook his head. "Amazing…"

"What?"

"You have a decent career and you still find something to complain about!"

"Believe me, no matter what you do, the gloss fades eventually."

"At least they pay you well."

"Oh yeah, I can't complain about the money. I even have enough to put some away. Rainy days, and all that."

"Very prudent. I wish I'd saved more years ago. The cash I wasted eating out and coming here…"

"Sorry, I guess I have to take the rap for that, since I kinda dragged you along."

"Nah, I could afford it at the time. It was my fault for being so short-sighted."

"At least you learned to cope, right?"

Jerin wasn't sure he could agree with that sentiment, yet replied, "Yeah. I don't completely regret not saving… I mean, we had a good laugh."

"Hell yeah. I miss those days like crazy."

"Yeah," Jerin sighed. "Everything was simpler then. Oh," he suddenly remembered, "before I forget…" he reached over to the other chair and unzipped his bag, passing Kol the movie he'd asked to borrow.

Kol smiled, examining the back of the box. "Brill,

thanks. I've been meaning to see this for ages. Is it any good?"

"It's alright," Jerin shrugged. "Not as good as Dark Nemesis, but it has its moments."

Kol laughed. "You say that about damn near everything!"

"That's because it's usually true," Jerin deadpanned. "I just think the studio should have waited until the Nemesis director had finished his side-project rather than rushing it. That Feldon guy is so overrated."

Kol glanced at his watch. "Shit, I better get going. It's been great finally having the chance to get caught up."

"Yeah," Jerin agreed, standing and leaning into another friendly hug. He couldn't help thinking there was something unusually off about Kol, but he couldn't put his finger on it. He wasn't his usual relaxed self; it was as though something heavy was weighing on his mind, but Jerin wouldn't push it: Kol was notoriously private and easily angered if interrogated. He would talk about it when he was ready.

They stepped apart, but Kol kept his right hand on Jerin's left shoulder. "Give my best to Juli. And hang in there. One day soon, all this trouble will be nothing more than a bad memory."

"Thanks. I hope so."

They waved a silent farewell to Tyrus and stepped outside. As Jerin watched his old friend walk away, he turned to face Hit Flix. For a few moments he couldn't tear himself away, wishing he could relive just one of those bygone days.

His meetings with Kol were always so fleeting that they only ever scratched the surface, and Kol so rarely said much about his own life.

Jerin finally broke free of nostalgia's hold and started the long, cold, lonely walk home.

IH
-Desperate Measures-

Upon finally arriving home, Jerin took another white capsule and fell heavily onto the bed, allowing it to take him away for a few more hours.

His relaxed mind drifted, myriad thoughts passing through, until he inevitably replayed the moment when the black hole had ensnared him. He wished he could just forget it, but it was just like when an annoying song got stuck in his head: the more he resisted, the stronger the pull.

He was once more standing on the plant's main floor for the pointless weekly meeting, impatiently waiting for the hog to wash over him.

But amongst the *blah-this, blah-that* drivel he hadn't been listening to was a little glimmer of hope that caught his attention, as Marv, whom he had been blessed enough not to know personally at the time, was ushered forwards to announce: "I'm looking for a team to work a night shift." This person looked far too young to be a manager, clearly lacking the life experience Jerin considered vital for such a role.

Even though it meant the corporation was bringing more jobs to Sendura, much low, indecipherable muttering and groaning rose from the assembled crowd.

"The new shifts will start at quarter past nine and finish at quarter to three. Of course, we don't expect people to work such hours out of the kindness of their hearts, so there will be an hourly premium as an incentive. Do I have any volunteers?"

Jerin nodded to himself. That would be *perfect*, allowing him to rebuild his ravaged savings, and it wasn't like he had a social life anyway. He looked around: not a hand was raised, but he was too self-conscious to be the first. He held on a moment longer, but when it became apparent no one else was interested, he gulped and reluctantly raised his hand, becoming hot under the collar as all eyes drew an accusing bead on him. More groaning. Someone mumbled, "There's always one," but there was no mention of additional work, merely additional money.

Another upside was that it would get him away from the crowd of morons surrounding him, many of whom frequently blighted his work life — the ones that weren't idiots he could count on one hand. But it wouldn't be long until he realised he was only trading one lot for another.

Besides, how hard could it be to sleep during the day and work overnight? The barrier's cycle meant it made no real difference, and he practically lived that way as a teenager anyhow.

He knew it would mean seeing less of Juli for a while, but it was only temporary, and it was the only way he was ever going to get a chance to put that ring on her finger.

*

With her fake magenta fingernails firmly secured in place, Juli drew an apprehensive breath before squeezing herself into her old hussy clothes. The skimpy underwear made her feel incredibly self-conscious, but she didn't have to strip if she didn't want to. That was what she kept telling herself, anyway. The purple side-buttoned boob tube and short pink multi-layered skirt she wore over it were just a touch tighter than she remembered, though given how well that emphasised her bust it would likely go down well with the crowd. She wore a more conservative knee-length black skirt and casual buttoned periwinkle blouse she didn't mind ruining over the top.

She looked at Jerin lying atop the duvet fully clothed, dead to the world. She folded a flap of cover over him and leaned over to plant a kiss on his inanimate lips.

She donned her thick coat, unlocked the front door, rested her hand on the cold golden-hued handle and baulked momentarily, slowly drawing and releasing several deep breaths. She felt like she was going to hurl. She had to go *now*. She stopped thinking and pushed down the handle, leaving the flat to meet Alezi.

Though she resolved to drive with extra care on the now-icier roads, she should have known to be more wary of others; after turning the corner and climbing the hill out of the cul-de-sac, she unexpectedly spotted an old-fashioned white hover-van careening down the middle of the road relentlessly towards her. She slammed on the brakes and tried to steer up the kerb on the left to avoid it.

As the car's tyres struggled for purchase, she looked up to see that the van was still heading towards her, slowly drifting sideways, its quantum braking mechanism trying to create anchorage points on the ice's surface, peppering it with tiny pock-marks — the curse of the first-generation hover-vehicles.

She tried not to panic as she gently released the brake, allowing the car to roll backwards. Though the van then came to a halt, there was no way she could get past it. She continued to roll towards a parked red van to allow the white one room to pass, tempted to make 'wanker' gestures at the moronic driver as he slowly drifted by. Once he'd passed without so much as a wave of apology, she tried to drive forwards, but the car continued to slide back towards the red van.

She tried again, unsure what gear to try, going up to third. Still she slid further back. She could feel the tears welling and told herself *I can do this*, no matter how tempted she was to abandon the car and go back inside.

She went up to fifth gear and pressed the accelerator down as slowly as she could. The engine roared in fierce protest. The car slid back a little further, then slowly began to edge forwards. Once on level road, she dropped to fourth, then third, finally able to continue on her way.

Thankfully, the rest of the journey went without incident, the roads largely empty as the sensible people remained safely inside, sheltered from the inhospitable conditions.

Juli eventually pulled up outside Alezi's place and beeped her horn. After a moment the door opened, revealing her friend's silhouette in an oblong of light. She was carrying a bag that was an unconventional and, in Juli's opinion, impractical shape.

Alezi ran over to the car, her stylish red waxed lunim raincoat flapping open to reveal her skimpy get-up beneath, not dissimilar to Juli's own.

"Aren't you cold?" Juli asked as Alezi climbed in.

"Not really. I guess I don't really feel it."

"Lucky you. I'm freezing!"

Alezi fastened herself in. "Right. Let's go!"

Juli looked her in the eyes. "You won't leave me on my own, will you?"

"I'll be right by your side."

"I mean it. Not even for a moment."

"I'll be your shadow."

Juli inhaled slowly, nervously, holding it before slowly exhaling, but it turned into a yawn.

"Keeping you up?" Alezi jested.

"Sorry. It's been a long and very tedious day."

Juli put the car into gear and set off for The Siren's Song. She'd be glad when it was all over.

Now that it was happening, the drive to *Sirens* seemed so much longer.

"What's bothering you now?" Alezi asked.

"How do you know something's wrong?" Juli asked, amazed at her friend's unusual display of astuteness.

"You're gripping the wheel so tight your knuckles are white, and your face is deathly pale. You look like you're about to throw up…"

Juli loosened her grip on the wheel but said nothing. She had to calm her turbulent stomach; she was pretty sure none of the bar patrons were depraved enough to be turned on by her vomiting all over them.

"We've been over this, Ju, I thought you were okay with it now?"

"I don't think I'll ever be okay with it, really. I just need to get through it. That's all."

"You just need to learn to switch your brain off for a

while," Alezi suggested.

"That's easier for you than it is for me." Juli suddenly realised how unintentionally bitchy that came across. "Alezi, I didn't mean…"

"You're not in a good mindset, so I'll let it slide, just this once. So what's the problem?"

Juli pulled over to the side of the road for a moment and looked Alezi in the eyes. "You really don't remember the last night I danced there, do you?"

"No, why—?" Then Alezi remembered, her eyes widening in comprehending horror. "Oh, shit! Ju, I'm so sorry, I completely forgot!"

"How could you forget a thing like that!?"

"I didn't even think about it… when you've done as much stupid shit as I have over the years, you learn to repress the worst of it."

"Lucky you. I wish I could forget…"

"You saved my bacon that night, you know."

"Your bacon never would have needed saving in the first place if not for me. I never even told Jerin… we hadn't been together long, but he knew something was up, but I wouldn't say what because I knew I wasn't going back, even before that, so it didn't matter… I had nightmares for months…"

"I can still lend you the cash if you'd prefer…"

It wasn't too late to turn back, but Juli was adamant that wouldn't solve anything. She released the handbrake, put the car in gear and continued onward to the club. "It's just one night. I'll earn enough to fix my latest mistake, then I'll finally get this damned promotion and everything will be back to how it was. Then Jerin can quit nights, return to the land of the living and finally get back to his art."

"Is he good?"

"I can't really say, I don't really 'get' art. I like his stuff. It's good to see him become so rapt in a world of his own creation, but then it's so disheartening when he pulls the image back and becomes depressed at what he sees.

He's found it hard since his brain op. Not just the art, but everything. He loses his temper far more easily than he used to…"

"I'm always here if you need someone to talk to."

"Thanks. I should remember that. So, what happened to that creep who attacked me?"

"Him? Oh, I er… I think he ended up in jail. The one people don't come back from."

Alezi's hesitation and tone led Juli to believe her friend wasn't being entirely honest, but as long as that creep was no longer around her concerns were somewhat assuaged.

"Here we are," Alezi needlessly announced as they pulled into the empty-but-for-an-overturned-supermarket-trolley car park behind the bar.

Juli flicked on the internal light to check her makeup in her rear view mirror as Alezi began rummaging around in her overstuffed bag.

"What have you got in there?" Juli asked impatiently.

"I know you're nervous, so I thought this might help. Put it on," Alezi insisted, handing Juli an electric blue wig before removing a second for herself. "No one'll recognise you and we'll look like twins. Trust me, men *love* that kind of thing!"

Juli shrugged. *What do I have to lose?* She tied her brunette hair back before tucking it beneath the bright blue hairpiece, trying to work out which side was supposed to be the front, its copious fringe covering her eyes. She couldn't see much through it, but she could see the floor if she looked straight down.

Alezi handed Juli a pair of matching high-heeled platform shoes, which were just a touch too small.

"Just my size," Juli said sarcastically.

"Sorry, they were all I had." Alezi applied some cerulean lipstick before handing it to Juli, who did the same.

Juli looked up at the entrance to the bar and sighed uneasily. "I guess we should head inside before we freeze."

Alezi placed her hand on her friend's shoulder. "Are you sure you're ready?"

"Let's just get this over with."

Alezi nodded and they silently exited and locked the car, the now-dry cold biting at their exposed skin as they hastily clip-clopped across the cracked asphalt, arms crossed tightly over their chests. Juli wobbled slightly as she walked, throwing Alezi a scowl.

"These shoes are ridiculous," Juli said.

"Haven't you ever worn platform shoes before?"

"No. Have you ever fallen over in these beasts?"

"Only once or twice," Alezi shrugged. "You'll do fine. You've always been more coordinated than me anyway."

"I suppose that's true, but it's not very reassuring. So, do the new clientele tip well?"

"That depends on how well you can hide your disgust when one unzips his fly and shows you how good you are at your job!"

Juli shuddered with disgust. "Ew! Please tell me that doesn't happen often?"

"Only usually towards the end of the night, when the stragglers are too drunk to stand on their own."

Juli paused for a moment, her hand resting on the door's cold metal handle.

"We'll start behind the bar before working our way onto the floor," Alezi promised.

"Okay," Juli replied with a long, deep breath. "Let's do this."

Juli pulled the heavy door open and they stepped inside.

Now that the thumping bass noise wasn't just in her mind, that corridor took on a malevolent presence, the red of the walls suddenly the shade of blood. They made their way to the dingy cloakroom. As Juli removed her coat, Alezi scrunched her face in obvious distaste at her skirt-and-shirt combo.

"I've got skimpier clothes underneath," Juli explained

in response to this wordless rebuke. "I just need to work up to it."

"Ah, good angle," Alezi nodded approvingly. "A little pre-strip tease usually results in big tips."

Just then, a boisterously enthusiastic cry of "Lady!" came from the doorway behind them.

Even without her trademark shock of fiery red curls, Juli would recognise Tegan Faramaugh's buxom body anywhere. She was the only woman who made Juli feel insecure about her bust. Alezi rushed over to greet her.

"Vix! Long time no see!"

"Fox didn't tell me you were back!"

"I only arrived a couple of days ago."

"And Crystal too! What is this, some kind of reunion?"

"Hey, Vix," Juli offered half-heartedly.

"Oh, come on, you can do better than that!" Vix teased.

"Juli's a bit nervous," Alezi replied. "Apparently she's all grown up now."

"Yeah, I heard our little Crystal was some big city corporate hotshot now… there's something I never thought I'd see. And yet she's back here."

"Yeah, she got all this from Fox too," Alezi said. "Ju fell on some hard times, she just needs a little extra cash. A one-off."

"Then I guess I'll just shut my evil little trap," Vix winked. "We've all been there, Ju. I'm just glad to see you again, that's all."

"Yeah, me too. I just wish…"

"I know. The circumstances aren't great. But you know we've always got your back."

Juli nodded. They made their way down the corridor, towards the violet velveteen curtains obscuring the entrance to the bar's public area.

"Perhaps we'll have to make a point of all meeting up one day for tea or something, so we can actually enjoy it," Vix suggested.

"Yeah," Juli smiled. "I'd like that."

"So how's your...?" Alezi asked Vixen, patting her stomach with her left hand.

"Better, thanks," Vix replied. "I just feel a little bloated every now and then. My doctor keeps telling me to drink less... maybe I should listen."

"Perhaps you should," Alezi scolded. "Believe it or not, they usually know what they're talking about."

"Yes, Mum!" Vix joked. Juli was still baffled by all of this, but it was forgotten the moment she found herself the subject of Vixen's attention. "So, do you still have the ever-elusive 'it'?"

Juli hoped so, but had no idea how to answer such a query.

"Well, we'll sure as hell find out," Alezi answered for her, wrapping her arm around her friend's shoulder, averting her gaze from the exit.

"Don't worry, it'll all come back to you," Vix said warmly. "The first hour's pretty quiet, so you've got time to settle in before the regulars arrive. We don't get many spontaneous visitors these days, so we know most of them on a first-name basis. Don't be offended if they take a special interest in the new girl. They're like kids with a new toy!"

Alezi took Juli's hand. "Come on, *Crystal*, let's go pour some drinks."

Vix gave Juli a pat on the shoulder as Alezi pulled her through the curtains. Even with only two men in the place, she felt so incredibly exposed in the suddenly-very-small room, quickly rushing to the left for the cover of the bar.

From her new vantage point, she spotted the familiar stage off to her right, but the old stripper poles atop squat round stages were conspicuously absent, and the four booths across the room were now framed with open violet curtains.

"What's with those?" Juli asked apprehensively, pointing.

"One of the bigger changes that have been made over

the years. If a guy gives you a fifty, you take him into one of those. He gets a pitcher of beer and a lap dance."

"You didn't warn me about that!" Juli yelled exasperatedly.

"Hey, it's a *sexy* bar. What did you expect?"

"I expected it to be how it used to be. What happened to the poles?"

"They're too common in the city's seedier venues, they lack a personal touch. Fox and Vix found that men prefer their scantily-clad ladies up close and personal."

Juli shook her head incredulously. "If you'd told me about this…"

"…Then you'd have phesaned out and been back to square one. Fox and Vix have to change with the times if they want people to keep coming back."

Juli conceded the point. She lowered her voice. "I don't even know *how* to lap dance!"

"It's really not that hard, you just grind your hips and shake your rear. They'll be too hypnotised by your curves to worry about your moves, so long as you give them a bit of leg or breast. If they slap you on the arse, don't discourage them. If you can, pretend to enjoy it. You'll get a bigger tip."

"Okay…"

"If they give you another fifty behind the curtain, you take your top off. Sometimes they like to pour beer down your chest. If they try, take the pitcher and do it yourself."

"Uh… okay… what if they try to lick it off?"

"Do the whole dominatrix thing. Take charge. Tell them no, but keep it sexy. This is Sirens, remember. We're in charge here."

"I don't know *how* to do the whole dominatrix thing… me and Jerin have never so much as role-played before."

Alezi laughed, "Oh, you'll have a few ideas after tonight, believe me!"

What have I gotten myself into!? What ever happened to just getting up on a table and dancing?

Juli hated the idea of arousing other men, even for

money. She knew it wasn't cheating, but it sure as hell felt like it. She would owe Jerin a lot to make up for this. There was no way she could keep it from him.

Then the fear returned. "What if they get violent? How will anyone know when a girl's hidden behind a closed curtain, the music drowning out her screams?"

"There's a panic button on the wall behind the curtain that activates the silent alarm. That'll summon Mack, the lead bouncer. One little tap, and he'll take care of them." Juli followed Alezi's gaze to the burliest man she had ever seen standing just inside the customer entrance, decked all in black, back to the wall, arms crossed, calm like a coiled spring, a veritable mountain of muscles. Seeing his imposing bulk allayed her concerns greatly. She wondered whether she could pay him to take care of Nate for her.

"*Nobody* messes with Mack. A few of the regulars are friends of his too, which is handy if a brawl breaks out. On the rare occasion that it does, Fox and Vix give them a free round of drinks for their trouble, though they have to be pretty frugal about it — their profit margins are smaller than their underwear!"

"Right. So has anything else changed that I should know about?"

Alezi mulled this over briefly, pulling the twisted 'concentration' face Juli used to mock. "Nope, I think that's about it."

"You *think*?" incredulously.

"I've never had to explain it all before… it just comes naturally to me."

Juli returned her attention to the bar as one of the patrons approached. Both he and his still-seated companion sported long, straggly beards that spilled over their black lunim jackets, which were adorned with decorative metallic flourishes. *Bikers*, she realised, wondering if they were a couple of these 'Misfits' Alezi had mentioned. She didn't know anything about the group beyond that recently-heard name.

"Hey," he said surprisingly bashfully, his polite tone

betraying his aggressive appearance. He laid down a twenty. "Two pints, please."

"I have no idea how to pour a pint," Juli discreetly whispered to Alezi.

"Oh, jeez… it's simple. Watch." Alezi grabbed two glasses. Juli noticed her take a dropper from a vial, putting a drop of a strange blue liquid in the bottom of each glass beneath the cover of the counter before filling them up, tilting the glasses at a forty-five degree angle to reduce the size of the head. As Alezi did this, Juli noticed the biker surreptitiously glancing at her friend's chest, quickly averting his gaze every time Alezi looked up. She gave the biker his change and drinks, and he thanked her before returning to his table.

"What was that blue stuff?" Juli asked.

"Just a little something extra to help them feel a little more generous."

Juli was stunned. "Isn't that unethical?"

"Everything about making money is unethical, but making it is essential to survival, so all's fair, right?" Alezi fixed herself a blue-green cocktail as she spoke. "We even have a pink one that helps nervous girls lose some of their inhibitions. Do you want one?"

"That depends… is it like being drunk?"

"Sort of, but not quite," Alezi replied. "Have you ever tried…" she lowered her voice, "pills?"

"Do you mean *drugs*?"

"Keep it down!" Alezi shout-whispered. "Well, have you?"

"What do you take me for?"

"Sorry, I didn't mean to offend such a fine, upstanding citizen!"

Juli stared daggers at Alezi.

"It gives more of a high than alcohol, but it does make you crash the morning after."

"Have you ever tried it?"

"Once or twice. It's fine, and it really helps the nerves just melt away. I'll even have one with you."

"What about your other drink?"

"It'll keep." She could see Juli was still hesitant. "Look, you need something to stave off the shakes if you ever want to get out there and earn enough money to avoid eviction, so just drink it already!"

Juli sighed. "Fine. Give me half a shot in some lemonade."

Alezi smiled and clapped with glee, hastily preparing two of them, giving them half a shot each, setting her other drink aside under the bar. They clinked their glasses together. "Bottoms up!"

They threw back their drinks and Juli waited.

*

Jerin awoke only once that night, and with a violent shiver, desperate for a piss. His head was spinning so violently that he almost fell over the moment he stood, struggling to balance, leaning against the doorframe for balance as he rounded the corner.

His head was filled with strangely vivid images of that vaguely familiar bar again, only this time he just couldn't shake it.

When he'd cleaned the errant urine splashes from the toilet's edge and the floor, he returned to bed. He glanced over at Juli's pillow, sure he saw a strand of bright blue nylon, picking it up. He closed his eyes and shook his head, opening them, seeing nothing more than yet another of Juli's wayward loose long brown hairs.

He dropped it into the bin and curled into the foetal position, mind slowly filling with visions of Juli, eliciting a warm smile. This was how he wanted his dreams to be: just the two of them, not a care in the world…

*

"What *is* that noise?" Juli asked, no longer able to ignore the annoyingly exuberant intermittent shrieks of head-splitting laughter outside the back door that somehow managed to be heard over the music, chatter, clinking glasses and wolf whistles of the drunkards in the now-gently-bustling bar.

"Those are the bimbos," Alezi replied matter-of-factly, sipping from what was either her third or fourth drink of the evening already. She seemed no worse for it to Juli. "They never turn up until it gets busy. Vix and Fox aren't keen on them, but they bring in those who lust after hot young idiots, so they put up with it."

Juli could smell the air slowly thickening with choking fumes as those idiots chatted over a billowing glass of water into which they poured their precious gunpowder, like witches gathered around a bubbling cauldron. Juli failed to stifle a reflex cough, wafting the air before her face. She had known enough bitches during her student days to know the derisive things they would say about the 'new arrival' when they saw her.

"If you want any chance of earning some tips before they get in here, you need to get out *there*," Alezi told her, gesturing towards the floor.

Juli knew this was true, and forced herself to remember why she was here: the money. She turned to Alezi. "Only if you come with me."

"You know I would, but I can't right now. Someone needs to watch the bar until the bimbos can be bothered to start."

"But I've never done this on my own before! You were always right by my side. You promised!"

Alezi sighed. "Fine. I'll do a quick round while you observe from here, but then it's your turn. Just don't mess up any drink orders while I'm away."

Alezi pulled her top slightly down and her tiny skirt up. She put on a sultry pout and waltzed out into the crowd, swaying her hips like a sexy pendulum. Much whistling and hooting ensued.

Juli watched in astonishment at Alezi's proficiency as she put on a sexy, sultry voice, uttering pleasantries such as "Hey, sugar," leaning forwards to offer an eyeful of her bountiful bosom, hands resting on her thighs. An amorous middle-aged man smacked her pert rear as she turned from him. She turned and winked at him, putting her right foot on the empty chair beside him so he could delicately place a rolled up note in the garter around her thigh.

This went on until Alezi had completed a circuit of the floor, briefly visiting every table.

"You make it look so easy," Juli sighed upon Alezi's return.

"It's not hard. Just smile politely and stifle every instinct."

"Didn't any call you to a booth?"

"Nah, they usually save that for the bimbos. But hey, you might get lucky. Now get out there and earn some cash!" she instructed, slapping Juli's arse. Juli flashed her an indignant look. "To warm you up!"

Juli still wasn't ready to strip to her smalls, but undid a few of the buttons on her blouse and hoisted her skirt up before putting on a sultry expression that she was sure made her look demented, swaggering out amongst the braying wolves, desperate to get their dirty paws on some fresh meat.

She quickly received her first arse-slap and accompanying tip, which was quickly followed by several more. Some of them were pretty enthusiastic; though none lifted her skirt to get the skin directly, she still hoped they didn't leave any red marks for Jerin to discover.

She continued round, but only got a few tips.

From the bar, Alezi remarked to herself, "Oh, I *know* you can do better than that!"

Without warning, the main lights dimmed and a familiar rhythmic beat pounded out of the speakers. Juli knew this intro all too well; she and Alezi had danced to this damned song every time it played at *Fluid* all those years ago.

"Work it, girl!" Alezi winked, *another* drink in hand. As the song proper kicked in, multi-coloured spotlights began swirling around the room.

Juli did her best, but was too self-conscious, her moves rigid and forced compared to Alezi, who was like liquid in motion. Juli imagined the crowd was cheering mostly for her incredibly flexible friend, but that didn't matter when they were happily throwing so much money around. Against her better judgement, she was beginning to enjoy herself, and though she was getting rather warm, she wasn't quite ready to acquiesce to the relentless chant: "Take it off! Take it off!"

As the first song wound down she bent over seductively and fluidly to gather her scattered earnings, ensuring she gave the men plenty of time to stare and grab and slap.

"Bravo!" Alezi cheered before sticking her little fingers into the corners of her mouth to emit a high-pitched whistle over the deafening cacophony of applause and drunken cheers.

Upon Juli's return to the bar, Vixen congratulated her with a hug. "Nice work, girl!"

"Thanks," Juli replied, wiping the sweat from her brow with the back of her hand.

"Yeah, not bad for an old lady," one of the bimbos snorted derisively from the curtained doorway. Juli almost laughed; they looked like quadruplets.

"Shut your mouth," Vix scolded. To Juli she quietly whispered, "I never even bothered learning that bitch's name. Probably something white trash."

"I think I'm ready for some more," Juli admitted.

"Well, someone's come out of her shell!" Alezi beamed.

"Go on, get out there with your friend, Lady," Vix insisted.

"Alrighty then!" Alezi cheered, only too happy to oblige.

As they sauntered sexily onto the floor, the ancient jukebox began playing another classic from their clubbing days.

"Nice," Juli nodded approvingly.

"I made this playlist a few years ago," Alezi said. "Just wait, it gets better."

Alezi started popping and rocking, her wig sashaying

yet staying firmly on her head. She progressed to bumping and grinding for the next song. Juli had never seen such seductive moves, not even in the most explicit music videos. Clearly Alezi hadn't lapsed on her exercises.

Juli tentatively joined her friend, quietly determined not to be shown up, but was relieved when Alezi instigated a series of moves that only a duet could perform. Juli followed Alezi's lead, leaning back just in time to avoid a facial collision as her friend leaned her head and shoulders towards Juli, a wave motion rippling up her body, which Juli did her best to mimic, hoping she wasn't coming across as a pale imitation. She tried to work the hand motions of readjusting her loosening wig into the rhythm of the dance with mixed success.

Without warning, Alezi groped her right breast to much cheering before just as suddenly kissing her passionately, catching Juli completely off-guard. Growing ever more uncomfortable as Alezi kept the kiss going, Juli was amazed to see dozens of notes raining down around their feet. Stroke of genius or not, it reinforced Juli's theory about her friend's sexuality. She didn't think she'd ever kissed Jerin for this long. Finally Alezi pulled away, and Juli saw the heavier crowd of men they had attracted.

Juli felt incredibly claustrophobic, noticing they were surrounded. Hoping no one could hear her over the bass-heavy music, Juli asked, "Do you know any of these men?"

"I remember a few nicknames, sure. The guy to your left in the eye-patch is rather aptly called 'Patches'. The guy to his left is 'Fisty McTavish'."

"Delightful," Juli remarked uneasily.

"There are worse," Alezi shrugged.

Juli hoped they weren't the violent kind. She focused solely on Alezi, doing her best to block all those men out. She'd never had a panic attack, but she was sure she could feel one coming on.

"Play along," Alezi said, dropping to her knees, slowly pulling Juli's skirt down until it collapsed around her ankles, revealing the tiny pink skirt beneath.

That wasn't as unnerving as what came next. Alezi's hands started working their way up and down Juli's smooth legs, cascades of notes landing everywhere. She then realised precisely what Alezi's evil plan was: at this rate, the men wouldn't have any cash left for the bimbos.

Juli blocked out everything and pretended she was back at *Fluid*, just dancing for the sheer thrill of it. She lost herself to the rhythm, flailing her arms and mouthing the nonsensical lyrics. She knew the song upside down and inside out, despite never having learned its name. As the song reached the bridge, she began to thrust her chest and gyrate her hips, just as they once did during those embarrassing clubbing days in front of crowds of brash young men, a routine which was always instigated by Alezi. Juli had been too self-conscious to ever dance that way with Jerin, but clubbing wasn't exactly his thing, and she'd been fine with that, but now she pretended he was the one she was dancing for. In a way, he was.

As she lost herself in the illusion, she heard Jerin's voice say "I love you" in her mind, feeling ephemerally light-headed, quickly shaking it off. *That must be that pink stuff*, she told herself.

She finished unbuttoning her blouse and dropped it to the floor, then took her boob tube off to reveal her barely-there black-string bra, immediately wondering why she'd done so. As her head became fuzzy again, she looked around and saw pointy-toothed horned demons clutching handfuls of notes leering at her, bulging eyes burning with fierce lust. She didn't look, but she could picture them rubbing their throbbing loins.

She glanced towards the bar and saw one of the suddenly-demonic bitches sticking her tongue out at her between rows of jagged teeth, another drawing a line in front of her neck with a ridiculously long false finger nail. Juli goaded them with a 'come on' hand gesture and began gyrating before Alezi's face as she pulled her skirt down, revealing Juli's black G-string.

Juli stepped out of her skirt and Alezi stood, motioning to Juli to do the same to her. As she complied, Juli became aware of a trio of men entering the bar, laughing amongst themselves, heading straight for the bar.

Juli hoped they might draw an even bigger crowd, but was stricken with panic as she glanced through a gap in the crowd that quickly closed. She was sure she'd seen Nate in that split-second and could feel her chest pounding. She decided it was time for a break.

"I'll be back in a few," she whispered to Alezi, quickly squatting to collect the notes littering the floor before darting towards the men blocking the curtained doorway, all of them stepping back immediately in a very gentlemanly manner. She hated leaving Alezi alone for a while, but was confident the old pro would manage. Juli raced through the purple curtains, bumping into Fox who was about to pass through in the other direction.

"Hey, what's up, hon?" Fox asked sympathetically. "You look like you've seen a ghost."

"One of the men who just came in..." she choked back the tears, glancing over her shoulder to ensure no one could see her through the curtains, which had firmly closed behind her.

"What about him?"

"I *can't* dance while he's out there."

"Why not?"

"He's the reason I'm here," she confessed through a veil of tears.

"Take a short break, get your head together." Fox gave her a comforting embrace before pulling back the curtain with one finger to assess the heaving crowd. "Which one?"

"The idiot in the shit-brown shirt with the piss-yellow tie." *So appropriate*, she considered.

Fox saw him and let the curtain go. "Oh, I know that fugada. He never buys a round, so you'll be safe if you want to man the bar for a while?"

Juli nodded silently.

"Alright. Just let me know when you're ready."

"Thanks."

"Hey, if we don't look out for one another, who else will?"

Juli sat alone on the bench in the tiny cloakroom, still shaking slightly, the blue wig resting on her lap. She felt so small and stupid sitting here in nothing but her black underwear, silently cursing herself for her lack of nerve. She looked at the crumpled notes in her left hand; half of it was Alezi's. She flattened it out to get an idea of how much was there. It looked pretty close, but she needed more. The sooner she got back out there, the sooner she could put this behind her, but right now she just wanted to go home.

Fox entered with a mojito in hand. "Here, this'll help you relax," she said, proffering Juli the drink.

"Thanks," Juli said, securing the money in the left side of her bottoms. She cradled the tall thin glass with both hands to avoid spilling its contents, taking a tentative sip. She'd never had one before; it wasn't bad, but it was noticeably watered-down, which was probably for the best given her low alcohol tolerance.

"It's so like that odious little fugada to come here," Juli grumbled. "He's my pervy landlord. I can't believe he actually has friends. Whenever I have to talk to him for whatever reason, I can *feel* his eyes on my chest." She shuddered. "He isn't even discreet about it."

Fox pulled up a stool and sat beside her. "Unfortunately we often have to dance for creeps like him, no matter how odious. Remember, we don't do it for the love. We're only in it for the cash. I don't mean to sound nasty, but it's not as if you haven't done this before. You know as well as I do that as long as you thrust your rack their way, no man here will remember your face. He won't even recognise you."

Juli nodded pensively. The idea of him ogling her chest wasn't an enticing thought, and if he *did* recognise her, things would only become more awkward at home.

Jerin was already close to coming to blows with the dolt, and if it wouldn't secure their eviction she'd be happy to let him do it.

"Is this your first drink of the night?" Fox asked.

"Alezi gave me half a shot of that pink stuff," she said, finishing her mojito in one hearty swig.

"Really? I've never seen anyone dance like that virtually sober before! Kudos!"

"Thanks. I don't really drink... I've always been a lightweight. This'll go right to my head. I must admit, having Alezi here has been a huge help. I still can't believe she came along tonight just to help me out."

"Is that what she told you?"

Juli was confused. "Why else would she be here?"

"It really isn't my place to say..."

"I'm sure there's something she isn't telling me. Please, I won't tell her you said a word."

Fox sighed. "Alright. But not a word!"

Juli mimed zipping her mouth, locking it and throwing away the key.

Fox nodded. "She lost her modelling contract a few days ago, but wouldn't say why. Before getting a string of regular jobs, she used to come here every other night. I guess she probably will again, until another company signs her up."

Juli was stunned. "I... I had no idea. I guess it makes sense... this must be why she's suddenly been behaving all humble. I thought she was lacking her usual tan."

"Tanning booths are hardly cheap," Fox noted. "Don't feel bad about it. Alezi doesn't like to talk about herself much."

"Not her real self. She hides behind the persona... I've known her for years, yet I know so little about the real Alezi. I think she might be gay."

"So what if she is?" Fox sounded almost offended.

"I don't mean it like that, it's just... if she is, I just want her to say so, so I can be supportive. It isn't a problem, I just hope she doesn't fancy me... she needs to understand that I'm straight."

"Just ask her. If she's really your friend, she'll tell you."

"Like she told me about the contract?"

"Hey, there's no judging here."

"You're right. I'm sorry... I'm just not in a good state of mind." She didn't mention that her head was already buzzing.

"Right. Break's over. Are you ready to go back out there?"

To her own surprise, Juli found herself rather keen to finish what she'd started. She was sure Fox had spiked her drink with more of that pink stuff, but if that was the case, it did the trick. She allowed it to melt her inhibitions away. "Sure thing."

Fox smiled at her. "That a girl!"

Juli found Alezi behind the bar, the bimbos waltzing around the floor giggling as they fell into men's laps, one of them sliding off and landing in a heap on the floor. Juli laughed, and the faller stared daggers at her.

"Look at those prissy little bitches," Juli muttered under her breath to Alezi, who sniggered. "They think they're some divine gift to humanity, but they're already pissed out of their tiny little minds."

"Trust me, they're not as dumb as they seem," came a voice from the curtained doorway. Juli looked over to see Vixen wearing a *very* short sparkling red skirt beneath a *very* low-cut black top, a loose triangular hang of material covering her midriff, plain black stripper's garters wrapped around her thighs. "They act drunk, but they only drink water. They know how to earn their keep. Some of us still have a few tricks up our sleeves though," she winked. She went behind the bar and grabbed a vial of purple fluid and downed it in one, ditching the empty in the small vial bin.

"So, am I finally going to find out what this is all about?" Juli whispered to Alezi, patting her own stomach.

"Oh, yeah," she smiled.

Vix shook her hips then picked up two barstools. "Do me a tray of three dozen shots please sweetie, whatever takes your fancy," Vix asked Juli quietly, a challenge over the noise.

Juli replied, "Of course," and Vixen headed over to the stage, placing the stools side by side.

Vix grabbed the stage mic and purred, "Good evening, gentlemen," as the music faded to a mildly hypnotic beat.

"Help me get some shots done," Juli told Alezi.

"Way ahead of you." Alezi had a dozen whiskeys ready on a tray and was preparing to pour a dozen more. "She does this every week."

Vix bellowed, "Some of you may have seen me do this before, but you newbies are in for a treat."

"Hurry up," Alezi scolded Juli, whose attention had been stolen by Vix.

"Sorry, this is my first time pouring shots!" Juli spilt drink everywhere as she attempted to fill a dozen lined-up shot glasses. She ditched the empty bottle and reached for another. Alezi quickly reached out a had to stop her.

"Not that one. Use the cheap stuff for freebies."

Juli nodded a silent apology, put the bottle back and took the one Alezi pointed to. She glanced up at Vixen as she sat on one of the stools.

"Vix's party piece is really quite something," Alezi teased.

"Is she going to hand out free shots while topless?" Juli asked, confused as to what was so special about that. She poured the last shot.

"In a manner of speaking. You'll see. Here." Alezi carefully handed Juli the tray of drinks. "Put these on the empty stool and come back."

Juli quickly but carefully crossed the floor, carefully balancing the tray of thirty-six clinking, overflowing shot glasses atop the slightly domed stool. She hastily departed after Vixen gave her an appreciative nod.

Vixen stood before her stool. The crowd applauded in wild anticipation while Juli, sure she was the only uninitiated one here, looked on in keen interest. She was glad to see the bitches knew their place, standing cross-armed along the wall opposite the stage with derisive sneers distorting what would otherwise have been pretty faces.

"Loosen your collars, boys... it's about to get hot in here!" Fox called over the speakers.

The music rose again, playing a song called 'Split Personality'. Vix leaned back against the stool, gripping its sides firmly with both hands. She wiggled her shoulders and hips with a grunt, which she managed to make sound orgasmic. Juli thought she could hear a kind of mechanical whirring and clicking, but it could have been the motorised lights for all she knew.

After a few moments, Vixen's shoulders relaxed and she straightened her torso, keeping her knees slightly bent. The hanging drape of her top shimmered up to better reveal her sparkling skirt, then moved further backwards, until it was pulling over an angular edge, a manoeuvre that would be impossible unless —

Juli suddenly felt so very woozy, raising a hand to her head. *What the hell has that pink stuff done to me?* "Did she just...?"

"Amazing, huh?" Alezi admired.

Vixen's truncated lower body stood on its own as she carefully lowered her upper body onto the stool. The crowd were hysterical, their cheers deafening.

Juli's vision seemed to go a little blurry, but she saw Vixen reach over and carefully lift the tray, placing it on the near-flat grey surface atop her legs, motioning as though she might be clipping something into place to stop it falling. The disembodied legs took a tentative step forwards, careful not to spill the drinks. Juli could see Vix was very adept at this, trying to imagine the coordinative dissonance. It must have taken many hours' practise to get this good at it.

"How many of you have seen a woman go topless like this before?" Fox called over the sound system, the whooping growing louder.

Vixen's legs performed a full circuit of the room as men fought past and over one another, either to grab a drink or just to touch her, perhaps to check the legs were real. Many were carefully placing rolled-up notes beneath her garters. Juli fought a gag reflex as she watched Nate lift the back of Vix's skirt, ogling her bottom beneath tiny black undies. If no one was watching, Juli had no doubt he would happily steal some of her tips as they came within snatching distance.

"Unbelievable," Juli drawled. "How is that even possible?"

"Let's just say there have been some interesting developments at Terrengus Corp, and Fox and Vix know how to procure a thing or two."

Juli was too distractedly in awe of what she was seeing to press this matter. In a roundabout fashion, what she saw and what Alezi said confirmed her suspicions about the company she worked for. Her jaw went slack as she watched in equal measures of awe and revulsion as a biker with a big bushy black beard lifted the skirt beneath the tray of drinks and gave Vixen's bottom a firm enough slap to slightly redden the skin, placing a rolled-up note beneath her left garter before grabbing the last shot glass after most of the contents had sloshed over the tray.

"Who even knew this would pay off?" Juli wondered aloud.

"Any girl who knows the truth about men."

"What's that?"

"That they're all perverts."

Juli considered this, realising just how little she really knew about Jerin, and how little he knew about her, as if such a thought had never occurred to her before.

She watched the young bimbos resume their entertaining duties as Vixen returned to the bar, back in one piece.

"Vix, I'm lost for words," Juli cooed. "That was *amazing*."

"Thanks."

"Does it hurt?"

"The separation doesn't hurt, but the mechanism gives me a little grief from time to time. The fluid helps."

"Can I see it?"

"Sure." Vixen lifted the flap of her top, showing an inch-thick metal band running around (and, evidently, *through*) her stomach, just below her navel. From a distance it could easily be mistaken for a fashionably thin decorative belt. Juli could clearly see the reddening of Vixen's skin around the edge of the cut.

"Why would you mutilate your beautiful body and risk your life just to make a living?" Juli asked. Alezi hit her to signal her personal disapproval of this question.

"It's fine, Lady," Vix told Alezi. "Many years ago, when we were in dire straits, I was very young and very stupid, and after a few too many drinks it seemed like a good idea. I wasn't worried about having kids, anyhow."

"Who would even perform such a dangerous procedure? I mean, no reputable piercer would work on a drunk, let alone anyone doing *that*…"

"We have plenty of discreet, disreputable contacts willing to take on any job, as long as it pays."

Juli decided not to ask precisely *who* could possibly perform such a procedure, instead remarking, "I guess it makes you pretty unique."

"That's the idea. My arse does get a tad sore from all the slapping, pinching and grabbing though!"

They all laughed. As the conversation continued around her, Juli's attention kept drifting over to Nate, difficult though he was to see beneath her blue fringe.

"Are you alright?" Alezi asked, placing a hand on Juli's shoulder. "You're a million miles away."

"I'm fine," she lied. As much as she wanted to pretend Nate wasn't there, she couldn't help eavesdropping on the conversation between that fugada and his 'friends'. Nate's choice of company was hardly surprising: one was morbidly obese, his bulbous belly poking between the buttons of his too-small once-white shirt; the other was a pallid, gaunt man with only a few wisps of hair, wearing a heavily food-stained turquoise business suit. His face was heavily blemished, eyes sunken in dark sockets. He looked like an animated corpse. Despite his appalling lack of fashion sense, Nate was the least-worst dressed of the three.

"It's your birthday, you gotta have a lap dance," the diseased-looking man insisted in a distinctly creepy voice.

Nate said nothing, pretending to be bashful, which his friends actually bought. Juli guessed they didn't know him the way she did.

"Go on, pick one," the big boy drawled, gasping for breath between handfuls of melted-cheese-dripping nachos, leaving a repulsive trail dribbling down his chin, his massive chest snowed under the crumbs.

"Alright, alright!" Nate conceded. He scanned the room. Juli quickly turned away. "That one," he said in a drunken drawl.

"Excuse me miss," the gaunt man said to one of the bimbos.

She squealed with delight and remarked in a forced airheaded voice, "What'll it be, mister?"

"Who's that girl over there?"

Please not me, please not me...

"Why would you want *her*?" she pouted. "She's way older than me. Wouldn't you prefer your fruit a little..." she pulled her top down, letting one boob fall out, "...riper?"

For once, Juli wanted the bimbo to get her way.

The attenuated man shook his head. "Sorry, you're a pretty girl, but our friend here has his eye on that one."

The bimbo covered herself. "Fine. That's Crystal, I think."

Shit!

"Hey, Cryyyysss-taaaaal!" the fat one called obnoxiously. There was no escaping it now.

She spun around wearing her most insincere smile.

"Hi, boys. What can I get you?"

"Come 'ere," the scabby one called, wafting a thick wad of low-denomination notes back and forth.

Shit!

"Go easy on him," Alezi smiled, promptly preparing a pitcher of beer and a glass. "Dead creeps can't settle up."

"You said you wouldn't leave me!" Juli shout-whispered.

"Sorry, I'm on my own here. If anything goes wrong, don't forget the panic button."

"But what if I panic so much I can't find it?"

"Ju, it's a massive red circular button on the wall. A blind person would be able to see it."

Juli hoped Nate was too drunk to recognise her, swallowing the bile down as she sexily sauntered his way with the tray, keeping time with the music's rhythm, never breaking the sexy-but-aloof persona she'd adopted.

"Hey, sugar," she forced in as sultry a voice as she could muster, his two cohorts whooping their approval, jostling him before pushing him unsteadily onto his feet. Juli took the money from the emaciated man. She headed towards the left of the two vacant booths without a word, not even pausing to check that he was following her. If he was so drunk he fell flat on his face, well that was just too bad.

Nate stepped inside and slumped heavily onto the violet faux-lunim crescent bench seat. Juli placed the tray on the small round table, held her breath and drew the curtain.

Shit.

Nate grunted his approval as she backed up, bending forwards to accentuate her rear, shaking her hips to the beat, wishing she could imagine it was anyone but *him* behind her. She adjusted her wig to better conceal her face. Maybe she could get away without doing the actual lap dance if she mimicked some of Alezi's more suggestive dance moves.

He'd been strangely quiet for a while, so she glanced

over her shoulder, only to see him holding up another bundle of notes, slowly unzipping his flies with his free hand as he laid the money on the table. He began masturbating. "Damn, you're hot, girl! Let's see those titties!"

Please, no...

She faced away and dry heaved. She glanced at the money in her peripheral vision as he clumsily poured himself a beer with his left hand. *Think of the money, think of the money...* as Nate put the pitcher down, his loose sleeve fanned the notes out, revealing five fives.

She wondered how many times he'd gotten away with this little scam. As much as she hated confrontation, she reminded herself she didn't usually have Mack to back her up. This thought bathed her in an all-encompassing calm.

She faced Nate as he downed half a pint in one long chug. He slumped back and spread his right arm along the back of the luxurious seat, leaving his repulsive member sticking up in the air. He exhaled a long, satisfied "aaaaaaahhh" before gesturing to his groin. "Finish it off for me, sweetheart."

"I'm afraid we don't do that, sugar," she replied, deliberately drawing his gaze to the fanned notes. "And a topless dance costs twice that."

He shrugged. "Do a good enough job and there's plenty more where that came from."

She smirked, "I don't think so," and scooped up the cash, but he seized the opportunity to wrap his hand firmly around her dainty right wrist.

"Finish me off," he drawled, pulling until her face was just inches from his, lowering her baulking hand towards his groin.

She smiled weakly, deciding to deny him the satisfaction of struggling or screaming. She'd deliberately positioned herself within reach of the panic button, which she discreetly pressed with her posterior.

He painfully tightened his grip and jerked her towards him. He wrapped a deceptively strong arm around her waist, pinning her between his legs, and smiled malevolently at her. "You weren't planning on leaving, were you? I'm not finished with you yet, whore!"

She struggled to maintain her composure as the nightmares came flooding back. *Come on, Mack!*

Tears welled in Juli's eyes as Nate leered at her, pulling her top down, exposing her breasts. She felt violated as he gave the left one a squeeze. "Nice. Pert. Now finish what you started!" he said menacingly.

The calm vanished and she was immobilised by fear. Her throat was closing so tight she could hardly breathe; everything she'd feared about tonight was coming true. A sudden kick of adrenaline sent her heart into overdrive, and she thought she might pass out. She'd never had a panic attack in her life... was that what was happening to her now?

The next thing she heard was the curtain flying open. Mack dived in, grabbing Nate firmly by the neck and left arm with his massive hands, but Nate's grip on Juli wouldn't yield. Mack said "Sorry," and rudely used his body to shove Juli aside before smashing Nate's face into the table top with a sickening *thud* that sent the pitcher and glass flying to the floor, the tempered glass bouncing harmlessly, beer spilling everywhere.

Juli looked on from the sidelines, unsure whether to stay or leave.

"You should leave," Mack glowered at Nate. From behind him came the scraping of chairs as a half a dozen bikers rose, all ready to step in if necessary. "And don't bother ever coming back. You're banned for life, mate. Every one of these men will remember your face."

Nate's newly-swollen brow creased in anger. "Fine."

Juli turned away as Nate zipped up before beating a retreat. She found herself hoping one of these bikers might bump into Nate when he was alone in the street, finding himself unable to contain his rage. The door banged open as he and his friends exited stage left.

"Are you alright?" Mack asked Juli softly as she

covered herself.

"I think so. Thank you."

"All part of the job," he said.

Vixen and Alezi came running over. "Ju-*Crystal*," Alezi fumbled, "what happened?"

"Chump tried to pay half for a topless dance," Juli explained, rubbing her sore wrist. To Vix she added, "He uses force to get the girls to touch him."

"I wonder how many times he's pulled that little stunt," Vix sighed. "Nice work, Crystal. Not many girls would have had the moxie to stand up to that fugada."

"I was petrified," Juli confided. "I thought..." she held back the tears. "I thought he was going to hurt me."

"It takes a special kind of girl to stand up for herself in a situation like that. Too many men think they can abuse us. I've seen far too many girls run out of booths with tears streaming down their faces during my time." Vix looked disappointed as she considered the true cost of this dark life.

"I wasn't far from it myself," Juli said, staring at the floor. "At least I have enough cash to call it a night now."

"You did *great*," Vix assured her, giving her a hug. "All you did was what you needed to do to survive. Welcome to the real world."

H
-One Fateful Night-

Juli awoke with a shiver despite being fully clothed. Her senses were dulled, she was completely disoriented and had no initial memory of the previous night. All she was aware of was that she was lying on her back, which was now very stiff indeed.

It was too dark to see. The top of her head was pressed against something hard, something that felt like wood under a coarse material so bobbled it snagged her hair. Her legs were elevated, bent at the knees, calf muscles draped over something angular and hard. She realised she was squashed onto a too-short sofa under a blanket too small and thin to trap her body heat.

Her mouth was so dry it hurt to swallow, and filled with the aftertaste of sick mixed with residual alcohol. She motioned to rise to get some water, realising a small weight was on her stomach. She reached her left hand from beneath the tassel-edged blanket to move it, only for it to erupt into a song of emphatic purring, fully stretching its needly paws out, raising its chin so she could stroke it with her extended index finger.

"Hey, Tabby," Juli said. Alezi's unimaginatively-named attention-starved old moggy adjusted herself so she was lying straight up Juli's belly, the way Nibbly used to lay on Jerin in bed. As much as Juli loved cats, she'd never bonded with Nibbly the way Jerin had. Tabby's prickly paws penetrated every layer of material.

"You're sweet, but your claws hurt," she told Tabby, who replied with a "myarrao" before jumping off and heading towards the kitchen.

Juli sat up, planting her feet on the floor, leaning forwards. She became woozy as the blood rushed from her head, the previous evening suddenly flooding back. At least it was behind her now. She inspected her wrist, glad that there was neither swelling nor pain. More than ever, she knew they had to find a way to get away from Nate.

When she had come here a couple of days ago, Juli had noticed a new shiny gold lamp sitting on the sofa-side table; she'd spent more time looking at that than engaging in conversation with Alezi's other 'friends' who had stopped by unannounced. She blearily spotted a feint yellow light, feeling the lamp's smooth base, fumbling for the switch, recoiling from the sudden burst of radiance.

When her eyes adjusted, she looked around. She was still amazed by just how small Alezi's new place was. *You certainly couldn't swing Tabby in here.* It was even smaller than her own tiny flat, the bulk of its character seemingly granted by the way the windowed wall leaned in at a forty-five degree angle, making the room that much smaller. It was that wall Alezi had chosen to position the sofa, requiring her to step forwards as she stood up to avoid hitting her head.

Juli suddenly panicked as a worrying thought crossed her mind. She frantically patted her empty pockets in search of the money she should have, sighing with relief when she saw it beside the lamp. She picked it up and had a quick count.

Two hundred and sixty-eight, not bad. It was enough to make up the rent shortfall.

Then she remembered some was Alezi's. She hadn't counted the takings from their duet, and had no idea how much she made on her own either. Even if she did, her head was way too groggy to work it out. Alezi was right about that pink stuff; it had well and truly done her head in. She wondered where it had come from; it certainly wasn't publicly available. Who in Terrengus Corp was making that stuff?

Alezi shuffled in from the bedroom in a pink robe and matching fluffy slippers, looking as dishevelled as any girl that time of morning, but surprisingly none the worse for the previous evening's activities. "Hey," she dry-croaked.

"Hey yourself," Juli replied, rubbing the crust from

her eyes. "Any chance of a cuppa? My mouth tastes foul."

"Help yourself." Alezi slumped heavily into the narrow gap beside Juli. Juli plucked a long strand of blue nylon that had woven itself into Alezi's blonde hair and placed it in her friend's hand.

"Your barnet is full of blue strands."

"Thanks. Those wigs are a pain."

"Tell me about it, I could hardly keep mine on straight! How come you're not hung over? You drank like a fish!"

Alezi shrugged. "I have a higher tolerance. Don't be surprised; I have a reputation to maintain. Let's not forget, the first three letters of my name do spell 'ale'! You were amazing, by the way."

"Thanks. I think I grabbed most of the cash from our duet, I guess I should give you your share."

"Ah, keep it," Alezi dismissed. "I earned a little more after your departure. I had that crowd eating out of my hands. Besides, you need it more than I do."

"Thanks, even if that remark was a tad backhanded!"

"Sorry, I was trying to be nice! It's hard not to sound like a bitch when you spend as much time hanging out with prima-donna models as I do."

Juli would bet her last few silvan that Alezi secretly enjoyed socialising with the prima-donnas she too often claimed to hate. This line of thought brought Fox's story back to mind. She considered confronting Alezi, but decided it wasn't the right moment.

Tabby returned to the front room, walked round in circles a few times then curled up in the corner beneath the HV bars.

"I'm glad old Tabby's still alive and kicking," Juli said.

"Yeah. Alive, anyway. Her kicking days are pretty much behind her now, though she has the odd try. I love her to bits. I don't know what I'll do when she goes. It seems like I've had her forever. Not having a cat would feel strange, but I feel so guilty that I hardly see her these days."

"Speaking of which, what do you do with her when you're off on a shoot?"

"There's an old dear who lives a few doors down the road. She has a small army of cats and was only too happy when I asked, but refuses to take any money, so I buy her bags of cat biscuits and litter every now and then."

"That's cool." Juli shivered again. "Don't you have any heating in this place?"

"Sorry, I'm used to it. You can put it on if you like, the switch box is downstairs."

"Since you know where it is, why don't you go flick it on while I make some tea?"

"But I just sat down…" Alezi groaned.

"Shift your lazy arse!" Juli jested, playfully elbowing her friend gently in the side.

Alezi made a bit of a drama about standing, pushing up from the arm of the sofa, then stretching her back until it cracked. She pulled a few more strands of blue nylon from her hair as she hobbled down the stairs.

Juli filled the kettle with fresh water before putting it on, then heard the cold pipes groaning to life. She glanced at her watch. "Shit!"

"What's up?" Alezi asked behind her.

"I need to go home to get ready for work." Juli groaned pitiably, clutching her head. "I probably shouldn't even be driving yet."

"Phone in sick," Alezi shrugged.

"I can't, I have to attend these stupid training workshops." If she hadn't drawn attention to herself, she probably could have asked Keresay to sit in for her.

The kettle clicked off and Alezi poured the water, filling the cold room with a growing cloud of steam. "This isn't as good as the stuff from the café, but it'll do," she said, throwing teabags into each mug.

"Thanks." Juli groaned again. "I think I need a spare head… I'd ask to borrow yours, but I'm not sure it'd be able to comprehend all the corp BS I'll be bombarded with today!"

"Thanks! You know, I never get tired of blonde jokes. You're such a charmer! It's no wonder Jerin loves you!"

"Sorry, I didn't mean it like that, I just meant it takes years of exposure to that crap to understand it. I miss the days when I didn't have a clue what any of the acronyms meant!" Juli gingerly sipped at the scolding-hot tea, burning her mouth slightly. She quickly added enough rehydrated milk to cool it so she could down it in one. "As productive as this conversation is, I better go find my car and get home. Jerin will be wondering where I've gotten to yet again." Juli paused to think.

"I'll walk with you if you like."

"Okay, cool. Umm… do you remember where I parked?"

Alezi smiled. "Oh, so now my blonde brain has a use?"

Juli squirmed. "I said I didn't mean it…"

"Relax, I'm just playing. Of course I remember. You left it behind the bar."

"How the hell did I forget a thing like that? I don't even remember walking home…"

"That'll be the pink fluid," Alezi remarked. "It may work, but it's hell in a bottle."

The hungover walk to the car beneath the twilight of the slowly illuminating barrier would be a long one, making Juli glad she had Alezi with her. They carefully dodged melting patches of ice on the cracked concrete pavement, passing a puddle of puke Juli suddenly remembered was hers. It brought back a vague memory of Alezi handing her a glass of water when they'd arrived at hers, which she remembered dropping during a momentary blackout.

The scuffing and clip-clopping of their heels was the only sound on that eerily quiet morning as they walked beside a road that in a few short hours would once again be heaving.

Juli finally decided to break the silence by asking

Alezi about Fox's story. When else might she get the chance?

"Alezi?" she began softly.

"Yeah?"

"Why didn't you tell me you lost your modelling contract?"

Alezi was stunned speechless for a moment. "Who told you about that?"

"It doesn't matter. Why didn't you tell me?"

"I... I messed up," she sobbed, tears rolling down her cheeks.

"Hey, it's not your fault," Juli said softly, then wondered. "Is it?"

Alezi squirmed. "Only a little."

"Alezi..." Even Juli was amazed by how reproachful this sounded. "What did you do?"

"One of the girls was being a bitch about how I was the wrong side of twenty-five, so I put some vinegar on her sanitary towels." She chuckled in spite of herself. "It was more like vineg-aarrgh!"

Juli squirmed as she imagined the burning pain. "Okay, she *probably* deserved it, but you have to remember not to act out like that! I told you that you'd get yourself in trouble one day!"

"That's why I couldn't tell you!" She wiped her cheeks with a tissue from the handbag she never left home without, smearing blue makeup residue across her face. Juli laughed. "What?"

"Here, let me do it," Juli said, stopping and taking out another tissue to wipe the mess away.

"Thanks."

They resumed walking. "So what are you going to do now?"

"I've got more than enough cash to tide me over until I find something else. That's the good thing about modelling; as long as you can handle money..."

"Rub it in, why don't you?" Juli interjected.

"I didn't mean it like that," Alezi replied.

"It's okay, you owe me one, remember?"

"True. Anyway, my point is, one or two high-profile shoots a year will earn you a damn sight more than any corporate job will, even the managerial roles."

"It's all well and good having the money stashed away, but it doesn't do you much good when you decide to go on a massive spending spree!"

"Touché. But I set aside enough cash for the bare necessities. Anything after that is disposable. I stick to a monthly budget, but I got sacked from my last job before I'd posed for a single shot, so I didn't get a cent. I'll work a few nights at the bar until something else comes along. It always does. I'll be fine, you just worry about yourself."

Juli nodded. *Should I change the subject...?* The car was still a fair distance away, so she decided it was time to ask that other burning question. But how to phrase it?

"Alezi, I keep meaning to ask you something..." she began uneasily.

"What is it, Ju?"

"Are you..." she fumbled for the right word, deciding it was better to just come out and say it. "Are you gay?"

Alezi laughed uproariously. "What?"

"It's just that it's been so long since you had a bloke, and you keep being really amorous around me, and you were all touchy-feely in the bar... I mean, it's cool and everything, but..."

"Ju, I'm not gay."

"Really?"

Alezi looked her in the eyes. "Really."

"Then you're straight...?"

"Ju, I'm asexual."

"Say what? *You*? Asexual?"

"It's a shock, I know."

"But you're so..."

"I know, the irony, right? Listen, just because I don't get turned on, it doesn't mean I don't know what turns others on."

"Well, I must admit, I am surprised."

"I don't really talk about it because it's really no big thing."

They eventually found the car, miraculously unscathed, behind the bar, just as Alezi had said.

"Safe as houses," Alezi chimed. "Well, I'll leave you to be on your way."

"Thanks for last night… and walking with me… and, well, you know…"

"Hey, don't sweat it. See you soon, chick." She gave Juli a quick hug. "You're probably still a little woozy, so take it easy. At least there aren't any cops around here."

"See you soon, Ale."

Alezi put her gloved hands in the pockets of her faux-fur lined coat and watched Juli drive away before starting the long, lonely walk back to her place.

Juli tried to get her brain in gear as she cautiously set off, glad the roads were empty. She badly needed a shower, but deep down she knew she'd never be clean again.

*

Jerin awoke with genuine surprise to see Juli standing before him, fresh from the shower. Wasn't she meant to be at work soon?

"Morning," he strained through a yawn.

"Morning, sleepy head," she replied, buzzing around the bedroom in a fervour, hastily climbing into fresh underwear while simultaneously drying her towel-wrapped hair, not really succeeding at either task.

"I didn't want to wake you last night, so I crashed at Alezi's."

"That's fine," he said, preferring to have been woken, if only to know she was safe. He'd seen too many fisticuffs outside clubs in his late teens. "At least I know you still exist!"

"Ha-ha."

"Kol says 'hi'."

Surprise lit her face up. "Kol stopped by? Crikey, I can't even remember the last time I saw him…"

"Me neither, but he's off again. He never sticks around here for long. Can't say I blame him."

Juli handed Jerin a bundle of heavily crumpled notes. "Hey, I got some cash out while I had the chance. When it's a more decent time, could you pass this onto Nate, please?"

Jerin was unsure whether or not he should feign surprise, deciding to remain stoic. "Wake him up. It'd serve him right."

"I haven't got the time to wait for him to clomp down the stairs. You know it always takes him an eternity to answer the door."

Jerin sighed. He *hated* dealing with Nate, but he knew it was better if he did it. He doubted that perv would spend the whole time looking at *his* chest. "Alright, fine. I guess I can find time to knock on the door literally around the corner. So, did you have a good night?"

"Yeah. I forgot how ridiculously flexible Alezi is… that girl can really bust some moves."

Jerin grinned. "Really? Hmm, perhaps she'll have to show me sometime…"

"Hey!" Juli chided, playfully smacking him. "Perv!"

"What? You brought it up!"

"Yeah, alright," she conceded before kissing him on the forehead. "I better get dressed and get to work."

"What, no proper kiss?"

She scowled at him. "Not when you have breath like a hobo's armpit!"

He glared at her. "Yeah, alright. I love you too!"

When Juli had departed, Jerin regarded the cash suspiciously. How had she obtained so much at such short notice? *Maybe Alezi loaned it to her*, he failed to convince himself. All he could see in his mind's eye were tiny fragments of that shattered dream. The money even stank faintly of alcohol and sweat. *I'm just being paranoid.*

It was still too early for most, but he decided it was the perfect time to pay Nate a visit, hoping to catch that fugada off-guard for a few choice words while he was in a confrontational mood.

He quickly got dressed in round-the-flat gear, donned his coat and slippers, and exited the flat. He headed down the short path, turned right, walked about the same distance again, turned right and knocked on Nate's door. It took a considerable time for the moron to answer, his feet falling from one step to the next more heavily than usual. When he finished fumbling with the lock and finally opened the door, Jerin saw he had a swollen forehead and a vague expression of what might have been guilt and shame. They both took a step back in shock. *If I find out you really* did *touch Juli...*

Nate smelled terrible and looked incredibly hungover. He hunched against the doorframe, his eyes unable to meet Jerin's as he distractedly picked at a piece of peeling wallpaper. "What?" Nate asked feebly.

"Rent," Jerin said. Nate reached almost blindly for the cash. "Nuh-uh," Jerin admonished, pulling the wad beyond his reach, Nate's eyes finally meeting his. "It comes with certain provisos."

Nate's weary face expression turned to confusion. He elevated the moronic look by allowing his mouth to hang open. "Like what?"

"Like, how about you fix our front door?"

Nate sighed. "I can't afford stuff like that…"

"Funny, I can. All I have to do is *not* give you this. What choice do you have? It's not like these flats are in high demand, is it?"

Nate paused as he struggled to process this. He sighed acquiescence. "What else?"

"Turn your damned HV down a few notches. Even better, turn it off once in a while so we can enjoy some peace and quiet and actually have some power. It'd be nice to be able to turn the front room light on occasionally."

Nate nodded slightly. He was being unexpectedly and annoyingly compliant; Jerin had anticipated more of a fight.

Jerin continued, "One more thing."

No reply.

"Stop harassing Juli."

"Youwhat?" The words ran together; "youoht?" Even then he didn't look directly at Jerin.

"I'm not stupid, and I'm not deaf. I've heard the way you speak to her when you think I'm not around. Cut the bravado, it's bad for your health, if you catch my drift."

Nate said nothing, but Jerin saw some vague semblance of comprehension in his eyes.

"Here," Jerin said, handing the money over.

Nate silently nodded and closed the door. No thanks, no witty remarks, no bravado.

Satisfied, Jerin headed back inside, just in time to hear Nate *clomp clomp clomping* his way upstairs.

Too depressed at the prospect of another long working week looming ever closer to be motivated to do something productive, Jerin decided against taking a black capsule, electing to sleep the day away by the numbing properties of the residual white substance in his system, and so he undressed and tucked himself back into bed.

*

By lunchtime, Juli's head was much clearer, but enduring so much tedious nonsense wasn't helping her stay awake. Safely away from the rest of the group, she let out an almighty yawn. Before last night, she'd become blind to just how overwhelmingly *grey* this place was, but now it was all she could see, on the walls and in the people.

She crossed back to the central building via the safer walkway and headed towards the refectory to get something to eat, when she heard some furore coming down the corridor from the open area of the floor ahead. Without consciously meaning to, she changed direction and picked up the pace as the commotion rose in both volume and tension, only to spot young Keresay arguing with one of the coders. They had drawn a few spectators of those with nothing better to do with their free time.

Not this again.

Keresay's youth-borne inexperience often made her act impetuously. Juli had been much the same at her age.

Juli baulked for a moment. Was she supposed to intervene? If not her, then who else would? She rushed over, telling the people to mind their own business. She was amazed to find the crowd quickly dispersed.

"Stop sticking your nose where it isn't wanted!" the coder, Niol, barked at Keresay.

"Stop deliberately making my job difficult!" Keresay yelled back.

"What's going on here?" Juli demanded, authoritative yet calm.

"Who are you?" Niol asked, throwing a rather disrespectful glance at Juli before returning his accusing gaze to Keresay.

"The most senior person here, so start explaining before I get Mr Manrose involved."

Niol scowled. "Fine. If you must know, this interfering little so-and-so has been tampering with our code!"

"He put a bug back in that I already reported last week," Keresay protested.

"Hang on, hang on. Let's go back to the start. Keresay, what happened?"

Niol rolled his eyes and threw his hands up in exasperation. Juli ignored him.

"I was playing a section of the new Aftermath mobile game that had already been extensively debugged on my break yesterday," Keresay explained patiently. "I was just playing for fun when I noticed a bug that had been quite problematic early on had somehow reappeared, but I was playing the latest code. It took me *weeks* to track down and fix that bug, it couldn't just come back."

"So you reported it?" Juli asked.

"Did she fuck as like!" Niol barked.

"Niol!" Juli scolded, her patience for this hateful man beginning to run out. "You'll get your turn!" She lowered her voice and turned back to Keresay. "Please continue."

"It was late before I remembered," Keresay continued. "The coders had all gone home, but one of their terminals was still on, so I took a look at the code. They'd literally copied and pasted the old code back in! They'd kept a copy of the new code, so I fixed it and deleted the borked version, and now it all works fine."

"*Technically*, it was the right thing to do," Juli told Keresay, meeting Niol's cry of "You what!?" with a steely gaze. "But you went about it the wrong way."

"Are you seriously encouraging this kind of behaviour!?" Niol barked.

"Niol, thank you for being so patient," Juli retorted sardonically. It was the kind of line she never would've used before meeting Jerin. "What do you have to say in your defence?"

"Why have I got to defend myself? I'm in the right here! If you must know, it was a test to prove that this little minx was snooping in our business! Why else do you think I left the terminal on?"

"That's not a particularly good argument for why I should let you keep your job," Juli told Niol. She had no idea why she said it; she'd never been one for such delusions of grandeur.

A malevolent smile crept across Niol's face. "Well, look who's gotten too big for her boots. You can't fire me. You even try and I'll have your job!"

Juli glanced over Niol's shoulder to see Mr Manrose watching silently. Niol followed her gaze, quickly backing down.

"Er, as I was saying… next time she needs to fill in the proper form and we'll take care of it."

Juli struggled to restrain a smile in face of his cowardice. "That *is* Terrengus Corp policy, but I do like to see people using their initiative. In the future, however, I would prefer it if you brought such a matter to my attention first, please," she said to Keresay.

"Yes, Ju. Sorry."

"It's okay. No harm was done. Go on."

Keresay disappeared quickly, leaving Juli with Niol.

"You're a gifted coder, Niol, but your conduct is highly unprofessional. We can't have software developers deliberately hindering a project that's due out in just over a month. I suggest you and your team take out the rest of your 'deliberate mistakes' and just focus on getting the software ready so we can get it on the servers."

Niol's voice became little more than a whisper. "There were rumours of layoffs once it's done. We just didn't want to lose our jobs. We thought this would buy us a little more time."

"Would the company be advertising a new position if that was true?" Juli asked.

"Who can ever tell in this place?" Niol replied. "Just because I'm the most senior coder on the team, that doesn't mean I'm immune to redundancy. That thought runs through my mind every time I teach someone one of my little tricks. If they knew everything I do, why would Terrengus keep me here for nearly twice the pay?"

"I understand your concern, but Keresay is also very good at her job. Since she joined the testing team, post-release fixes are down seventy-five percent. I get the feeling it would be even higher if not for your team. If you all want to keep your jobs, I suggest you get your house in order."

Niol nodded solemnly before finally leaving. Juli noted that he never actually apologised.

Mr Manrose approached, standing beside Juli with crossed arms, both of them watching Niol disappear from sight. Juli smirked as the tea boy Doon rushed over to ask Keresay if she was alright.

"Good work," Mr Manrose commended quietly.

"Thank you, Mr Manrose," she replied just as quietly. "I wasn't really sure what to say."

"I would have said much the same." He looked at her. "And call me Andivus."

"Thank you… *Andivus*. Since you're here, I promised Keresay I would have a little word with you about that coding vacancy..."

"I think she would make a fine addition to the team," he smiled. "It's about time someone jerked Niol and his team from their complacency."

*

Jerin's alarm blared for a full minute before he could be bothered to roll over and turn it off. His sleep had been typically bitty and restless, but he deliberately set his alarm early so he didn't have to jump out of bed the very moment that herald-of-doom song played. It was much warmer now than when he'd climbed beneath the covers, and he was hot and sticky.

Juli rolled to face him, throwing an arm around him as she wearily croaked, "Hey, honey."

"Sorry, I didn't mean to wake you."

"It's fine. Did you sleep well?"

"Not really." Juli stretched her arm. "Ah!" he winced.

Juli looked concerned, lifting her arm off Jerin. "What's the matter?"

"My stomach hurts slightly." He looked at the time. He had no desire to get up whatsoever. "Can't I just phone in dead?"

"I'm not sure they'd buy that."

"Why not? Most of the staff are like reanimated corpses anyway."

"So be the king of the drones."

He laughed. "The king of the drones gets paid a damn sight more than I do! Just five more minutes."

"You'd better not fall asleep again!" she warned.

"Relax, I snoozed the alarm." She carefully laid her arm on his chest and he wrapped the arm she was lying on around her side, revelling in her touch. After less than a minute, she was gently snoring.

After two snoozes that miraculously didn't stir her, he reluctantly gave in, slowly sliding himself from beneath her. His eyes were bleary and his mind foggy. He got dressed with all the fervour of a man lowering a hangman's noose around his own neck, considering that preferable. At least it would be over quicker.

Before her early starts, Juli would wake him every night with a steaming mug of fresh coffee, but now he had to hastily make it himself, when he had the time.

That was just one of the little things he missed. He didn't want to deny her the company of friends, but Alezi wasn't just keeping Juli from him, she actively encouraged her reckless spending, adding yet more bricks to their financial prison. He sighed despondently; he knew he was never going to get out of that damned plant. They might be okay for now, but what would Juli do when things got really bad again? Strip for a bunch of fugadas. He just couldn't shake the image from his dream of her pushing him aside and wriggling for those cash-clenching demons.

When he was dressed and standing in the hallway about to depart, he saw the ingrained dirt on Juli as she staggered out of the bedroom in her diaphanous nightie to bid him goodbye. In his dark mood he couldn't stop himself from asking, "So when exactly were you planning on telling me about your new job?" His tone was perfectly calm; they could have been talking about what to have for lunch.

Shock and sorrow struck her face. "You know about that?"

"Did you really expect me to turn a blind eye while you whored yourself out?"

Juli cast her eyes down at the ground, too ashamed to speak.

"You knew I knew when you gave me that money. Why didn't you tell me?"

"I wanted to, I just... I was ashamed." Her eyes met his. "I made a mistake. I'm sorry. I just did what I needed to do to keep a roof over our heads."

He threw his hands up, curling them into frustrated fists that hung in the air impotently. "All the times you assured me you wouldn't do this again... and I was stupid enough to believe you."

"It was a one-off!" she yelled, crying. "The dates just didn't align. You know what that bank is like, they don't negotiate." She tried to calm herself. "I just needed a little extra this month, that's all."

He told himself he was a fool if he believed it. "It always starts like this. And now I've run out of cash to loan you, you resort to taking your clothes off for money... where will it all end? With you laying in a gutter with your throat slashed?"

"I *won't* do it again," she reiterated, eyes downcast once more.

"I have to go to work."

She sobbed, "Please don't go to work mad."

"I'm not mad, I'm disappointed." That was true.

She said nothing.

He donned his coat, grabbed his heavy backpack from beneath the coat rack by one strap and opened the door.

"See you in the morning," he said coldly, closing the door, hearing her burst into tears the second it closed. He stood there for a few seconds wondering whether to open the door and apologise, but he was already running late.

He closed his eyes for a moment; his head was still so thick. He was so weary that even the flat grey glare of the barrier was harsh to his eyes. He donned the peaked cap from his bag in favour of his bike helmet. He knew eschewing the helmet was reckless, but he was more likely to crash due to that glare than anything else, not that the cap did much to block out that omnipresent light. Besides, if he fell and bashed his head, what harm could it do him? It might even knock something back into place.

He opened the warped metal gate and limply hopped onto his unsecured once-silver-and-black bike. He kept wishing someone would steal it just so he had an excuse to be late for once. He was always the first to arrive despite living farthest away and not having a car — what was that all about? — yet he was the only one who ever got pulled aside over his 'bad' time-keeping.

He mounted the rock-hard seat and rode past the

heavily-rusted module that powered the almost-unpopulated block during the dark days, hearing the familiar dull buzz of the worn-out circuitry within as it struggled to take the charge. He wondered how much more it could take before it blew and they were plunged into darkness. What would they do then?

As he rode he tried not to think about Juli, but the more he tried, the harder it was. Perhaps she would blame work apprehension for his dour mood; it was usually true. But this was something else. He hated feeling like this.

A peaceful, happy life... why was it so unattainable?

Now that his eyes had adjusted to the light, he could lift his gaze up from the broken road. By tomorrow night the sky would be bright white, the very last of the ice would be gone, and he'd be pedalling to work in a t-shirt.

The roads a few streets from their flat never got too busy during his travel time, but the drivers that did use them tended to be dangerously moronic. It was quieter on the way home, which was just as well considering he struggled to maintain his balance by then.

An articulated hover-lorry full of booze began to overtake Jerin, the force of the grit-laden air it kicked up from the road making him wobble perilously close to its side. Jerin pictured himself being sucked under it, the driver barely noticing the mild bump as the force of the hover mechanism chewed up the bike along with Jerin's comparatively fragile body, casually discarding the mangled pile of bloody mess behind it. Part of Jerin wanted it to happen. Perhaps if it did, Marv might show some sign of empathy, were he capable of such a thing. But the lorry roared ahead of him without incident.

During the rest of his long, mostly-uphill cross-town journey, he pedalled along more heavily cracked and dilapidated roads, past whole streets of crumbling derelict houses, their valuable glass doors and windows long gone. He bypassed the junkie-infested estate, oft-rumoured to be an area of frequent stabbings for any unfortunates that unwittingly passed through. He rode through an abandoned-in-mid-development housing estate, complete with roads to nowhere. As he crested the hill, dead chimney stacks of a bygone era dotted the horizon below him.

He arrived at the last corner, overlooking the sprawling plant complex adorned with the gargantuan red-glowing GMM logo, and baulked, his feet refusing to pump the pedals just a few more times.

He didn't *want* to go any further, but he knew he had to. Whatever shit inevitably awaited, he couldn't be bothered with it. Why couldn't he ever just come in and do his shift without any hassle? All he wanted to do was turn around and go home.

I can get through this, he told himself. *I won't let them get the better of me.* But even this thought failed to motivate him.

He sat there for a moment longer before sighing with weary resignation. When he finally forced himself to pedal that last short distance he found it physically and mentally harder than the journey that had preceded it. He parked his bike around the corner, approached the entrance on foot, and felt his heart sink a little deeper as the gloom consumed him once more.

*

Jerin squeezed his way to an empty locker in the crowded changing room, pulling out a fresh pair of light grey coveralls to wear over his clothes. They were some kind of obsidian-dust-weave material that somehow blocked the radiation of the module cores, the company very insistent that all safety precautions be taken these days. For Jerin, it was too little too late.

Jerin stuffed his gear into the now-vacant locker, cursing upon realising he'd uncharacteristically left his phone on his bedside cabinet. His set-to with Juli had left him in a particularly pugnacious mood, so he grabbed the dog-eared scrap of paper from the front pocket of his backpack before clocking in and heading to his station. He grabbed a clean helmet from the repository, still feeling a touch light-headed as he stepped onto the rattling metal-mesh floor of the plant.

Before he could don the helmet, he heard that annoyingly smarmy voice gleefully announce, "You're late," from behind.

"Not by my watch," Jerin replied as he spun on his heels. If Marv wanted to start shit tonight, Jerin was damned sure he was going to finish it.

"It's two minutes past," Marv said. "Get dressed in your own time."

"I do, every morning. At night, it comes out of company time. Only fair, right?"

"Everyone else does it in their own time."

"Do they really? That's an interesting theory, because I was just in there, and I saw everyone else getting changed at the same time." Just then, a colleague came out of the locker room, walking by unaccosted. "Really?" Jerin asked Marv.

"So... how's your head?" Marv asked without any hint of concern. "Did you see the doctor? You remember our agreement...?"

A sudden panic rose in Jerin as he realised he never took a black capsule. He tried to remain calm. "I should have known you had an ulterior motive for stopping me. I did see the doctor actually, and he gave me some new capsules. Thanks for asking, I didn't know you cared."

"The only thing I care about is whether or not your supposed 'noise sickness' has passed. There's always one problem or another when it comes to you."

"You're a lovely person, Marv. I appreciate your deep concern."

"Just get to the point. Are you going to be complaining of a headache if I put the music on?"

"I wouldn't know, since I don't listen to the shitty noise you call 'music' at home."

"Well then, I guess there's only one way to find out, isn't there?"

At that moment, a welcome sight loomed into Jerin's

view behind Marv; a feisty, just-past-middle-age diminutive woman with ever-changing brightly coloured hair, currently fluorescent pink, which made her initially difficult to take seriously unless you knew her better.

Marv continued, "As I said the other night, I'd better see an improvement in your productivity…"

"Evening, Roz," Jerin interrupted with a smile.

Marv smiled wryly, as though calling his bluff, when Roz replied, "Evening, Jerin."

Marv jumped in shock, spinning around. "Roz!"

Jerin quickly marched off, chuckling to himself as Roz tore Marv apart, yelling, "What have I told you about bullying Jerin? You're on thin ice as it is!"

He couldn't understand why some people had to be so hateful. He tried to reason that they couldn't help being stupid, likely born to morons who raised them that way.

Was it so much to ask for Marv to just say "good work," or even offer a simple "thanks"? Not just for him, but anyone who deserved it, few and far between as they were. People like Jerin were the ones who kept the company afloat, after all.

Arriving at his station, Jerin bumped into the day shift idiot, just as he'd hoped. Jerin usually made a point of avoiding him and his hyperbolic boasts, but today he was going to give that dipshit a piece of his mind.

"Oh, hi," the moron whose name Jerin had never bothered learning greeted derisively. "I packed another five hundred today, so you might as well go home."

Jerin wanted to smash the idiot's teeth out on the edge of the conveyor belt until he was shitting enamel, but somehow remained calm, sticking to the plan.

"You know, that's *really* interesting, because last time you said that, I found *this* little gem." Jerin carefully unfolded the month-old sheet of paper, the creases having worn thin, and handed it over.

The idiot studied it uncomprehendingly. His signature was scrawled at the bottom beside Kaxan's. It was a warning for only managing a pathetic workload of two hundred and twenty modules.

"It seems you needed help, drastically reducing the productivity of the entire plant that day. It's really quite remarkable how one weak link can break the entire chain, isn't it?"

The shocked idiot stuttered, "Wh-where d-did you g-get thi-thi-this?"

"You really shouldn't leave such paperwork laying around, you know. You never know who might find it. I guess you're lucky that it was me and not Kaxan. You know how he feels about people disrespecting him. Hell, he'd probably have given you a second warning just for that. But I digress. What I find really funny is that I manage twice that on a slow production day."

The idiot said nothing, scrunching his face as though he was about to cry. He screwed up the sheet, discarded it in a nearby bin and hastily departed without another word.

"What, no witty retort? I'm disappointed!" Jerin heckled as the idiot disappeared from his sight.

Jerin donned the helmet and quickly packed the accumulated modules into the waiting trays, clearing the idiot's backlog as Marv's tedious playlist crackled into scratchy life over the PA speakers, starting at the same song it always did, some crappy modern-day pop number. It would be less wearisome if he just shuffled it once in a while.

Jerin perfunctorily squeezed each head-sized unit into the ill-fitting foam lining, placing each full tray atop the ever-growing stack, careful to line them up right. When it reached eye level, he wheeled it over to the waiting area by the wall and pressed the call button to alert Falz, if he could be bothered to do his job. Jerin hadn't even seen him yet. Before old age had necessitated a move to a less strenuous area of the plant, Biln had been a brilliant backdoor man. Jerin just wished Marv realised that; he'd given the old man nothing but grief.

Jerin performed this repetitive task over and again, wondering how anyone was supposed to do this for an hour straight without their mind wandering, which of course his already was. It was inevitable when performing the most menial job imaginable.

During his mental meanderings, he remembered one of his better flashes of inspiration from a while back, when he had visualised himself working in the belly of a warship that had come under heavy enemy fire. To him at that moment, the only way to maintain the faltering shield was to keep feeding new power modules into the grid. The lives of the crew depended on it!

He smiled. Perhaps it was absurd, but he loved the additional ideas this inspired. He resolved to dedicate an entire sketchbook to the project he would call 'Ship Under Fire'.

It felt like he'd been going for almost an hour, but it had only been eighty minutes. The first night of the week was always the longest, but at least there were only twenty minutes to go until first break, *at long last*.

Suddenly, the belt came to a screeching halt. This was met by a cacophony of groans from around the expansive room, because it signalled either yet another fire drill or a pointless meeting. A series of crackles accompanied a high-pitched squeal as the music stopped. Marv announced: "Attention please, would all staff report to the meeting wall. Thank you."

The staff reluctantly shuffled like the drones most of them were over to the grey breeze-block wall, adorned with laminated sheets displaying various 'inspiring' propaganda-style messages that ran around the warehouse.

Most of the assembled mob restlessly shifted their weight from one foot to the other, muttering about this-and-that. Jerin was sanguine about such pointless meetings; the more time they wasted here, the less work they had to do. Marv marched over, accompanied by his 'pet', Falz.

"We'll get this out the way quickly, then you can all have a slightly longer break to celebrate," Marv declared. Celebrate *what*, Jerin didn't know, but it was a rare, if small, concession to sweeten what was to be a very bitter pill. Marv then proudly announced his most egregious error to date: "I've called you here to announce that Falz is now officially the new conveyor floor supervisor! I hope you'll all make him feel welcome in his new role, and treat him with the same respect you have for me."

Most of the crowd was indifferent about this, and Jerin would have thought, *Well that's easy... I have no respect for you either*, but he was too preoccupied, struggling to contain his rage as his mind screamed *fan-fucking-tastic*.

After break, Jerin was busily minding his own business when Marv made an unwelcome appearance. At least this time his little pet wasn't in tow.

"Jerin," the cheery persona in full swing as though their earlier confrontation had never happened. "Could you just hop in the forklift and tidy warehouse for me? It'll only take about two minutes, there's a good lad," worded as though he had a choice.

The alarm bells in Jerin's head immediately started clanging, *Setup! Setup!* What fall was Marv lining him up for now? Nevertheless, this was the closest he ever got to receiving praise. "What's stopping Falz from doing his job *now*?" he asked incredulously, continuing to place modules in trays.

"He's busy with some paperwork. All part of his new role." Marv's erroneous pride was sickening.

Jerin looked Marv in the eye. "How can he be too busy to do his own job?"

"Just get on with it." And voila — just like that, the persona was gone.

"No," Jerin refused. Marv didn't react. "It's above my pay grade. Besides, I've never been trained to use the forklift. And then there's the fact that, given my health problem, I'm not supposed to operate heavy machinery…"

"But you've used it before."

"Once, very reluctantly, about two years ago, and only

then because Falz was on holiday and no other bugger would do it. I was told I'd be paid the difference, but it never happened, so I resolved never to do it again. And to top it off, as soon as Falz came back he chastised me for mistreating his 'pwecious yellow baby'," he mocked. "So the forks bent, big whoop. Maybe they'd have to be changed more often if Falz ever did his job properly."

"Yes, you've made your point perfectly clear, now stop carping and get on with it." He spotted Jerin's odds tray. "What's this?"

"The incomplete modules that need to go round again."

Marv was genuinely baffled by this concept. "Why are they incomplete?"

"Because your 'amazing' staff are too busy chatting away to do their jobs properly."

"Do you think there's time to send them round again?" No mention of Jerin using his initiative. Jerin had expected no less.

"Even if there isn't, I figured it was better not to send faulty modules out. That might give the company a bad reputation."

"Alright, smart-arse. Go clear the warehouse."

Better to be a smart-arse than a dumb-arse.

Offering a sarcastic "Yes, sir!" salute, Jerin turned from his station, allowing the modules to build up behind him to illustrate his point as he asked, "And who exactly is going to do this while I'm gone?"

Marv beamed, "I'm sure I can manage."

Jerin eyeballed him. "If that's the case, what exactly is stopping *you* from tidying the warehouse?"

"Because *I'm* telling *you* to do it."

You power-tripping little turd.

Jerin took a leaf from his old friend Riccardo's book. "Fine, whatever," resentfully waltzing off with no sense of urgency whatsoever. *At least I'll get a laugh out of Marv's ineptitude when I return.*

He crossed the floor, turned left around the corner of

the grey wall, and his heart became leaden at the sight of the palette dumped in the mouth of the roller-door. That was always an accurate indicator of just how shit a state the warehouse interior was in.

He squeezed through the narrow gap between the metal frame and the pallet, scratching a small hole in the coveralls over his right shoulder blade on the corner of a tray. Inside was even worse than he'd anticipated: dozens upon dozens of pallets were haphazardly dumped everywhere. He threw his hands up and exasperatedly declared, "Oh, come on! This'll take a damn sight more than two minutes!" He wished he had his phone to snap a picture to show Marv when he inevitably got berated for taking too long. "And this is the work of the person you chose to be supervisor." When did the best workers, the life blood of the company, become the ones who were left behind? *When the corporation realised they were too valuable to promote*, he realised.

He searched between and around the too-tall stacks for the wayward forklift, eventually finding it in a tiny clearing with barely enough room to manoeuvre.

He almost slipped on the dusty floor as he moved a stack of wheeled dollies out of the way. When was the last time Falz swept in here? He approached the ancient faded-yellow rust-patched counterbalance forklift truck, accumulations of dirt-blacked grease in every nook and cranny.

He grabbed the overhead guard and pulled himself up, landing heavily on the foam-spewing pock-marked seat. He quickly re-familiarised himself with the control layout: accelerator, brake handle, levers to raise and lower the forks (sideways for tilt), and the all-important reverse flick-switch.

He pressed the ignition button, but it wouldn't start. *Damn you, Falz. Replacing the battery really isn't that hard.* He hopped off the seat and walked round to the back of the filthy machine. He pressed the red release catches either side of the massive battery to eject it, lifting the foot-wide black cube out, hauling then dropping the weighty thing onto the navy blue metal counter with a solid *clang*, swapping it for the long-charged one.

This time the forklift violently juddered to life, making its familiar metallic rattling noise. Jerin tried to reverse, but the switch rattled loosely in its surround. After six attempts he finally heard the telltale click, slowly depressing the accelerator so it didn't suddenly jerk forwards. The balding tyres kicked up thin clouds of dust as they fought for grip. It finally began to ease back, allowing him to pass through the narrow gap between stacks so he could assess how to begin sorting this unbelievable fuck job.

He lined up with the first stack. He carefully moved forwards, pulling the lever, the chain straining under the weight of the over-stacked load as it raised it. He pictured the forklift tilting forwards, but remarkably it remained level. He raised it as high as possible, confirming his suspicion that it wouldn't rise above the other stacks, severely restricting his movement options.

The turning circle of the truck was so ridiculously wide that he had to perform a twelve-point turn to manoeuvre this first pallet around the others before he could place it snugly into the empty corner it was supposed to occupy. If only the corp had bothered to spend just a little more and got one of those trucks that could spin on the spot.

It took Jerin about four minutes of careful manoeuvring to move half of them, the warehouse slowly becoming ever more traversable.

Just as he was on a roll, Marv marched in. *So who's packing the modules now? It better not be Falz...*

"Haven't you finished this yet?" Marv shouted in dismay over the noise of the engine.

"You know, if Falz had just done it properly the first time, I wouldn't be here doing this at all. I'm sick of having to clean up his mess just because you're happy to pander to his laziness. It isn't my job. And don't give me that 'you know Sundrosians aren't as clever as us' shit, because you know as well as I do that he just uses that as an excuse."

"I told you, Falz…"

"Doesn't have time to do his own job," Jerin interrupted. "Doesn't that make him kind of pointless?"

"I prefer to think of it as him making others more productive," Marv said without a hint of irony.

"Yeah, you would say that when there's no union rep around, wouldn't you? He's an encumbrant buffoon, Marv. Why would you promote someone who can't outperform a trained orangilla?"

"Just get on with it," Marv sighed, storming off without another word.

Good riddance. Piss off and annoy someone who deserves it.

With only one unbalanced stack left to move, Jerin heard an unwelcome voice. "Whuh oo doo'un?" The noise of the truck had masked his shoe-scuffing approach.

"Your job, you lazy bum-nut!"

"Oo sez oo can oose mah twuck?"

"Your boyfriend. If you have a problem with that, take it up with him."

"Ha-ha. No funny. Oo twy mayk mee luke bahd?"

"You what? I can't understand what you're saying! Speak properly, you mush-mouthed moron."

An expression of incomprehension lowered his prognathic jaw and wrinkled his sloping brow, raising his already Neanderthalic countenance to a whole new level. "Whuh oo cahll mee?"

"You heard, you ineloquent moron!"

Falz's mouth opened and closed several times as he fumbled for words before barking, "Oi'll zack oo!"

"You *can't*, dink, you're a *supervisor*, not a manager. Which is a point, I haven't gotten around to congratulating you on your ill-gained promotion yet. It's amazing what some brown-nosing will do for you, eh? Clearly you're a better man than me."

"Shuwup! Oo stop takin' tuh piss."

"No, I'm serious. You must have done something right, since you managed to get Marv to somehow look past your astonishing ignorance. I guess now the corporation will do all that heavy thinking for you. Oh wait, you never let such things burden you in the first place, did you? It's all a load of crap anyway, since all you actually get to do is tell Marv why we haven't achieved his impossible goal yet again."

Falz pointed a finger at him as he slowly remarked, "Oo hass tah doo whuh oi tells oo nah!"

"No, I don't. Do you even know what a supervisor actually does? I didn't think so." Then a thought crossed his mind, and he smiled malevolently. "You know what, forget it. I'm in a generous mood, Fabulous Falz, so this one time, I *will* listen to you. What do you want me to do?"

"Furst, oo no call me 'faboous'! Secund, muve 'at dere!" he pointed, moving his whole arm rapidly back and forth to emphasise the point, just in case Jerin was as stupid as him and couldn't figure it out the first time.

"Fine. Let me just go round to the far side…"

"Nah! Nah!" Falz insisted. "Doo at nah!"

Jerin glanced at the sign emphasising the importance of a balanced load, and smirked. Falz couldn't read a word of it. Hell, he wouldn't care even if he could, he just wanted to wear the big boy pants. How this illiterate moron ever got his degree was a mystery greater than that of the fabled temple of Zengothenia.

"What, like this?" Jerin asked faux-compliantly. Falz nodded as he manoeuvred the forks beneath the stack. He lifted the load as directed, the forklift's right-side suspension bowing, the left wheels lifting off the ground. Jerin quickly leapt off the seat to his left, the sudden removal of his weight allowing the load to topple, the truck landing with a heavy *clang* on its side.

"Good idea, Falz," Jerin nodded, patting him on the shoulder. "You know, I did not see that coming."

"Ahhh," Falz scolded in an infantile manner, "I tell Marv. He luv to zack oo."

"Aww, hush little cry-baby, it was your idea, remember?" Jerin leaned intimidatingly close to Falz and with quiet malice told him, "Now clean up your mess, moron."

"Juss oo wayt." Falz stormed off in a huff.

*

Jerin was second to arrive in the refectory for lunch, Falz already sitting near the door, sipping an obviously ineffective energy drink from a brightly-coloured can, chuckling as he gawped at who-knows-what on his phone.

Jerin's stomach was aching too much to eat, likely a symptom of him forgetting to take that black capsule. He wished he had time to cycle home and take one, but he simply didn't. He was too honest to pull a sicky, possessing a strangely misplaced sense of duty. Even if he had an appetite, the sight and smell of the over-done deep-fried foodstuffs would kill it anyway. The terrible Sundrosian cook wore his usual expression of pride as he stood behind the counter in his grease-stained apron.

Jerin placed his small tatty sketchbook and *Dark Nemesis* novel on the table in the far corner while he fixed himself a mug of tea. He would be alone there, and at the furthest point from the source of noise that would soon ensue.

He opened the novel Juli had bought him at a car-boot sale years ago; it was a collectible of reasonable value, but a little dog-eared, with a creased spine.

He read the first sentence: *Jannao skulked along the dark, dank corridor, silently stalking her prey.*

As he read, the gears of his mind became unstuck and began turning. In his mind's eye, he saw a dark-clad warrior brandishing an intimidating, intricately-detailed crystal sword. He closed the book's yellowed pages and cast it aside, opening his sketchbook at a fresh page, hurriedly sketching a broad outline. He was perfectly happy in his own little world, but the peaceful silence was abruptly broken like a bulldozer crashing through a brick wall by shrill squeals and uproarious loquaciousness as Hinges, Motormouth and Shit-For-Brains came tumbling in together.

Jerin sighed. He yearned for the agreeable break-time silence of Vahirinese workers that Jezebel had told him about.

The wenches often directed derisive remarks at Jerin for having aspirations beyond being stuck here his entire life. Whether he ever escaped or not, he needed to believe it was possible, and though he didn't care if people thought him deluded, he found their undeserved sense of superiority intolerable.

He closed his sketchbook and resumed reading, ignoring them for as long as he could, but as they passed loud, ignorant commentary on various stories on the table-top news screen, they spurned one another to ever-higher eardrum-piercing pitches. After just two minutes, Jerin could take no more, slamming his hand on the table hard enough to get their attention.

"What the hell is so damned funny that you can't shut up and give us some peace and quiet?"

"Excuseusforhavingasenseofhumour!" Motormouth hollered, her booming voice bouncing off the walls, her words running together, forcing him to concentrate to differentiate them.

"What's it to you anyway?" Shit-For-Brains chipped in.

"The refectory is for everyone, not just you lot. Would it hurt you to be considerate and keep the volume down?" He hoped the others would have the balls to stand up for themselves, but he knew they wouldn't. That was why Marv hated Jerin specifically.

The wenches glared at him, the room tensely silent. As he resumed sketching they resumed speaking, initially softer, then Hinges read aloud in her flat, nasally tone, "He groomed her by pretending to be a teenager on BestBuddies, then invited her over for a party. When she arrived he tied her to his bed and didn't let her go for three days! Oh my word, that's horrible!" They all gasped in their typically exaggerated fashion.

"That website has so much to answer for," Shit-For-Brains opined.

Jerin had heard more than enough *BestBuddies*-bashing over the years. He could easily have spent several minutes patiently explaining that sites like that were tools, that it could be used for good or bad and that people had to take responsibility for their own actions. He could have even pointed out that bad people would always find ways to achieve their nefarious ends, but it would be a waste of both logic and breath. Besides, the wenches were well known for broadcasting such fallacious opinions, and so help you if you corrected them. To Jerin they were the ultimate proof of the theory: tiny brain = big mouth.

As their ruckus once more reached full volume, he slammed his palm on the table again. "One minute! You couldn't even make it that long, could you?"

"Excuse us for feeling sorry for a girl being raped!" Hinges remarked.

"And does your loudly-expressed sympathy do anything about it? What if she cried rape so she could sell her story and become a minor celebrity for a while? What if it was a slow news day, so the editor decided to fabricate a story about the perilous times we live in? It wouldn't exactly be the first time now, would it?"

"Idoubtjournalistsarethatirresponsible," Motormouth opined.

"I disagree," Jerin replied. "My mate Kol was taking pictures for *Motoring Monthly* at the speedway a while back, and he overheard a driver jesting another about joining their team next season. They all laughed of course, and the driver joked that he'd think about it. The next issue of that magazine featured a story about how he *would* be racing for them the following year. That's the problem with daily news. When nothing happens, people either invent it entirely or exaggerate something meaningless or insignificant. Always have, always will."

"It'shardlythesame," Motormouth replied.

"It's exactly the same principle," Jerin countered. "We don't *know* anything, really, only what other people tell us. That's why it's important to think for yourself. Have you never heard the expression, it isn't what we don't know that's the problem, it's what we do know that just ain't so?"

"Socynical," Motormouth chimed.

"So you think I should be like you and unquestioningly believe everything I read? Did you forget that no news is good news? I mean, who'd pay any attention to the news if all they ever wrote about was how everything is fine? No, they sensationalise shit and create a climate of fear so people will keep coming back for more."

"Wellifyousaysothenitmustbetrue," Motormouth said obstinately.

Jerin shook his head. "You just…"

"Nonono," she interrupted, "whatwouldthewritersofthenewsknow?"

He rose to his feet. "Fuck all, that's what." He held his novel up. "Do you know what the difference between the author of this novel and a journalist is? The author will admit his work is fiction. Here's a newsflash for you: the articles you're reading were written by people like the rest of us, not some high and mighty super-being. People with bills to pay. And if their boss tells them to write something they know is false or get sacked, what do you think they'll do? Now why don't you all SHUT THE FUCK UP and have a little think about that for a while!?" he shouted at the top of his lungs, creating his own echo. He hated being the centre of attention, but damn if it didn't feel good to just let it all out.

The room fell silent, all except for Falz, who was still grinning like a burke and laughing at some unnecessarily loud video clip on his phone.

"Turn it down or turn it off, Neanderthal!" Jerin

bellowed.

Falz looked up uncomprehendingly, his toothy smile fading.

"Whydon'tyoustoppickingonhim?" Motormouth yelled, her companions adding a cowardly, "Yeah!"

"When the fuck did you become a member of the Falz fan club? I've heard you call him worse things than that!"

"At least we're not racist!" Hinges added.

"Oh, fuck *you*," Jerin replied. He impersonated her monotonous tone: "My boy bought this shirt, but it wasn't the right size, so he took it back, only he'd lost the receipt…" he resumed his normal voice. "Who the hell even cares? Don't you have anything interesting to say? You're boring as fuck!"

"It'snoneofyourbusiness!" Motormouth yelled.

"When you pollute my airwaves with your incessant mindless drivel, you make it my business."

"Whoaskedyouanyway?" Motormouth demanded.

Jerin sighed, but said nothing more, trying to calm himself as he waved at them dismissively. As he sat down, he heard Hinges say, "Mind your own business and go back to your colouring in."

"You got something to say?" he confronted.

"She didn't say anything!" Shit-For-Brains protested.

"I fucking heard her as clearly as I hear you now!" he replied.

"I didn't say a word!" Hinges whined.

"If you've got a fucking problem, why not just come out and say it?" he challenged, rising then slowly marching towards their table.

Shit-For-Brains' eyes darted around the room and she got up and bolted for the door, saying, "I better get Marv."

"Whatthefuckareyougoingtodo?" he heard Motormouth add, spotting that her lips never moved.

"Get out of my head, you evil wench!" he yelled, grabbing at his once-more throbbing head. He decided to go to the toilet to calm down and escape these idiots for a moment, when Roz met him at the door with Marv, Shit-

For-Brains squeezing back in without a word.

"Maybe we should all have a little get-together after lunch," Roz suggested.

Jerin nodded ashamedly and the air filled with the wenches' no-doubt derisive mutterings once more.

Him and his damned temper; how he wished he'd never opened his mouth in the first place.

Roz spoke with Jerin alone in Marv's office before the shit could hit the fan proper. They leaned their rear ends against Marv's desk, facing the door, both with their arms crossed.

"What's this about you toppling the forklift, Jerin?" Roz asked.

"That was Falz's fault," he shrugged. "I did exactly what he told me to."

"You know that's never a good idea."

"Haven't you heard? He's the new supervisor! Now I *have* to listen to his idiotic ideas…"

"Supervisors have no real power, you know that as well as I do. I just think you were looking for an excuse to do something stupid to let off some steam." Jerin didn't admit she was right. "Then you had that little set-to in the canteen… you're not yourself tonight, Jerin, what's the matter?"

"I don't know," he sighed. "I guess I'm just in a bad mood. Maybe it's the new medication, but those idiots just piss me off. This is why I want to take my breaks at different times."

"I tried reasoning with Marv about that, but he thinks it's antisocial."

"So what if it is? Is it so wrong that I want to be alone? Being forced to spend my free time with those idiots isn't going to make me like them. It's more likely to make me want to *kill* them."

"Marv also thinks there's no way to accommodate you going for breaks at different times."

"Bullshit! He has time to get me to do Falz's job. Biln isn't unreasonable, he's perfectly happy to fill the trays while I come out for a break. Then when I go back while the belt's off, I can return the favour by doing his job for a while. What's the harm in that?"

"Biln's old, Jerin. He isn't as strong or nimble as he used to be. He may be willing, but his back can't take the weight of those trays."

"There are other ways around it, Marv just doesn't want to know. You know what he's like. If not for you, he'd have sacked me ages ago. It's all so stupid. We wouldn't even *need* a union if not for insufferable pricks like him."

"I agree, it's a shame, but it's by Lazarus Terrengus's grace that I'm here at all. If his son wasn't so busy enjoying his father's wealth, he might pull the plug on people like me just to save a few bob. So I'll do my best to help you while I can."

Jerin nodded. "Thanks. So what do we do?"

"You and Marv need to talk it out. There's really nothing more for me to say, but I'll be here to listen. Hopefully, you two can get to the crux of the matter and nip it in the bud before it escalates any further. Okay?"

Jerin sighed. He couldn't see Marv being able to talk on his level, but he really had no choice. "Fine. I don't think it'll accomplish anything, but let's get it over with."

Roz nodded, and opened the door for Marv to enter.

Falz stood to Jerin's right, arms crossed, leaning against the old metal filing cabinets. Marv stood opposite, leaning against his desk, while Roz stood to his left.

"Does *he* have to be here?" Jerin asked, throwing a disdainful glance at Falz.

"I think he should go," Roz agreed. "This is a private matter."

"I want him here," Marv insisted. Falz flashed his moronic, toothy grin. "So, Jerin, we keep having these little set-tos, don't we?" Marv was trying on the persona again. It didn't fit him well. "Let's discuss this like adults and see if we can resolve the situation once and for all, shall we?"

"I'd love to," Jerin beamed. He waited for Falz to react, but he didn't.

"In your own words," Marv said to Jerin, "would you care to start by explaining the obvious problem you have with Falz?"

Jerin eyeballed Falz, staring straight at the idiot as he spoke to Marv. "You really don't know?" He snorted a brief laugh as his composure faded. "He's amazing, isn't he? I mean, he's a model colleague… he spends most of his time doing exactly what he's doing right now, propping up that filing cabinet there, and yet he gets promoted to a position that sees him getting paid more for less work. He's clearly much smarter than I am. Honestly, I could learn *so much* from him!" Jerin stopped.

Marv smiled insincerely. "Please, continue."

Jerin was aware this might be a trap, but had plenty more to say. "On the rare occasion that Falz can be bothered to work, he makes such a hash of it that people like me have to step in and do the job properly, as perfectly illustrated by that whole warehouse situation earlier. I mean, I can think of a dozen people right off the top of my head far better suited for the supervisor role, and yet you mysteriously choose this incompetent buffoon. I can only assume the Sundrosian you're wooing is his sister!"

Marv blushed. "Alright. That's quite enough of that." He was remarkably restrained, symptomatic of having Roz present.

"I disagree!" Jerin yelled, temper rising, his piercing gaze still firmly fixated on the subject of his frustration while he addressed his enabler. "I think we should discuss why this idiot is allowed to keep his job at all!"

"Enough of these asinine remarks," Marv yelled. "I want you to say something *positive* about Falz."

Jerin considered this, the answer coming to him in a flash. "Okay." He turned his gaze to Falz. "Falz. You are genuinely amazing at improving the general work atmosphere when you are not here."

"Jerin!" Marv barked. Roz shook her head disapprovingly, yet remained silent. Jerin wished she would speak up already, but she remained true to her word.

Jerin continued unabated, "Productivity improves tenfold and there's less waste. Oh, and we meet the weekly quota. In fact, I'd go so far as to say that your absence is so beneficial, the company would profit from paying you to stay at home. It really is quite a feat if you think about it."

"That isn't what I meant," Marv said through gritted teeth.

"Oh, but the same is true of you, Marv," Jerin said, turning his gaze to the bigger idiot. "This used to be a good company before you came along. People talked and laughed, and still got the job done. And then *you* decided it would be more productive to treat us like automatons whose very humanity was an inconvenience. When you can't handle someone, you shift them to another station, hoping the problem will resolve itself. When you're not here, people go where they fit best and we leave on time. You do no good for this place, but if you want to sink this ship, that's fine by me. There was a time when I might have given a shit, but not anymore. And let's not forget that you're the dolt who hired then promoted Falz. You're king of the idiots. I just wished there was a crown we could give you." Jerin folded his arms triumphantly.

Roz stifled a laugh. Marv's face flushed florid with anger as he glared at her. She shrugged unapologetically.

"You think you could run this place better?" Marv barked at Jerin, the persona well and truly discarded.

"*Anyone* could run this place better than an impotent buffoon like you!"

Falz finally broke his silence. "We hass degwees, whuh bowt oo?"

"Proving once and for all what a pointless joke they bloody well are!" Jerin said through gritted teeth, his anger building with every moronic syllable that left Falz's lips. He fought harder to restrain his hands as the rising red mist rolled them into fists. "I mean, what did you have to do to get yours, show up and hand over some money?"

Falz's eyes seemed to glow red, his voice sounding mechanical as he said, "Oo juss jehwus oo no haff wun cos bwain scwewy!"

The face became angular before Jerin's disbelieving eyes, Falz's skin dissolving to reveal angular metal plates beneath. Jerin realised this was all just another dream, and was damned if he was going to put up with it.

"Arf-bwained fuhwit!" Falz-o-tron goaded.

"It's still half a brain more than you've got!" Jerin yelled, forcing every ounce of his anger into his right fist, ferociously smashing it into Falz's face, breaking his nose with a loud *crack*. Blood dashed Jerin's fist as Falz flew sideways, falling towards the sharp corner of Marv's desk, on which he hit his right temple with the sickening sound of his thick skull cracking.

Falz hit the floor like a rag-doll, near-black blood pooling around his head.

No one spoke, all looking on in shocked, fascinated horror.

Jerin wasn't dreaming at all. He turned tail and ran without looking back.

*

Jerin pedalled furiously until his legs burned and then pedalled harder, as though accepting the pain as retribution for his fuck up. He pedalled through a skin-dampening fog made thick by the white glow of the warming barrier, limiting his field of view. Hazardous was an understatement, but at least there was little traffic about.

The adrenaline was pumping too hard for his mind to form cohesive thoughts; all he could think was *shit, shit, shit*.

The cops would come. He'd lose his job. He'd go to jail.

He'd lose Juli.

Fuck, fuck, fuck.

Be calm. There's a solution to every problem. Perhaps if I go back and apologise...

But what if Falz was dead? Then there'd be no escape. Perhaps if he and Juli fled into the city and hid? Kol might be able to help, Jerin was pretty sure he knew a few unscrupulous individuals who could make such problems disappear. Okay, so they'd be in debt to someone else, but that was a bridge on the horizon.

He had to get away from the plant; cops still patrolled this area from time to time. He headed deeper into Sendura, down streets no right-minded individual would dare travel, down streets he had never travelled his entire life until now.

He had no idea where he was going, but he couldn't stop. Even if he *could*, he *wouldn't*.

He narrowly avoided cycling over a forcefully-peeled-back strip of asphalt that would likely have sent him straight into or over wrought-iron railings, crashing in the abandoned bakery's drainage ditch beyond.

He came to a clearing in the fog, and the strength drained from his entire body when he realised where he was: *that* street. Ferrelus Road. He became numb to all sensation, not even registering that he was saturated to the skin, transfixed by *that* house.

For all the mistakes Juli had ever made, his was far, far worse.

As he followed the leftward curvature of the road, he was appalled but not shocked to see that the street that had once buzzed with fervent life was now desolate, the windows of the many houses as dark as the empty eye-sockets of a skull.

He reached the sharpest point of the curve, spotting number thirty-five wedged between thirty-three and thirty-seven. He stopped, stepping unenthusiastically off his bike, leaning it against the garden wall. It was the only house that was boarded up. *Typical.* The rest were likely filled with squatters. He and Juli should have done that; it was preferable to dealing with that avaricious bastard, Nate. Just another grain of a mistake in a desert full of them. The idea of seeing Nate's face twist in horror as he told him they were moving out brought a spiteful grin to Jerin's face. At least it was one potential solution to the quagmire he had created.

He stood there for an interminable time, dozens of memories breaking through the floodgates of his mind, some good, many bad, until he was too overwhelmed to look any longer.

He turned his back on that place for the last time.

Streets came and went in a distant haze as Jerin walked his bike along, mindlessly tracing the path they once walked together, desperately seeking a solution from within his enfeebled mind. There was no denying the fact that he had fucked up royally.

He passed closed-down shops and restaurants they used to frequent: the pizza place, the sweet shop, even the convenience store where they bought overpriced milk, all victims of the attrition. *Nothing stays the same.*

He came to a familiar sight that tugged the heartstrings more than he expected: the old park they had once walked through, hand in hand, at every available opportunity. So many little things… he'd forgotten just how much he missed their old life. Their new one was delicate and fragile, yet had become so heavily scored over the years that he'd long considered it beyond repair, but he'd never once thought he'd be the one to shatter it entirely.

He walked across the scabby remains of the old tarmac path cutting through the park, avoiding the slick mud, passing between two thick-grey-trunked long-dead trees, each lined with deep cracks. He came to rest on a soaked slightly-bent metal bench beside the path, leaning his bike against its side.

It was too soon for him to go home; there was no way he could slip in unnoticed. He held his head in his hands as it began to throb again. *How the hell can I explain this?*

She'll never forgive me...

He could crash here until Juli left for work. It was warmer now; the fog would lift soon and he would dry out. Perhaps sleep was what he needed to formulate a solution. He could feel the fluid building up inside his skull cavity again, sloshing with every little movement.

Just then, he saw a middle-aged Vahirinese man in a beige mac walking along the path. He was too well groomed to be a gangster. Besides, they'd have better things to do than walk the streets this early in the morning. All he could think was that this man looked like a cop, but surely none would dare wander here alone? Jerin couldn't fight the thought that he looked strangely familiar for some reason.

The man nodded at Jerin as he walked by. Jerin nodded back. Perhaps he would just assume Jerin was an errant drunk.

Confident the by-passer was far enough away, Jerin allowed sleep to take hold of him, only it came far quicker than he expected. He was too numb to stop himself from tilting to the left. He slipped from the bench, distantly aware as he hit his head on a protrusion of tarmac, feeling neither the pain nor the rush of warm blood on the side of his face.

As his vision faltered, he heard faint foot scuffs as the man in the mac ran over to him.

"Are you okay?" the man asked, but to Jerin the words were distant and muted. "That's a hell of a gash you've got there. Just hang in there!"

He took his phone out of his pocket, his mac flapping open to reveal a cop badge poking out of the top of his trouser pocket.

The man spoke to someone, but everything was growing ever darker and quieter, until it all faded away.

-Midlogue-

Horran Venura picked up the phone. In his panic, his trembling fingers were barely able to navigate the menu.

It rang, and Vincenul answered almost immediately. "What is it?"

"I'm at the hospital. There's been a complication."

A pause. In an eerily calm voice, Vince asked, "Have you made a backup copy?"

"Of course, I'm doing it now." Computer simulations run on a map of a person's mind were a useful tool, but nowhere near as accurate as the real thing.

"Then there's no need to panic."

"You promised you'd fix it if anything went wrong."

"And you have my permission to do whatever is necessary to achieve that goal, as long as you get that data. Is there anything else? I'm rather preoccupied right now."

"No."

"Good. Keep me posted." He hung up.

It sickened Horran to know that was the only value Jerin's life had to Vince now.

HI
-What Could Have Been-

Jerin awoke dazed and confused, splayed out of his front, hands either side of his left-facing head. Pushing himself up, his weary eyes were greeted by hazy red and black squares arranged in a checkerboard pattern on a surprisingly smooth blanket. His shadow was clear-cut beneath the harsh glow of a strange spotlight in the sky, from which he shielded his eyes, his vision filling with dark spots when he blinked. He came to rest on his knees, looking behind himself, astonished to see a massive smooth blue rock wall towering over him.

He dropped onto his bottom to sit upright, feeling the warm, gentle breeze caress his skin and ruffle his short hair as he stared straight ahead at the dreamily idyllic paradise before him: a field of fervent purple grass, which rolled away after only twenty metres or so, giving way to a massive drop, beyond which were numerous not-too-distant mountains topped by thin halos of mist. The seemingly boundless view took his breath away and replaced it with awe.

He glanced up at an unusual tree, the long golden trunk thin and peeling, its massive angular leaves a deep red. They bent at the middle, coming to sharp orange points.

Strange high-pitched calls came from nearby, and he glanced over to a group of brightly coloured flying feathered creatures he had never seen in his life. They were like quollings, only not quite. One was red, another yellow, one green, one blue...

Where the hell am I? he wondered as he rubbed his disbelieving eyes.

"Beautiful, isn't it?" a softly well-spoken woman said.

He jumped, glancing around, seeing a beautiful face framed by two tendrils of brunette hair. She held a book in her left hand, absently playing with the plait hanging over her shoulder with the right. His gaze was drawn to her piercing blue eyes.

"Jezebel?" he croaked.

She smiled, passing him an open half-filled bottle of water. He took it, realising how parched he was. It was so cool and refreshing, somehow slightly sweet. In his haste, he spilled it down his chin. He gasped when he finished, handing back the empty bottle.

"Thanks," he panted. "I needed that."

"You're welcome, sweetie. Did you have a good nap?"

"Yes, thanks," he replied, head still foggy. He spotted a woven basket with a handle and two hinged flaps, one open.

"I guess you really did enjoy my special breakfast picnic," Jezebel smiled, sighing happily as she admired the view. "What a great way to start the day."

"The best," he agreed, following her gaze over to the horizon. It didn't feel real somehow, but he put the sensation down to the receding fog of sleep.

He smiled widely, the sensation of serenity filling him to the brim as he stretched, inhaling a deep lungful of the freshest air he'd ever breathed. "So what else do you have planned for the day?"

"Nothing at all," she said contentedly, putting her book down. She sidled along the blanket, wrapping her left arm around him, laying her legs over his, resting her head on his right shoulder.

He leaned his head gently against hers, absently playing with one of the picnic blanket's tassels. "I wish every day could be like this."

"When you get your series finished, I'm sure it will be," she replied without a hint of sarcasm, uncertainty or derision.

His mind progressed from a slow trickle to an all-out torrent as memories flooded back. *That's right,* he thought. His friends had been kind enough to have agreed to pose for photographs in the nearby picturesque *Amaldus Valley*. He was in the midst of translating those images onto canvas as part of an ambitious project to create not just a story, but a tangible *world* in around twenty panels. If memory served, he had completed ten so far; *a good milestone.*

He felt so incredibly lucky to have such great friends willing to donate their valuable time to indulge him.

"Yeah," he said. "It'll be done soon. Then we can have a few more weeks of this before I start the next one. I might even have to put *you* in that," he teased.

"Oh, really?" she asked, moving her head away so she could look at him.

"Well, *parts* of you…" he joked.

She slapped at him playfully, a mischievous glimmer in her eyes.

He placed a hand atop her soft hair and gently pushed her flat onto the grass, falling on top of her, pinning her wrists either side of her head and kissing her passionately, so confident in their privacy that he intended to undress her and make love right here, but as they kissed again and again, the whole world felt as though it was tilting. Twisting sideways with this shift, Jerin's lips broke from Jezebel's. She reached a hand out, grabbing his loose red t-shirt.

"Are you okay?" she asked, concerned.

He shook his head as the ephemeral sensation passed. "Yeah. I think so."

"Don't lie to me, Jerin Endersul. What's wrong?"

"I don't know. I feel light-headed… dizzy."

"Come on," she said, wiping the grass from her flowing white skirt as she rose. She held her hands out, arms criss-crossed to help him up. "Let's go home."

They walked hand in hand between sporadic sprigs of brightly-coloured flowers lining the gently declining mountain path.

"This place will look so amazing in your next project," Jezebel beamed. "I'm sure you'll make it look great."

"If it comes out half as well as it looks in my mind, it'll be well worth the effort."

The plants here were big, strong and vibrant. It truly was perfection. Even the insects were too preoccupied to pester them.

"I know you like to keep your projects wrapped in a cocoon of secrecy until they're done," Jezebel said, "but could you please tell me a little about the story of the one you're working on now?"

He glanced at her with a playfully mischievous glint in his eyes.

"Just a little," she pleaded, indicating how little by pinching her thumb and index finger together so they were almost touching. "*Please?*"

"Oh, alright," he conceded, "but only because you're so *cute* when you beg!"

She slapped him so softly it was as though she brushed him with a feather.

"It's about two people who can't escape this small town called Sendura, which is nothing like here. Everyone's miserable because it's so dilapidated and destitute..." he stopped, suddenly feeling light-headed again, taking Jezebel's hand to steady himself as he swayed with a "whoa."

"What's wrong?" she asked.

"Just another dizzy spell."

"We'll be home soon, then you can take another nap if you need to. I'm intrigued, tell me more," she requested as they resumed walking.

"I... uh, I don't know," he said, shaking his head. "My mind's gone blank." Visions that had once been so vivid eluded him now, as though lost to the wind.

"You've been working too hard, you're just burned out. You need a good night's sleep. You were tossing and turning so much last night. Take today off, spend some time with me."

"Yeah, maybe you're right." He smiled at her. "Maybe

we need to spend the whole day not-sleeping!"

She slapped him again. "Is that all you ever think about? You're insatiable!"

"Is it so bad that I find you so attractive I just want to rip your clothes off and violate you repeatedly?"

"How romantic," she chided. "Some days I wish I could just give you my legs and leave you to it."

"That would work," he smiled. "How shall I remove them?"

She pushed him away facetiously.

"No, I'm serious," he said in the same joking tone. "Our saw is a little rusty though, it might take a while. They could just sit in the guest chair in my office for whenever I need a bit of... *inspiration*."

She shoved him again. "Even if you *could* have them, I wouldn't give them to you!"

He faux-whined, "But you just said..."

"I'd never get anything done! For one thing, I'd have to walk everywhere on my hands. For another, I'd be sitting there painting, minding my own business, and I'd suddenly have to stop until you finished getting your 'inspiration'!"

"If you enjoy it so much, you could always just come to bed with me..."

"Then I'd get even less done!"

They laughed as they walked in the shade of the dense canopy of various trees lining the path down into the tiny town. They passed the post office, the two restaurants, and the sheriff's outpost, the deputy tipping his hat to them from his rocking chair on the porch. Jerin nodded and Jezebel curtsied back.

Jerin saw a two-storey log cabin before them, behind a still-newly-white-painted picket fence, and well-trimmed lush violet lawn. It had a roomy wood-slat porch with a chair hanging from chains rocking in the gentle breeze. The windows were spotlessly clean, the reflection of the brilliant sunlight forcing him to avert his gaze. He realised then that he should have felt hot, perhaps uncomfortably so, yet somehow the weather was absolutely perfect.

They walked down the neatly tiled path. Jerin opened the unlocked door and they stepped inside.

Their home was so palatial, much bigger than it looked from the outside. The generously large windows allowed the light to fill every corner.

Jerin walked along the wooden floorboards to the open-plan living area, admiring every little thing. It should have all been so familiar, yet everything seemed somehow new. The furniture, which of course all matched, was exquisite and obviously expensive, the many chairs all covered with genuine maroon soft lunim. The ornaments adorning the shelves were trinkets from around the world; an ornate hand-carved desk with a bowl of fruit in the centre sat below the front-left window; the stereo seemed to be the only piece of technology in the room, and was like nothing he'd seen before. There was a disc inside it, but it was enormous, maybe a foot across, and black. There was a needle on an arm suspended above it rather than a small laser beneath to read it. *Weird*.

He admired the floor-to-ceiling picture on the wall — Jezebel's famed Vahirinese behemoth, worth more than their entire home, but strictly not for sale. It was intricately and lovingly painted, larger than life, so enormous he doubted his pokey old flat would even accommodate it.

Hang on; what pokey old flat? He felt woozy again.

Something didn't make sense. He sat down on the enormous right-hand corner sofa.

"Would you like some tea?" Jezebel asked.

"Please, spiced sachi with a spoonful of honey."

"Coming right up," she smiled cheerfully, disappearing into the kitchen area.

As he lay back to think, something caught his eye. He looked at a shelf that held only a lone carved wood sculpture of another Vahirinese behemoth. He noticed that though pictures hung on every wall, they were all painted by Jezebel.

He followed them along, admiring each one. She blushed as she brought in two gently steaming mugs of tea.

"Jerin..." she sounded embarrassed.

"What? They're good," he smiled, still wondering where his were. Perhaps he'd been too busy with his current project to create a standalone piece to display.

"But you admire them every day."

"That's because I love them. But I love the person who created them even more."

She sat his mug on a coaster on the opulent wooden side table, laying on the sofa beside him. They embraced, sharing a quick cuddle and a few light kisses. He couldn't shift the niggling thought that something was amiss.

"Let's go up to the bedroom," she suggested.

"At least let me drink my tea first!"

He threw back the fragrant liquid, savouring the way the sweetness brought out the fruity spices. Jezebel unbuttoned her baggy lilac top before leading him up the surprisingly non-creaky wooden stairs, stepping out of her skirt, letting it drape over the stairs. His eyes traced their way up her gorgeous long legs to her just-right rear, which he grabbed with one hand. She slapped it away, turning and ascending the stairs backwards, waving a faux-scolding index finger at him before turning away again, undoing her plait, cascading her long brunette hair down her back.

On the landing, she turned around, removing her long-sleeve white blouse.

Huh?

He glanced down the stairs at the skirt and saw that it was a grey business one that someone might wear if they worked in an office.

But she doesn't work in an office... and she wasn't wearing that earlier... he shook his head. *I must be more tired than I thought.*

He looked at her as she turned around, and her face was different.

"Come here." Her voice had changed from the typical Vahirinese accent with its elongated vowels to something else. Something more like his.

He paid it no mind as they entered the bedroom, the open window filling the room with cool air, the white satin curtains dancing joyfully in the gentle breeze.

He fell onto her as they landed on the soft, deceptively deep lilac bedspread, which engulfed them.

*

When the end of another gruelling day finally came, Juli greeted it gladly. The last hour had dragged on unbelievably slowly as the instructor spoke patronisingly about the importance of following strict austerity measures, which they had already covered ad nauseam. Considering the affluence of the building and its décor, especially the lavish executive offices, it was incredibly hypocritical.

On the drive home she detoured into a supermarket, hoping to snag a reduced-price treat to cheer Jerin up. She didn't blame him for the mood swings; she knew all too well what he'd been through and that, at times, he was in the passenger seat, unable to stop himself from saying hurtful things. She had told him many a time that she would always love him, come what may.

Once inside, she made straight for the bakery.

She preferred donuts, but Jerin was more of a cookies and brownies person. Luckily there was a bag of triple-choc cookies going for just a few pennies, so she grabbed it and proceeded to the tills, where she had to use one of those dreadfully slow, ever-crashing self-service machines.

As she dispensed a few low-denomination coins into the slot, Juli glanced up at a well-dressed man queuing behind her, catching his face in her peripheral vision.

Oh, no. Why him?

"Julianos, what brings you here?" he asked in his trademark cocksure manner.

Moron. What does it look like I'm doing!?

"Hey, Seran," she replied unenthusiastically, still adamant that it sounded more like a girl's name. She said nothing more, hoping she had successfully conveyed her lack of interest.

Nope, he wan't that astute.

"How goes the training course?" he asked.

"Fine."

"Good stuff. You know, keep it up and in a few years you could be like me," he grinned in a self-satisfied manner.

Lordy, I hope not.

She hadn't seen this reprehensible prick since he'd moved up a floor, and was glad for it. He'd quite openly and unashamedly brown-nosed his way up the ranks, and it probably didn't hurt that his big brother Vincenul was a member of the board.

"We'll see," she replied.

"Well, if you need any help, I'll be glad to have a chat with you sometime." He flashed that comic-book superhero-aping smile again.

No thanks, she thought, feigning an unconvincing smile, quickly putting him behind her.

*

Jerin donned his navy blue robe and headed for the bathroom, suddenly noticing the serendipitous lack of noisy, smelly children, walking past a closed door — the only one in the house. He back-pedalled and tried the rattly handle, but it was locked.

It occurred to him that the key was on a high shelf to the right of it. He had no idea what the point of that was, but he picked it up and unlocked the door, too curious to just walk on by.

Inside was pitch black, the air musty. He flicked the dusty light switch, the bare bulb slowly coming to dim life, struggling to push back the pervading gloom that clung to every corner. Dust particles hung lazily in the air, dancing and swirling as he disturbed their slumber as he stepped inside, the ill-fitting floorboards creaking noisily.

As his eyes adjusted, he saw dozens of neatly-stacked columns of boxes. They were *everywhere*. He grabbed the top box from the nearest stack to his left and lowered it to the floor, crouching over it, pulling the flaps open.

Inside were many of the old sketchbooks he'd filled during his schooldays with amateurish, juvenile images of demons, robots and spaceships. They paled in comparison to the magnificent works strewn on every wall elsewhere in the house. He looked around the room. His canvasses hung askew on the walls with the kind of disdain typically reserved for a child's drawing stuck to a fridge door with a magnet strategically placed to obscure the most terrible part of the image.

He grabbed another box. This one was full of loose papers, from when he still lived with his mum, staying up until two in the morning to take advantage of the peace and quiet.

Then he realised the truth: this was his room of shame.

He stood up and turned around, seeing Jezebel leaning coyly against the doorframe.

"Don't worry, sweetie, soon you'll have time to create a piece we can display downstairs."

Time... that was always his excuse. There was never enough to go around. Except there was; he was just too damn good at finding other excuses for never producing anything. An expert in the art of procrastination.

"I thought living somewhere like this would inspire me."

"It's normal to doubt yourself. Some consider it a sign of intelligence." She took his hands in hers. "Never forget, *I* believe in you. I think your project will turn out to be *amazing*."

He stared straight through her in that introspective manner. "Will it? Or am I just fooling myself?" He was slowly getting worked up now, ever angrier at himself. "Nothing I dream up ever comes out the way I see it in my head. It just ends up being unintentionally derivative of something far better... what if I'm never happy with my own work? It's nowhere near as realistic as your stuff."

"We all have different styles. That's what makes art exciting!"

"But I want to convey more realism."

"Then take a picture! Sometimes, people like art that shows them things that don't or can't exist. I envy your imagination."

He looked at her incredulously. "Really?"

"Really. Now stop beating yourself up," she soothed.

"I just feel like… dead weight."

"Then stop being such a damned perfectionist. You're too hard on yourself. Let it flow. Don't over-analyse everything."

"Maybe you're right. But if I can't, what good am I?"

"You're good for me, because you inspire me," she smiled warmly. "Come here, silly."

He stepped into her arms, dubious about her last remark, but glad to share a long embrace, her head resting on his right shoulder. He *was* happy, yet he harboured so much regret.

She tilted her head up to meet his eyes. "I'm heading back to bed to get some more shut-eye; are you coming?"

He nodded, turned off the light and closed the door, not locking it.

*

Juli parked in a different space, her usual one occupied by an unfamiliar black hover-car, a rare occurrence in this neighbourhood. It made her nervous. If it was a friend of Nate's, were they planning to ambush her? As she walked round to the flat, she kept glancing at the few ominous shadows, mostly cast beneath front door overhangs, wary of any would-be assailants. She fumbled for her keys with her right hand, holding a can of pepper spray in her left, wishing she had a psi-pistol.

As she approached the path to the front door, under the overhang bridging their flat and the one opposite, she spotted someone wearing a beige coat that stood out despite the darkness of the shadow. She jumped back with a scream, almost dropping the cookies, holding the pepper spray at arm's length. Her heart was pounding so hard she thought she might have a heart attack.

"Who's there?" she yelled. "Show yourself!"

"Relax," the man said as he stepped forwards into the harsh light, hands raised. "Sorry, I didn't mean to scare you." His face bore the haggard look of a long and weary day, but his voice was soft and kind. She would listen, but wouldn't readily lower her defences. "I'm sorry to approach you like this, but are you Jerin Endersul's spouse?"

"I'm his girlfriend, yes," she answered, growing ever more wary. This man's face was vaguely familiar, but she just couldn't place it. "What of it?"

The man waved a hand, dismissing Juli's distinction as neither here nor there. "I'm detective Haikyo Tinjima, DCPD," he said barely audibly, pulling his mac open slightly and sliding his badge out of his inside pocket.

It was a name she would never forget, and it instantly exhumed a very painful memory. "I thought I recognised you," she said.

He nodded forlornly. "It's been a long time. I'd hoped never to see you again, but I'm glad I finally found you. I've been popping round periodically, but it isn't safe for me to linger. Could I please come inside?"

Juli spotted Jerin's bike leaning against the wall behind the detective. "What's going on?"

Haikyo's gaze followed hers to the bike. "I have some news that you must hear, but not out here. Please."

The desperate look in his eyes frightened her. What had happened to Jerin? Panic had firmly jammed the gears of her mind. She unlocked and opened the door, gesturing for him to follow. He was risking a lot just by coming here. Members of the DCPD rarely came here these days, and for good reason: the gangsters had expanded their boundaries since she and Jerin had first moved here, and they enforced their own laws, and one of those was to scare off or kill any cops who stuck their noses in.

Juli quickly glanced into the bedroom, spotting the phone Jerin had forgotten, but no sign of its owner. Deep down she'd known he wouldn't be there. "Where's Jerin?"

"Perhaps you should take a seat," Haikyo insisted, following her into the front room.

Juli sat on the sofa, absently dropping the cookies on Jerin's sofa-side table, finding herself struggling for breath as her mind flooded with the fear of myriad dire situations that may have befallen her love. Had he attacked Nate? Had Nate attacked him? Had someone run him down on his way home from work? She sat there in silence as her mind considered the many possibilities, each more grim than the last.

Haikyo sat beside her. "I was pretty sure I knew where to find you, but I hoped I was wrong. As soon as I saw the address on his provisional driving license, my heart sank. He didn't have a phone on him, or I would have tried to call you."

Juli shook her head. "Sorry, I'm confused... what's happened?"

"Sorry. I'm no good at these things... I came across your partner, Jerin, while patrolling the park early this morning. He passed out, hitting his head quite badly."

She was quietly panicking now, fearing the worst. She tried to calm herself by remembering his own words: *prepare for the worst, hope for the best.* "So is he alright?"

"He's not in a great way. I called an ambulance. Last I heard, he hadn't regained consciousness. I spoke to your upstairs neighbour..."

"Landlord."

"Right. Sorry. He wasn't very helpful."

"Yeah, it's in his nature to be an arse."

"I noticed that."

She could only imagine what damage he may have done by hitting his head, but what preceded it, who knew? "You said this was this morning?"

"Yes."

"What time?"

"Around two, give or take."

"That can't be," she shook her head vehemently. "He would have been at work." She looked down, her hands shaking as this slowly sank in.

"There was a call from the GMM plant logged with base around the time I found him. A Sundrosian named Falz suffered a similar injury after Mr Endersul allegedly assaulted him. The DCPD want to formally interview Jerin, but I haven't told them where he is, not even that I've found him. I didn't think it would be fair on you to visit him flanked by armed guards."

Tears began to run down Juli's shocked face. *What has he done? He's ruined everything...*

Haikyo put an arm around her, doing his best to comfort her, to no avail. "Would you like me to take you to see him?"

"Yes... please..." there was a tremor in her voice. *Please be alright... I can't do this alone.*

"Is there anyone you can bring along for emotional support?"

"Alezi. She lives in the suburbs."

"Would you like to give her a call?" He offered her his mobile.

"It's okay," she replied, putting on her phone-glasses and dialling Alezi.

Alezi groggily answered, "Hello?"

"Hi Alezi, it's me."

"Hey, Me. How are you?" she drunkenly replied.

Of all the days to be drunk...

"Could you please come to the hospital with me?"

A pause. "What's wrong?" The silliness had vanished in an instant.

"There's something wrong with Jerin."

Another pause. "Okay. Sure thing. Let me just get a coffee or ten in me. I'll be ready when you get here."

"Thanks," Juli said, hanging up, bursting into a flood of tears. Haikyo gingerly patted her on the back to comfort her as she threw her face into his shoulder.

After a moment she lifted her head and he asked, "Are you ready to go?"

"Just a minute," she replied, the bile rising.

"Take as long as you need."

She jumped up, rushing to the toilet to throw up. She was aware of Haikyo following as she closed the door, shutting out the world for a moment.

She kneeled before the bowl and let it flow, hoping it would be over quickly.

"Would you like a glass of water?" he asked through the door.

She said nothing, unsure whether or not she was done.

"Are you alright?" he asked. In the silence that followed she imagined him wincing as he realised what a stupid question this was.

"I'm fine," she replied unconvincingly.

She flushed the toilet and opened the door without stopping to consult the mirror.

"Do you feel dizzy?" he asked, softly placing a hand on her left shoulder.

"A little."

"Sit down for a moment." He offered his arm for support, which she took. "I've got you. Nice and easy."

He walked her back into the living room.

"No," she said. "Let's go."

"Are you sure you're ready?"

"No. But I won't ever be ready for this."

*

Jerin was lying on his back with the covers half off, wide awake, staring at the ceiling, listening to the soft sound of Jezebel sleeping. His mind was still buzzing; all this seemed so *new*, so *wrong*, somehow indefinably *thin*. He quietly slipped off the bed and headed downstairs.

He went to the fridge and found it virtually bare but for half a bottle of milk, from which he took a mouthful, and a cling-film-covered white plastarch bowl containing two whole phesan breasts marinading in a strangely familiar sauce. He closed the fridge and absently rubbed his right temple, stopping himself when he realised what he was doing. He had no idea why he even did it.

He toured the house again, admiring the neatly-planed wooden floor, the fine-weave maroon rug with the shiny golden border. It was all so affluent and impossibly clean, not a speck of dust or dirt anywhere but in that room of shame.

It occurred to him then that with no technology with which to communicate with the outside world, he had no idea how he kept in touch with his friends. Did they all live nearby? Come to think of it, on the walk back with Jezebel, he hadn't noticed any other houses... he suddenly felt so alone.

He reached the exquisitely luxurious sofa, running one hand along the cool, smooth surface before falling onto it, staring up at the ceiling, admiring the ornate gold-and-crystal chandelier he somehow hadn't noticed until now.

He needed a distraction, something to help him clear his mind so he could get some sleep. He grabbed an art magazine from the hand-carved wooden rack beside the sofa, guessing it was likely the usual pseudo-intellectual overly-analytical crap, flicking through the many colourful pages until he came across an article about the works of several undiscovered talents, hoping for some encouraging words and secretly desiring to see something inferior to his own work.

The first picture was so incredibly simplistic that he couldn't believe he hadn't thought of it himself; white silhouettes against a black backdrop, wispy hazes in the background adding an eerie touch. But it was lacking a central element to tie it all together, as though the artist couldn't think of anything, leaving it unfinished.

Several arty-farty luminaries had offered their opinions on the works printed. The first wrote: 'I admire the simplicity of this piece. There's a conveyance of isolation, even desolation, which comes across with somewhat mixed results.'

That's because it isn't finished!

'I disagree,' wrote another. 'There's no central focus. It looks too much like a student project for my taste.'

Thank you!

The third commented, 'I admire the ambience, it conveys such dark emotions. I think this artist has a lot of promise.'

Jerin flipped to the next double-page spread, seeing a massively detailed picture that looked like a still from an action movie. A man and his dog were walking by nonchalantly as all hell broke loose around them, another man apparently leaping backwards firing twin pistols, a ninja sex kitten slicing a steel blade through three foes. It was good, much implied to be happening out of view by the presence of explosions and debris flying in, yet there was so much wasted space filled with a flat sky blue wash, which screamed of laziness. The overall image lacked subtlety to Jerin, presenting a somewhat juvenile view of conflict. Maybe that was the point.

'I admire the conveyance of the tenacity of the Silandrian spirit in the face of overwhelming adversity,' the first luminary had noted. Jerin was tiring of the repeated use of the words 'I admire.'

'I would agree,' the next wrote, making Jerin think, *either you agree or you don't*. 'But it implies so much more can be revealed on one canvas. A panoramic version could be phenomenal.'

Really? Even though it would then lose its focus? And no mention of the fact that the artist is too lazy to fill the blanks?

'The retro style makes me nostalgic for my misspent youth, when I read far too many comic books,' the last noted. 'It heralds back to a simpler time.'

Jerin shook his head in dismay, turning to another article, noticing the thumbnail photo of the writer, a cute brunette by the name of Julianos Miriandus. *Why does she look so familiar...?* He shook the thought from his mind and began reading.

'Some would-be artists toil their lives away trying to convey complex ideas and simple emotions on canvas, but simply lack the talent. While I admire their tenacity, perhaps they should accept their limitations and move on to something better suited to their abilities,' Julianos had written.

The story was continued over the page from this short introductory paragraph, so he turned it, his heart stopping as he saw one of his older works: his version of the Vahirinese behemoth, the very one he'd seen hanging in that dark room.

How the hell!?

He read the accompanying text so quickly that the only words he took in were 'amateurish', 'poorly realised' and 'a waste of good paint'.

He closed the magazine and his eyes, massaging both temples as his head throbbed and the world tilted once more. When the sensation passed, he opened the magazine again, feverishly flipping through the pages, but that story was nowhere to be seen.

He cast the magazine aside, wishing he'd never opened it. He was no more tired now than he had been before he'd picked it up. He got up and crossed to his desk in his small partitioned 'office' in the back corner, picking up the twenty large-print photos of his friends in various costumes, smiling at the first few. He placed them aside and ducked beneath the desk, grabbing his massive silvery metal box storage case to review the completed images.

He took out the first, depicting a ground floor apartment in a dreary cul-de-sac, surrounded by houses with dark windows, the sky a flat grey. There was something about the idea of that barrier that fascinated him.

He took out the second, showing his main protagonist drinking with an old friend in a ramshackle bar, deciding to move it to third, bringing one of an incredibly vibrant underground park to second. It seemed to flow better, but something needed to come between the first two.

He flipped through the rest, happy with the world he'd created, yet unable to escape the feeling that the manner in which he had decided to tell this story was rather crap. Perhaps if he created enough additional panels he could salvage it.

He sighed despondently. He would never be satisfied with it, not really.

*

The inside of the gleaming black unmarked police car smelled of sterilised lunim. Juli guessed it was cleaned quite frequently; a lot of drunks had likely sat where she was now. Though it made her feel like a convict, she insisted on sitting in the back, to be with Alezi.

Juli hated not being in control, especially in a car without wheels. The lack of that familiar rumble as it glided smoothly above the ground was disconcerting, and she kept expecting the whole thing to fall to the ground. She'd seen it happen many years ago, wireless power points being non-existent in Sendura. The complete silence of its photonic engine was also strange.

Haikyo drove much more cautiously than she ever did, adhering strictly to the speed limits and yielding for every other driver. In her heightened emotional state, she would have been cutting everyone up left, right and centre, so it was probably for the best.

The silent journey seemed to take forever. Neither of them said a word, Juli staring with disinterest at the world passing by as they crossed the bridge into the city. She wondered what stories the people walking around might have to tell, sure none were as sad as hers right now.

Alezi was anxiously waiting when they arrived, quickly running over when she saw the car coming up the street. Under different circumstances the idea of Alezi impatiently hurrying over to numerous incorrect cars might have made Juli laugh.

As soon as the car stopped Alezi opened the back door and sidled in beside Juli, fastening her seatbelt before throwing her arms around Juli, who was too numb and distant to react, pallid beyond belief, as though the very life had been drained from her.

*

Jezebel came downstairs to find Jerin lying on the sofa, eyes closed, right leg crossing his left, bobbing up and down. She abruptly drew back the curtain, dazzling him with brilliant sunshine.

He was stunned: *no way is it morning already.* It was as though the night had skipped forwards in the blink of an eye.

"Hey, what happened to you?" she asked.

"Couldn't sleep. Creative crisis," he shrugged.

"Just make sure you get some sleep before you go back to work tonight."

Wait, what? Oh, yeah. That...

"Holiday's almost over," she sighed. "Sucks for me as much as it does for you. I've *loved* having you here this week."

"Me too. But you gotta do what you gotta do, right?"

"You know, you don't *have* to go back if you don't want to," she suggested, sitting on the sofa's short side, beside his head. "I mean, we do earn a pretty comfortable living from the money selling my work brings in alone."

"I know, but it isn't fair on you if I don't."

"You know that doesn't bother me."

"I know. But it bothers *me*. Maybe once this project is done my work will begin to generate at least *some* revenue."

"Jerin, I get that, really, but you won't get it done anytime soon if you insist on working full time… you could always cut your hours if you like. Surely that makes sense?"

It did, but some mysterious force seemed to answer for him. Was it his sub-conscience? "I know, but sitting around here for hours or days on end does me no good. It just leads to procrastination. Sometimes, being alone and miserable is great motivation. It gives me something to aspire to." The words sounded empty and hollow to his own ears. "Many of the best artists say that misery is the best source of inspiration."

"I know. Many of the most pretentious ones say that too," she added bluntly. "You make it sound like success is the worst thing that could happen to you."

"What if it is? What if having to do it day in and out to earn a living kills my love of it?"

"Sometimes I think you'll never be happy."

"You make me happy," he said as he stared lovingly up at her gorgeous inverted face. He kept flicking a glance at the clock above the far window: the hands moved normally whenever he looked directly at them, yet jumped forwards disproportionately every time he looked away then back again. In what felt like just a few minutes, the clock's hands moved from early morning to almost noon.

He figured he should probably heed her advice and get some sleep, but he still wasn't tired. Not even slightly. In fact, he hadn't felt a moment's fatigue since waking up on that picnic blanket, reinforcing his theory that none of this was real. Even if that was the case, he wanted this to last. He couldn't fight the feeling that he was happier here than he would be elsewhere, so long as he didn't peer behind the invisible curtain.

*

"I'll wait out here," Haikyo said as he pulled up outside the gargantuan hospital's main entrance. Alezi uttered a single word of thanks, and they headed inside.

Juli approached the deserted receptionist's desk and waited anxiously for someone to notice her, even coughing a few times. One nurse walked by and Juli softly called, "Excuse me," but despite a cursory glance, the woman walked on by.

Alezi's jaw was agape in shock. "What the fuck?"

"Calm down," Juli said.

"I'll calm down when one of these bitches takes notice of us!" Alezi shouted. The many people sitting in the waiting area glanced her way. "Sorry," she soothed. They responded by averting their gazes back to magazines, phones, or just the floor.

While several nurses dealt with the throng of patients, another nurse and a woman who looked like she might be the receptionist stood over to one side, having a good old chin-wag.

Juli approached them, meekly calling, "Excuse me?"

"Do you want tea or coffee?" the nurse asked the suspected receptionist.

"Coffee. I need the caffeine!"

"Um, excuse me?" Juli asked as she tentatively stepped closer.

"I don't like the coffee here, it tastes weird."

"It's drinkable, as long as you add about ten sweeteners."

Alezi's blood was boiling now. She stepped in. "Excuse me!" she yelled, once more drawing the attention of everyone. "I realise it's so important whether you have tea or coffee, but I'm rather more concerned about the pressing matter of the health of my friend's partner!"

Both women's faces wore an expression of indignation.

Juli stood silently by as Alezi continued, "We're looking for Jerin Endersul. Tell us where he is and you can go back to your so important hot beverage debate."

A middle-aged eloquent male voice asked, "Did you say Jerin Endersul?"

Juli and Alezi turned to face him. "Yes," Juli replied to the well-groomed grey-haired doctor in his immaculate white lab coat.

"I'm Mr Venura, his consultant. I'll take you to him."

"Thank you, Mr Venura," Alezi chimed. "It's good to see someone around here is capable of doing their job." The two women stared daggers at her as she walked away.

Their urgent footfalls echoed against the bare walls as they followed the consultant down one near-identical corridor after another in the labyrinthine complex, arranged in easy-to-navigate-once-you-know-them blocks. Their guide never hesitated, Alezi throwing the occasional cursory glance at the manifold signs passing overhead.

During the walk, Alezi introduced herself and Juli, offering to speak on Juli's behalf.

"It's a shame to meet you both under such circumstances," their courteous host noted.

After several long minutes they reached the isolation ward in the intensive care wing. As Mr Venura stepped over to the vacant nurse's station to grab the datapad, Juli was drawn to Jerin's room. She stared longingly through the thick lead-infused glass, saying nothing. He looked so pitiful. His head was heavily bandaged. An IV drip kept him nourished and hydrated. Oxygen was being pumped through tubes inserted up his nostrils. A large metal dish-like device, attached to a length of pole wrapped in differently coloured wires, was curled around the space just above his head. More tubes carried his blood to and from a dialysis machine. All these intimidating machines beeped and flashed esoterically.

"Most doctors might dismiss his injuries as the result of the concussion he sustained in the fall," Mr Venura stated. "Thankfully, I know better, though if he had to hit his head, he picked the worst side."

Alezi was baffled by all of this; Juli had only told her so much. "So what's wrong with him?" she asked on behalf of her still shock-silenced friend.

To neither of them in particular he answered, "Radioactive particles from his new capsules have built up around the cerebellum and pituitary gland, causing extensive damage to both the cerebral and prefrontal cortexes. His mind has shut down, putting him into a coma to limit the damage, which caused him to fall. He's unresponsive to all external stimulus, but his brain activity is through the roof. Two things are certain: he's dreaming... and he's in pain."

Juli was stricken by a new shock. "Hang on, *what* new capsules? Why were they radioactive?"

Mr Venura's face registered surprise. "He didn't tell you? He came to me a few days ago, complaining of recurring headaches and a general lack of wellbeing. The radiation is a very small dose, designed to promote brain activity. Our analysis reveals that he forgot to take a black capsule to counteract the white. This allowed the radiation to permeate his soft brain tissue. I told him he mustn't forget…" he trailed off, shaking his head, casting his eyes downward. "His spleen is also pretty heavily damaged… did he mention any stomach pains at all?"

"Once or twice…" Juli considered. How could she have been so blind?

"Can we go inside?" Alezi asked.

Mr Venura looked at Juli, whose stare never broke from Jerin. "Of course. But you'll have to suit up." He nodded towards the white hazard protection coveralls hanging on nearby hooks. "We're doing all we can, but he's still emitting radioactive particles, and his immune system is so weak we can't take any chances."

Alezi nodded, then asked Juli, "Do you think you can get into one of those?"

Juli nodded silently. Her limbs were leaden as she fumbled clumsily into a pair of the form-lacking coveralls with Alezi's help. After Alezi donned her own outfit, they placed the cylindrical helmets with face-sized viewing windows over their heads and were ushered through the first white-trimmed glass door into the ante-room.

"I'll operate everything from out here," Mr Venura told them via in-helmet speakers. "Please be patient while you're both sterilised."

As the room filled with the quiet hiss of invisible germ-killing gas, Mr Venura explained, "The helmets have always-on mics if you wish to talk to me."

Alezi nodded, and after an agonising moment the door to the main chamber opened. Alezi waited patiently for Juli to work up the courage to enter first, which took a while.

When Juli finally found the courage to move, she slowly walked over, weak knees quivering, stopping several feet from him. She stared longingly at his still, lifeless face. Her mind froze, unable to accept that this was happening.

"What are his chances of recovery?" Alezi asked softly.

Hope for the best, prepare for the worst.

"He's critical, but stable for now. I wish I could say he'll make a full recovery, but I'm afraid the prognosis doesn't look good. But don't give up hope, there's a slim chance he may pull through. Once his blood is cleansed we'll administer the antidote incrementally to remove the errant radioactive particles from deep within the brain tissue. After that, we may need to replace his mind-chip. I wish I could say it's all very routine, but we've simply never had a case quite like this before."

Alezi looked at Juli, who remained silent. "I'm sure Juli trusts you to do whatever you need."

Mr Venura said, "There really is nothing more we can do at the moment. You two should go home and get some rest."

Alezi nodded, walking over to Juli. "Come on, Ju. Time to go."

Juli slowly approached Jerin, gently stroking the side of his face with her gloved hand. "No." Her voice was shaky and barely audible.

Alezi asked, "What?"

Juli's calm composure finally broke. She turned to face Mr Venura through the glass. "*You* gave him those damned pills! *You* did this to him! Get in here and fix him *now!*" She frantically looked around, grabbing an empty metal tray and hurling it at the window, screaming, tears of rage streaming down her face.

"Juli! Stop!" Alezi cried.

Mr Venura looked forlorn. "You're right. I'm sorry." His eyes widened in terror as Juli lunged towards a table littered with valuable medical equipment. "No, don't!"

Alezi grabbed Juli's arms in a vain effort to stop her. "Juli! This isn't helping!"

Mr Venura pressed a button on the wall, the speakers

inside their helmets emitting a crippling high-pitched squeal, dropping them to their knees, cradling their heads in agony. Mr Venura quickly suited up and entered, hooking his hands under the handles formed by Juli's arms, Alezi trying to protect him as they dragged her kicking and screaming from the room.

When they reached the lobby, Juli stared at the ground in silence as Mr Venura stood before her, doubled over and panting from the effort of battling her. The nurse and receptionist gawked at them, but made themselves scarce when Alezi glared at them.

Venura looked up as Haikyo entered. "Afternoon, officer."

"Afternoon. Are you alright?" Haikyo asked Juli. She didn't reply. Haikyo looked at Venura in silent understanding. "Let's get you home," Haikyo suggested.

Alezi grabbed a small notebook from her bag, giving Venura Juli's phone number on a ripped-off scrap. "I'm sorry for what she did, but could you please keep us informed if anything changes?"

"Of course," Venura said respectfully, tucking the number into his shirt's breast pocket. "I don't think any major harm was done. With any luck I can keep the board in the dark."

"Thanks, I'm sure Juli's sorry for what she did," Alezi replied.

Juli nodded, then Alezi led her out to the black car, sidling in beside her for the long, silent journey back.

Juli was vaguely aware of the unmarked police car pulling up outside Alezi's place, her mind lost, her thoughts nebulous.

"Juli?" Alezi's voice passed through Juli's mind like a distant whisper. She felt a hand on her shoulder, then Alezi asked softly, "Do you want to stay the night?"

As much as Juli dreaded the prospect of spending another night squeezed onto Alezi's tiny sofa, it was preferable to going back to her own place. *Their* place. She nodded weakly.

Haikyo got out and held the door for Juli. She slid out and Alezi exited through the same door, nodding a thanks to their chauffeur.

"Will she be alright?" Haikyo asked Alezi.

"I don't know. I'm scared of what she might do. I'll stick to her like glue."

"Yes, I think that would be best."

He watched them enter the flat, then went on his way.

Alezi put her arm around the small of Juli's back, guiding her up the stairs and into the front room, where she sat on the tiny sofa beside Tabby, who opened one eye, one fang on display, a comical look that would usually make Juli smile. Not today. The fluffy grey cat stretched emphatically, rolling onto her back so Juli could rub her belly, which she absently did.

"Let's spend the evening chilling out," Alezi suggested. "I know it's hard, but you need to rest. I'm here for you, Ju."

Juli nodded her appreciation almost imperceptibly.

"Do you want a drink?" Alezi asked.

"No," barely audibly.

"Do you want to watch a movie? Some light-hearted stupid chick flicks usually cheer me up when I'm down."

Juli was more than down, but she simply shook her head and insisted, "I'm fine." Tabby's purring was drowning out the screaming in her head, if only for a short while.

"Okay." As though a thunderbolt had shot through her mind, Alezi then asked, "What about work? Do you want me to give your boss a call for you?"

Juli nodded, handing Alezi her phone-specs. Alezi put them on and found the number quickly, heading towards the kitchen.

"Oh, hi, I'm Alezi, Juli's friend..." was all Juli heard.

The life had been completely drained from her, leaving her with barely enough energy to sit there staring into space; not quite dead, far from alive. How was she meant to sleep tonight? Everything felt like a bad dream as it was. It felt like there was something intangible lodged in the back of her throat. She needed to vomit, but there was nothing to bring up, and the very idea that she would ever feel hungry again seemed completely implausible. The rug had been pulled from beneath her world. How long would it be until she hit the floor? Every time she moved she felt like someone's puppet, going through the motions, never feeling in control. Whatever might happen, for better or worse, she just wanted to get past this debilitating depression, for Alezi's sake as much as her own.

Perhaps she did need a night of cheesy chick flicks to take her mind off things. If there were such things as small mercies, perhaps she'd fall asleep in the middle of one.

Alezi finally came back in, the sound of the kettle boiling rising behind her. She returned Juli's specs. "Mr Manrose said to take as long as you need."

Juli nodded. She knew he'd understand.

*

Lying on the sofa in quiet contemplation, Jerin could hear distant voices, but couldn't make out the words. He listened intently, but the voices fell silent before the sudden shock of an ear-splitting, high-frequency warbling noise jolted him so harshly he fell onto the floor, struggling to rise onto his knees, hands pressing against his ears until it felt like he was about to crush his own skull. It was no use; the sound was *inside* his head. After a moment it finally faded. He dropped his hands, resting them on the floor, panting.

A moment later the room around him grew dark. He felt a sharp scratch in the crook of his left elbow. He curled into a tight ball and clenched his eyes shut as a pinching sensation coursed up his arm, intensifying as it moved up to his shoulder and into his neck before settling in his brain, freezing it from within. His head felt like it was going to explode.

He tried to scream but could make no sound. The pressure was so intense he couldn't move.

If you're going to kill me, just get it over with already!

Then the pressure slowly faded. He slowly uncoiled, opening his eyes. The darkness receded, revealing muted colours. He was lying on a sparkling granite floor, distinctly *not* that of the cabin. He looked up to see a glass wall, beyond which were several other glass-walled rooms. Wherever he was, it was impossibly clean and sterile.

He realised he had no reflection. Why the hell was that? Then he spotted a nurse walk behind the glass, and he realised where he was. He'd heard about out of body experiences, but despite his frequent bouts of ESP he'd never really believed in them. Was it real, or just a product of his highly-fevered imagination? He had no way of knowing.

He lacked the strength to stand, an unseen weight pressing him to the floor. He struggled to shuffle using his arms and legs, slowly turning around, seeing a meticulously-polished metal trolley nearby. He could hear a familiar rhythmic high-pitched 'beep' he knew from HV shows; a heart monitor. His gaze met the locked casters of a wheeled bed, but he was too close to be able to see over the solid metal footboard. He spotted light turquoise trousers draped over white trainer-like shoes on the other side from underneath.

"Is it working?" an unfamiliar female voice asked.

"Yes, but very slowly. We likely won't see any change in his condition for at least a few hours." That voice wasn't so unfamiliar. *Is that you, Venura? What are you doing to me?*

"Any sign of consciousness?"

"Not yet."

He tried to scream *I'm here, I can hear you,* but he could make no sound.

Jerin tried harder to stand, but what little strength he had drained from him as the fluid was flushed from his body, every muscle beginning to tense until he was in the most excruciating agony.

He closed his eyes as it became too much to bear. Then there was only silence as he felt the world around him once more fade away.

*

Midway through the second happy-go-lucky chick flick, Juli finally passed out on the sofa.

Alezi draped the thin tassel-edged blanket over her before sitting cross-legged in the single round-backed chair over to the right of the sofa so she could stop her friend if she awoke with the intention of doing something stupid.

Alezi was dreading tomorrow; she had a strong feeling that things were going to get a whole lot worse.

*

Jerin was back in the wood cabin, but it was different now. The wooden slats that comprised the floor were warped and gappy, beams of darkness seeping in from below. Dust fell heavily through the air, laying thickly on every surface. The once-vivid mindscape was becoming too thin to last; gaps appeared everywhere now that he knew for sure it was an illusion.

Jezebel approached from the kitchen, adorned in sexy white silken negligee that left absolutely nothing to the imagination. Safe in the knowledge that he could skip imaginary work without consequence, he was determined to make the most of what little time remained.

"Here's your lunch," she declared, handing him the old-fashioned grey metal lunchbox covered in scabs of blue paint. "Shouldn't you get dressed?"

He glanced down, seeing that he too was in nightwear, only his was far less flattering: baggy navy blue bottoms and a white long-sleeve t-shirt.

He stared lovingly at her gorgeous face as she flashed her perfect smile. He put his hands either side of her head, pulling her towards him, kissing her passionately.

She was getting right into it, then pulled back, protesting, "Stop," playfully pushing his hands away. "There's no time for that now, you have to get ready for work."

"I decided you're right. Who needs that place?"

"But you said you *wanted* to go, as hard as that is to believe."

"You changed my mind. We should just spend the night fooling around."

She smiled coyly. "Why the sudden change of heart?"

They were wasting precious time; he wanted to cut to the chase. "Let's just say, when you walk around wearing something like *that*, you can be very persuasive!"

She playfully ran upstairs and he gave chase, reaching out to undo her tiny outfit, his fingers unable to get ahold of it. She ran into the bedroom and closed the door, giggling.

"Oh, we're playing this game, are we?" he asked, reaching for the handle. "Perhaps I'll just go back downstairs…" he faked, yanking the door open abruptly. He was baffled by what he saw: a dark concrete room filled with gigantic rapidly-hammering pistons.

"What the—?"

He slowly walked inside, stepping onto the metal-grille floor, the initially distant noise rising to a pounding din. The door slammed behind him. He turned, seeing the door was no longer wood but metal. He opened it, revealing only a long concrete corridor.

He looked down and saw that he was adorned in his work gear; heavy-duty denim coveralls with thick black rubber gloves that came halfway to his elbows. He focused on the sight beyond the grilled floor, spotting dozens of identically-clad workers pushing handles to turn giant wheels, sending gargantuan drills burrowing deep into the ground. As one worker began to flag, a burly shirtless man unfolded his arms from over his dirt-blackened chest, unfurling a long black lunim bullwhip, the sound of it hitting the floor enough to motivate the worker into finding a second wind.

What kind of nightmare is this? This isn't a plant, it's a mine… but for what?

Whatever it was, it was toxic enough to require them all to wear intimidating gas masks. The vision elicited a mild throb in his head, and he heard that voice from a once-forgotten dream shout, *At last he has returned to us, now I will reclaim you.* The voice did not reach his ears; it came from *within* his head.

He decided to turn tail and run, heading down the corridor outside the door, his ears filled with the echo of his feet pounding on the hard concrete.

A shout of "Hey!" came from behind, followed by "Get back here!"

He glanced over his shoulder to see a slimmer shirtless man with a whip bolting after him, gaining fast.

Jerin ran as hard as he could, but in true dream fashion it just wasn't enough, his legs turning to jelly, his pace slowing despite no drop in effort. He could almost feel his pursuer's breath on the nape of his neck.

He reached a long flight of stairs, summoning all the coordination and strength he could muster to run up them two at a time, assured he couldn't hurt himself if he slipped.

He was making good progress, but could feel fingers clutching at his black boots, trying to snare his loose laces. The pursuer got a strong enough hold to pull him down, the bridge of his nose smashing with incredible force on the edge of a step, the shock enough to incapacitate him.

"Aargh!" he shouted. *Wait a minute — that* hurt*!*

He wiped blood from the gash as his pursuer scooped him up, draping him effortlessly over one shoulder. Jerin was in too much pain to struggle, groggily raising his free right hand to his head, which was now pounding like one of those pistons.

The journey back was far shorter, his assailant taking him through a previously unseen side door into a dingy office, dropping him heavily onto a wheeled chair, kicking up a cloud of choking dust from its filthy cushion.

An eight foot tall man wearing an intimidatingly

massive gunmetal-black gas mask entered, slowly approaching Jerin, his heavy footfalls shaking the ground. The whip on his hip had at least six tips. He leaned over Jerin, that imposing mask hovering mere inches from his face. This was the boss.

"Get to your station," a deep, muffled voice told him.

The pressure on his mind forced his gaze downward, back to that whip. He could feel the cold rush of liquid coursing through his body again. His head felt like someone was slowly piercing it with long needles. He dropped from the chair onto his hands and knees, the boss stepping back.

Jerin glanced up, seeing the boss's mask twist into a disapproving glower as he towered over him. He pointed so his finger was only an inch from Jerin's face and demanded, "Get to your station!"

Jerin tried to stand, but his body wouldn't obey. "I... can't... move!" His head pounded with crippling agony, forcing him ever closer to the concrete floor.

He heard the multiple whip heads hit the floor.

"Get. To. Your. STATION!"

"No!" he yelled defiantly. He gave up, sprawling onto his front, his face resting on the dusty ground.

The next thing he knew he was being hoisted up by the collar, his dangling feet kicking ineffectually.

"Pathetic," the boss said contemptuously.

He tossed Jerin towards the far wall. Jerin anticipated a blow that never came, the wall giving way as though made of air. He was falling into darkness, the boss staring down at him as though from atop a well.

Jerin closed his eyes and waited as he fell and fell and fell. After several moments, he finally hit the ground with a spine-jarring *thud*. At least the headache was gone now.

He opened his eyes and was astonished to see that he was back in the tiny Senduran flat, laying on the bathroom floor, head next to the toilet bowl. He pushed himself up on a soggy patch of carpet in disgust, spotting a drop of water falling before him. He traced its path upwards to a bulbous protrusion on the ceiling, dangerously close to the large glass bowl that surrounded the lightbulb.

He stood up and examined it closely, realising that the bowl was filling with the water that was leaking from the flat above. *Nate's flat.*

Typical. That insufferable oaf is always too busy sticking his nose in other people's business to pay any attention to his own.

Jerin stood on his tiptoes and cautiously reached up, trying to unscrew the still-filling bowl, trying not to panic as it buzzed alarmingly.

The ceiling suddenly gave way to a torrent of water and plaster chunks. The bowl flew from his hand, shattering against the sink's edge.

Tempered glass doesn't break... water continued to pour into the small bathroom. *Oh, fuck this!*

Jerin went out into the hallway and tried to open the front door, but it wouldn't budge. He frantically looked for a key, but there wasn't one. The entire hook was missing, two lonely holes marking where it should have been. He glanced around at the water slowly filling the flat, reasoning that if the glass bowl could break, so could this window. He kicked the door's lower pane as hard as he could, bouncing back and trying again, wading through the ever-deepening water. It took seven attempts, but he succeeded, the window exploding, taking much of the water with it. Once enough water had drained, he ducked through the gap and ran down the street.

He knew then that the dream was over. The nightmare was only just beginning.

HU
-Natural Selection-

Jerin wandered in darkness until the road before him became that dreaded one. He realised there was no escaping it now; some demons had to be confronted. He walked down Ferrelus Road until he reached the gate to number thirty-five.

He stood at the foot of the small concrete-slabbed garden and drew several long, deep breaths. When he was as ready as he would ever be he opened the gate, proceeding down the path. The blue-paint-flecked wooden front door was ajar, as though waiting for him. He pushed it open with a creak and crossed the threshold, wondering what horrors might await within. He was unexpectedly bathed in a brilliant light.

He suddenly felt younger. He turned right, walking into the front room, dust particles floating lazily through the barrier-shine pouring in through the windows. He felt a tap on his shoulder, jumping and yelling simultaneously in shock.

"Hey," Juli soothed, "it's only me."

"Sorry, I didn't hear you."

She took his hands in hers. He was so glad to see her, much more than he thought he'd be. He freed his left hand, wrapping it around her neck to pull her in for a kiss, dragging his fingers through her long, silky brunette hair.

"Save that sort of thing for later," she whispered.

He reluctantly stopped. "Sorry. Is it my fault that all I want to do is hold you in my arms and kiss you?"

"Maybe," she smiled. "Come on, let's look around."

She led him by his right hand through the hallway and into the spacious kitchen, then back into the hallway and up the stairs, where they glimpsed briefly into the bathroom before visiting both virtually-mirrored bedrooms, their gleeful smiles widening constantly. That the whole house narrowed towards the back only enhanced its character.

It was very old-fashioned, with quaint wooden supports proudly visible, making Jerin wonder whether this was what the Jester looked like in its prime.

"I can't believe nobody's snapped this place up yet," Juli cooed.

As they stood looking out of the bathroom's tiny high window at the minuscule triangle that was the rear garden, Juli talked about what colours they might paint the various rooms, where they could place the wardrobe, bookcases and drawers, but Jerin was lost in thought over the room he would have all to himself, his own private studio in which to create in peace to his heart's content, free from distraction.

They walked through to the second bedroom. "This room will be great for the kids," Juli said, snapping Jerin from his daydreaming.

"What?"

"I thought that might get your attention!"

"Ha-ha," he said dryly. "Besides, I didn't think you wanted kids yet?"

"Well, not yet, but a few years down the road, who knows…?"

"But they're so…" there were so many words to choose, but which to pick? "*Expensive*. Not to mention noisy, smelly…"

She grabbed his hands and stood in front of him, looking into his eyes. "I know you have your doubts, but trust me, you'll make a great dad."

He said nothing, looking down at the floor. His father had never been that loving, and had died before Jerin really got to know him. Maybe he hadn't been as hard on Jerin as he remembered.

"One day," Juli added. "But for now, this can be your studio. But I expect to see some amazing works of art in return for my investment!"

"We'll see. Hang on, let me get this straight… so

when the sprog comes along, I have to give it up? Typical!" He threw his hands up in an exaggeratedly facetious manner.

She playfully slapped him. "You'll feel different once she's born."

"Oh, so it's a girl now, is it?"

She laughed. "Maybe it is, maybe it isn't. Who knows?" She did a little twirl, her skirt rising with the motion, his eyes checking her out.

"You keep doing that and junior might come along sooner than you think."

The bedroom's lower and larger window gave a far better view of the garden, allowing them to see that the path was formed of hexagonal concrete slabs, little grey islands in a sea of loose gravel. "We have to get a kitten."

Juli laughed in surprise. "I didn't realise you were so soft!"

"I *love* cats. Think of all the space it'll have to explore and play."

"Cats are cool and all, but I prefer dogs."

"Nuh-uh, no way!" he protested comically.

"Aww," she faux-pouted, "why not?"

"They stink!"

"They do not!"

"Yeah they do. It's even worse when they get wet, they smell like baby sick!"

Juli burst into laughter. "No they don't!"

"Near as damn it! Besides, when would we find the time to walk a dog?"

"Yeah, alright, fair point," she conceded. "We'll get a cat. But when it shits on the floor, you can clean it up!"

He shrugged. "I can live with that." He'd regret that the night he stood barefoot in a cold pile of the stuff on the bathroom floor.

They headed back downstairs, the estate agent pacing around the front room, chatting away on his phone. He excused himself and hung up, then started rambling to them about cavity wall insulation and other such tedious nonsense, most of it washing over Jerin as he pictured where the under-HV cabinet and sofa would best be positioned, what trinkets they might line the marble heater surround with, and so on.

"So what do you think?" the estate agent asked through a hopeful smile.

"It has doors that open and close!" Jerin beamed. The estate agent's smile faded, replaced with an expression of incomprehension. Jerin elaborated, "The last place we viewed was a tip. The only internal door was held in place by two nails in the doorframe. The rather dopey seller showed how functional it was by sliding it out and putting it back."

"I can't imagine anyone selling a house like that for much," the agent remarked.

"That's why we pulled out. But this place is so..." he looked at Juli.

"Perfect!" she finished, her excitement reaching bursting point. "We'll take it," she beamed, rocking on her heels as though restraining herself from jumping for joy.

"Alright, I'll fill in the documents when we get back to the office." He extended a hand and Jerin shook it. "Congratulations!"

Jerin turned to Juli. They wrapped their arms around one another for a big hug and kiss, giddy with child-like glee.

Juli had one last look back, as did Jerin, following her gaze. For a moment he could have sworn he saw what he was sure she saw: a baby's crib with a mobile hanging over it.

He shook the image from his mind, having to yank Juli away with a disappointed "aww."

He opened the car door for her, and she playfully stroked her belly as she climbed in. She smiled at him, saying: "The oven's always warm whenever you want to put a bun in it."

"What a corny line!" he chuckled. She looked at him with a theatrically exaggerated frown. "Let's get moved in first and worry about that later," he said to appease her. Of course, that particular later would never come.

Jerin stepped free of his younger self, intangibly wandering the house, suddenly surrounded by a flurry of sped-up fervent activity: the new fridge-freezer, oven and hob all appeared in the kitchen, purchased using the credit account he'd been reluctant to open, eventually caving to Juli's insistence that they would have to make do without appliances for years otherwise, and her assurances that they would 'easily' be able to pay it off before the interest hit cripplingly high levels.

Then the walls were patched, smoothed, cleaned and painted, shelves went up, ornaments appeared... it had been too much temptation. Before long he'd bought larger HV bars and a then state-of-the-art compu-phone, just a few months before the price was infuriatingly slashed by almost half.

Despite that annoyance, he definitely got his money's worth from that phone, finding myriad uses for it in just about every situation imaginable: photography, note taking, navigating to a new restaurant, anything and everything. He drove Juli mad by making it expand and shrink ad nauseam.

When everything in the house settled and slowed back down, apparition-Jerin wandered into the kitchen, admiring what he and Juli once managed to pull off together, when the younger versions of them arrived home with a pet carrier, which they carefully placed on the kitchen floor before opening.

They crouched in hushed awe as the tiny black and white furball nervously emerged, taking in his surroundings with his wide blue eyes.

They offered him food, but the rattle of the kitten biscuits sent him cowering into the corner beneath the cupboards. Jerin quickly found an old shoelace and dangled it before the as-yet-unnamed cat. After a few moments he was throwing his prickly paws energetically forth, grabbing the plastarch-coated tip and chewing on it fervently as he fell onto his side, rolling onto his back. They smiled at him like proud parents.

Once he came around, the kitten was so hungry he almost fell face-first into his massive bowl, voraciously devouring his first meal in his new home. This was quickly followed by a long drink and the production of the smelliest litter box log imaginable, leading to Jerin scrambling for a can of air freshener from the bathroom upstairs.

After that, the kitten ran into the hallway with something of a skip, sniffing at the shoes on the rack, playing with a loose lace, grabbing it in his mouth and pulling with a comical sneer, scaring himself witless when the shoe inevitably tumbled to the floor as a result of his incessant tugging.

The kitten soon settled in, tearing around the house like a mini tornado, climbing the patio door curtains and sitting proudly atop the railing before mewing to be rescued when he realised he didn't know how to get down. They even arrived home to find him asleep up there one day.

Apparition-Jerin was suddenly whisked to the bedroom for reasons he didn't know. When he was free to move again he felt rather dizzy, and so decided to take a quick lie down on their still-new bed, hoping this weird trip through his own psyche would end soon. Juli appeared beside him as he segued from phantom to interactive subject, yet he remained a puppet, controlled by the memory.

She smiled at him as the little black and white kitten tentatively made its way up the valley of duvet between their covered bodies, both of them encouraging him with outstretched fingers and sucky-mouthed noises. Jerin glanced at the tiny black spot on his nose and went to tickle it, receiving a playful nibble on the tip of his finger.

"Oi! Little nibbler," Jerin faux-scolded.

"I like it!" Juli beamed.

"Huh?"

"It's a good name."

"It's more of a description really, but I guess it works." He turned his attention back to the cat. "Do you like the name 'Nibbler'?"

The tiny tomcat meowed enthusiastically, which they took as him signalling his approval.

They smiled and laughed and petted Nibbler, a name which was soon replaced by the affectionate nickname 'Nibbly', even though it was no shorter.

They were so stupidly in love, so sure that nothing could possibly go wrong. It was a high no drug could have provided.

But it wouldn't last.

Apparition-Jerin watched from the sidelines again as Juli came home after a whole day spent with Alezi. She had so many canvas shopping bags that it took all three of them a good five minutes to unload the lot.

Juli explained to Jerin what it all was — ornaments, shelving she would later ask him to put up, curtains, rugs he would put away after tripping over the sticking-up corner of the one in the bedroom one time too many. Alezi had also bought them a few "house-warming gifts," which occupied two full bags.

"You don't mind, do you?" Juli asked.

Jerin looked at her, somewhat offended. "It's your money, and you work hard for it. Why would I mind how you spend it?"

Juli smiled and gave him a big hug, moving towards the first bag.

"Let's leave it 'til the morning," he insisted, pushing the nagging doubts aside. "You've been gone all day, you owe me some alone time in the bedroom!"

Juli smiled widely, leading memory-Jerin up the stairs.

*

Jerin knew that the key to happiness was when life gave a person more ups than downs. Enough highs could cancel out the majority of the lows, clearing them from a person's mind entirely. But the inverse was also true;

when the troughs were more frequent than the peaks, even the good parts became joyless.

Not every person has a key moment in their life they could pin-point as that precise moment when everything went wrong, but Jerin certainly did. If there was one moment he could go back in time and avoid, it was this one.

The house was consumed by darkness, replaced by the plant.

Their move had necessitated Jerin's finding of a job that was both nearer to home and better paid, and so with a leaden heart Jerin had quit Hit Flix and started here as a stop-gap, then both young and naïve enough to believe that he would soon move on to bigger better things.

He didn't hate the job at first: though it was tedious his colleagues were mostly a good bunch, always ripe for a laugh, but that soon changed. As one shuffle followed another, these genial people were replaced by sullen ones, which made his move to an area where he was all alone something of a relief, for a little while.

Then only twenty-three, he was also quite reckless. As rock music blared through his headphones to drown out the annoying pop-shit on the radio, he grabbed the fist-sized glowing liquid cores from the overhanging dispenser, dextrously twirling them in one hand before dropping them into the open modules as they slowly rolled by, the black gloves providing more grip than his bare hands.

They had been told time and again that the substance inside the cores was dangerous, but no one took health and safety *that* seriously; back then they didn't even have to wear helmets.

One day Jerin noticed that the dispenser's spring-latch was getting loose, the cores often coming two at a time. He filled in the necessary form on the staff terminal to report the problem, but despite his use of the precise words 'accident waiting to happen', nothing came of it. Unhappy at being ignored, he took the matter directly to

Kaxan, who confirmed his ignorance of the situation, following Jerin dutifully to inspect the faulty unit, making a note of it on his work-issued datapad and assuring him it would "be dealt with as a top priority."

But still nothing came of it.

On a day like any other, Jerin was at his station, quietly minding his own business, when he had an unusually strong premonition that something very wrong was about to happen. Without conscious premeditation, he sprang to his feet just as the loose latch finally gave way. He stood with both palms rammed against the opening, struggling to hold the glowing glass ovoids back — the force of the impact from that height would surely eject the stop-caps, exposing him to their toxic contents. All he could see in his mind's eye was a glowing puddle growing larger and larger.

"If anyone can hear me, HELP!" he yelled as loud as he could.

No answer. The radio was drowning him out.

He glanced around frantically, twisting his body this way and that, spotting no one.

"HEEEEELP!" he yelled at the top of his lungs. The weight of the cores as they continued to build up was becoming too much, his arms quivering under the strain.

"FUCK!" he barked, jumping back and hitting the red alarm-come-shut-down button before running to the nearest cleanup point, quickly throwing scoopfuls of the cat litter-like black granules onto the spreading mess as dozens of cores continued to fall, most ejecting their caps on impact, the brightly glowing puddle growing ever larger. He hadn't even noticed it spreading around his feet; his senses were being bombarded by flashing red lights and that infernally blaring klaxon that had caused his ears to start ringing. He ripped the granule bag open wider, spilling its entire contents over the mess, but it just wasn't enough. In his haste to get more he slipped as soon as he tried to run, falling hard onto his back and left elbow, yelling in excruciating pain. He could feel the slimy gunk seeping through his thin coveralls, through his street clothes, soaking him to the skin. He tried to roll away from it, but simply covered himself in more, and all the time that stuff just kept coming.

As he tried to stand again his foot slipped, and he hit the right side of his head hard enough to give himself an instant headache. He lay incapacitated on the ground, his hair soaking in that ooze.

At long last the cavalry arrived, a team of three decked in hazard suits with an incredulous manager in tow. One of the three manually shut off the core dispenser with the key while the other two dragged Jerin clear of the mess. One of them escorted him out back with the manager, where he was taken to the showers for a scrub-down before being offered some musty-smelling clothes to replace his own.

He was given a mug of dark herbal tea that was supposed to flush errant radiation from the body, which he slowly sipped at while telling Roz the full story. She said very little as she took notes, grumbling under her breath. He was sure he heard her say "Heads will roll," but he knew as well as she did that the omnipotent Terrengus Corporation wouldn't admit liability easily, if at all.

After that very brief sit down he was hurried back to work by Kaxan's boss, who assured him that he would "be fine."

A few weeks later, Jerin came down with a migraine that just wouldn't shift, but he kept it quiet for fear of upsetting Juli. He hadn't mentioned so much as a word of the accident to her, but he couldn't hide the increasingly frequent headaches from her. She had to have noticed.

On a typical day off together, they were in the kitchen preparing a healthy stir-fry; Jerin made the teriyaki sauce in which to marinate the phesan strips while boiling some dried noodles, while Juli chopped the flavourless hydroponic pepper, mushrooms and pak choi. Nibbly sat with his front paws on the very corner of the dining table watching, tilting his head hopefully, the white tip of his long tail dangling off the table's edge, swishing back and forth cheerfully.

As Jerin finished the sauce, taking the hot pan off the heat, the strength left his body and he fell forwards with a pained grunt, quickly dropping a hand to the counter to steady himself, his hand mere inches from the red-hot glass-topped hob he'd just been using.

Juli spun around, dropping her knife on the counter in her panic. "Jerin! What's wrong?"

"I'm fine," he lied unconvincingly. "I just feel a little light-headed. Probably just a bit of a cold, there's one doing the rounds at work again."

"You haven't been right the past few weeks. If you're not well you should go back to bed, get some rest."

"I'm fine!" he insisted through gritted teeth, bracing himself with both arms.

She nodded uneasily and silently resumed chopping the veg. He poured the sauce over the bowl of phesan strips before draining the starchy water from the noodle pan. There was a sharp pain behind his right eye, momentarily blurring his vision. He couldn't clear it, no matter how many times he turned away from her to rub it.

He saw that she was watching him, deep concern etched into every line of her face. "I've got something in my eye." He could see she didn't believe him. "It's nothing, honey, really." He remained calm this time. They resumed cooking.

"There are some headache tablets in the drawer if you need some," she suggested.

"I've already taken some," he said more aggressively than he meant to, massage his temples with the thumb and middle finger of his right hand. "They're just taking a while to kick in."

"Do you want to go for a walk after lunch? Perhaps the fresh air will do you some good."

"I'll see how I feel after we've eaten. Maybe you're right, maybe I need to sleep it off."

She turned back to the counter, looking down at the

veg, pretending to chop them even though they were done. "You never want to go for a walk anymore."

"That's because it's so fucking hard!" He yelled so loud it scared Nibbler from the room. *Damn these mood swings!* He took a few deep breaths to calm himself. "Sorry. You're right, I haven't been right lately. My head hurts nearly all the time. The cold aggravates it. Going for a walk is likely to make it worse."

"This isn't like you," she said. "You should see a doctor."

"What good can come of it?"

"Please, Jerin. No good can come of ignoring this." She placed her hand over his on the counter. "I'll make the appointment, but you're going."

He nodded, deciding not to argue. She was right.

"I'll finish making lunch. Go sit down for a bit," she insisted.

He sighed. He reluctantly acquiesced, giving her a kiss, promptly falling asleep on the sofa.

*

Jerin watched and listened in increasing dismay as the various arrogantly dismissive doctors faded in and out before him in turn.

A studious rapidly-greying middle-aged man, his name long forgotten, told Jerin, "The odd migraine is nothing to worry about, it's just growing pains."

A somewhat pretty young woman, not much older than he was then, still very green, said, "Your brain is still developing."

At twenty-three?

The first thing Jerin had done was tell each corporate doctor about the accident, but none of them took his concerns about residual radiation sickness seriously. He didn't expect any of them would be keen to advise the monopolistic, all-powerful corporation to pay for its mistakes. They each had their own bills to pay, so why would they risk their own necks for him? And so Jerin had even begun to accept that the company would simply let him die. After all, it was cheaper.

An older man with thinning hair, wearing an awful grey sweater appeared. "Your brain is too large for your skull, but not to worry, it should sort itself out."

Say what? That sounds like it could be kind of serious!

The last in the line of incompetent doctors stared at his computer screen for a few moments. "You suffer regular headaches." It wasn't a question.

"Migraines," Jerin corrected.

"It's probably just stress."

"I've had stress headaches," *usually when dealing with people like you,* "I know the difference."

All he had wanted was for one of them to admit that they *didn't know*, and to refer him to someone who might.

He gave up after that, until the night he had a migraine of such intensity that it laid him out on the bedroom floor, barely able to open his eyes as he vomited into a bucket. Juli sat by his side, rubbing his back through the blanket she'd draped over his shoulders. He stopped puking so long as he remained nil-by-mouth — he couldn't even keep water down.

He repeatedly assured Juli he would be fine, then suddenly asked her, "When's my dad coming over?"

She was bewildered. "Jerin, your father's dead," she reluctantly told him.

"Don't be silly," he giggled in a suddenly child-like manner.

Juli's voice wavered as she said, "Jerin, stop playing, you're scaring me."

"Daddy's taking me to the zoo today!"

"Jerin, he isn't coming."

He looked up at her without recognition. "You're pretty. Who are you?"

She was stilled by shock. "Jerin, it's me, Juli."

"Juli," he repeated. "I like that name. Are you my aunt, Juli?"

After a few hours of this, Juli bundled him into the back of the car and took him to the hospital, where only one consultant was working the graveyard shift: a man named Mr Venura.

Jerin saw Juli by his younger self's side, holding his hand while they waited for the consultant to return. Jerin's gaze was inexorably fixated on the inactive wall-screen that would finally reveal the source of his pain and misery. He remembered the heavy feeling in his heart. If ignorance was bliss, he had a feeling he was about to be very miserable indeed. Prior to the scan, Jerin had taken the opportunity to explain the incident at the plant to the consultant while Juli was safely out of earshot. The expression Mr Venura wore upon hearing this hadn't filled Jerin with much confidence.

"It'll be alright," Juli whispered as he involuntarily squeezed her hand. Was she trying to fool him or herself?

"Prepare for the worst, hope for the best, right?" The graveness of his tone surprised himself.

Juli said nothing, drooping her head, unable to look him in the eye.

Approaching footsteps signalled Mr Venura's return. He offered a courteous semi-bow as he walked through the curtain, his apologies made as he had left. He switched on the wall-screen and loaded Jerin's profile. The fateful scan appeared, a cross-section of his skull in flawless detail that could only be bettered by physically cutting his head open.

There were six bright white dots surrounded by grey hazes scattered randomly around his brain, one directly behind his right eye. Mr Venura's sullen expression confirmed Jerin's worst fears.

"You have several solid intracranial neoplasms," the consultant said flatly. "They're a form of benign tumour."

Tears welled in Juli's eyes, which she quickly wiped away, perhaps hoping Jerin hadn't seen them. Her mouth became a straight line, her diffident expression conveying a 'we'll get through this' determination.

"Though they are not cancerous, they slowly kill brain tissue, converting it into pockets of solid mass, but they're localised to the right hemisphere, which is a small blessing. These are undoubtedly the cause of the bouts of delirium you have been experiencing."

Numbness filled Jerin from head to toe, and everything felt like someone else's bad dream. *Is this really happening?* "What does that mean?"

"It means we need to act quickly and aggressively. We'll have to remove the affected brain tissue and the immediate surrounding area to prevent further tumour growths from occurring."

Jerin looked at the scan glumly: that was a *lot* of brain tissue. "How much would you need to remove?"

"Worst case scenario? The entire right hemisphere."

Disbelief stilled his mouth.

Jerin considered now, as he had then, how an animal with such a condition would either be put down or given strong pain-control medication until it died of its own accord.

"Given your unique situation, Terrengus Corp has requested we try an advanced prototype to give you the best chance of resuming a normal life as quickly as possible," Mr Venura explained, opening the top drawer of his metal filing cabinet, retrieving a small glass box containing an inch-square microchip. "This will be the invisible crutch for your remaining brain. It's a learning chip, configured to read from the right hemisphere."

It was all too much to take in, and there were so many questions. "Isn't the right side of the brain responsible for creativity?"

Mr Venura's eyes averted from Jerin's, focusing on the box in his hands. "Yes. But the left side controls all major bodily functions."

"But will I ever be able to draw again?"

"It's hard to say for sure. Motor functions won't be adversely affected. The mind is astonishingly resilient. The left hemisphere will learn to compensate for the majority of cognitive functions, but can easily become fatigued by the extra workload, and there will likely be a little memory loss. That's where the chip comes in; it works in conjunction with your remaining organic brain to restore normal functionality by handling many minor logistical processes. Though it isn't designed to do so, it's not beyond the realm of possibility that it could help the left hemisphere adopt a certain degree of creative functionality. It may even enhance your overall thinking speed and help you remain more alert. You may actually end up being smarter."

Jerin wasn't particularly won over by this. Logical thinking and creative thinking weren't the same. What good was there in having a hundred brilliant ideas if he couldn't get any of them onto the page? "And what are the chances of brain damage?"

"I won't lie, they're reasonably high. Medical science has come leaps and bounds, but there will always be risks."

Jerin stared pensively at the chip for a long time. "What if I say no?"

"Jerin…" Juli whispered. He placed his free hand atop hers, sandwiching it.

"In all likelihood, you'll die in less than two years. Listen, I understand your concern. I'd feel the same in your position." He hunkered down in front of them, meeting Jerin's gaze. "Look at it objectively, and all it comes down to is a choice between *probable* life and *certain* death."

Jerin nodded unenthusiastically.

Mr Venura handed him the chip. "Take this with you. I'll show you how to hook it up. By connecting it to your mind prior to the operation it will calibrate to your mind, recording everything that makes you who you are. Wear it whenever you sleep. It needs to communicate with the subconscious mind to really work."

Jerin wondered now whether he made the right decision… *perhaps death would have been better?* Nature had tried to kill him, and he'd defied it. But even now he could see the fear in Juli's eyes. He couldn't have said no.

"Okay," his younger self reluctantly conceded. "When will the operation be?"

"Hopefully in around six to eight weeks. It all depends on the schedules coinciding. I'll get you in sooner if I can." He typed on his computer before turning back to Jerin. "Stop by the dispensary on the way out. I've prescribed you some pills that will help when the headaches get bad, and may help slow the growth of the tumours. Don't worry about the cost, we'll pay for them. Just be warned, they'll lay you out. I'll give you a sick note for work. You need to get as much rest as you can. It's important."

Jerin nodded silently and they left, saying nothing all the way home.

Jerin couldn't afford as much time off as he needed, but what choice did he have? He'd spoken to Roz on the phone, and she'd assured him Kaxan was fine with it all.

He could hardly stand for ten minutes before becoming dizzy. He spent weeks crashed out on the sofa, bored out of his mind despite gradually working his way through his pile of previously-unopened movies. The drugs did little to quell the increasingly frequent migraines. He could hardly keep any food down, quickly becoming dangerously gaunt and weak.

Nibbly became as much a permanent presence on his lap as the woollen hat lined with myriad thin metal strips did on his head, his hair shaved off to enhance contact while it collected its data, wirelessly beaming it to the chip in his top bedside drawer.

Could such a device really work? For all the advances in quantum science, could a chip really replace living brain tissue? For better or worse, he was going to find out.

As fear and doubt flowed frequently through his mind, rest often eluded him, leading to him spending much of his time in a half-asleep stupor. He wondered if this was the feeling of death. When sleep did come, all his dreams featured him in a wheel chair, too brain damaged to even know his own name as Juli pushed him around, stopping occasionally to wipe the drool from his chin.

As the weeks wore on his depression deepened. One night in bed, staring at the ceiling, eyes bloodshot from exhaustion, he removed the uncomfortable cap, throwing it aside in frustration.

Juli jumped out of bed to retrieve it, handing it back to him. "Put it on!"

He took it and held it in his hands, staring through its internal golden strands despondently. "What's the point? It works best when I sleep, and I can't sleep."

She got back into bed and cuddled over him. "Put it on," she repeated, reaching for it, but he yanked it away, holding it beyond her reach. "It *will* help."

"Will it?"

"You've only been wearing it for a few weeks. You *have* to wear it if you want to keep your mind intact. A mind which I happen to like very much." She stretched her slender neck and kissed him tenderly. "I love you, Jerin. I don't want to lose you. Do it for me, please?"

He looked into her beautiful grey eyes, then at the cap as it swayed on his fingertips. "I can think of things worse than death."

"Like what?"

"Like not being able to wipe my own arse."

"Is that what's bothering you?"

"Not as much as the idea that I might be aware that I'm a vegetable. I'd rather participate in life than be relegated to a spectator on the sidelines."

"If the worst happens, I'll look after you," she promised, reaching her hand up to stroke the side of his face.

He brushed her hand away. "Please don't."

Shock struck her face and she sat bolt upright. "What? Why?"

"If the worst happens, I want you to promise you'll euthanise me."

"Why?" She couldn't hide the tremble from her voice.

"I couldn't live like that. I already feel like your

burden without that. If I'm paralysed, I want you to kill me and get on with your life." He looked her straight in the eyes. "*Please*."

After a moment's contemplation, she said, "Okay. I promise. But only on the condition that you at least give it a fighting chance."

He nodded. "That's fair. I can do that."

He brought the hat within her reach, allowing her to place it on his head. She kissed him softly, three times in rapid succession, like a pecking bird.

"I can't believe we still don't have a date from the hospital yet," Juli said. "What if it takes longer than eight weeks?"

"I'm not exactly relishing it either, but I guess we'll just have to wait."

"But you can hardly look after yourself now, and with all the overtime I'm hardly here…"

"I'll manage," he insisted.

"But you're so thin. And what about the mortgage? Even with the extra money, I can't afford it on my own…"

"We'll just have to tighten our belts, buy cheaper food. I can't eat much, anyway," he jested, seeing the concern in her eyes. He took her in his arms, holding her close. "It'll be fine. We'll get through this."

If only he could have believed his own hollow words.

*

Juli arrived home from another day at the office with a bag full of pencils, notebooks, acrylic paints, and a set of four small canvasses. "They were on offer, and you know what it's like when you pass up a bargain then reconsider, some other bugger always gets it first."

He studied the contents of the bag with mixed feelings, unaware that he must have been wearing a hangdog expression until she spoke again.

"They're no good, are they?"

"No, they're fine… it's just… can we really afford them?"

"They really didn't cost that much, and I thought since

you had so much free time, it would be a shame not to do something productive."

"*Please* stop spending so much," he pleaded.

She was momentarily unsure how to react, settling for, "I knew you were getting bored, and I thought they might help, that's all."

"It doesn't matter how much I have to occupy me, it still gets unbearably boring. When I am well enough to draw or paint there's only so much I can do until it loses its appeal. It wouldn't be so bad if any of my friends were ever free to visit, but whenever they are, I've always arranged to spend the day with you."

"If you'd rather see your friends, I don't mind. I'll just see if Alezi's free."

And spend even more money, he thought, keeping it to himself. "I'll bear it in mind, not that anyone replies to my messages anymore. It's like they've all forgotten about me."

She leaned over to kiss him, which he unenthusiastically returned. "Well, *I* still love you," she told him. "I'll always be here for you."

He smiled wanly back. "Thanks. I love you too."

Jerin tried to take his mind off of how dire things were by sketching and painting, but it was getting increasingly difficult to concentrate, let alone keep his hand steady. A month later, he was doing virtually nothing every day, and still had no appointment owing to delays with the corporation dealing with the necessary forms, and Jerin's delirium was getting worse. He spent the days in as much darkness as the closed curtains would allow, even the slightest light making him feel nauseous at that time.

Looking back, he remembered this day, and not fondly. Juli had asked him if he was okay with her going out with Alezi, and he had given his blessing, but had completely forgotten that conversation by the time she'd gotten home with another two full shopping bags.

"Hey, honey," she greeted.

He studied the bags contemptuously, but chose not to

say anything, still aware enough at that moment to know he was liable to snap.

"Alezi treated me to a few things," she explained upon seeing his gaze.

He remembered feeling angry about her reckless spending. He had no reason not to trust her, but his mind was incapable of reason by that point. Looking back now, he wondered how much of this tumour-induced anger had been learned by the chip. He felt the need to escape to clear his head before they had a full-blown argument, so he got up, sat on the second-from-bottom-step to put his shoes on, only to become frustrated over his inability to remember how to tie his laces.

"Where are you going?" she asked.

"For a walk."

"You're not well, Jerin," she said softly. "You need to stay inside. Take a pill and sleep it off."

He slapped her hand away as soon as she placed it on his shoulder. "Leave me alone! I can go for a walk, damn it!"

Juli withdrew her hand. "You're mad, aren't you?"

"Of course not." He was struggling to concentrate on tying his laces. "I mean, it's not like you frequently neglect the chores so you can go and short-sightedly spend all of what little money we have on stuff we don't need, is it?"

"I did the chores, Jerin, then I asked you..." she patiently began to explain, but trailed off. He'd always blamed the illness, but how much had he used it as an excuse?

Young Jerin stood up and reached into one of the bags, knowing she wouldn't wear half the contents, her wardrobe still groaning with all the unworn clothes Alezi had supposedly bought her previously. He pulled out a maroon scarf. "Since when do you wear a scarf?"

"Jerin, listen to yourself! You aren't exactly in a position to lecture me on finances when you bought yourself that new video game the other day!" What little fight she had left in her had gone into that rebuttal, and now she looked even more like a broken woman. Spirit-Jerin had such a strong sense of empathy now, feeling her exasperation, frustration and futility. He knew all too well that nothing she said would get through to him when he was in such an obstinate mood; she'd tried many times before, but he always felt she wasn't understanding him. How wrong he'd had it.

"You know I saved for months to get that game, and I made sure I had more than enough left in my account afterwards. Why blow money on a needlessly overpriced scarf when a cheaper one is plenty good enough?"

"You have your games, I have my clothes. Anyway, like I said, I didn't pay for it. You know how cold I get on dark days, so it seemed like a good idea, and Alezi insisted on treating me to one that didn't make me look like a hobo... she sure has a way with words..."

He threw it back on top of the bag. "No friend is that generous. I bet all the receipts have your debit card number on them."

"There aren't any receipts because Alezi has them," she explained patiently. Apparition-Jerin felt horrible; she was trying so hard to maintain her composure, and he knew it couldn't have been easy.

He crossed his arms and nodded sardonically. "That's right, she would, wouldn't she?"

Tears of frustration were welling in her eyes. "If you must know, I treated us to lunch. That's all."

"Uh-huh... and how much was that, exactly?"

"Only twenty-five."

He scoffed, "*Only.* You know, *only* a little here, *only* a little there, and before you know it, we've *only* lost the house," he remarked.

"Don't be so dramatic! Give me some credit, I'm not that stupid."

"So where did I fit into all this, sitting here starving, not knowing when you were going to come home since you couldn't be bothered to reply to my message?"

"What message?"

"Yeah, that's what I thought. Why did you get lunch out? What about the food in the fridge we were going to have for dinner?"

She tried to calm herself again. "There is no food in the fridge, Jerin. We buy frozen food now because your appetite is so fickle…"

"Great. So we'll just throw away more spoiled food. Fantastic. Well, at least you had a good day!" memory-Jerin yelled as he exited the house to cool down. He remembered that walk; stopping to puke into a roadside drain, the bright light intensifying his headache until it crippled him. He'd cursed his own impetuousness for not grabbing his peaked cap and shades on the way out. Juli found him leaning heavily on a wall just a short distance down the street, then patiently and slowly lead him back home, him cursing under his breath the whole time.

As memory-Jerin stormed upstairs, apparition-Jerin watched as Juli ran into the living room, crying into her hands in the dark. He hadn't realised at the time just what she'd had to put up with. He knew it hadn't been his fault, but he felt like such a callous bastard.

*

Jerin saw himself sitting at home watching the HV in 2D mode, the added dimension only exacerbating the nausea, the pain making his head feel like it was in a slowly-tightening vice. His feet were resting atop a small blanket-containing ottoman, Nibbly stretched along his legs, shedding his hair all over another pair of trousers, one outstretched paw resting on the inside of Jerin's loose slipper. Apparition-Jerin crouched before Nibbly's contented face, his intangible hand passing through his little face as he tried to give him just one last fuss.

"I love you, little man," spirit-Jerin told Nibbly.

Without warning, a sharp pain rose up memory-Jerin's entire body, so painful he was silenced by shock. Every muscle tensed at once and his head felt like it was going to explode. "Fuck!" he barked. He didn't swear all that often, but there were times when he felt it was justified, and this had most definitely been one of those occasions. Nibbler looked at him with wide eyes, but didn't budge.

When he could move again, Jerin placed Nibbler on the sofa and stumbled through to the kitchen to take all the pills he could. He lost his balance upon hobbling back into the front room, falling so heavily onto the sofa he heard a spring go before he slipped onto the floor, semi-conscious. Nibbly climbed onto his back, sniffing his sideways face, pawing gently at him with a faint "mew" of concern.

He couldn't move a muscle. For a while, Nibbler and pain were his only companions.

It seemed like an eternity until Juli arrived home, horrified to discover him lying there completely immobile, dropping her work bag and spilling its contents as she ran over, yelling "Jerin, what's wrong?"

He couldn't answer. She donned her phone-specs to call an ambulance, and all fell dark and silent around Jerin now just as it had then, when he had been drifting in and out of consciousness. The only words he could faintly hear were her saying, "Hang in there, Jerin... *please* be okay."

When the darkness receded he saw he was in a large room, a mysterious female voice saying they needed to "relieve the pressure" inside his skull. The numbness receded enough to allow him to feel every painful moment as four screws slowly penetrated skin and bone with an intense burning sensation, like a lit match pressed against then *into* his skin as a black metal restraint was screwed into place. The doctors gave him a shot of local anaesthetic, then prepared to drill behind his right ear.

But the anaesthesia did nothing. His screams of agony would have dominated the room if not for the deafeningly high-pitched whine of the drill as it bored its way through bone with unrelenting ferocity, a pain that eclipsed all other sensation. His right eyeball had felt like it was going to eject itself from the socket, causing him to squeeze his eyes shut tight.

The next thing Jerin remembered was waking up in a hospital bed, head heavily bandaged, eyes covered to avoid overloading his delicate mind too soon, giving him no sense of time but an overwhelming sensation of boredom and isolation.

There was an incredible pain in his penis: a catheter. It felt like a rod of fire.

Looking back now, he realised that there was one other thing he could remember between the drill and waking up: a city falling from the sky. Had he dreamt that on the operating table? He thought anaesthetic-induced sleep was meant to be dreamless...

Mr Venura visited him, of course, informing him just how lucky he was. They'd had no choice but to go ahead and remove half his brain: the drugs had done nothing to halt the growth of the radiation-born tumours. He was informed that by some miracle they had saved not only his life, but his right eye too.

"If it had been a day or two later, you'd have lost it for sure," Mr Venura informed him.

Jerin said nothing. Right now, he didn't feel especially lucky. When he would later ask about the sloshing inside his head he would be told this was normal and that it would subside on its own, but it kept occurring annoyingly frequently, and would often wake him as he rolled over during the night. As if that wasn't bad enough, the incision mark behind his right ear was maddeningly itchy, the antihistamines doing little to ease it. He was tempted to barricade himself in the bathroom so he could peel off the thick wad of bandages just for that brief moment of relief, and to hell with it if it would take longer to heal.

Time passed so very slowly, the tedium only momentarily interrupted by the arrival of a drink or a foul-tasting insubstantial meal.

Various doctors came and went, commenting on his remarkable progress, though he was reduced to the indignity of having to ask for help whenever he needed to take a dump, a chilling reminder of the fate he had narrowly avoided. He loathed every lonely, long minute.

As the weeks wore on, he was subjected to one exhausting cognitive function test after another, to ensure he still had his faculties and to prevent brain atrophy. These ranged from the laughably simple to the absurdly difficult.

"Name a shape with four sides," the annoyingly perky nurse said.

"A trapezium," he answered.

She laughed, "Alright, smart arse!"

"Better than being a dumb arse!" he answered.

As his progress continued to improve, he was asked to answer trivia questions about the city and its controversial, oft-disputed history. Since he didn't trust the hospital staff — they *were* corporate employees after all, no matter how polite their bedside manner — he fed them the answers they would be happiest with.

One day, he couldn't recall an answer he knew he should have known, and became so frustrated he yelled out, "I don't know, alright?"

"Hey, calm down," the tester soothed. "Some of it will take a while to come back to you, okay?"

"I've had enough of this! I just want to go home already."

"I understand your frustration, but you have to remember that you went through a very serious procedure. It will take time for all your faculties to return. The chip is still adjusting, give it time. You must be tired, get some sleep. I'll come back tomorrow."

"Yippee," he remarked, more sardonic than sarcastic.

Juli's visits were all-too-rare bursts of colour in a world gone grey.

On her first visit she told him, "I didn't know whether to go into work or not. I was so scared of losing you, but I knew I'd only worry more if I sat at home all day, waiting for my phone to ring." He could hear by her tone how shaken she had been.

He reached blindly for one of her hands. She took it, holding it tight. "I won't leave you," he told her. "Not if I can help it."

"I know… but that was too damned close. I *can't* go on alone."

He aimed his bandage-blinded gaze in the direction of her voice and tried to smile. "I'm going to be okay."

"I know. Now it's just the long road to recovery…"

"Don't worry about that," he insisted. "That's my worry, not yours." Listening to his younger self say that made him realise how naïve he had been at the time; of course it was her concern.

"I'll put your phone in your bedside cupboard," she informed him. He heard the cabinet's cupboard door open and close as expected. "Your headphones are in there too. I downloaded a few audiobooks onto it. If you ask one of the nurses I'm sure they'll play one for you."

She then placed something in his hands, a roughly cuboid plastarch something, each nearly-flat surface about the size of his palm. It had rounded corners.

"What's this?"

"A speaking clock."

A smile of pleasant surprise tugged at the left corner of his mouth. He felt for a button, pressing it.

"Four. Twenty. Six," the stilted mechanical voice informed. Even though his phone had that very function, the lack of tactile buttons on the touch-screen ensured he would be unable to use it.

It was equal parts blessing and curse; he knew he would press it far too often now, but nevertheless he was grateful. "Thanks," he said with genuine gratitude.

"You're welcome," she replied, a little choked up. He realised now that the reason for the surprise in her reply was because it was the first time he had thanked her for anything in weeks without admonishing her for wasting money.

One morning a two uneventful weeks later, Jerin awoke, pressing the button on the clock.

"Two. Thirty. Two." The city would slowly be coming to life as thousands of people descended upon their various workplaces while he rotted away in here. He wished he could sleep longer. His long uneventful days were punctuated by snatched unsatisfying naps.

"Ah, you're awake," the perky young-sounding female nurse chimed. "How do you feel?"

"Okay, I guess," he croaked. "Can I have a glass of water, please?"

"Certainly," she replied cheerfully, handing him the glass. He downed it in one. "I've got some good news for you, Mr Endersul. Your bandages can come off now. Are you ready?"

"I think so," he said, thinking *about bloody time.*

"Don't move," she advised, placing a pair of ice-cold scissors against the side of his head, cutting the bandage in one smooth *snip*.

She carefully unravelled the bandage before slowly peeling the taped pads from over his eyelids.

He opened his eyes, even the control-dimmed light initially blinding. He blinked repeatedly and wiped two weeks' crust from the corners of both eyes.

"Can you see?" The haziness passed and the nurse was revealed to be a petite blonde.

"A little. Everything's a little bit fuzzy."

"That's normal. Your vision should return fully by the end of the day."

He was glad for that; he'd run out of audiobooks, and just listening to the overpriced pay-per-view monovision had long lost its appeal, and there was no discount for the blind. He was grateful just to be able to read again. He'd gained a newfound appreciation for books, and now desired to read them in his own voice.

But his joy was short-lived as he was immediately subjected to more tests.

The nurse held a primary-school-looking sheet up. "Please point to the blue triangle."

He stared at her derisively. "Could you *please* stop

treating me like a child?"

"I'm sorry, we have to ascertain full restoration of cognitive function, including the ability to recognise basic shapes and colours."

"At least give me a semi-translucent cerulean dodecahedron," he smirked.

"And what's one of those?" she asked in her test-voice.

He sighed. "A three dimensional shape with twelve pentagonal faces."

"Alright, I'll let you off." She started to walk away then looked back. "Smart arse." He smiled, saying nothing.

When he was finally alone, he picked up his phone and called Juli to give her the good news.

"That's great," she chimed.

"I can't wait to see you tonight. It seems like an eternity since I last saw you."

"It'll be good to see you without those bandages, but I'm afraid I can't come tonight."

He was stunned; she'd found time to visit him every single day so far. "What? Why?"

"I'm sorry, I've got this stupid work thing I can't get out of. It's all about the management training scheme."

"Sounds exciting," he deadpanned. He'd be secretly happy when she later revealed she hadn't been signed onto it.

"I know, it sucks." As if that wasn't enough of a gut-punch, she was about to inadvertently hit him where it really hurt. "Hey, somebody else wants to say hello." She held her phone close enough to Nibbler for Jerin to hear his purring.

"Hey, Nibbly." Tears welled in his eyes. "Listen, I'm tired so I better go, okay?"

"Okay. Take care, honey."

He hung up and rolled towards the wall, quietly sobbing to himself. He missed that little furball.

The next day, Jerin's sight was remarkably clear, so he

tried to utilise some of his interminable stay to do some drawing on his phone, struggling to find inspiration, deciding to just doodle to see what came to mind, but when he tried to draw his finger wouldn't move.

If his mind was going to adjust, it hadn't done so yet. He figured it was the artists' equivalent of writers' block.

Juli came to see him early that day, with two 'get well soon' cards. He wondered who the second one was from, deciding to open that one first without enquiring.

There was a picture of a fluffy grey cat on the front, a real jingling bell attached to its collar. He smiled, laughing as he opened it, greeted by the words, 'Get well soon, miss laying on your lap Daddy, meow meow, lots of purrs and cuddles, Nibbly,' with a crudely-drawn paw print beneath.

"You're stupid," he told Juli, unable to wipe the dopey smirk from his face. Cards weren't cheap, but it had warmed the cockles of his weary heart.

She laughed but said nothing, watching patiently as he opened her card, with the expected message and a, 'P.S, I can't wait to help you "recover".'

"Thanks," he said, giving her a kiss.

She shook her head. "If you had to fall ill, you couldn't pick anything simple, could you?"

He laughed until he coughed. She poured and passed him a glass of water from the pitcher atop the bedside cabinet.

"How are you?" she asked.

"Bored," he sighed.

She smiled. "I know. But other than that?"

"Fine, I guess. Only…" he trailed off.

"Only what?"

"It seems like a really trivial thing to mention, given what I've just been through, but… I used to have the most vivid dreams. But since the op, I haven't had a single one."

Juli was astonished. "None at all?"

"None that I remember."

"Mr Venura did say your memory might be affected. Perhaps you're just forgetting them?"

He shrugged. "Maybe. I hope they come back soon, they inspire most of my art."

She said nothing more on the subject, offering him a small bag with string handles.

"What's this?" he asked.

"Just look inside."

He took it, reaching in with one hand and pulling out a small blue cuddly bear with a bandaged head holding a tiny fabric 'get well soon' card.

"I couldn't resist," she said.

"He's adorable," Jerin smiled, leaning over to give her a kiss, placing the bear beside the cards already atop the bedside cabinet.

"There's one more thing," she told him.

He looked into the bag again as he felt something slip, removing a *Ranger* bar.

"That's to get rid of the taste of dinner later," she winked.

"The food here *is* pretty terrible," he agreed. " And I guess the extra calories couldn't hurt, either."

She quickly looked around to make sure no one was watching then sat on the bed beside him, taking his right hand between hers. "When you get out, we'll go to a restaurant for dinner to celebrate, anywhere you want," she promised.

They heard a nurse cough deliberately to catch their attention, and she slid from the bed back into the cheap plastarch bucket chair.

"Naughty-naughty," Jerin faux-chastised.

When he was finally discharged, Jerin was advised to avoid stress and given a huge supply of super-strong painkillers. To celebrate, Juli took him to *Perfect Pizza*. At that moment it was the best meal he'd ever tasted. He ate until his stomach felt like it was going to burst, waddling back to the car.

When they arrived home, Nibbly was initially very

wary of Jerin, hiding behind the cabinet below the HV, but his feline friend came around within half an hour, settling down on his 'daddy's' lap for hours. Over the following weeks he would hardly leave Jerin's side, perhaps afraid of losing him.

Despite the feeling of relief, Jerin had an irreconcilable sensation of dread that would not turn out to be unfounded.

UO
-Broken Dreams-

Juli stood alone beneath an ethereal spotlight, beyond which was a wall of unwavering darkness. She walked away from the light, blindly feeling for a wall or door that wasn't there.

"I'm sorry," she heard Jerin say.

She spun around to see him standing beneath the light. "You," she said, her tone clearly conveying how welcome he wasn't.

"It wasn't meant to be this way. I was trying… but…" he trailed off.

"I don't need dreams like this right now," she dismissed.

"This is no dream," he told her. "It took a lot of effort, but I'm here. Now. Inside your head."

"No you're not," she scoffed. "What a preposterous notion!"

"You know I am. I don't have much time, so please listen."

"Why should I? You left me! You said you'd never do that… not if it was up to you."

"I know. I'm sorry. But *please* listen. It's important. It's something I should have told you a long time ago."

"Then tell me and be gone," she demanded, turning her back to him. "I have better things to think about, like getting on with my life."

"You have every right to be angry," he soothed. "I wish I could have stopped myself from saying those hurtful things to you. If I could take it all back, I would. When you get the chance, look in the top drawer of my bedside cabinet. Find the black box with the silver trim." He cast his eyes downward. "I bought it so long ago. Find it. Open it. Treasure it. I wanted to give it to you in the underground park, but I didn't think of it before we left. If nothing else, I wish I could go back and change just that. It wouldn't make up for my mistake, but you might think better of me. I'm sorry, Juli."

Juli could think of nothing to say. After a moment, she turned back for one last look, but he was gone.

*

Jerin returned to his own mind, mentally drained after his emotional confrontation with Juli, wishing he could rest, but once more he saw his younger self in their old home. He was doing his mind-restoring mental therapy exercises, scoring a depressing 56%, reportedly due to his low computational speed, the mind-chip clearly not yet properly attuned to his synaptic rhythm. He sighed despondently. *How long does it really take to fully calibrate?*

Much as he did before the op, he spent most of his time in a state of lethargy, wasting entire days sat in front of the HV, phone in hand, idly surfing the 'net and scouring *BestBuddies* for anything of interest, only ever rising to eat, sleep or shit, more often than not in no mood or state for visitors. When he was feeling up to it, Kol, Jalzon and Desra came by one day, but their visit was all too fleeting. Despite the more agreeable surroundings and lack of noise, it was exactly as tedious as being stuck in the hospital.

Even messaging to his online friends quickly lost its appeal. His lax memory kept losing track of conversations. It didn't help that people quickly ran out of interesting things to say when he spoke to them all the time.

Late one morning he received an email from the city council refusing his application for tax relief. It stated that if he wished to appeal he would need to do so in person with yet even more bank statements and proof that he had no savings left, but after four attempts he just didn't see the point anymore. What enraged him most was how frequently the news was full of stories about benefit cheats playing the system for thousands to fund lavish lifestyles, yet he couldn't get so much as fifty silvan a week. Statutory sick pay just wasn't sufficient.

Nibbly came along just in time to replace his foul mood with a smile, purring and mewing as he paced back and forth head-butting Jerin's dangling hand. The stress of the letter brought on a pressure headache, then the scar behind his right ear began to burn as though someone was prodding him with the tip of a hot needle. He reached for the bottle of painkillers on his sofa-side table, fumbling with the child-proof cap for a moment before finally being allowed to take a couple. He then decided it was time to get some lunch.

He scoured the freezer and cupboards for anything remotely palatable, but everything was so unappetising. Corned boumive, peami slices in sugar syrup to give them some semblance of flavour, dried noodles that were more powder than food. Other than that he only found an ancient half-bag of flour, a near-empty bag of brown sugar, and ice-encased boxes of 'fish' and 'sausage meat' in the heavily-frosted freezer. The 'meats' were so cheap he expected the back of the packets to read 'any resemblance to actual food is purely coincidental'.

None of it appealed.

During this fruitless search, memory-Jerin had found a notepad beneath the plastarch tubs containing all the jars of herbs and spices on the middle shelf of a waist-high chrome kitchen tidy. The wrinkled top page displayed an old curry recipe they had made once, speckled by orange-brown splashes of that very curry's sauce.

He smiled to himself. *I forgot to add the jojanas milk.* Juli hadn't written it down, but he blamed himself because it was his customised recipe, and he'd cooked it while she'd chopped the onions, garlic, ginger and other veg they'd decided to throw in to make it a healthier, more complete meal.

Memory-Jerin flipped though the notebook's pages, desperate to find *something* to make out of these limited ingredients. He saw recipes for brownies, flapjacks, caramel and such, all of which he'd modified as he'd seen fit. In his overconfident haste he'd misread the original flapjack recipe's prep time of five minutes as the baking time, only to discover that they were far more delicious under-baked. Beyond those were blank pages. Apparition-Jerin remembered wishing he'd had the imagination of a chef enough to invent something. He'd watched entire seasons of various cooking shows during his lengthy convalescence, but he doubted any of the contestants could make something appetising out of that poor selection. Even the world's top chefs would have been hard pushed.

Young Jerin sighed as his hollow stomach grumbled; there weren't even any beans in the cupboards for him to currify with some of the spices.

It's my fault we never have money for decent food.

There was only one solution, but was he really ready yet? *What choice do I have? It's not like I'll see her any less than I already do.*

With uncertainty in his heart, he picked the phone up and dialled.

"Hi, Kaxan? It's Jerin. I'll be back tomorrow."

"Are you sure? You can take as much time as you need… you can come back on reduced hours if you like, to ease you back in?"

"I'm fine," he lied convincingly. Jerin appreciated the offer but he couldn't afford anything less than a full-time wage. "What time should I be there?"

"The usual, if you're sure you're up to it?"

Back to the old midday starts; he could live with that, though it was going to take a while to get used to the old routine again. "Yeah, that sounds good. See you at five."

"See you then, Jerin. I'm glad you're okay. It'll be good to have you back."

The next morning, Jerin was back on his trusty old pushbike, feeling incredibly unsafe as he wobbled to and fro during every excruciating pedal push of the suddenly-long journey.

His leg muscles burned ferociously. He hadn't expected the muscle atrophy to be so bad, but he'd forgotten just how much time he'd spent over the last couple of months either laying in bed or sitting on the sofa doing nothing, so focused on rebuilding his mind that he'd neglected his body. What had once been easy was now excruciatingly difficult.

Near the midway point he mounted the curb, deciding to walk his bike instead. At least the return journey was mostly downhill.

He arrived with barely a minute to spare, locking his bike up. Juli had urged him not to go back so soon, but he'd assured her he was fine. She saw through it but he insisted, citing his boredom as another reason, deciding not to mention the obvious financial aspect.

"Jerin!" Kaxan called cheerily down the corridor. Jerin had a soft spot for the middle-aged Jorandixan. Despite the majority of people insisting his kind were not to be trusted, harbouring much bitterness and resentment over the loss of their country following their instigation of the revolution, Jerin found Kaxan to be one of the kindest and most trustworthy people he knew.

Jorandixans had a naturally bronze skin, giving the appearance of a permanent tan, and the men customarily sported thick black beards, of which Kaxan's was always so well maintained. Kaxan had once told Jerin that though he was born and raised in Darina, he had been strictly raised only to speak his native tongue, but when he'd reached his teens he'd admitted to his parents that he'd been learning to speak Darinian in secret, realising that not doing so would only be a hindrance. He spoke it fluently, harbouring only the merest hint of an accent. He still struggled with Darinian pronunciation, but that was to be expected. After all, in Jorandixan, 'j' was pronounced with an 'h' sound, 'g' with a 'y' sound, and 'x' sounded like 'sh'.

"How are you?" Kaxan asked.

"Ambivalent."

"I understand," Kaxan replied, throwing an arm around Jerin's shoulder, walking with him. "I know this place caused your suffering, but new safety measures have been put in place. Since it's been a while I thought I'd ease you in gently, rather than throwing you back in at the deep end."

"How so?" Jerin asked, suspicious that this 'gentler' job would be even more tedious than his old one, which was boring enough.

"I'll show you," Kaxan insisted, leading Jerin to an area of the plant he'd never seen before: the end of the long production line. "You take the completed, fully-shielded capsules and place them in the foam-lined trays. You stack the trays on the palette and one of the warehouse crew will take them away post-haste. How's that for you?"

"Seems simple enough," he sighed, knowing then that it was going to be a very long, very boring day.

"I'm sorry, I know it's going to be tedious, but you have to understand we have to minimise the risk if you have an episode. It was all I could do to get the corporation to agree."

"Don't get me wrong, I'm grateful for what you've done," Jerin replied. "It's just... why did it have to happen at all? If the company had just listened to you in the first place, taken my relayed concerns more seriously... this whole thing was easily avoidable, and I'm the one who paid for a pen-pusher's mistake." *And I'll go on paying.*

"I know. I assure you, I reported it to them many times. In the end they got sick of me; they told me to get lost and stop wasting their time. It's sad that they simply won't act until an accident happens. They never learn that prevention is better than cure."

"If there's one thing I've learned in all my years working here is that the corporate overlords lack the capacity to learn."

And so Jerin started his new job, watching as every second slowly ticked by. It was the longest day of his life so far, and spells of dizziness kept fading in and out, leading to him wondering whether he had been foolish to come back so soon, but though he knew his health was more valuable than money, if he didn't earn he wouldn't be able to afford the basic essentials like food and shelter, things that, as far as he was concerned, should be free for all.

Upon returning home that evening, his head pounding with a new-found ferocity despite the high-strength drugs, he lay on the sofa in the dark with his eyes closed, fighting the urge to rush to the bathroom to throw up. How he would last the rest of the week he didn't know.

I'm fine, he tried to convince himself. *I* can *do this.*

*

Jerin saw his younger self and Juli walking through the park near their house, wearing thick coats on a dark day, determined to make the best of what little time they had together, even if it was so cold the ground was white with fine ice crystals. Their clasped hands swung wildly back and forth like a caffeine-fuelled pendulum. Young Jerin was actually in a good mood, brought on by a rare but very welcome alleviation of pain.

With careful painkiller management he had struggled on and received his first full month's pay. Things were on the up again, but the road to recovery was to be a long one yet.

"You're sure the cold isn't hurting your head?" Juli asked.

"Absolutely," he smiled back. "I've never felt better." His stomach gurgled. "I am famished though."

"Then let's go home and get some dinner," Juli suggested.

"But I'm not ready to go home yet."

"No need. There are plenty of take-outs. What do you fancy?"

He shook his head. "We can't afford it. I'll just have to wait."

"But I'm hungry too," she insisted. "I was ignoring it

until you spoke up! Now it's all I can think about!"

"Oh I see, it's my fault you're hungry, is it?"

"Damn right!" she laughed. "I don't know about you, but I could go for some Vahirinese!"

"We can make that at home."

"It isn't the same."

His face was stricken with mock-shock. "Is there something wrong with my cooking?"

She pushed him aside playfully. "No, but it's nice to eat out once in a while."

"You know we can't afford it," he reaffirmed.

"I've got some cash left over from the overtime I did last month."

"Do you actually have the money in your account yet?"

"Of course. What do you take me for?"

He couldn't tell from her tone whether or not she was being spurious. "It's just that you have a habit of spending money before you have it. Then they fail to pay you properly, then you end up short…"

"It's fine. I've got it. I *do* learn sometimes, you know."

"Yeah right, that'll be the day!"

Though his tone was one of thinly-veiled frustration, she decided to take it in jest. "Cheeky sod! We work hard for our money, we deserve the odd treat every now and then."

His belly gurgled again, so he gave her the benefit of the doubt. "Alright. But I'd rather go to a restaurant than get a greasy take-out. But nowhere too fancy. Besides, we're not exactly dressed for the occasion."

She clapped excitedly, doing her happy dance. "Where do you want to go then?"

"How about Katana? It's been ages since we last went there."

"Okay, why not? A girl at work told me they've updated the menu."

"As long as they still do their barbecue phesan

skewers, they can do whatever they like."

They kissed and happily marched to their destination. Upon arrival, the waiter saw them to their table and brought them their drinks, but mistakenly brought Jerin a beer rather than a relaxing green tea.

"At what point in time does 'green tea' sound like 'beer'?" he asked incredulously, temper rising. Juli placed her hand over his and he calmed again. "Sorry. Sometimes my temper gets the better of me."

The waiter bowed slightly. "It's okay. I'm sorry sir, I'll sort it out for you," he said in a thick accent.

Jerin wanted to say *too bloody right you will*, but the soothing effect Juli had on him had extinguished his rage. Besides, he was determined not to let one act of idiocy ruin a perfectly good day.

*

Juli dreamed she was sitting on the sofa in the spacious living room of their old house, half-watching something on HV she wasn't that interested in, using it as an excuse to cuddle up to Jerin. The lights were off and she was close to falling asleep. She hadn't noticed at the time, but the bright glow of the HV cast long ugly shadows around the room, highlighting every little fray on the carpet, every dent in the walls, every claw pluck on the sofa, and every little imperfection on the wooden beams running along the ceiling. All she had seen at the time, glancing up at Jerin's face, were the tiny reflections dancing in his pupils.

During an ad break, Jerin vanished into the kitchen to get a cup of tea. She decided to quickly and covertly review her ailing finances on her phone-specs. That little bit here and there had left her short of meeting this month's mortgage payment, and she had already fallen into arrears. Another short payment would be enough to bring down the bank's proverbial hammer.

There was no hiding it from Jerin anymore. She had to admit he was right, though she knew it wouldn't go well.

Jerin returned with two steaming mugs, despite her

not asking for one. Her face bore a contrite expression as she asked uneasily, "Jerin, do you have any spare money?"

"Why?" She could hear the suspicion in his tone immediately.

"I'm a little short this month."

He looked crestfallen. His tone became short and accusing. "How short?"

"Just fifty..." she said sheepishly.

His expression turned to utter incredulity. "I thought you said you could afford that meal at Katana?"

She began to sob quietly. "I'm sorry, I thought I could, otherwise I wouldn't have said so. I forgot my mobile bill hadn't gone out yet."

He sighed. "I thought you said you'd worked out all your outgoings?"

"I did, I just lost track..."

"But if you know what your monthly disposable income is, how can you lose track?"

"I'm just not as good at it as you!" she yelled, falling immediately silent with shame.

"How exactly will you learn from your mistakes if I bail you out whenever you mess up?"

"I'm not blaming you," she said, meaning she was about to do exactly that, "but while you were off we just didn't have enough cash coming in, so I borrowed a little from the savings for us to go out..."

"You dipped into the savings to go out when I suggested we stay at home?"

"You were so miserable, I thought it might do you some good to get out of the house..."

"So how much of our savings do we have left?"

"Just under twenty..."

He threw his hands in exasperation.

"I'm sorry! I'm doing overtime to make it up!" she cried. "The office has just been slow in paying it..."

"So you did count on money you didn't actually have?"

"I'm sorry. I know you told me not to…"

"Then try *listening* to me." He sighed. As furious as he was, what choice did he have? By refusing, he too would suffer the consequences of her mistake. "Fine."

"Thank you."

"But just this once. If you mess up again, it's your mess to fix."

"I promise I'll try, but… what if it means losing the house?"

He callously answered, "So be it."

With that he stormed off, presumably to find Nibbler for a comforting fuss, leaving her alone to cry in the dark.

Juli woke, her thoughts still swimming in the turgid mire of her dream.

How dare he treat me like that!

She sat up and glanced around as if to hit him, stopping as she remembered it was only a dream. Her eyes adjusted to the slight light and she realised she was on the sofa at Alezi's place. Reality came flooding back, bringing only a debilitating numbness.

He was right… it was *my fault.*

As if on cue, Alezi entered in her pink robe and slippers, stretching emphatically as she yawned, "Morning. Sleep well?"

Alezi cringed, clearly realising what a stupid question this was. There was nothing Alezi could say or do to ease Juli's dour mood. Mercifully, Alezi fell silent and headed into the kitchen briefly before sitting beside Juli, turning on the HV, watching over a bowl of cereal.

Juli was in no mood to eat, and was far too distracted to care that her hair looked like she'd slept upside down. She spent the rest of the day drifting in and out of progressively more nightmare-riddled sleep.

She kept seeing herself wearing a black dress, her mascara running beneath her black veil. She was holding a black and grey marbled urn. Its silvery plaque bore the inscription: *Jerin Malkin Endersul, 13/05/25005 — 33/07/25032.*

*

Just over a year after his not-so-triumphant return to work, Jerin took the opportunity to migrate to the new night shift, and though the novelty quickly wore off, a cursory glance at his once-ailing bank balance was all the motivation he needed to keep doing it.

The wedding was slowly coming within reach.

But, one morning after work, he arrived home to an empty house, dropping his then-new bag in front of the cupboard under the stairs, spotting a rare sight in these digital times: a white envelope protruding from behind the small cabinet by the front door.

He picked it up, realising it was a final notification for module maintenance tax. Whether it had ended up there by accident or design he didn't know, but once more he gave Juli the benefit of the doubt, picking up the phone and paying it himself, deciding not to mention it for now. If she did need help, he knew she was too damn stubborn to admit it.

That wasn't the only carelessly discarded bill he would find over the coming months. Pretty soon, what little savings he'd managed to accrue were gone once again.

He should have said something, but it wasn't that easy. If only he had, maybe… just maybe…

*

Juli dreamed she was walking with Alezi around *Radiance*, Darina City's largest and most exorbitant fashion boutique. Alezi had recently hit the big time in the world of modelling, and was picking out increasingly garish party clothes. Juli kept expecting Alezi to admit she'd picked some of them up as a joke, but her expression remained fiercely stoic as she scanned the innumerable racks.

Alezi stared at her left arm as her loose tan suede sleeve fell back while reaching for another outlandish top. "I really need to top up my tan," she sighed.

"I don't get the whole tanning booth thing," Juli

replied. "I mean, is it really worth risking your health just to look a little more trashy?"

"Don't believe everything you see on the news. Besides, it's expected in the world of fashion. Not that I'd expect someone like you to understand."

Juli wasn't keen on the scathing new persona Alezi had recently adopted. She replied with a derisive, "I don't think I want to understand it, thanks."

Alezi placed the maroon boob tube with printed fake nipples atop the pile in her basket, then scrutinised Juli's getup with a sneer. "You're not wearing *that* to the party, are you?"

Juli glanced down at her cat-hair-strewn claw-plucked purple knitted jumper. "What's wrong with it?"

"It makes you look like a crazy cat lady! It's so tatty!" Alezi tugged at a fraying edge.

"Thanks! I'd love to treat myself to something, but I just don't have the spare cash at the moment."

"That's what credit accounts are for, sweetie," Alezi winked.

"I'd rather not fall into that trap, thank you very much. Besides, I'm not even sure I want to go to this party. Just you and a bunch of your idiotic model 'friends'..." she made the finger-quotation marks in the air when she sarcastically said *friends*.

"I don't really want to go either," Alezi replied unconvincingly, "but I have to keep up appearances now. And it's nice to have a friend come along for moral support. At least there'll be lots of free booze, that should make it more tolerable."

"You know I don't really drink."

"Oh. Yeah. Umm... there'll be lots of free food... and lots of hunky men to admire!"

Juli sighed facetiously. "Well, it all sounds like far too much hard work, but I guess I'll do it for you..."

They both laughed. They would likely spend half the night taking the piss out of the bimbos and the other half admiring the beefcakes.

As for the outfit, Juli decided she *had* been working hard, and since Jerin was back at work now, surely she could afford to treat herself to a little something.

Alezi picked up a jumper remarkably similar to the one Juli was wearing and handed it to her. "This is nice…"

Juli took it from the enthusiastically quivering hand. "But it's almost identical to this one…"

But Alezi was gone, rushing over to grab a matching pair of purple trousers, draping them over Juli's arms before excitedly rushing off towards something else.

"This one's so you!" Alezi chimed, adding more and more to the pile, until it was so high Juli couldn't see over it, her arms beginning to shake under the strain.

"But when would I wear them?" Juli asked.

"You need an outfit for every occasion! Ooh, this'll go perfectly with almost anything!" Alezi threw an amethyst necklace atop the pile.

"It *is* cute," Juli agreed.

"Now you need shoes! So many shoes! Dinner shoes, dancing shoes, party shoes…"

"Isn't there like a one-style-suits-all-occasions pair?" Juli enquired.

"Ooh, no no no, you can't do that!" Alezi scolded. "You need high heels, low heels, formal, semi-casual, lace-ups, buckles…" she flitted around, throwing pair after pair atop the now-perilously-high stack.

"But I've got plenty of shoes at home!" Juli protested.

"But yours are so *old*," Alezi pouted. "And they're scuffed. I won't be seen with you in scuffed shoes!"

"These parties sound like more trouble than they're worth."

Alezi ran off again. "You'll need a new bag, and some accessories… ooh! Cute belt!"

Juli didn't hate the shiny black belt with the oversized square silver clasp, but wasn't sure it was her, but Alezi was unrelentingly insistent. Juli couldn't believe Alezi's nonchalance as she made the payment of

§1198.88, as if she did it all the time.

"You have to invest in yourself," Alezi naïvely insisted.

Juli handed her own items to the till operator, jaw dropping ever lower as the cost spiralled ever higher.

"Look at how much I'm spending!" Juli yelled.

"But look at how much you're saving!" Alezi remarked.

"I don't *need* all this..." she protested, but before she could reconsider the till operator was asking her to make the wireless payment from her phone-specs, and she absently complied.

How could she have been so stupid? She loved Alezi, but she was a terrible influence. All Juli had wanted was one party outfit, something she could wear whenever she and Jerin went out; he wouldn't judge her for wearing the same outfit twice. Even if she'd sold her reckless purchases, she wouldn't have made enough to pay back the unauthorised overdraft fee, and Alezi would guilt her into keeping every single one. She would eventually become too ashamed to wear them.

The shop vanished and Juli appeared before her wardrobe of shame, compelled to open it for the first time in as long as she could remember. The moment she did, manifold outfits spilled forth, cascading like a waterfall, the force of the deluge sending her hurtling backwards. She spun in the air, falling face-first towards the multi-coloured pool of outfits, falling straight into it...

She was falling into an abyss, landing with a violent splash in a dirty puddle on a dark and dreary street. She saw the reflection of neon lights, glancing up to see a twisted version of *Sirens*: a castle built from black bricks. Vertical strip lights lining the walls crackled with audible *snaps* and *pops*. The sign promised people *topless girls like you've never seen.* Beneath it stood Alezi, wearing nothing more than tiny black underwear, gesturing to Juli to come inside.

As Juli stood, the long coat she was now wearing

flapped open, revealing nothing underneath but her own tiny black underwear. Her skin was hard but smooth, like the soft plastarch of a girl's doll. Her joints seemed to be articulated like a doll's too: ball-and-sockets at her hips, levers at her knees. Her neck was stiff. She raised a shaky hand to it, feeling its strange joint, realising she could turn her head completely backwards.

Alezi stepped into the entrance of the bar and a massive bouncer held her under the arms while another used a filthy chainsaw to cut her in half. Blood and guts sprayed everywhere, but Alezi just smiled and giggled. Her legs went left and the rest of her went right, effortlessly walking on her hands.

A massive hand wrapped itself around Juli's right arm. She looked up to see Nate towering over her. "Rent," he grunted Neanderthalically through a maliciously toothy grin.

"Get lost!" she protested, trying to pull back, her arm *popping* completely free of its socket, remaining in his hand.

She gasped as he effortlessly scooped her up, carrying her into the bar over his shoulder. "Rent. Dance."

Juli kicked and punched with her remaining hand, but it was futile. Nate relentlessly marched her into the bar. "Dance. Rent."

He threw her across the room. She collapsed like a rag doll as she landed on the main stage, her arm landing before her. She flexed the fingers on her disembodied arm then took her coat off, shoving the ball end of the limb back into the socket.

She rose to her feet, the faceless mob of men barely visible through the bright array of spotlights concentrated on her. In a drone-like fashion, the crowd rhythmically chanted, "Dance! Dance! Dance! Rent! Rent! Rent!"

She reluctantly complied, dancing as seductively as she could to the awful metal music, her moves stiffly rigid. The chant changed to, "Take it off! Take it off."

She removed her bra, noticing her lack of nipples, but

still they chanted. She reluctantly removed her only other item of clothing, a skimpy gee-string, noticing a lack of naughty bits beneath that too. Still the mob chanted, "Take it off! Take it off!"

Vixen and Fox stood either side of her. Vixen removed her own legs, shuffling her torso onto a barstool, and Fox took off her own head, holding it out in one hand. "Take it off," they spoke in unison.

"Take what off?"

"This!" Vix yanked Juli's head off with a *pop*.

Juli's hands flailed wildly. She closed her eyes, hoping to wake up, but still it went on. There was much cheering. She could feel unseen hands caressing her naked body, opening her eyes to see it pulled apart with a series of accompanying *pops*, the various pieces vanishing into the crowd. She tried to scream, but could make no sound.

Vix held Fox's head while Fox's headless body carried Juli's head over to Nate, who was sitting in a booth, his erect member awaiting her delicate mouth. It was far too big for her in this twisted mindscape.

"No," she protested as Fox lowered her mouth towards it. "No! NO!"

She awoke abruptly, frantically feeling her soft and sweaty body, eyes darting around the room. She was alone on Alezi's bed. She couldn't even remember coming in here.

She went into the front room, spotting Alezi sleeping in the single chair, regarding her so-called 'friend' with accusing eyes.

She needed some fresh air. She had much to think about. She crept into the bedroom and quietly got out of her pyjamas and into her not-so-fresh street clothes.

Juli returned to the sofa fully dressed to retrieve her phone, when she heard the chair creak as Alezi stretched.

"Where are you going?" Alezi asked sleepily.

"I have to go home," Juli replied without making eye contact.

Alezi was baffled. "Why?"

"Because this is all your fault!" Juli shouted, snatching an empty mug from the table and hurling it across the room, narrowly missing Alezi's head. It exploded into a shower of ceramic shards against the far wall. Alezi watched in stunned silence as her fragile friend hastily departed, slamming the door on her way out.

*

Jerin was abruptly woken by the clamour of the front door as Juli burst in, running upstairs into the bedroom, sending a frightened Nibbly jumping off Jerin's stomach and scurrying under the bed. Tears were streaming down her face.

"Jerin... I need your help again... I've messed up," she blubbed.

"What have you done *now*?" His tone was one of sheer exasperation.

"I fell into arrears on the mortgage, and the bank added late payment charges, and now they're demanding I pay them in full or they'll repossess the house..." she paused to wipe the tears away. "Jerin, they're demanding nearly a thousand silvan!"

His long, emphatic sigh grew louder until it became an angry bellow of sheer frustration that sent Nibbly running out of the room in a panic. "Why didn't you tell me this back when we could have done something about it?"

"I'm sorry, I know I should have, but I knew you'd get mad at me... I was too scared to say anything... I didn't want to worry you and hinder your recovery..."

He threw his hands up in frustration, quieting his freshly-hoarse voice. "You said you wouldn't do this again... and I was stupid enough to believe you."

"Can- you- *please*- help me?" she struggled between sobs.

"Even if I wanted to, I can't." He sat on the edge of the bed, facing away from her. "I don't have any spare cash left. It went on all those unpaid utility bills I found."

She was stricken with renewed shock. "Shit! I forgot

about those!"

"And all those clothes you wasted your money on…" he shook his head in dismay.

"I know! I'm sorry! I don't know what to do."

He turned to face her. "There's nothing you *can* do. It's an insurmountable amount." He sighed. "Now we lose the house."

"I'm so sorry! *Please* don't hate me!" she bawled.

"What *should* I do, Juli? I thought we were back on track, yet somehow you managed to ruin everything!"

Juli fled the room in tears, leaving Jerin alone to contemplate her egregious error. He hadn't seen it coming, though looking back now it seemed numbingly inevitable.

He placed his face in his hands, considering their next move.

He opened his top drawer and took out the small black box with the silver trim, but couldn't bring himself to open it. It was too late to return it. He tensed his hands around the box as though throttling it. He almost wanted to throw it at the wall, but what good would that do? He put it back and slammed the drawer shut.

Did he still love her? Could he honestly say that?

*

"Do we have to?" Jerin protested, stopping a short distance from the bank's front door, glaring at the people inside through the tinted glass. "They're always so unreasonable."

Juli looked at her own reflection in that darkened glass, adjusting her grey suit to make herself look as professional and presentable as possible. "Look, it's got to be worth a try. I'm sure they don't really want to kick us out of our own home. Just sit, try not to look too bored, and try not to get stressy."

"Too late for that."

They stepped through the automatic sliding doors into the cavernous, insultingly opulent building. The stairs, floor and pillars were all marble. The few offices had glass walls, but the main floor was largely open-plan. The air was filled with the echoing chatter of dozens of conversations. Juli scanned the innumerable besuited people milling about, spotting a stationary, clearly highly disciplined security guard, stun-staff in his right hand, shield braced on his left arm, just waiting for trouble. Something about his stone cold stare gave them the creeps. They gave him a wide berth.

"Excuse me," Juli said as a young woman in a posh silken red blouse and smart black skirt walked by. She stopped, greeting them with a wide plastarch smile. "Could you please direct us to Mr Farr?"

"I can do better than that, madam. What's your name?"

"Julianos Tenzalin."

The woman glanced at Jerin expectedly, but he said nothing. She gestured to two chairs sitting before an empty desk. "Please take a seat, Mrs Tenzalin, and I'll fetch him for you."

They decided not to correct the woman, sitting and waiting while she darted up the stairs beside them with a very echoey *clip-clopping*. Juli rummaged in her handbag atop her lap, noticing Jerin was wincing slightly.

She whispered, "Do you need a pill?"

"I already took two."

"Sorry. Just trying to help."

Jerin didn't reply, seeming to be reasonably composed. Juli couldn't stop fidgeting, closing her bag to place it beneath her seat before absently tapping her fingers on the arms of her chair. Jerin shot her a silent glance and she wrapped her fingers tightly around the ends of the arms. She didn't like dealing with these avaricious people anymore than Jerin did.

A man of approximately their own age finally appeared from behind, as if from nowhere, his footsteps so soft he could have been gliding on air. He was clean-shaven with short, ungelled hair, predictably wearing an expensive suit, the jacket of which he buttoned as he ran his fingers down the lapels.

"Chilly in here," he remarked with a theatrical shoulder-shudder. Neither Juli nor Jerin replied. "Jisento Farr," he introduced himself, proffering his right hand. Juli shook it wanly; Jerin didn't even move, regarding this overpaid man with undisguised contempt. He slowly withdrew the hand. "I hear you have defaulted on your mortgage payments?" he asked with a sickening air of smugness as he took his seat.

"Yes," Juli said in little more than a whisper. "But we've been paying what we can afford."

"You both signed the agreement at the time of taking out the loan, stating that you would be able to afford the full payment each month."

"Yes, but we were told that we would be okay as long as we were making contributions if we fell on… *difficult* times…" Juli said diffidently.

Jisento sighed through his nostrils. "If only you'd taken out our insurance policy…"

"We have a very limited income," Juli interrupted. "We couldn't afford the insurance as well."

Jisento stared at his computer screen. "Okay. Well, I see you owe a thousand. We might be able to wrangle a fix here." He tapped at his keyboard. "If you were to resume full payment, how much extra could you afford to pay each month?"

"We can't afford any extra, that's the point!" Juli explained. "The best solution for us would be to extend the period of the mortgage so that we can add it to the end."

"Ooh, I'm afraid we can't do that."

"Why not?"

"You'd have to apply for a remortgage, which you won't get, not in your financial situation. Even if you did, it comes with considerable fees."

"So the only way out of this is to pay you more than we already owe? We're already paying virtually double what we borrowed!"

"Like I said, if you could pay just a *little* more each

month… a hundred silvan can't be too much, surely?"

"Maybe not for an overpaid prick like you!" Jerin snapped. Juli was amazed he'd remained silent this long. "All you greedy bastards want is more! I mean look at you, sitting there in your expensive suit, so damned assured of your financially secure future, gold-plated pension and all! I bet you and your ilk make a killing cheating schmucks like us out of our hard-earned cash!"

Juli had to step in before this got ugly. "Jerin, don't…"

Jerin sprang to his feet, banging his fist on the desk as he shouted, "If this fugada is going to ruin our lives, I'm going to give him a piece of my mind!"

Jisento glanced up at Jerin indifferently, not only assured of his financial stability but of his personal safety too. He glanced at one of the numerous armed guards standing close by, who had gone from dutifully surveying his surroundings to watching Jerin intently. Jisento signalled him to remain where he was.

Jerin laughed derisively. "What I admire most," he continued, staring at his own fist rocking back and forth atop the desk, voice quietly malevolent, "is that you're so professional, you'd rather have this little meeting in front of everyone rather than in the privacy of one of the back offices."

Jisento seemed genuinely stunned by this. "My apologies, you're right. We can relocate, if that's more convenient…"

"What's the point?" Jerin asked, throwing his hands up. "You've already got everyone's attention! Isn't that the point, after all? To show everyone what happens if you fall behind? To show these *little people* how pathetic, how far beneath you they really are?" He leaned on the desk's edge, his mind feeling heavy, staring intently into Jisento's slowly comprehending eyes. "You're so out of touch, you can't even feel the approaching storm of dissidence. When it comes tearing through here, stripping away everything you hold so dear, what will you do?"

Just as Jisento signalled for the guard to apprehend him, Jerin staggered, falling heavily into his seat, staring up at the bright lights hanging above, feeling like he was about to have some sort of seizure. Perhaps he just had.

"Jerin! Jerin, are you alright?" Juli's voice was muffled, as though in another room. She swatted ineffectually at the guard as he lifted Jerin up by the armpits. Jerin heard Juli tell the guard, "Please don't, he has mental health problems, you wouldn't understand," but he didn't care a jot, carrying him outside and unceremoniously dropping him on a concrete bench before marching back inside, standing sentry just inside the door.

Juli sat beside Jerin, crying. He could feel the warm touch of her hands on his, but it was distant. After several moments he was able to stand, but couldn't walk far. Juli hailed a taxi to take them back to where they'd parked, and damn the expense.

Later, when Jerin's head had cleared, Juli asked him, "What was all that you were talking about at the bank earlier?"

He shook his head and wrinkled his brow in confusion. "What bank?"

*

The two of them stood firm the day the bailiffs arrived, refusing to answer the door. They had decided that the bank was being unreasonable, not them.

The knocks and muffled threats kept coming, but the bailiffs eventually left.

However, the cavalry soon arrived. As a SWAT van pulled up out front, Juli hurriedly placed Nibbler in his pet carrier and shut him in the kitchen along with what they'd been able to pack into boxes, reluctantly accepting that the rest would be left behind.

They silently watched events unfold outside the window under the dull glow of the street light, holding hands as half a dozen intimidating armed and armoured officers leapt out of the van's back doors.

One of them started walking down the garden path, then they heard him knock on their front door in that firmly authoritative manner. Through the door he shouted, "Sorry folks, you have to leave."

"We're not going anywhere!" Jerin shouted back. "We're staging a sit-in!"

"Okay. What if you let me in? Just me. The squad will stay out here, and we'll discuss the matter like adults. How's that?"

Jerin and Juli looked into one another's eyes for a moment.

"Okay," Jerin conceded. "But no weapons."

"Done," the cop answered, telling his men, "Stand down."

They opened the door and the cop stepped inside. He removed his helmet, revealing a kindly but weathered Vahirinese face. "Evening, folks. I'm officer Haikyo Tinjima."

"I'm Juli. This is Jerin," Juli said glumly.

Jerin stepped towards the officer, staring him straight in the eyes. "Does this make you feel good? Coming in here, separating people from their dreams. We've done nothing wrong. We even tried to be reasonable."

"I'm sorry," the cop said earnestly, resting his bulky black helmet on top of a nearby bookcase. Even though her heart was breaking, Juli could see the genuine displeasure etched into every line of that man's middle-aged face. "I'm just doing my job. I admire your tenacity, but you must realise this is an effort doomed to failure. If I don't evict you, the bank will send in a gung-ho team of psi-pistol-wielding morons. Believe me, you don't want that. They'll use a disproportionate amount of resources to get you out, and pass the cost onto more innocent people. It really is best that we just get this over with now."

"Maybe he's right. Maybe it is time to go," Juli whispered to Jerin, who nodded sombrely.

"What about our belongings?" Jerin asked. "We bought them... they belong to us. The bank can't take them, that's abuse of power!"

"I agree, I think it's shameful that the bank will take it. They have no right. But they can't prove what is and isn't here, you know. I'll help you load what we can in the back of the SWAT van," the officer suggested.

Juli nodded solemnly, turning to Jerin as tears rolled down her cheeks. "I think it's time to go."

Jerin nodded his reluctant agreement. To Haikyo he requested, "Just... give us a minute. Please?"

The cop nodded and headed back outside, telling his assembled team, "They'll come out on their own when they're ready."

They wandered around for one last look. Jerin ran his fingers along Nibbly's claw marks on the doorframe. He sat at the desk in his office, spinning slowly in the chair, while Juli went into the bedroom for a moment.

He wouldn't let the tears flow, not now. There would be time to grieve over their loss later, though many tears had already been shed as the inevitable had approached.

They collected what they had prepared and packed it into the car, in full view of the waiting SWAT officers, grateful that at least the expensive HV bars were slim and robust enough to lie safely in the rear footwell. They fastened Nibbly in last.

The friendly cop approached Jerin, still unarmed. "What can we take for you?"

They had taken time during their wandering to discuss this. "There's a desk and a chair in the second bedroom," Juli answered.

The cop nodded.

Jerin added, "If I help take it apart, will you be able to fit a bed in there?"

"Probably a sofa too," the cop suggested. "But that would be about it."

"So the kitchen appliances would be left behind?"

"I'm afraid so."

"But they're virtually new!" Juli protested, sobbing, "It isn't right..."

"Maybe I can convince the squad to come back…"

"You'd really do that? That'd be great!" Juli replied in pleasant surprise.

"Do you have a place to go?"

Jerin answered, "Not yet, but a friend told me about a place down south. She said it was quiet and cheap."

"I know it," the cop said. "It's out of gang territory. If you lead the way, we'll follow."

About an hour later, the car and van were fully loaded and they were on their way.

Jerin held his phone sideways, plotting their course. Nibbler's strained protests during the entirety of the journey flanked by the SWAT van made Juli feel incredibly guilty, as though she was committing an act of severe cruelty. After all, it was Nibbler's home too.

"You could just load the route onto my specs," Juli said. "I don't even know where we're going."

"Just drive," Jerin replied icily. "I'll tell you when we're there."

She abhorred the long silence that followed as she drove past one identical street after another.

"Who told you about this place?" Juli asked. He said nothing. "Jerin?"

He sighed. "I had plenty of time to talk to people online while I was off sick. It turns out Lucille used to live out this way. When I spoke to her about our finances, she mentioned it as a possibility. I figured it wouldn't hurt to have a contingency plan… I just hoped it wouldn't be necessary."

"I'm sorry," she sobbed.

"It's too late for that. There's nothing left to say."

Another long silence. Finally, she asked, "Do you still love me?"

Silence.

"Do you?"

"I don't know."

She began to cry again, reaching for a tissue from the box on the dashboard to wipe the tears from her eyes.

When she couldn't reach, Jerin silently passed her one. She took it with a subdued "Thanks."

Many more streets came and went with no need to issue directions, but Jerin could see a turn finally coming ahead. "Take the next left," he said quietly.

She turned as bade, clearly astonished by the lack of cars on the road and driveways. "Where is everyone?"

"This place is pretty desolate. That's why it's perfect for us." It was so quiet it almost felt like they were the only people for miles around.

She drove along the winding road, passing many turns.

"Next right," he said.

She turned into a cul-de-sac, parking in an unmarked bay wide enough for four cars, the SWAT van pulling up alongside them.

"Wait here," he told her, getting out and disappearing into the darkness for an interminable time, leaving Juli to fuss Nibbler, sticking her fingers through the squares in the door of his carrier. Though he was still frightened, he brushed his furry cheeks against her fingers, nibbling one gently.

After about twenty minutes, Jerin finally returned with a key in his right hand. "It's sorted. Number thirty-two. Come on."

She got out of the car and followed him down the path. They entered after a bit of a fight with the front door. The inside smelled musty. They glanced into the tiny bathroom and bedroom before walking around the far more spacious living room, which backed onto a fairly sizeable garden, the patio doors not all that dissimilar to those of the house they'd just lost.

"At least there's somewhere for Nibbler to run around," Jerin observed as the SWAT team dutifully brought in the sofa and pieces of bed, assembling the latter for them while Juli had a look around the tiny kitchen.

"There are appliances in there, but they're ancient,"

she remarked.

She saw that Jerin had sat on the sofa, staring blankly at the wall opposite where the HV would eventually go. He didn't utter a word as people came and went around him.

The hardest part of all was handing over their old house keys. Juli held them above the cop's waiting palm, unable to let go. She made a pained sound as she finally released them.

"I'm sorry for your loss," the cop said earnestly before departing. "We'll haul these old appliances off to the recycling plant and bring the ones from the house over post haste."

Juli smiled weakly at this very welcome concession. "Thank you so much for your kindness," she replied, Jerin too upset to speak.

"I just wish we could have done more," the cop sighed sadly.

But as harrowing as the loss of their house was, for Jerin there was worse yet to come.

It took Nibbler longer than they'd expected to settle into the new flat. After inheriting his descriptive name, the exuberant feline had quickly developed his funny little quirks: running around the house half-sideways, half-forwards, prompting Jerin to call him a "two-dimensional puddy cat"; he would sit on Juli's bedside cabinet, waiting for her to hide beneath the covers. When she did, he would tilt his head quizzically before pouncing on her, causing much mirth before retreating back to the cabinet and waiting again. He quickly learned the art of smacking the rattling snack ball around the carpet and sniffing enthusiastically to consume the dispensed biscuit treats, only to realise he could trap it in a corner and get treat after treat with remarkable ease; he would often run through the living room and collide noisily with the patio door, walking away as though nothing out of the ordinary had occurred, as if to say "nothing to see here."

Jerin snapped countless pictures of Nibbly, choosing

his favourite — playing with the shoelace — as the basis for a painting to keep him occupied in the boring weeks prior to his operation, finally using those paints and the first of the canvasses.

But the move had seen the quickly-growing slinky cat become even more restless, which hadn't seemed possible. Not long after Jerin had started working nights, Nibbly had taken to waking him in the middle of the day to be let out, growing increasingly insistent, refusing to let his 'daddy' sleep, smacking him in the face repeatedly, retreating when he stirred. Nevertheless, Jerin refused to let him out on dark days for fear that any passing drivers might not see the predominantly black cat if he wandered into the road.

On the day before Jerin's last shift of the week, Nibbly simply wasn't taking no for an answer, incessantly meowing and jingling the front door keys, which soon became too much to ignore. Perhaps Jerin should have just shut him in the kitchen, but he was too tired to think straight, and since vehicles rarely came by here anyway he relented, opening the door and watching Nibbler vanish into the gradually darkening day.

That night before work Nibbler wouldn't answer Jerin's repeated loud calls or shaking of the biscuit bag. There wasn't even the telltale jingle of his collar's bell, and Jerin didn't have time to wait indefinitely. With a leaden heart, he had no choice but to leave Nibbler out, leaving Juli a post-it note regarding the matter on the living room door.

He thought about it all night, regretting giving in. Once that cat decided he wanted something, he was a persistent bugger.

When Jerin arrived home the next morning, Juli had already left for work, adding to his note that Nibbly still hadn't come home.

Jerin panicked, going on a hunt with a torch, calling his name into the silent darkness over and over, to no avail. He walked until his feet and his voice were sore, then he walked and he called some more. He adopted Nibbly's own policy, refusing to give up.

Not far from their flat was an old fence separating the residential area from the road. Jerin had seen Nibbly scale it more than once, and it scared him witless every time. *Please, no*. There was no quick way around and it was too high for Jerin to confidently jump, so he hastily jogged the long way around, a sudden panic rising through him. When he finally reached the other side his torchlight passed fleetingly over a tiny patch of white fur, and he realised it was a cat's belly. His heart seemed to freeze in his chest. *Please, no...* He almost couldn't bear to do it, but he aimed the torch at it and saw Nibbler's perfectly still body, laying along the dead-dirt verge, the side of his mouth slightly bloodied by the car that had doubtless hit him.

Jerin suddenly knew what people meant when they said they had felt their heart breaking. The pain was intense. He knelt before his beloved companion and wept in silence, gingerly stroking his tiny head before cradling his rigid, cold body in his arms.

Whoever was responsible and whether it was intentional or not didn't matter; it was himself Jerin would never forgive.

Reliving these hate-inspiring memories in such vivid detail had left Jerin both mentally and emotionally exhausted. He needed to escape. He looked around, spotting the way he felt he was supposed to go next, slowly starting to walk that way before quickly taking a hard left, running down a heavily-fogged street. He pushed past myriad repressed memories of moronic colleagues and so-called back-stabbing 'friends', all of them pawing ineffectually at him in drone-like fashion. He brusquely brushed their hands from his sleeves without slowing. Streets came and went. Flashes of things he recognised well and many that eluded his immediate recollection faded in and out, giving him no clue as to where he might end up next.

But the visions were cruel, and they took him back to the scene he'd fled, to that street where he'd found Nibbly dead, only now he was alive, tentatively sniffing something on the edge of the road as a hover-car came flying down the long straight road way too fast. It was a mid-blue douchebag-mobile with white go-faster stripes running from bonnet to boot, and Jerin watched helplessly as it bore down on tiny, fragile Nibbler. Jerin so badly wanted to look away, but some unseen force held him in place as the car struck his beloved companion, throwing him aside like a tiny rag doll, killing him instantly.

The car pulled into a nearby driveway and the driver got out, a late-teens idiot without a care in the world for the life he'd just taken. The unseen force released Jerin and he rushed over, tackling the driver to the ground. Rage surged through Jerin, and he began punching the driver in the face over and over. His nose erupted bright red spurts on the driveway, left then right and over again with every strike, before exploding entirely. The young man became comatose, his eyes rolling back to reveal only the whites. Jerin rose to his feet, took a step back, then jumped onto the idiot's head, reducing it to a puddle of bloody pulp. He'd imagined doing this to the person responsible for the death of Nibbler more times than he could remember, and every time it felt so good. He wanted someone else to come out and pick a fight so he could kill them too. He almost wished he could bring the idiotic driver back to life, just so he could kill him again. If only he had that power, then he could simply wish his beloved companion back to life. *If only cats truly had nine lives...*

With that done and his anger momentarily satisfied, Jerin screamed at the sky, "There! Are you happy now?" and the fog cleared, revealing the way forwards. He began walking again, finally permitted to escape that street. As he continued ever onwards, he felt that cold sensation surging up his left arm again, but he was determined not to let it stop him this time.

He saw flashes of moments from his earliest days at the plant, back when he'd handled boxes of components that were to be checked before being delivered to the appropriate stations, in the days before the headaches had begun blighting his existence.

A particularly oblivious and dim-witted ex-colleague knocked a stack of trays in his path, missing him by mere inches.

Jerin came to a stop, narrowly avoiding tripping. In an instant the anger was back, and he barked, "You *idiot*!"

This drew even more unwelcome visions to him. A former boss emerged as if from nowhere, a skinny bespectacled young man who knew exactly what to say to his own superiors to continue rising despite his overwhelming ignorance and naïvety. "Jerin, please don't call your colleagues idiots."

"If he wasn't an idiot, he would have secured the load! It isn't rocket science!"

"I feel your frustration…"

"No you don't! How could you? Did he almost flatten you?"

"Don't call him an idiot."

Jerin snorted in frustration. "Fine. Brain dead. Mentally deficient. Intellectually challenged. Dip shit. Pick one."

Before the too-green boss could reply, Jerin glanced to his right, saw his chance to escape, and was off again.

As he ran ever faster he heard the most irritating sound in the world: whistling. He looked for the annoying so-and-so making the sound, quickly telling him, "Cram a sock in it, or I'm going to be arrested for murder." That did the trick, the now-silent "oh" expression left on the whistler's face suiting him to a tee.

"You've got a real problem with authority," barked an idiotic, clearly alcoholic woman he despised with every fibre of his being. She floated alongside him. Even though he knew she wasn't really here, seeing her haughty 'everything is below me' down-the-nose expression sent rage coursing through his body. He hated that anyone could make him feel angry enough to want to hug their face between two bricks.

Jerin offered her no reply, running with all his might, ignoring the creeping, now near-crippling cold rising within. A momentary drop in concentration resulted in him barking back, "You have no authority!" which had only led to more trouble when he'd said it first time around. She disappeared in a puff of smoke, which reformed to present him with another former boss, a vertically-challenged slowly balding middle-aged man named Mildew, a very apt name indeed.

"You don't have what it takes to be a manager," Mildew derided. "You have to learn to swim with the sharks without getting eaten, and you've been chewed up and spat out."

Jerin slowed as the fluid in his system finally became too much to bear. Through gritted teeth he replied, "You're no shark, you're a mindless sheep! You're full of shit. Why did you always have to be so patronising? When I said I'd suggest someone took three or four boxes at a time to improve efficiency…"

"I said I would tell them, 'I have to pay for my shoe lunim'," the echo replied.

Jerin fell to his knees, crawling now. "Then you took three days off sick for a sniffle while I was here through worse, doing *your* job for less money. And where did it get me? Fucking nowhere! Now get lost, you waste of space."

That boss's boss appeared. "Jerin, while you were looking after things, productivity was up and waste was down. Unlike Mildew, you contribute to the workload rather than hiding in the back office all day. I must say, I'm rather impressed."

Jerin was practically pinned to the ground now, struggling just to hold himself up on his hands, his elbows quivering, jaw clenched in sheer agony. "So- why- did- you- never- promote- me?" Every word was an effort to get out.

"Because you forgot to leave him to do his own job when he came back. You made him look good. And when you had the chance, you said too much in the interview, remember?"

He summoned the last of his strength to speak, falling to the ground and rolling onto his back. "Everyone else who applied was told what to say, but not me!" he panted. "All you ever did was use me... if you hired people based on what they can *do* rather than what they can *say*, this place might actually be worth the corporation's investment!" He was as incredulous now as he had been back then.

"But don't you understand? That's how the corporation likes things done..."

Jerin was too weak to reply. He watched helplessly as the myriad visions gathered around him, slowly closing in, their incessant droning chatter blocking out all thought. He closed his eyes, drew a deep breath, and shouted as loud as he could, "Shut up and leave me alone!"

The voices fell silent. He opened his eyes, seeing them all standing over him, jaws slack, bony fingers on outstretched arms pointing at him accusingly. They said in unison, "Heathen! Be gone!" He felt the ground suddenly give way beneath him, and was falling deeper again.

No more, please... I can't take it. If you're going to kill me, just get it over with already!

10
-Lost & Lonely-

After a long walk's slowly-petering stewing across early morning Darina, Juli finally arrived back at the tiny flat in Sendura. She went into the bedroom and sat on the cold bed. She hadn't wanted to come straight home, but just as she felt now she'd had absolutely no idea what to do with herself. She hated being in moods like this; she didn't feel like doing anything, but she felt the need to do *something*. She'd never felt so lost and alone. Without Jerin here, this tiny flat felt surprisingly massive.

In an effort to distract herself she opened her top bedside drawer, recoiling at the mass of mess within. She decided to tidy it up, beginning to sift through ancient loose papers, finding a near-empty box of condoms near the bottom. One envelope in particular stood out like a sore thumb: the one containing the letter she'd received a few weeks after they'd lost the house, the one she couldn't find the courage to tell Jerin about.

She'd considered not giving the bank her new address, but the cop was likely obliged to pass that little nugget of information on. Even if neither of them had told the bank, she knew they'd find her, no matter what the cost. It was what they did.

She regarded the Bank Of Terrengus logo with burning hatred before rereading the short message.

'Your total legal fees, less your reimbursed deposit and payments made to date, amount to §15,065.49, which will be deducted from your account automatically on the 1st of each month, at a rate of §150.51, with interest applied.'

The crooks had gotten away with it again, adding insult to injury by piling interest on top of these already lofty fees, which surely couldn't be legal. But what could she do? They were the *only* bank.

Her mind kept turning to what Jerin had said during that weird outburst about dissidence amongst the people of the city over the bank's behaviour. She had no idea what had prompted it, but she knew then that he was right.

The shit was going to hit the fan, and likely sooner than later.

She put the letter away and thought about all the money she'd wasted again. Jerin had been right about so much, and she'd never told him so, mostly for fear of inflating his ego. *What ego? It was frustration... why couldn't I see it?* Why hadn't she realised before now that he simply cared? *Maybe I was the one with the ego... or maybe I was too stubborn... oh, I don't know!* All she did know was that he had been right all along: she *should* have just listened to him.

She promised herself to tell him that when he woke up.

Juli realised that she suddenly had a pretty good understanding of what Jerin had been going through on a regular basis as she once again found herself with nothing to do. As he often had, she donned her phone-specs to check her much-neglected *BestBuddies* page, noticing she had a voice message from Keresay that had been sent yesterday.

In the message, Keresay informed Juli that Andivus had told her about Jerin's condition (but neither had told anyone else), and offered her sympathies and best wishes, thanking her for speaking to Mr Manrose on her behalf. Juli dictated a short reply, saying that she hoped all would be well soon and that she would be back "before she knew it," not really sure how much truth was in it. It was just nice to have some sense of continuity with all that was happening in the world. *Whatever happens, life goes on,* she reminded herself.

She was raising a hand to remove the specs when she was startled by the abrupt, deafening wail of an incoming call.

That'll be Alezi, she thought, about to reject the call

when she noticed the caller ID read: 'Mum'.

She hadn't heard from her in much longer than usual. No doubt she'd be worried about Juli if she didn't answer, but she wasn't sure she was in any fit state to talk, and their conversations were rarely short.

Juli answered with no idea what to say, deciding to let her mum take the lead.

"Hullo," the disembodied voice greeted, "I haven't heard from you in a fortnight, are you alright?"

"I'm fine," she lied, hoping her mum would buy it.

"Don't lie to me, Juli. What's wrong?"

"It's nothing. I'll be fine."

"It's just that Alezi came over saying she was worried about you…"

"Tell her it's none of her concern."

"She's your friend. She's worried about you. I would say that makes it her concern."

"I'm fine, really," she reiterated, welling tears blurring her vision. *Damn you, Alezi, what have you told her?*

As if reading this thought, Juli's mum said, "Alezi wouldn't say what was wrong, just that you weren't in a good way. Would it be better if I came over?"

"No, don't worry about me, I'm sure you're busy."

"I'm never too busy for you, you know that. I can hear you're upset. You won't feel better until you spill it."

Juli grabbed a tissue from Jerin's side of the bed and wiped beneath her phone-specs. "Jerin collapsed… he's in hospital again."

There was a long pause; whenever Juli hadn't been at work or with Jerin, she'd been with her mum through the last scare. She knew how serious it was. Juli was glad her mum wasn't the sort to do an overly dramatic, gormless-sounding "oh no."

"Do you want me to come with you to see him?"

"No. I'm not ready to go back yet."

"Alright. Is anyone else there to keep you company?"

"No. I was staying at Alezi's, but I lost my temper and ran out. It's not her fault. She was only trying to help, she didn't deserve it."

"If you apologise to her, I'm sure she'll understand."

"I guess."

"You need company. I know how down you can get at times. I worry about you, you know."

"I know. I'm scared, Mum. It's too similar to how we lost dad."

"I know, sweetheart. I don't know what else to say."

"I hate just sitting around here doing nothing but moping… maybe I should go back to work tomorrow…"

"I don't think that'd do you much good. All you'd be thinking about all day is Jerin. You'd be too distracted. Speak to Alezi," she pleaded. "You need a friend right now. Listen, I better get going. Impatient client."

"Okay. Bye. I love you, Mum."

"I love you too. Bye-eee."

She knew her mum was right about Alezi, but she wasn't ready just yet. She just needed some time alone to clear her head.

The sudden silence felt like her worst enemy. She went into the living room, drew the curtains to block out the worst of the harsh barrier shine and turned the HV on. She didn't care that there was nothing worth watching, she just needed the background noise to drown out the dark voices in her head.

*

Jerin slowed to a gradual halt as he fell, landing on his feet surprisingly gently. All around him was cloaked by a thick veil of black fog.

He glanced around, straining his eyes, but nothing came into focus. Gingerly, he walked forwards, feeling the space before him; the empty blackness was absolute.

His head was ringing, not painfully so, but very uncomfortably, like one of those annoyingly insatiable itches where the source is nowhere near the sensation.

Just then, an indistinguishably hazy white radiance penetrated the thick gloom. He approached until it came into focus, realising it was the Hit Flix sign. His heart skipped a beat; when was the last time he'd seen that sign illuminated? The bent metal panels straightened with creaking protests and the boards over the doors fell away as he walked closer. He climbed the four concrete steps and peered into the middle set of the three lots of metal-rimmed glass double doors, astonished by what he saw: old colleagues milling about, just as he remembered. Lucille, Purvil, Jalzon, Vessan, Riccardo… it was like something out of a movie, a million memories all coming together simultaneously.

This place had been his first full-time employer, and though it didn't seem all that significant at the time, the people he would meet while working here would change his life in an unexpectedly profound way. Life seemed so much simpler back then, when the days were longer. He had been young and naïve enough to believe that anything was possible, but too stupid to know how to apply himself. Perhaps he could have avoided his dire fate, if only he'd known.

But if the mythical manual to life existed, and all the talented people were able to realise their dreams, who would serve the popcorn?

As he reached for the right door's handle, he caught his own reflection: his not-quite-twenty-year-old face stared back at him.

He pulled the door open and stepped into the past, setting his feet on the red, violet and black patterned carpet.

A strange, indescribable sensation filled his entire being, like he was suddenly as young as his reflection. That black fog was thinner here, but still present, clinging at every corner as though holding the very building up. This wasn't some warped version of his memory either; everything was exactly where it was supposed to be. Suddenly, young Kol appeared before him from nowhere. Jerin looked down at himself, seeing that he was now adorned in his all-black uniform, complete with purple stripes running down the long shirt sleeves. He saw the name 'Jerin' etched in white on his oval purple name badge.

He hadn't noticed the prevalent silence until sound started to emerge, like someone slowly turning an HV up from mute.

He entered the fray, transitioning from observer to part of the vision, living it almost as if for the first time.

Jerin ran up the two flights of stairs, using the cold metal handrail to propel himself up faster. He'd been so sprightly then, and was determined to make the most of it while it lasted.

When he reached the third floor of the old cinema he spotted Kess sitting on one of the cushioned, metal-pole-armed chairs, her right leg crossing her left knee, a compu-phone in tablet mode resting on her open left palm. Jerin remembered that she often did her university homework during the many quiet periods.

"Hey, Jere," she smiled.

"Uh, hey, Kess," he replied, trying to act nonchalant. He quite liked her, but knew so little about her. He would happily have taken the time to resolve that problem, if he wasn't so lame around pretty girls. He was even worse around ones who were nice to him; he could never tell whether they were flirting or just being friendly. Riccardo had once insisted those were two sides of the same coin, but Jerin wasn't so sure.

"Are you here to take over?" she asked, glancing at her watch.

"Yeah."

"Where am I next?"

"Screens down."

She nodded, bringing up the showing times she'd loaded onto her phone. "Ah, I'll stay up here for a while, I've got a little time."

He sat beside her, staring straight ahead through the glass wall overlooking the street below, watching the people milling about, catching her in the periphery of his vision every now and then. She absently brushed her brunette straight shoulder-length hair away from the side of her face with one hand, drawing his eye right to her. He'd forgotten just how strikingly beautiful she was. She looked at him and he quickly looked away, sure he was probably blushing.

"What's up?" she asked.

"Oh, uh, not much. Just bored. You?"

"Much the same!" Her jubilant laugh made his heart flutter. "Now, what were we talking about last time? Oh yeah! Have you decided what you want to do with your life yet? You know, you really should go to university."

"I don't know... maybe I should... I just wish I knew what my calling was." He didn't tell her that he lacked the motivation and inclination to look for something else; he was contented enough now that he'd settled into a groove here. After all, he was earning enough money to get by, the job had plenty of downtime in which he could strive to perfect his art, it was near and handy, and he would eventually earn even more if one of the two team leaders would ever leave. He'd proven himself to Desra by filling in for them in their absence more than enough times to be a shoo-in, but he'd lacked the foresight to realise that, with the gradual attrition of Sendura, this wouldn't last forever, or that he'd quickly grow sick of it if it did. It never occurred to him to ask Desra whether she was actually happy in her job.

It was strange the effect talking to Kess had on him; he never thought about what he was going to do in the future until she brought it up, like she snapped him out of some kind of trance.

"Well, you need to do *something*, and soon, or life will pass you by and you'll regret it," she told him.

How right she'd been; if only he'd listened. But whenever she spoke, he was too busy admiring her beautiful hazel eyes. All he wanted to do was kiss her. Jeez, why did he have to be so pathetic? If only he'd had the courage to ask her out, who knows how different his life could have been?

"Once I pass my course there's no way I'm sticking around here," she told him. "I've seen way too many people spend years of their lives earning qualifications only to waste the effort by taking menial jobs. Worse yet is to never try. Don't waste your life, Jerin."

He didn't realise how much she cared. "I wish it was that simple," he sighed.

"So make it simple. You're a smart guy, but that can be bad as well as good. You over-think things. Don't."

"But raw intellect is worthless without a stupid piece of paper to say I can do a given job," he despaired. "It just seems to make me more aware of what a fuck-up I've made of my life."

"So fix it. Go get that piece of paper. The time will pass whether you do anything or not, so you have to ask yourself: when you look back in five years, would you rather feel proud of accomplishing something you once thought impossible, or ashamed that you never tried?"

He broke his gaze away, looking pensively at the floor. "You're right, I just have no idea *how*…"

"I'm sure you can find a way. Use your intellect for good," she urged him. "I know you're a pretty good artist, but it's nigh impossible to earn money doing that, and even then it's hardly a comfortable living. And it's such a competitive industry. A good mate of mine is a really great artist, and he's done quite a few high-profile jobs over the last year, yet he practically lives hand-to-mouth."

Jerin said nothing. He knew she was right; art was his crutch, his excuse for never trying to pursue anything harder. It was his escape into a fantasy world, nothing more, yet it made him happy. He was far too passive for him to even contemplate trying to competing with a million other artists; though he didn't doubt many weren't up to his level, he knew more than a few would humble him well and truly.

"You pick up anything you try with such ease," she continued. "You have a very scientific mind. Pick a course and follow it."

"The problem is I don't even know what I really want to do, or how to even go about finding the kind of job I could be happy with," he confessed.

"You'll never know if you don't try. Stop making excuses, Jerin. If you want to study art, go to uni and do it."

He snorted a short laugh. "I did study art a couple of years ago, but I dropped out after a few months when I became disillusioned."

"Why was that?"

"I wanted to explore and develop my own distinct style, but they wanted me to do everything *their* way."

"Oh. I can see why that would be so frustrating. Why didn't you try something else?"

"I guess I crashed, and... started working here."

"The only ones who work here full time are the ones who have given up on themselves."

Like me, Jerin considered. When they had lived together and had a few drinks, either at home or down the Jester, a rather drunken Kol had often spoken of picking up a part-time university course to put his life back on track. What ever happened to that?

Kess stood, suddenly adorned in chef's whites. "I have to go get on with my life. Take care, Jerin."

He watched silently as she descended the stairs, never to return. He stood up and crossed over to the chrome railings, watching her walk down the street, when he noticed someone leaning beside him. Jerin glanced to his side to see it was Ric, seemingly having appeared out of thin air. They exchanged nodded greetings.

Ric had gone through the rigmarole of further education. If anyone could tell Jerin the best way to go about it, it was him.

"Ric, how did you afford to go to uni?"

"I struggled," he confessed. "I took out a student loan, back when I was young and dumb enough to think it would change my life."

"So why didn't it? If you spent all those years getting

a degree in filmmaking, why haven't you done anything with it?"

Jerin expected Ric to offer a typically flippant reply before answering such a delicate question, especially one asked in such a blunt manner, surprised when he sighed deflatedly. Ric averted his gaze, never making eye contact when he spoke seriously. "Look, as long as I earn less than twenty grand a year, I never have to repay a penny of my loan. If I move to Solaria, if I'm really lucky I might be able to get a job working on a film set, but even with my degree I'd likely have to start at the bottom and work my way up. I might earn twenty-five grand a year doing that, but the cost of living and loan repayments would bankrupt me in less than a month. I'd need at least fifty grand to make a reasonably comfortable living, and that's highly unlikely. Contrary to what many people think, people in the film industry have to work for a living. I mean, have you seen how expensive everything is in Solaria? A sandwich that costs three silvan here costs eight over there. I'd be broke within a month. It just isn't worth it. For every big-shot director, there are a hundred washing cars just to make ends meet."

"So it was nothing more than a waste of time and effort?"

"Yeah, but whatever, right?" That was more the kind of response Jerin had expected.

With this knowledge, Jerin was even more conflicted; did he accept the life of mediocrity that lay before him, or delude himself into believing he could do better? Was Kess simply naïve, or did she have what Jerin lacked: loving, supportive parents who sacrificed their own comfort to give her a better chance? He never got the chance to ask, but that was the only way for someone like him to stand a real chance at self-betterment.

The best in life, it seemed, was meant for the wealthy, who had spent their lives creating a system that favoured only them, and shat all over everyone else.

The best things in life are free... my arse!

*

Juli dreamed of Jerin sitting on the sofa in their tiny flat watching HV. As she neared him he glanced up at her, a strangely demonic look about him. His short brown hair turned black and his eyes glowed like a cat's. He regarded her with a cold, piercing glare reminiscent of the one she'd seen the last time they'd spoken.

"Why did you leave me?" she asked.

"Because you ruined my life." His tone was stone cold.

"I ruined *your* life? Before me, you didn't even *have* a life!" she yelled.

"I had a future. You took it away."

"Your future? What about *my* future? It was your fault we lost the house! You and your fucked-up head ruined my life!" she screamed.

"I suspected you resented me. You just didn't have the moxie to tell me while you had the chance."

"Yes, some days I did resent you… I just needed some time and space to myself!"

He stood and walked towards her. "So that's why you kept going to the city with Alezi, is it? You like keeping your little secrets, don't you?" He grabbed her collar and pulled off her clothes, revealing her skimpy strippers' outfit. "Like this tawdry little gem, surely your proudest moment. All that time spent climbing the corporate ladder, all those 'invested' hours away from home, and this is all you have to show for it."

She looked down at herself, feeling nothing but the deepest shame. Nothing she could say or do would make this better.

He turned away from her. "I left you because I can't even look at what you've become anymore."

With all her pent-up rage, she bellowed, "At least I did something besides sitting on my arse all day wallowing in self pity!"

Juli snapped awake on the sofa, the HV still on, that parasitic idea gnawing at her mind, twisting her thoughts into pure hatred.

He abandoned me... he chose *to leave me...*

She glanced at the mess adorning Jerin's sofa-side table, piled almost half a foot high. The whole place was littered with more of his junk than hers, but that could be remedied. She peeled off the stubborn coaster, stuck in place by the visible tea and coffee stains which had seeped through the annoyingly porous cork base, then glanced at the untidy stack of books beneath mounds of built-up dust and sighed. She wasn't exactly a neat freak, but she couldn't understand how he could ever let it get *this* bad. She unceremoniously swept the whole lot into the top of the nearby half-empty bin, along with the now-rock-hard cookies.

She got up and filled the kitchen sink with soapy water, in which she left the long-dirtied crockery and cutlery to soak while she noisily and agitatedly vacuumed the flat, not even caring if it was too early for the dick living overhead. She worked until she was hot, and too exhausted to feel rage's grip on her any longer.

When she was done she sat on the sofa, her gaze drawn, to the bin now filled with Jerin's crap. She spotted a lone sketchbook amongst it, and wondered how many secrets its many pages might harbour. What else had she missed in her blind haste?

She knelt beside the bin, and with slow determination she callously pawed through everything, carelessly discarding it on the floor around her until the carpet was only visible between islands of litter, becoming ever hotter under the collar, pausing to cool down and survey all that she had scattered.

Wrinkled novels and reference books, a few movies, the odd squiggle on a loose sheet he'd likely torn from his sketchbook. It was all trash. None of it helped.

She glanced at the bookshelves heaving with her work folders and his art books. *What a waste of money...*

Her eyes darted around the room as she wondered where to look next. It was suddenly so obvious. She headed to his desk, yanking the packed top drawer open so hard it almost fell to the floor, turning its entire contents onto the floor.

As she sifted through the ever-collapsing pile, she was filled with a sickening sense of dread at the prospect of clearing up all that remained after he had gone, which at the back of her mind seemed inevitable now. She dreaded the prospect of being alone more than anything else.

There were so many little things of his dotted around the flat; the essence of him was spread throughout every inch of that place. She needed to cleanse both the flat and her mind of it all.

She headed into the bedroom, spotting his phone on the bedside cabinet. She picked it up, intending to throw it at the wall, but something stopped her. She dropped it into her trouser pocket in case one of his friends called to ask where he was. *Like that'll happen.*

She opened the wardrobe, sweeping floor-wards the heap of stale-smelling clothes from atop the old board games that had all once been meant for a charity shop. She moved a few half-rolls of old wrapping paper, finally revealing the small dog-eared flattened boxes, audibly scraping them between the remaining clutter and the sides of the wardrobe as they stubbornly refused to budge, like a defiant child who didn't want to go somewhere.

She took four into the living room and made them up, running a length of thick brown parcel tape along their bottoms. She started by clearing the bookcase, kneeling beside it and taking an armful of Jerin's art books, calmly and carefully placing them into the first box.

She scoured the mess from his desk drawer next, carrying his dog-eared sketchbooks over to the sofa, sitting down and putting them away, taping the box closed and grabbing the next. *Considering how much shit he sold, there's a hell of a lot of his crap left.* She was so enrapt in her activities she didn't notice his phone slip out of her pocket, falling down the side of the sofa.

She placed video games, obsolete-format movies and

books into each remaining box as she came across them, unsure what she intended to do with it all as she sealed each filled box before pushing it aside and moving onto the next.

The things they had bought together had to go, along with all the trinkets she had wasted her hard-earned money on, and especially all the little nothings he had bought her that, at the time, had seemed so sweet. She could no longer bear to look at them.

How many of them had been bought out of genuine love? How many out of guilt, or a sense of routine? He was with her, so he had to buy her gifts. After all, that was one of the basic rules of relationships, right? It was so wasteful. They could have saved hundreds.

She boxed, tidied and cleaned for hours, until he was all packed away, as though he had never existed. She was sure every last thing was gone, then would find that one small thing she'd overlooked, and would begin the search all over again.

*

Jerin casually wandered around Hit Flix, not a care in the world, when he saw Purvil approach, greeting Jerin warmly with a friendly yet typically exaggerated cry of "Hey!" which Jerin returned in his typically faux-unenthusiastic manner. Purvil was holding an old-fashioned digital camera, which he preferred for its ease of use rather than the end result (which he maintained was meant to be slightly grainy anyway!)

Purvil asked Jerin to don his coat and gurn as he shuffled along like a brain dead drone as part of his latest home-movie project, to be uploaded to the then-fledgling *BestBuddies* social networking website.

Jerin complied, getting the laughs out between takes so as not to ruin the movie. Where else would they have had enough idle time to do something like this?

With that recorded, Purvil asked Jerin, "Can you film me?"

"Sure."

Purvil donned some dubious-looking cyclist gear, then began shuffling and groaning like a demented drone himself. Jerin fought hard not to shake the camera as he laughed.

Purvil reviewed the footage with a massive grin creeping across his tall face. "Awesome."

Next, Purvil produced two small black replica guns, changing their outfits to make them look like rogue-drone hunters, masking their faces in turn with a crudely wrapped-around scarf.

The finished video appeared instantly on Purvil's camera, Jerin unaware of the time-skip. They watched it in fits of hysterics. It had been edited so that they were shooting at themselves.

"That's awesome," Jerin drawled.

Jerin had been amazed by the positive online feedback upon the video's upload. It renewed his own desire to create, but once he sat down to do exactly that inspiration once more decided to go on vacation. He tried to relax his mind, to allow an idea to materialise organically, but nothing came, and once more he became disheartened. Not even a quick game of word association could jolt an idea from his lethargy-dulled mind.

Time jumped again, and he was taking up position behind the popcorn counter at the head of the small shop area filled with brightly-coloured bags of confectionary and inviting self-serve fizzy drink dispensers. The central focal point was the tall glass self-service dispenser filled with ever-stale sweet popcorn.

Confident that he would be doing very little work, he sat on the silver-taped black-topped stool, took his sketchbook from the cubbyhole beneath the counter, placed it atop his lap and began doodling whatever came to mind. Nothing amazing came out, but he soon had a series of circles that were beginning to form cartoon robots.

Just as he'd settled into a groove, an entourage of ten customers chose that precise moment to bother him, highly unusual for the time of day, each of the four who ordered choosing the most time-consuming foods imaginable: one portion of nachos with cheese sauce that had to be heated, accompanied by a generous dollop of salsa and jalapeños on the side, and three hotdogs that each had to be microwaved in turn, the token lone one on the rollers looking rather desiccated and unappetisingly wrinkled, having been on there all day.

The customers all groaned as they waited, three of Jerin's colleagues standing around the box office across the foyer, too engrossed in idle conversation to take any notice, let alone offer help. On his lonesome, Jerin dutifully finished preparing the dubious-quality snacks, took the extortionate amount of cash for them, then resumed his seat as the customers waddled off.

Jerin always likened working in the cinema to being a keeper in a human zoo, feeding and entertaining the animals, then cleaning up after them. One day, he even found a candy floss tub dumped in the corner of the toilets, empty but for a lone lump of faecal matter at the bottom. As much as it had disgusted him, it came as no surprise. He guessed he should be grateful the culprit didn't just shit on the auditorium floor. That wouldn't be a first.

Lucille suddenly appeared at the far end of the counter, obscured from customer view by a fibreboard divider, tucking her hair beneath one of the unflattering black peaked caps and donning her pointless below-the-waist apron before sitting beside Jerin, offering a quiet friendly greeting in her dulcet voice followed by her warm smile, which he returned.

They were both single, and he kept trying to work up the nerve to ask her out, but the fear stopped him every time.

The only previous time he'd asked a girl out, many years ago outside the school gates, a cute brunette named Darolane, she'd simply dismissed his request with, "Nah, you're alright," three simple words that would send a damaging shockwave to the very core of his near-non-existent confidence, ensuring it would take him years to summon enough courage to ask another girl out.

Lucille wasn't anything like that girl, and her appeal was deepened by her interests: movies, games, even comics. For a self-confessed nerd like Jerin, she was perfect. They talked all the time, but never about anything meaningful. The only time they'd gone out was as part of a group of six, when they'd ended up downing shots together. He and Lucille had wrapped their arms around one another's before sending each shot home. He'd considered giving one of his to her, hoping she would return the favour, but even with copious amounts of alcohol swilling around inside him he couldn't work up the moxie. He drank shot after shot in the hope that the next would grant him the courage he needed, and she kept up with him. It was remarkable neither of them succumbed to alcohol poisoning. She passed out, the two stronger lads in their party carrying her home while Kol passed out on some steps and he puked, the only time he'd drunk enough to do so.

Lucille looked at his fresh drawing and chuckled at the large woman with a feeding bag strapped before her huge mouth. "Who's that?"

"A woman who came in last week. She bought six bags of chocolates, all for herself."

"I like it!" she smiled, nodding enthusiastically. "You should send some of your pictures to a comic company!"

He remembered agreeing that it was a good idea, deciding to use it to start a portfolio, but despite her praise he never followed through on it.

Or had he missed something? Was she paying him a kindness because she liked him? He was so very bad at reading women. On a holiday he, Lucille and five other colleagues took to the cheapest part of Solaria a few months ago, a cute girl had splashed him in the pool at the resort, but he'd missed the hint spectacularly. Riccardo was determined never to let him hear the end of it. It wasn't Jerin's fault: these things never happened to him.

To hell with it, he thought, his voice trembling as he asked, "Luce, do you want to go out for a coffee sometime?" He couldn't look her in the eye as he spoke, but his shoulders felt so much lighter as the words finally left his lips.

"Like... a date?" she asked with such affable faux-innocence.

He chuckled nervously. "Yeah, I mean... if you're free sometime."

"I'm flattered." Was she blushing? "Sure! But only as friends, if that's okay?"

Shot down, but not heartbroken. It wasn't a surprise after her recent breakup with an ex-colleague. Jerin just wished she'd give him a chance... he wasn't like Klin. They could be so perfect together.

"Sure," he said, failing to sound cool.

"It's just, after things with Klin went wrong..."

"I understand."

"I just don't want to risk ruining another friendship."

"Luce, it's fine. Really."

She smiled at him and he did his best to smile back.

Klin had been obsessively possessive of her, demanding she cover up, insisting that her skin was for his eyes only. She wore a short skirt to work one day just to piss him off. Jerin remembered wishing Klin would piss her off enough to do that more often. Needless to say, she didn't stay with him long after that, and he left the cinema soon after.

Lucille suddenly vanished, replaced by Riccardo, who stood the other side of the counter, holding his trademark fruit smoothie from Café Jouran. This one was vibrant orange, probably faux-mango flavour. They were expensive, but Ric rarely had anything better to spend his money on. They weren't exactly light on calories either, which didn't help Ric's slightly bulky figure, but that didn't seem to bother him. Jerin envied that carefree existence, but suspected Ric's wisecracks were his way of dealing with all the crap life had thrown his way. Sometimes, you just have to laugh at the absurdity of it all.

Jerin leaned forwards, banging his head on the countertop lightly in an exaggerated expression of frustration.

"What's wrong with you?" Ric asked.

"I'm so tired of being lonely," Jerin sighed.

"Then why don't you find a girl and ask her out?"

"Because it isn't that easy, okay?"

"Why not? I never struggle and, well, look at me."

"Yeah, well, I guess confidence is a big part of it."

"Whatever." Typical Ric.

"Yeah, but you must know what to say... I'm just crap at it."

"Yeah... I heard Lucille shot you down," looking into his drink and playing with the straw.

"She told you about that? Great."

"Hey, don't sweat it. She said no to me too. It sucks, but I'll move on. Eventually."

"How do you cope with being single?"

"I go out occasionally, I just don't broadcast it."

"But how do you meet people?"

"You don't swim away when they splash you!"

"Thanks, mate. How very droll."

"Sorry, couldn't resist. Why don't you try a dating site?"

"Don't they cost money?"

"*Loveless Pyjahns* is free. Plenty of people use it. I've met several girls on there."

Jerin looked at Riccardo skeptically. "Any good ones?"

"A few."

"I don't want to end up meeting a load of berthas."

"What have you got to lose?"

Jerin nodded. "You have a point. Alright, you win. I'll look it up." Ric motioned to walk away, and Jerin quickly added, "Hey. Thanks."

"Don't mention it," Riccardo said as he casually sauntered off.

Jerin considered it. He wasn't sure he trusted these services, but Ric was right: what did he have to lose, except his misery? It was time to do something proactive.

*

Juli looked at all the boxes surrounding her, feeling more dolorous and pensive than ever. She dug her fingers deep into the hair at the base of her skull and slowly dragging them through her long locks, sighing in despair. If he loved her as much as he proclaimed, why was she so conspicuously absent in all that she saw?

Did he love someone else? Had he *ever* loved her?

She was startled by a sudden knock on the front door. Expecting it to be that abhorrent creep Nate, she sprung up and marched over to the door, ready to give him a piece of her mind, but upon violently wrenching it open she was greeted by a rather meek-looking Alezi.

"Hey, Ju. Can I come in?" she asked diffidently.

Juli paused for only a brief moment. "Sure."

Alezi stepped inside and entered the living room in silence, tentatively navigating the maze of boxes to sit on the sofa. Juli sat beside her. She had stood outside for a full ten minutes before knocking, wondering what to say, but it hadn't come to her. She'd hoped it might click once Juli answered, but it hadn't. She felt she had to say *something* just to break the increasingly tense, palpable silence.

"Juli, I'm sorry. I never meant to make you feel inadequate or pressured or…" she was fumbling, trying to feign acceptance of blame so they could just get past this.

Juli virtually whispered, "It wasn't all your fault, I should have said no… I was stupid to indulge in so much retail therapy."

"It's an easy mistake to make… you were going through so much, and I…" Alezi realised a simple truth. "I was too self-centred to pay it any mind." She looked her friend straight in the eyes. "I should have been a better friend. I really *am* sorry." Juli could see she meant it.

Without another word they spontaneously grabbed one another for a big, emotional hug.

"You don't need to be sorry. *I* was in the wrong, not you. I shouldn't have snapped," Juli replied. "It was my fault for constantly burying my head in the dirt. I'm sorry."

"I forgive you," Alezi told Juli with firm conviction.

"Really?" Juli asked in astonishment as she leaned back from the embrace, her hands still on Alezi's arms.

"Of course. That's what friends do, right?"

Juli smiled weakly for the first time since before Haikyo broke the dire news of Jerin's predicament to her.

"I guess. Thanks for not leaving me to rot in a pit of my own despair."

"You know, if you needed help, you shouldn't have been so stubborn when I asked. I'm always here for you, even when I'm away doing a photo shoot. All you have to do is pick up the phone."

Juli nodded. "I know… I'll try to remember that, I promise."

"Shall I put the kettle on?" Alezi offered, already heading to the kitchen in anticipation.

"Sure."

"Hang on, how come I always end up making the tea?" she asked as she filled the kettle and switched it on.

"Because you're just so good at it," Juli remarked.

"How can anyone be 'good' at making tea?" Alezi asked as she sat on the arm of the sofa for a moment.

"Oh, believe me, you should try the tea at the office sometime, it's *awful*. I didn't think it was possible."

"Who makes it so bad?"

"This young lad. I think his name's Doon. He's pretty new."

"And does this young lad have his eye on a particular girl?"

"Boy, does he! He follows Keresay around like a lost puppy."

"There you go then. He's too enamoured to pay any attention to the simple task of pouring hot water over a few teabags in mugs. He's probably too stupid to realise he's letting the water get hot enough to burn the leaves. Ruins the flavour."

"See, you're a veritable tea-making expert!" Juli exclaimed.

There was a brief pause, but not an awkward one, somewhat like wearing a comfortable old jumper that was too tatty to wear out and about, but perfect for the privacy of home.

"How are you coping?" Alezi asked in a serious tone, hoping to better convey her genuine concern.

"Nate is paid off," Juli announced.

"Glad to hear it," Alezi replied with a sigh. "But you know that isn't what I was talking about."

"I know," she sighed. "I don't know what to do with myself. I hate this. I hate to say it, but one way or another, I just wish it would be over."

"I know what you mean."

There was a long pause. Juli knew that there were a million comforting words Alezi could offer right now, but none of them would make a bit of difference.

"You can stay with me," Alezi offered. "If you need to. I could always use someone to feed Tabby when I'm away."

Juli nodded. "Thanks."

"Any time, any place." Alezi surveyed the boxes littering the room, deciding it was safe to stop ignoring them now. "So what is all this?"

"I had to do *something*, so I packed all of Jerin's junk away. I guess you're going to tell me I've gone too far, right?"

"Everyone reacts differently to shock. You just did what you felt you needed to. So, what now? If things go bad... are you going to throw it all away?"

"Like he threw our lives away? No. I'll donate most of it to charity. Someone might as well benefit from his selfishness, I guess."

"You're angry. I get it. Don't think of every moment you spent with him as a waste," Alezi pleaded. "He might yet recover. It happens. Then you two can figure out what comes next together."

Juli stared into the mid-distance and felt a cold sensation rising through her. She shuddered. "He won't recover," she said numbly. "Not from this." She didn't know what had drawn those words from her. It was as though they'd come out of their own accord. Was this how Jerin felt when he experienced his mysterious bouts of intuition?

Alezi moved in front of Juli, looking her in the eyes, placing her hands on her friend's shoulders. "Well whatever happens, he isn't gone yet."

A single tear flowed from Juli's right eye and down her cheek.

"What is it?"

"I just need to know that he loved me!"

Alezi took Juli in her arms as she erupted into a fountain of tears once more.

*

Jerin was reliving just another typically slow day at the nexus point that was Hit Flix. The place had been open for half an hour and there were two people in screen one, one in two and another in four, and not a soul in either three or five.

Kol sat in a chair behind the box office, staring derisively at his bank statement. He uttered a single syllable: "Shit."

"What's the matter?" Jerin asked from the swivel chair beside him, lazily rocking side to side hypnotically.

"Ah, my credit bill's due and I haven't got enough. So I'll be overdrawn again, and the bank will levy a charge of five silvan every day until payday. So by the time we finally get paid, I lose a load on the accrued charges, then don't have enough again come next month. And so the cycle continues."

"How much do you need?"

"Just fifty would be great. A hundred would be *fantastic*. I guess I should ask Desra about picking up some overtime."

Jerin shrugged. "I can loan it to you."

Kol paused, stunned, his gaze meeting Jerin's. "Really?"

"Why not? You'd do the same."

"Well yeah, but... are you sure?"

"I wouldn't offer if I wasn't."

"I really don't know what to say. Thanks! You're a lifesaver!"

"Hey, no worries. We can go to the bank at lunch."

"What would I do without you?" Kol rhetoricked.

"You'd be down a well without a ladder," Jerin laughed.

Jerin and Kol headed to the bank together and completed the loan, which had promptly been repaid the very next payday. As they were about to leave the bank, Jerin quickly stopped, putting an arm out to stop Kol taking another step. Without warning, a ladder fell sideways from out of sight, crashing with a loud bang followed by a clatter on the pavement.

Kol looked at Jerin in wide-eyed astonishment. "How the hell did you know that was going to happen?"

"I don't know... sometimes I just... *know*."

"Something told me you were going to stop... maybe I just read your body language."

"Maybe."

That incident made them closer friends, establishing a deeper, unspoken bond. Jerin refused to talk about it, no matter how much Kol asked, and Jerin never got drunk enough to bring it up himself.

Jerin returned his attention to the events replaying around him, watching as his younger self and Kol grabbed lunch from Burger Barn before heading back to Hit Flix, Kol treating Jerin as thanks for saving his bacon. Afterwards they still had time to spare, so Jerin suggested a quick glance in the VideoGame Emporium.

As Jerin glanced over shelves heaving with invitingly eye-catching boxes, an overwhelming urge to buy *something* took over him. He worked all the overtime he could since he had nothing better to do and had the cash to show for it, currently having close to a thousand silvan sitting in his account doing nothing, so why not? What good was money sitting in an account anyway?

Then he saw the Eclipse, a gargantuan games console he'd long had an eye on. It'd had a slow launch, but there were enough decent-looking exclusive games out for it now to make it a reasonably worthwhile purchase, and the price had dropped considerably, so he treated himself.

Back then, he could afford whatever took his fancy. Before he knew it, he had more games than he had time to play, and was so reckless he often bought anything of interest before it had a chance to drop in price, which most of his purchases typically did before he even got as far as unwrapping the cellophane.

If only he'd been wiser, he could've had thousands sitting in his account, easily enough to weather the worst of storms. Looking back now, he realised how addicted he'd become to the escapism offered by video games, but at the time he could find no other way to cope with the mundanity of existence. All those times he'd criticised Kol for the money he wasted on gunpowder; he felt like such a hypocrite. Juli had been so right to berate Jerin over it, but he'd been so blind all he'd told her was that she wouldn't understand. If only he'd had the imagination he thought he had, maybe he could have avoided each and every one of these short-sighted, short-term solutions and found a better way, side-stepping that whole financial trap in the first place.

'Living for today' could be a highly pernicious philosophy. Once money was spent, it was worthless. And none of it had changed the fact that something meaningful had continued to elude him. Looking back, he wondered whether he'd ever really expected material things to give him the same kind of happiness the love of a good woman undoubtedly would, but you couldn't miss something you'd never had. To have someone with whom he could share ideas and cuddle up to on the sofa... he had been too blind to see that the things that couldn't be bought were worth so much more than the things that could.

*

"Dammit, you've made my mascara run!" Alezi jested.

Juli pulled back, smiling through her veil of tears as she saw her friend's blue-hued cheeks. "I've got your shoulder wet too!"

Alezi looked at the dark patches on her green jumper. "Typical! This is dry-clean only!"

"Stop moaning and go make the tea," Juli ordered as she dropped to the floor amongst the boxes.

As Alezi stood, something caught her eye down the side of the sofa: a phone. Was it Jerin's? She picked it up to give it to Juli, spotting her looking from one box to another, and decided that perhaps now might not be the best time. She slipped it into her pocket for safekeeping.

Juli opened the box to her left and spotted a sketchbook she'd missed in her packing haste. Though it was Jerin's most recent, the spine was dated just after his operation.

She opened it and was shocked at how child-like his first post-op pictures were. As she flipped through the pages she saw gradual improvement, but felt that perhaps she finally understood why he had always been so frustrated. She never realised how important his art was to him. Alezi wasn't the only one who was blinded by her own concerns.

Juli looked at picture after picture until she froze on one of a crudely-drawn girl she didn't recognise.

Alezi returned from the kitchen with two steaming mugs, spotting Juli staring in silence at the picture. "What's wrong?"

"Who the hell is *she*!?" she demanded as though Alezi should know as she aimed the page at her.

Alezi studied the image intently. "It's a bit crude, but..." she leaned in closely, as if studying every line. "It kind of looks like you."

"It *isn't* me," Juli insisted exasperatedly. "*Who is she?*"

"Does it really matter? Just because he drew a picture of a pretty girl, it doesn't mean he loves you any less."

Juli stared at it for a moment. Was she being obsessive now? "Maybe you're right... I guess..." she put the book down and took her tea from Alezi, who sat on the edge of the sofa.

"How many times have you thought another bloke was alright-looking since you two got together?"

Juli squirmed. "Only once or twice..."

"There you go then. Don't admonish him for something you do. Not every picture he draws of a girl has to be an indicator of some secret desire."

Juli said nothing, staring at the shimmering reflection in her tea. "Jerin knew about Sirens."

"What? How? Surely you didn't tell him?"

She shook her head. "I never told him. I hid the outfit, but... he told me once he sometimes *saw* things, like he was psychic. I was always a little skeptical, but..."

"It might just be that it was the logical conclusion," Alezi suggested. "He knew of your past, knew you were still sexy, and you handed him an envelope of money. If you'd paid Nate yourself, perhaps Jerin would have been none the wiser."

"I don't know," Juli replied. "That night, it was like I was dancing for him... and with that pink stuff, it was like I got some sort of weird psyche-feedback or something." She decided not to mention the dream where he had asked her to look in his top drawer, which had escaped her until now.

Alezi said no more on the psychic issue. As they drank their tea, she asked, "Where did you find all these boxes?"

"We still had them from when we moved here. Jerin insisted we kept them for when we moved on again. I would have thrown them away ages ago."

"I guess he never gave up hope."

Juli's head drooped sombrely. "He hated admitting defeat."

"This can't be good for your mental health. You need to give it some time."

"We've been together for seven years. How did I not see this coming? I feel like I never knew him." Tears of despair once more broke through the dam of numbness.

Alezi cast her mug aside and sat on the floor beside Juli, wrapping her arm around her. "People don't tell each other every little thing. You each have your own lives. He probably didn't know himself. Sometimes, things just... get too much. Think about the things you've done. Did Jerin know every little thing about you?"

Juli nodded, conceding the point. "I just need to find that sign..."

Alezi sat beside her, picking two books from the open box, handing one to Juli. "Well, there are a lot of books here. It can't take that long to find one little thing I guess. Let's see if we can find the real him buried in one of these, shall we?"

Juli nodded, taking one of the books.

As they flicked through image after image, Alezi added, "Just remember, the creative process is very esoteric."

Juli raised a silent eyebrow that couldn't be ignored.

Alezi barked, "What?"

"It's just... I never thought I'd hear you say a word like 'esoteric'!"

"People surprise you sometimes," Alezi shrugged.

"Ain't that the truth."

"You've thrown me off now... where was I?... oh yeah; sometimes art may give you a window into the soul of its creator, but that's not to say that it necessarily *means* anything. Some of it is just whimsical." She fixed Juli with an unblinking, steely gaze. "Don't read meaning into something that might not be there."

"But how will I know the meaningful from the not? How do you decipher this stuff?"

"I don't know. I know it's hard, but try to remain objective and I'm sure we'll figure it out."

Juli put her book down and reached into the box, pulling out another. "This is his oldest one. They all have years on the spine."

Alezi glanced at the spine of hers, figuring it was somewhere in the middle, placing it aside. She took the book Juli was holding and opened it, revealing a full-page collage of ink sketches, some drawn all in red, some in black, some in blue, the basis of each image clearly defined.

"It's so *intricate*," Alezi cooed. "All that detail… it must have taken ages."

"He spent years adding to that," Juli remembered. "Whenever he was bored, he just built and built until the page was full."

Alezi flipped through the pages one at a time, past pencil concept images, fully-coloured ones and a few more ink ones.

"There's nothing helpful there," Juli noted.

Alezi came to the last page. "There's this." She tapped the delicately-drawn portrait of Juli. "This was drawn with love."

Juli remembered the first and only time she had previously seen it, when he'd left the book on his desk when he departed for work. Many mixed feeling stirred within her, a fresh pang of pain permeating her heart. She slammed the book shut. "Seven years ago!" It came out more abruptly than she'd meant.

"But it proves that he *does* love you. Surely that was the kind of thing you were looking for?"

"Of course he loved me when we first got together! We had sex nearly every night, it was only natural. I need to find something more recent." She put the book to one side and picked up the next. "Keep looking."

"Did he draw many pictures of you?"

"I guess we'll find out. He never talked about his art unless I asked, and even then he never said much. He was always so self-conscious."

Alezi began flipping through the next book. "Does he have any books before these?"

"Not that I know of."

Alezi said nothing, smirking wryly.

"What?" Juli asked, spotting the smile.

"It's just that it's kind of sweet."

Juli's brow furrowed in confusion. "How is that 'sweet'?"

"It's like it's his way of saying his life didn't start until he met you."

Juli turned her gaze from Alezi, looking through the pages. Maybe Alezi was right.

"Who is this?" Alezi asked.

Juli looked at the young woman, depicted as a demonic succubus surrounded by corpses lying in pools of blood, her expression the epitome of stoicism. "Oh, I remember her. Remy." She said the name with the air of disdain one might use when saying *shit*.

"Did he love her?"

Juli shook her head assuredly. "No."

"How can you be so sure?"

"It's a long story."

"I've got time."

And so Juli told the long story and Alezi listened intently, hanging on her every word.

*

Jerin arrived home at the tiny flat he shared with Kol and Jalzon. It was rather crowded when they were all there at once, but when those two were out doing who-knows-what it was almost unbearably quiet. Privacy was Jerin's friend today though. He took advantage of it by registering on *Loveless Pyjahns*, a venture that quickly bore unexpected fruit: two prospective ladies replied to his advances, the anonymity of the online environment imbuing him with enough courage to ask out a pretty girl called Remy. She was a couple of years younger than he, not quite out of her teens.

Jerin was so exhilarated when she accepted his request to meet up that he didn't even mind clearing the overflowing sink of the dirtied pots and pans and the cluttered counter of plates and dishes from the curry Kol and Jalzon had made the previous night, which Jerin had missed out on due to his working late. It was a rare night that Kol got off without him; their shifts were paired, but Kol had taken a week's holiday to watch some motor sports event Jerin didn't mind missing out on. It was the hardened-froth-coated mugs Jerin minded... was it *really* so hard to rinse them out?

Jerin wasn't usually in the habit of cleaning up their mess, but he was buzzing with adrenaline and needed an outlet. Every once in a while he'd stop, check his messages, find one from her, and reply excitedly. He felt like a schoolboy again.

A few days later he was approaching their rendezvous point, watching her nervously fiddling with her fingers as she came into sight beneath a lamp's light after rounding a corner. Nerves made his heart pound so hard he thought it might break through his ribcage at any moment. She was quite short and very petite, endearingly bearing the uncertainty of her youthful inexperience, warily stopping in her tracks as they stood only a few feet apart.

She wore a dark green big-buttoned coat with a grey faux-fur lining circling her head on that chilly darkening day, neither of them knowing what to say. He soon discovered that the confidence he'd amassed behind a screen of anonymity didn't extend beyond the online realm.

"Thanks for coming," he finally said quietly.

"I almost didn't," she said so quietly he had to strain his ears to hear, without even a hint of a smile tugging at her lips.

Though she wasn't much younger than him physically, it would soon transpire that there was an insurmountable age gap maturity-wise; many of her mannerisms were still so child-like, and not in an endearing way. She often displayed almost unbelievable levels of naïvety, insecurity and indecisiveness, traits he should have recognised as warning signs, but he was too excited to notice them.

"Sorry I'm a little late," she said.

"It's alright."

"It took me ages to park… I only passed my test a few weeks ago. I'm crap at reverse parking. I had to call my friend Juan for help."

Ah yes, her soon-to-be-infamous friend and colleague Juan, who had so heroically driven across the city to come to her aid. He knew better now, and this revelation had made him feel rather uneasy at the time too. After all, what kind of man did such a thing for a girl he hardly knew? *Only one who wants to get into her knickers,* he thought. So annoyed would he become with this older man intruding in their fledgling relationship that Jerin would come to refer to him derogatorily as 'Juarez', which Remy absolutely despised.

In the back of his mind, younger Jerin couldn't fight the feeling that this man was to become Remy's partner, despite her protests to the contrary.

Though he didn't want to seem a cheapskate, something about that revelation kept him from investing too heavily in their first 'date' (she insisted it was just a 'meeting'), so they went to Hit Flix to see a (free) movie. It wasn't a very good movie, but he hadn't expected to see much of it, but Remy had maintained her aloof demeanour throughout every attempt at getting her attention, even throwing off his arm after the old yawn-and-stretch, after which they sat and watched the rest of the film in a somewhat contemptuous silence. Despite the heat in the cinema she never so much as unbuttoned her coat, the skin of her hands and face all that she ever revealed. *Now there's an ice queen if ever I saw one,* his older self thought.

Despite this, he somehow became besotted with her. Perhaps it was just the idea of finally being with someone. Either way, when he burst into work the next day he had an enormous smile on his face, proudly declaring to his friends and colleagues: "I have a girlfriend!"

The two of them walked hand in hand through the neon-lit funfair in north-east Darina, the many spinning rides so wonderfully colourful and radiant in the cold darkness. Remy suddenly took her fingerless-gloved hand away from Jerin's to scratch an itch before placing her hands in her pockets. He glanced at her out of the periphery of his vision, his attention drawn to the multi-coloured scarf trailing from her coat's collar, and begrudgingly did the same.

They didn't talk much; he had no idea what to say. Did she want to be with him or didn't she? They didn't seem to have much in common.

In an effort to thaw the rapidly thickening ice, he opened his wallet and bought them both some lunch. She begrudgingly accepted, but insisted on spending her own money in the arcade, expecting him to do the same, reluctant to give him so much as a single coin, forcing him to break a note, as though in retribution for his first-date reluctance to invest in her.

He found a soft toy grabber machine, surprising himself by easily winning a *Fuzzy Bear*, which he didn't even hesitate to hand over to her.

A faint smile tugged at the corners of her mouth; it was the first and last time he would see it, and it actually suited her quite well, but when he complimented how beautiful it made her look, the smile promptly melted away.

After a boring ride in the tea-cups (everything else was far too intimidating for her, though he was a tad wary of the funfair's notorious safety record), they decided to get away from the discord, heading to a near-desolate park littered with fairground trash, more joining it as a small group of teenagers passed through, eating burgers and drinking illegally obtained alcohol as they sang merrily into the night. Jerin and Remy sat on a crumbling stone wall a safe distance behind them, staring at nothing in particular, waiting for the idiots to complete their exit so they could enjoy some peace and quiet.

He desperately wanted to love her, if only to know how it felt, but could someone ever feel that way without that love being reciprocated? There had to be some way he could reach her.

"I had a good time tonight," he told her.

"Yeah."

He wasn't sure what that meant. Without pausing to think he added, "I think I want to kiss you."

"No." Stone cold.

"Why not? Don't you like me?"

"I'm not sure yet." What the hell did that mean?

"But I thought we were on a date?"

"I don't know."

He tried to remain calm, which wasn't easy. "What *do* you know?"

"I know that I like candy floss."

"Do you want me to go back and get you some?" he offered with genuine intent, but she said nothing. She was so damned impossible to read, and he wasn't any good at that as it was.

They sat there for quarter of an hour in complete silence.

Upon returning to Sendura, he thanked her for the date, which was followed by another long, uncomfortable silence.

"Can I at least kiss you goodnight?" he asked innocently.

She resisted initially but then nodded. He leaned forwards and kissed her so gently their lips barely touched. She made no effort to kiss him back; she didn't even purse her lips. When he pulled back he saw that her eyes were closed and she was as rigid as a statue. Tears were welling in her eyes.

What was so wrong with him that she didn't want to kiss him?

He decided not to say another word on the subject, bidding her goodbye and watching her drive off into the night in the fancy new hover-car her dad had bought her as a gift for passing her test.

At the time, Jerin had no idea how he was supposed to feel about any of this. With no basis for comparison he had no idea whether all women were like this or whether she was particularly awkward. He liked being able to say he was half of a whole, but what was the cost? Kol had kept his opinion of Remy to himself; was he simply allowing Jerin to make his own mistake, or had she got them all fooled? Maybe young Jerin's happiness eclipsed all other emotions, blinding him from the simple truth that it would be better to get out sooner rather than later. After all, what kind of girl told the man she was dating that she didn't find him attractive? And what kind of man would just let that slide? *Only a fool*, his older self thought, but that was the problem with hindsight: it was always crystal clear.

Perhaps if he invited her for lunch at the Onyx Dragoth he might finally break through her shell. Who knew, perhaps she might even relax enough to take her coat off.

They had quite a nice meal in the pub, but were destined to meet just once more afterwards. Before that came the most uncomfortable phone conversation Jerin would ever have.

"There's this guy at work," Remy told him.

"That guy who drove across the city to park your car?" he asked uneasily.

"Yeah," she said with an almost lovelorn sigh. "His name's Juan."

Jerin's silence said more than words ever could.

"He's always so nice to me. He asked me out."

"And you said no?"

"I said yes," she confessed.

That sinking feeling. It was the end, and he knew it.

"Why would you do that?" he asked, failing to mask his anger.

"He's just a friend, that's all."

She was so damned naïve. "Please don't go," Jerin pleaded.

"I'm going," she insisted.

"How old is he?" he asked, for some stupid reason.

"Thirty-eight," she said nonchalantly.

Thirty-eight! You're nineteen! There was nothing more he could say that wouldn't make it worse. He bade her farewell and hung up with aching despondency in his heart.

That evening at Hit Flix, he came downstairs to see her in the foyer, waiting for him. As he neared the end of his descent, the wall moved relative to his motion to reveal the interloper Juan standing beside her. Why would she do that?

'Juarez' extended his hand, and Jerin reluctantly shook it, knowing he should have snubbed him. He envisioned snapping the fugada's arm at the elbow, bending it backwards and gouging his eyes out with his own fingers.

Jerin could feel his friends closing in, but he knew the fight was worthless. Remy was worthless. If 'Juarez' wanted her, he could have her. At least Jerin could take some small solace in knowing it wasn't his fault.

He feigned geniality before watching her walk out of his life.

Kol asked if he was alright. Most of him wasn't, yet part of him was. At least the niggling pain caused by all the doubt was finally gone.

The next day, she had the audacity to phone him. He contemplated rejecting the call, but took it simply to say goodbye, no matter how much she didn't deserve such a polite send-off.

"Jerin?" There was a tremor in her voice.

"How was your date?" He mirrored her aloof tone

perfectly.

"It wasn't a date," Remy insisted unconvincingly.

"Oh? So what did you do?"

"We went to the Onyx Dragoth for lunch, then we went to the fair for a while," she told him. Her voice successfully conveyed a cold shrug.

The same things we did. How much salt do you want to rub into this wound? How can you not know what you're doing? "Sounds like a date to me."

"It wasn't."

He snorted a short nasal sigh. "We should stop seeing each other."

A pause, perhaps of disbelief. "Why?" with a quiet sob.

"You know why."

"But I don't want to lose you as a friend," she said, now sobbing fully.

"You betrayed my trust and acted like you didn't want me around, why would I want you as a friend? You'll end up with him, mark my words."

"No I won't!"

"Who are you trying to fool?"

Silence but for the sniffling of tears.

"Goodbye, Remy." Before she could say another word, he hung up. He could easily have thrown his phone in rage, but it would have been a pointless waste. She was neither worth the expense nor his tears. He didn't consider her an ex so much as a speed-bump on his road to love, though it was hard to ignore the pain. He'd heard the cliché many times in his life, but he knew for himself now that there really was no pain worse than that of a broken heart.

He wondered what to do now. His mind felt different suddenly, as light as it was before he stepped into the memory of Hit Flix. No matter how much he wished it, there was no changing his fate. *Which is kind of a shame... if ever anyone deserved the pain of mourning me, it was Remy.* Instead he'd ended up pulling Juli into his nightmare.

He hated feeling like this, but what he hated more was the sensation that was creeping up him once again. But it was different this time... there was no cold rush.

Only falling.

*

Juli's story had been longer than Alezi had expected, but she understood now why Jerin hadn't been keen on Remy, using his art to exaggerate her callousness. What was that girl's deal?

Just then, Juli's phone rang. Alezi answered it for her without hesitation.

"Hello, this is Mr Venura. Is Miss Tenzalin there?"

"This is her friend, Alezi. I can speak for her."

"Okay. That might be for the best, actually. Mr Endersul's condition has taken a turn for the worse. She should come in to see him. And she needs to be prepared."

Alezi didn't have to ask *prepared for what?* She glanced at Juli, who regarded her with widening, comprehending eyes, pools of darkest despair. She was sure her heart stopped for a moment.

Alezi asked quietly, "When should we come?"

"As soon as you can."

Alezi hung up and looked glumly at Juli, who looked at all the boxes. She had packed him away, and suddenly felt responsible for his deterioration. Perhaps if she had been more supportive, visited him more, perhaps he would have heard her... perhaps she could have aided his recovery and brought him back from whatever brink he had been on.

Now it might be too late.

All she could think in that moment was, *Shit, what have I done?*

O
-Starting Over-

Jerin fell through darkness, between visions, hearing disembodied voices come and go, echoed and distant as if through a tunnel. One became clear enough to understand, one that he'd never expected to hear ever again. One that was very unwelcome.

"You're an ungrateful brat, Jerin!"

Jerin closed his eyes. *Why did it have to be him?* "What do you want, Dad?" He spat the last word; as far as Jerin was concerned, he was his father in name only.

"A lot of good all that spanking did you. Didn't I tell you that you'd never amount to anything? Head always in the clouds. Didn't I tell you to pay attention to what you're doing? As if it wasn't enough that I saved you from being run over because you didn't look before crossing the street. Now look what you've gone and done!"

"It's no worse than what you did. It was your temper that got you killed in the first place!"

"Maybe it was, but at least I went down fighting. At least I died with honour."

"Honour? Honour! What honour is there in being stabbed by a drunk *you* decided to pick a fight with? What honour is there in leaving mum to raise me all by herself? I may have messed up, but at least I didn't go looking for trouble!"

"No. But you did lose your cool. And that was your failing."

"Maybe if you hadn't taught me to hate I could have been better!"

The voice vanished. Jerin suddenly saw Juli appear, a bright beacon amongst the darkness. She could only have been fifteen or sixteen. She was wearing a white blouse and black skirt with black tights. Her hair was plaited, and a navy jumper was folded over the back of her chair. The

world slowly appeared around her, as if painted in. She was leaning over a bed... someone was lying on it... her father.

He was connected to both a dialysis machine and a respirator, and was raggedly struggling for breath. He was so emaciated he looked older than sixty. A fine white stubble covered his chin and head. Tears were running down young Juli's face. Her mum watched from behind Juli, one hand over her mouth, her face twisted in anguish.

Juli's father nodded. Her mother switched off the life-support machine, and her father's weary eyes closed. His chest stopped rising. Juli stood and spun around, clutching herself to her mother, both of them bawling.

"This is what you're doing to her all over again," Jerin's father's voice said.

Jerin hung his head as the manifestation disappeared.

A clearer voice followed, something not said directly to him but near him, an overheard snippet of conversation.

"Is there any response?" a female voice asked. She sounded like the perky young nurse who had performed his cognitive tests after the operation all those years ago.

"None," Mr Venura said solemnly. "I don't understand... I thought it would work. But the damage is just too great."

"Should I contact Mr Endersul's partner?"

"No... it's best that I do it. It's my fault, after all."

Why is it your fault? What was in those pills? What did you give to me?

But there was only an indistinguishable background chatter that seemed to come and go, like someone tuning a radio.

After a moment, Jerin heard: "Falz will be fine. He's got a thick skull, and it isn't like he's got enough brains to damage anyway!" That sounded like Roz.

"Jerin will swing for this!" Marv. *What an arsehole.*

"Unlikely, I spoke to his consultant and he's prone to bouts of delirium. No judge would ever send him to jail."

Marv shouted something indecipherable, and the

sound faded away again as the cold rush subsided, returning him to where he left off.

*

Juli had gone into the bedroom to be alone after being sick again. Alezi could only imagine how she felt; even to her, it just didn't feel real. These things only happened to people in books and on HV shows. Alezi paced up and down the narrow passageway running up along the over-cluttered living room, wondering what she could say or do. Time was of the essence, and Juli would be even more inconsolable if they arrived too late.

Alezi suddenly remembered Jerin's phone in her pocket, realising that it held the key. She took it out. The moment she touched the screen she was greeted by a picture of Jerin and Juli smiling widely, the sides of their heads pressed together, the absolute picture of love and contentment. She attempted to navigate its unfamiliar menus to find his photo album.

She smiled upon seeing pictures of a mother quolling followed by a string of babies; a perfectly-timed snap of a skwarril round-housing a pyjahn; Juli laughing as she tried to catch trails of melting ice cream with her tongue before they reached her hand; Juli playfully sneering at him as he snapped her time and again, typically when she was least expecting it. There was even an ancient one of Juli lying on her bed with her now long-dead black cat, Tiggy. If Juli needed proof of Jerin's love for her, why hadn't she looked at his phone?

Then Alezi realised the truth: Juli wasn't looking for proof that he *did* love her, she was looking for proof that he *didn't*, perhaps so it might be okay to hate him, to ease the unbearable pain.

Alezi's heart broke as it finally dawned on her just what Juli was about to say goodbye to.

Everything.

Today was going to be beyond hard. The coming days, weeks and months would be harder still. Perhaps losing her contract was a good thing; it allowed her to be here when Juli needed her most. *Funny how things work out sometimes.* It was time for Alezi to be the friend she should have been all those years ago. She owed Juli that.

She slipped the phone back into her pocket and resumed pacing, heading towards the large window at the back of the room, staring out over the cracked-dirt lawn, when something caught her attention out of the periphery of her vision: a striking blue.

She turned towards it, spotting the corner of a small canvas poking from under a dust-sheet. She drew it back to be greeted by a wash of that pleasant blue surrounding several black and white splodges arranged into the ill-defined shape of a cat playing with a shoelace. It was so unfinished that the eyes were empty blue sockets.

"He started that before his operation," Juli noted, having approached so quietly Alezi hadn't even heard her, the muteness of her voice making her jump in the prevalent silence.

"Ju, crikey, you snuck up on me!" Alezi gasped.

"Sorry." She smiled weakly as she took hold of the picture for a closer look. "I wanted him to finish it, but I guess it was too painful after Nibbly died. Perhaps now they'll..." she couldn't find the courage to say *be together*. She wouldn't count him for dead while he still had a chance, however slim. She'd made that mistake with her dad.

Juli didn't know what to believe when it came to death. Would she one day see Jerin and her father again? There were countless tragic tales of lovers taking their own lives to be reunited with their deceased partners in the spirit realm. Juli was pretty sure Alezi wouldn't let that happen to her. That was why her friend was here... Alezi was every bit as frightened of losing her as Juli was of losing Jerin. When she was up to it, she would have to remember to thank Alezi.

There was a sudden heavy clunk from the flat above, and they looked up in unison.

"Is he always like that?" Alezi asked.

"Yep," Juli replied. She placed the canvas atop Jerin's desk, in plain sight. "Nate drove Jerin mad some days. The arsehole knew Jerin worked nights, but do you think he cared?"

"What a dick." She looked her friend in the eyes. "So... as much as I hate to ask this... are you ready?"

Juli cast her eyes down at the sickly green carpet. The finality of it was eating her from within, making her stomach churn again. It was even worse than the last time. "I'll never be ready."

"I know. Take a little longer to get your head together if you need to, but remember, we don't have all that much time."

Juli nodded silently, heading towards the bathroom again. She had no idea how she was going to get through this.

*

In the weeks following his escape from Remy's selfish love, Jerin had been lovelorn in a really bad way. Though there were plenty of other girls he could approach on *Loveless Pyjahns*, he just didn't feel up to starting over again so soon. Sure, the rush of finding a date would break him free of his depression, but if it went badly it would only plunge him deeper into it. It didn't feel like a risk worth taking, and with his luck the odds were stacked against him.

He replied to a short message from a girl called Julianos. She was just looking for a friend, nursing her own heartbreak after a similar failed attempt at finding love. Jerin had to admit that having someone to relate to helped a little, even through the typically limited and rather impersonal barrier of the internet.

During those typically quiet work days, Jerin found plenty of time to keep texting her on the sly, much to Patras's chagrin. On the current day he was revisiting, their cantankerous boss was squawking about the fact that he and Kol were sitting behind the box office doing nothing while Vyrus was noisily struggling with a banner on the balcony above. Since neither of them cared a jot about the selfish git, given that he acted like he owned the place, neither was willing to offer Vyrus help. It wasn't like he would have accepted it if they had.

Despite her vociferous criticisms about the laziness of many of her subordinates, Patras insisted on sitting behind the box office while Kol and Jerin built the display stand for the impending re-release of the original *Dark Nemesis* movie, *The Light Within*, an adaptation of the first novel, which, confusingly, was the second part of the second trilogy. Since this menial task would kill some time they decided to humour her rather than mention her hypocrisy, lest she have a full-blown psychotic episode, like the one she'd had when she found that video clip of her slipping over in the sweet shop.

Kol and Jerin took the half-metre wide, two-metre high, two-inch deep box into the spacious foyer and opened it up on the floor. They laid out all the pieces, then laughed until their faces hurt as they read the poorly-translated instructions: *inert tab a into slut b*.

As they did this one-man job between them, Jerin kept glancing over at the box office to ensure the large digital poster display was between him and Patras's line of sight before reading the next of Juli's many messages on his phone. He discreetly typed a shorthand reply to each, much as he abhorred text speak.

"Who's that?" Kol asked with an air of suspicion.

"Not Remy," Jerin assured him.

"Glad to hear it. Then who?"

"A girl called Julianos."

"From the same site?"

"Yeah."

"Bloody hell, you don't hang about do you? And you reckon I get all the girls…"

"It isn't like that. We're both working through some stuff… it just seemed easier to work through it together."

Kol nodded insincerely. "Right, sure. So she's single?"

"I guess so, but she's interested in some other bloke. She plans to ask him out."

"Mmm," Kol said, sounding defeatist. "Shame."

"I guess. Maybe it's for the best. I don't think I'm ready for all that again just yet. Besides, there are plenty of other girls out there. I'm sure I'll find someone when I'm ready."

"Yeah, no doubt."

When the stand was assembled in all its glory, Kol and Jerin stepped back to admire it.

"Another job well done," Kol beamed. "Even if I did do about ninety percent of the work!"

Jerin shrugged it off and they returned to sitting on their rear ends. There was nothing else pressing enough for Patras to moan at them about, so she retreated back to the managers' office without a word of thanks.

Over the next few days, Jerin and Juli continued to console one another over the failure of their respective relationships. She then revealed that the person she was interested in had spurned her advances.

'Nobody wants to go out with me,' she bemoaned.

'That's a shame,' he replied. 'Chin up, you'll meet someone. I'm sure you'll be very happy very soon,' he typed, having already told her about his occasional strong intuitions, most notably the incident with Kol and the falling ladder. Maybe she was humouring him, but he was just glad she didn't feel the need to call him a superstitious idiot. He knew he'd successfully predicted too many things over the years for it to be dismissed as simple coincidence.

'I hope you're right. I'm tired of being lonely. Some days I just feel like giving up. What do you see in your own future?'

He hadn't given it much thought, and tried to calm his mind. He didn't make a habit of trying to predict the future; when he did that, he could never be sure whether he was seeing the truth, what he wanted, or what he feared, and was frequently wrong. 'Hmm... I see a loving, lasting relationship… and for some reason, I see it happening soon.'

'If that's true, then I'm happy for you. I wish somebody wanted to go out with me' :'('

'Hey, do you want to go out for a drink?' he replied. 'It'd be nice to meet the person behind the countless messages!'

She sent him: ' :-) that'd be great! How about the Onyx Dragoth tomorrow night?'

The time was fine, but not that place.

'How about the Firebrand?' he replied, hoping he wouldn't need to elaborate.

'Okay.'

He realised he was grinning like an idiot as he put his phone away. Maybe it was nothing. Maybe it was everything.

*

Juli was startled so violently from her introspective staring-into-space by the clattering of the letterbox that her face slipped off her left fist, almost connecting with the arm of the sofa.

Alezi headed into the hallway to retrieve the item without a word, handing the lone letter to Juli upon her return. "It's for you."

Juli regarded her with an expression of confusion and took the envelope, tearing it open unenthusiastically, spotting the letter header GMM Ltd., expecting it to be from Marv berating Jerin for his absence. *That would be so like him*, she considered, ignoring a scrap of paper that fluttered to the floor as she pulled the letter out.

She scanned the letter somewhat dismissively.

"Dear Miss Tenzalin,

It is with great regret that I write this… *blah blah blah*… unfortunate circumstances… *get to the point*…

Upon starting his job at the Grid Module Maintenance plant, Jerin Endersul signed up to Terrengus Corporation's life insurance policy, naming you as sole beneficiary…" she skipped some more. "…our occupational health assessor has posthumously declared him unfit for work, *something about pension contributions, boring...* in the event of terminal illness or death... I hope this in some way helps alleviate your burden as your move on from this turbulent period, and wish both yourself and Jerin the very best of health.

Yours sincerely,

Lazarus Terrengus."

None of it sank in. Only later would she read the letter properly, but in the next moment she was stunned speechless as Alezi handed her the errant piece of paper: it was a cheque made out in her name for the sum of §85,000.

The money might make things easier, but without Jerin every penny of it was completely worthless.

*

Jerin had a strong niggling feeling during that long tram ride that tonight was going to go beyond friendship. He had prepared himself as if for a date: he was freshly washed and groomed, and dressed semi-smart in a short-sleeve dark grey shirt and black jeans. Formal shirts and polished shoes just weren't him.

His younger self fidgeted impatiently for the entire duration of that journey. Even now, spirit-Jerin remembered that anxiety well.

The Firebrand was situated almost directly between where he and Juli each lived, and was far enough from the city's core to avoid the loud throngs of drunken revellers they both abhorred.

He alighted sprightly at his destination, stomach in knots as he saw her for the first time, sitting on a bench just a short distance away. Her hands were sandwiched between her knees as she stared off to her right at who-knows-what, giving him time to admire her beautiful face and luxuriously long dark hair, which shined beneath the neon glow of the tram-stop sign overhead. Her gaze was suddenly on him, as though someone had flicked a light switch, and he continued to walk towards her slowly and automatically as their eyes met. He could easily get lost in those gorgeous deep brown pools; he loved the way the corners creased when she smiled.

He tried to smile back, but was far too awestruck to pull it off without making it goofily lopsided. She wore a maroon coat with big black buttons above a knee-length skirt that wasn't exactly flirty, but showed far more than he'd ever seen of Remy. Her hair was far longer too, cascading over her shoulders, finishing just above her very pert rear.

Juli rose to her feet but was quiet and meek, and for just a brief moment he was reminded of Remy's demure demeanour, but he put this down to first-meeting nerves. He cast that negative thought aside and offered a feeble, "Hey."

"Hey," she replied. "This is the first time I've actually met someone I've met online," she confessed. "I'm so nervous... I almost didn't come."

"I'm glad you did. You, uh... you're beautiful, by the way..." they both blushed.

"Thanks. You're not so bad yourself."

He smiled. "Shall we get going?"

They hesitated for a moment before heading to their destination in awkward silence side by side, each too shy to hold the other's hand.

The Firebrand was upmarket yet not too snobbish, busy but not bustling, the friendly atmosphere somewhat reminiscent of the Jester in its heyday. Jerin didn't lament being put off of the Dragoth: it was fast becoming the place of choice for loudmouthed yobs and idiots alike.

He hadn't been to the Firebrand in years; he'd forgotten how soothing the red and orange lighting was, atmospheric yet bright enough to see by. The music was pleasant and upbeat but not obnoxiously loud, certainly quiet enough to be able to enjoy intimate conversation in the privacy of the recessed booths that didn't make you feel completely isolated. It was *perfect*.

Juli took her coat off to reveal a very low-cut red top

beneath, offering him a more than ample view of her cleavage, which he could hardly take his eyes away from. This girl was hot, and she knew it.

Jerin offered to buy the drinks, and though Juli accepted, she insisted on returning the favour by ordering a large sharing plate of chilli cheese fries. They laughed like idiots as they made a complete mess of themselves consuming this repast, lifting the dripping fries over their gaping maws, using bundles of napkins to wipe the orange grease from their chins, both of them expressing their relief at not getting it all over their clothes.

Though Jerin was frequently stunned silent by her mesmerising beauty, when talk did come it did so naturally rather than having to be forced. They were like old friends catching up, chatting about everything and nothing. She imbued him with enough confidence for him to risk looking like a complete idiot by complimenting her sexy legs, and not only did she not take offence, but she stunned him by remarking on how good his rear looked in those jeans, even adding that it was just a shame the dark colour hid it so well.

What he had initially hoped would be a good few hours soon turned into one of the best nights of his life. Before he knew it, the small hours were upon them, him more intoxicated by lust than alcohol, though he daren't say so at that point. It made him realise what a waste of time Remy was, but perhaps her legacy was that she made him appreciate Juli more. Whatever did or didn't happen with Juli, she had given him a glimpse of what love could be.

They left the bar, deciding to give the nightclub a miss; Jerin was in no mood, and Juli claimed she wasn't either, though he didn't entirely believe her. Nevertheless, he was glad she chose to stay with him.

They walked down dark, deserted streets, arms hooked around the smalls of one another's backs. He stared into her eyes, smiling like a loon. He couldn't help it; in that moment a strangely vivid vision rushed into his head, and he knew he was looking at the girl he was meant to spend the rest of his life with.

Though he found it much easier to talk walking beside rather than sitting opposite her, he still didn't know what to say. He considered that may be the biggest stumbling block of why he struggled to talk to girls: the perennial problem of finding a suitable topic.

"So, this ESP of yours...?" Juli said, finally breaking the increasingly awkward silence.

"What about it?"

"Is it really real, or are you just pulling my leg?"

"I don't really know. It seems too much to be coincidence, but maybe it is. But I see things... just little flashes, glimpses... and then I see them later that same day, usually within a few hours. It happens so often I tend to forget what I've seen, but I get déjà vu all the time."

"Can you give me an example?"

"It's not something I'm particularly comfortable talking about. I don't even talk to my friends about it... it just sounds so stupid." He shook his head. "I don't even know why I mentioned it in the first place."

She looked at him with a faux-pouty expression. "*Please?*"

"Oh, alright. Just for you." She clapped happily. "One of my many part-time jobs before starting at Hit Flix was at the corp's audio-visual delivery warehouse in Sendura. I was opening the side of a van to put a forgotten holodisc player inside, and I instinctively reached a hand out and caught a set of HV bars that came sliding right out."

"Really? That's kinda cool."

He shrugged. "Maybe. But maybe I just knew the idiot who stacked the van would have done a bad job and I expected it."

"But if you caught it, part of your mind knew exactly where it was going to go. Have you ever foreseen any disasters or anything?"

"No. At least, not that I remember."

"My mum had a bad dream about a hover-tram crash

the night before that big one over in Bassara." Jerin didn't say anything. "I heard they never even cleaned the mess up. Someone even said there are still dead bodies trapped inside the mangled wreckage."

"I doubt it. People like to say such nonsense just because they have nothing else interesting to say."

"Maybe. But do you think my mum's dream was a vision too?"

"I couldn't possibly say."

Silence resumed as they walked ever onwards.

"Do you... want to come back to my place?" Juli asked Jerin demurely. "To sleep," she hastily added. "I can drive you home in the morning. My mum's away visiting some relative, so we'll have plenty of peace and quiet."

"That's very kind of you," he blushed. Should he mention his obvious lack of sleepwear?

During the journey in her passenger seat, he slowly became ever more nervous. He was sagacious enough to know that they wouldn't be getting much sleep that night, despite her claim, and he'd never been with a girl before. That he was here now was, frankly, a miracle. He felt that something didn't belong, and couldn't help but feel that something was *him*. That he was twenty and his only kiss was the botched attempt with Remy was testament to just how lame he already was, without her finding out just how terrible he was bound to be in the sack. He could imagine being kicked out of the house by a girl in fits of malevolent hysterics. But Juli wasn't the girl he pictured doing the kicking... that was what 'being with' Remy had done to his mind.

All he said during the entirety of the journey was, "I can't believe that a girl as gorgeous as you, a girl so beautiful she dances in her underwear for extra cash, could ever be single."

"That's not going to be a problem, is it?"

"Hey, you were doing that before I came into your life. I'm not going to tell you to change just for me. I want you to do whatever makes you happy. I just find it hard to believe you aren't already taken."

She replied, "Believe me, the kind of man who typically frequents strip bars tends not to be great boyfriend material."

He chose not to mention his incredulity over the idea that she would choose him. What was so special about *him*? How could he score a girl like her? He was a nobody...

He told himself to stop being so pessimistic. Juli wasn't like that. But she was *beautiful*, the kind that people wrote songs and poems about. There was *no way* she didn't have plenty of experience under her belt. He was suddenly very dubious about her claim that she only had a double bed because she liked to spread out. Not that he considered her a slut, despite the manner in which she supplemented her wages, which was kind of sexy in a way, since he was pretty sure he would soon be the only one who got to touch her where it counts... he tried to stop his racing mind.

Before long, they were parking outside her mum's vacant house, Juli leading him up the path and inside. The décor was a touch garish, but he mostly noticed how spacious it was compared to the pokey bedsit he lived in. He made a mental note to upgrade to a house one day.

Focus! There's a girl here to worry about!

Juli headed straight up the stairs, ascending in a surprisingly flirtatious fashion, slowly pulling down her skirt, casually dropping it on the stairs.

Jerin followed her up, quickly arriving at her bedroom. He stepped inside while she vanished into the bathroom. Her room smelled of soothing lavender, the walls were a calming lilac and her bed sheets were cream with bursts of purple flowers. A black cat was sleeping in the bottom corner of the bed, curled into a tight ball. Shelves were adorned with cat and delphino ornaments. Jerin approached the bed to fuss the cat. Tigger rolled onto his back so Jerin could rub his belly but soon grew agitated, taking a playful swipe at his botherer before vanishing downstairs.

Juli appeared in the doorway wearing a diaphanous white nightie over black underwear, looking far sexier than he could have imagined. He looked a right scruff in his boxers and T-shirt, which was what he was accustomed to wearing to sleep: when you lived with two other blokes, getting up to go for a pee in the buff wasn't the done thing.

She got into bed first and he nervously followed, ridiculously unsure what to do as he settled on the surprisingly soft double mattress beside her. Did he lie down facing away? towards her? Or would it be better to just lie on his back? Had she noticed the bulge in his boxers?

He just did what felt natural, fixedly staring into her eyes as she stared back into his, stupid grins etched upon their faces.

The dim light of her lamp was strangely romantic, somehow making her even more attractive, though he was pretty sure no light could make her look otherwise. He was such a nervous wreck, his eyes constantly flicking down to her pink-glossed lips. He might not have been any good at reading women, but it was plainly obvious even to him that she wanted him to plant his lips on hers.

Stop being such a wuss, he told himself. *All you have to do is lean forwards...*

Time and again he failed to muster the courage to simply kiss her. He gulped heavily, making her laugh in a very affable, jubilant way.

You are lying in bed opposite a beautiful girl that wants to kiss you. Just do it already! Hell, she wants to do a damn sight more than that. She won't care if you're a bit rubbish at it; you'll get better.

He kept expecting it all to go wrong; this sort of thing just didn't happen to him. Yet, against all odds, after what seemed like an eternity, she finally said, "So are you going to kiss me or what?"

No girl had ever made him so self-conscious before;

in her presence he felt so safe yet so afraid; so strong yet so weak.

"I want to," he admitted. "I'm just... *really* intimidated."

"Then you'll have to get over it," she shrugged.

What does that mean? "Couldn't *you* kiss *me*?"

"Now where's the fun in that?" she teased.

What am I supposed to do? He considered something he'd read somewhere years ago concerning the infinite cosmos and how infinitesimally insignificant the actions of a single person were, and was amazed to find that it helped. One day, everything would be gone, and all will have been for nothing.

And the majority of the fear just evaporated.

From somewhere deep inside, he finally summoned the courage, thrusting his lips towards hers, kissing her as passionately as he could manage. He was so, so bad at it, but her lips were so silkily smooth that he just couldn't stop. He let her guide him as she reached a hand around to the back of his head, pulling him to her, pushing her tongue into his mouth.

They pulled away panting frantically, his lower member throbbing with a desire he dare not mention.

"At long last!" she gasped happily.

"Sorry I was so bad..."

"I've had far worse. You'll get better," she winked.

Without warning, she reached into his boxers, slowly working it. "Well, someone's ready for something more!"

He froze, unsure what to say or do. Was he supposed to just lay there and enjoy it, or should he return the favour? She pulled down his boxers and went down on him, and he almost jumped in shock. It was a whole new echelon in sensual pleasure. That she was a little clumsy at it reassured him that she hadn't done it much before.

Just before he climaxed she stopped, looked him in the eyes and whispered, "I want you inside me."

Whoa, hold on, what just happened? If he was that bad at kissing, precisely how terrible was he going to be at sex? A nervous "Uh-huh" was all he could manage.

She opened her top drawer and took out a condom, placing it on him before removing her underwear, laying beside him completely naked.

After that came a heady whirlwind of passion, the likes of which he'd never expected. That he wasn't her first allowed her to teach him all he needed to know, giving him the time of his life while cementing his love for her forever.

Afterwards, he stared lovingly into her eyes and asked with childlike innocence, "So... do you want to be my girlfriend?"

She pretended to think about this while making an "umm..." sound. With the flash of a gleeful smile she declared, "Okay!"

They kissed some more to celebrate.

All he kept thinking to himself over and over was: *I have a girlfriend... an actual, real, genuinely loving girlfriend.*

As they finally prepared to sleep after a few more sweaty frantic bouts, they were once more staring stupidly into one another's eyes, their faces the epitome of contentment.

"Psst!" he said.

Her smiling face scrunched in confusion. "What?"

"I think I love you!"

She laughed. "Soppy bugger!"

"Perhaps... is that such a bad thing?"

"Hmm..." she teased, looking up as if giving it serious thought. "I suppose not, as long as you're my soppy bugger!" she chuckled.

"I'm all yours," he told her. "Forever and ever!"

They kissed over and over before cuddling closely, Juli falling asleep in Jerin's arms, breathing so softly. He lay awake for so very long just holding her, far too buzzed to sleep. The time until his next shift was growing ever shorter. He knew he'd pay for it the next day, but it was so worth it.

He felt like a far better man for being with her that night, knowing what he'd been missing out on, knowing that he didn't ever want to let it go.

In that moment, she was his and he was hers, and that was all that mattered.

*

Those early days seemed so long ago now, back when he and Juli had been so young and so stupidly in love. They walked down streets hand in hand; dressed up semi-smart when they went out just because they wanted to look good for one another. Jerin even took to shaving more regularly, despite the inconvenience, regular bleeding and minor skin blemishes that it resulted in.

She wore revealing clothes "for his eyes only", choosing tops that gave him an even bigger eyeful than on their first date when she sat opposite him in a fancy restaurant. When they went to the cinema she always wore a short skirt, placing one of his hands on one of her impossibly-smooth thighs.

He bought her flowers and chocolates for no reason.

They swam together, cycled together, ate together, slept together. No inconvenience could come between them.

They went out and danced all the time.

They would hear a song they both enjoyed, and it became *their* song.

They went to the cinema almost every week.

They would see a movie they both adored, and it became *their* movie.

They went to expensive restaurants at every opportunity.

When they found the dishes they enjoyed the most, they became *their* meals.

He learned the recipes and made them for her whenever he could. He'd never been much of a cook, but he gladly learned for her. As they ate, one song from a playlist of their music would play quietly in the background.

He knew in his heart that these would become the songs, films and foods that Juli would eventually become unable to enjoy ever again, each and every one bringing fresh pangs of pain and sorrow to her deeply scarred heart.

*

When Juli finally summoned enough courage to get going, Alezi convinced her to pack a few things so she could crash at her place until she was over the worst of it, promising her plenty of chick flicks, ice cream, chocolate and alcohol. Juli felt she'd be needing the last thing on that list most of all. She dared not hope... the fall would be far enough from here as it was.

As Juli carelessly shoved baggy tops and bottoms into her holdall, that niggling itch returned to the back of her mind. She couldn't ignore it; she *had* to know.

She sat on Jerin's side of the bed and opened his top drawer. Alezi watched in respectful silence as Juli sifted through swathes of loose papers, dead pens and other random odds and ends. Anything could get lost in all this clutter — it really was the perfect hiding place.

Amongst the loose papers were several screwed-up bank statements he'd printed off for some reason, dated a few months after his op. A cursory glance revealed the steep plunge his savings had taken, deepening her misery. If she found what she sought, she knew exactly what he'd been trying so desperately to save for.

She gasped as she found the small black box with a double-line of silver trim running around the opening. "I can't believe it... it really is here."

Alezi was baffled. "How did you know?"

"I saw it in a dream. You remember I told you Jerin said he had some kind of extrasensory perception... he came to me in a dream, and I didn't believe it was real, but he told me about this..." she trailed off, not wanting to wonder whether or not he knew of his impending fate. She held the box sideways between her palms, cherishing it as though it was the last remaining piece of him.

"What is it?" Alezi asked.

"We spoke of marriage in passing, but we never went into specifics... before I messed everything up, he was secretly saving for our wedding."

She raised the box to eye level and slowly peeled back the lid, seeing exactly what she had anticipated inside: an engagement ring. The moderate heart-shaped amethyst's ethereal glow stole her breath. It was set atop a white gold band. She choked, and tears ran down her cheeks. "It's beautiful." She took it out and placed it on her right ring finger.

"It's a perfect fit," Alezi gasped. "You really weren't kidding about ESP, were you?"

Juli didn't answer this rhetoric.

"Are you ready to get going?" Alezi asked.

Juli smiled unexpectedly, her heart a maelstrom of emotions. "Yes," she replied through tears as she admired the shining purple stone. "I think I finally am."

Before they left, she picked up all of her heaving folders of corporate crap, dumping them in the recycling bin outside.

*

Jerin returned to work the day after his night with Juli with a spring in his step and an ache in his crotch (but in a really good way).

He told Kol all about it, save for the most intimate details, and was glad to see that Kol was happy for him.

Jerin was truly happy for the first time in his entire life. He wondered how he'd lived before now, questioning whether, in fact, he *had*. Until now, life had been an endless struggle devoid of joy. Even the unnecessarily bitchy remarks from Vyrus and Lessani didn't bother him anymore. As far as he was concerned, they were bitter, twisted people who deserved to wallow in their own misery. Purvil and Lucille expressed their congratulations and most no one else uttered a word about it. The only downside was that the fevered anticipation of seeing Juli again made every working day feel unbearably long.

Whenever her mum was away, either visiting that

well-to-do relative in the ritzy city core or wooing new clients for her small-scale marketing firm, Juli would picked him up and take him back to her place for a night of private intimacy.

The fact that Jerin would eventually move out of the bedsit was inevitable, considering he already spent more time during those first few months at Juli's mum's place than his own. They only stayed at his when her mum was home, eager to meet at every opportunity. The only problem was that the bedsit was hardly an ideal location. His bed was too small to comfortably accommodate them both, meaning they had to sleep in the cramped space on the floor. At least they couldn't fall off of that, he guessed, but even worse were the paper-thin walls that allowed every little sound to pass through. In the prevalent silence of night, no matter how well Juli managed to stifle her moans, if they could hear Kol and Jalzon ruffling their duvets as they rolled over in bed, he was damned sure they could hear them.

Jerin knew Kol wouldn't resent him for moving out when the time came, though. The lease was almost up on the bedsit, and the rent was due to rise, so they'd already briefly discussed finding a new place anyway.

Jerin had forgotten about Remy entirely until, roughly two months into his new relationship, he received a text message from her out of the blue. He gave it a cursory glance — something about still wanting to be friends — then promptly deleted it.

Juli asked, "Who was that?"

He replied, "Nothing, junk text."

As their relationship continued to blossom, these unwelcome intrusions persisted. He stopped reading Remy's occasional messages after noticing she was sending the same ones again and again. She was completely oblivious to the strong hint given by his silence.

Yet the messages slowly started to arrive more frequently. After a week of multiple messages a day, he read one which mentioned that she was with her work colleague *Juan* now, prompting him to smile maliciously to himself. *I knew it!* But apparently 'Juarez' wasn't the kind of man who could help her get through a tough time in her life that Jerin really didn't care about. In his view there were convicted criminals more deserving of empathy than her.

He sent only one reply — 'I really don't care, leave me alone' — but she was undeterred.

As more messages continued to arrive, she annoyed him more and more, and Juli was becoming rather agitated too.

"Who keeps texting you, honey?" she asked.

"No one," he dismissed.

"*Who?*" she asked; not forcefully but insistently. "I can see it's bothering you, I just want to know who's annoying my man."

"Just my not-really-ex."

"You can be friends with your ex if you like, that's fine. I won't get jealous."

"It isn't like that. I don't *want* to be friends with her. She just won't leave me alone."

"What did she do to make you hate her?"

"Well, for a start, she was the complete antithesis of you. Dull, selfish, uncaring." He gave her an abridged account of the hell Remy had put him through.

"How could anyone do something like that?" Juli asked in blatant disgust.

"I have no idea. I guess I should thank her though."

"Yeah," Juli smiled. "Otherwise you wouldn't have found me."

They smiled, kissed, and the phone buzzed again. Before Jerin could delete the text, Juli took his phone, typing her own reply, which Jerin read before hitting 'send' himself.

'Jerin doesn't want to be friends with a heartless wench like you, so why don't you kindly fuck off and leave my man alone?'

They never heard from Remy again after that. As the widest smile imaginable slowly crept across Jerin's face, he assured Juli that she would have to be "punished severely" for such an impetuous act, promptly leading to several more bouts of energetic, sweaty lovemaking.

Jerin wondered whether new love was always fraught with difficulty. A few weeks after the Remy incident, Juli mysteriously began waking in the middle of the night, rolling over and frantically grabbing for him the way a child might reach for a teddy bear, burying her face in his chest, falling asleep in the comfort of his embrace.

When she would finally roll away again he would notice wet patches on his skin from her tears. He never asked what made her cry, figuring she'd tell him when she was ready, but she never did. As the weeks went on these occurrences became less frequent and the topic eventually vanished from his mind entirely, until now. Upon seeing a twenty-year-old Juli entering a decidedly different-looking Sirens, he had a feeling he was about to discover the why of them.

Juli rushed over to meet Alezi in the changing room, ignoring her comments about them wondering where she'd got to and being ready to send out a search party, enthusiastically telling her all about her "amazing new guy." Weirdly, Jerin could feel all of Juli's emotions; the dizzying joy and the sudden rush of guilt competing against one another. Her stomach was churning. Was it just that she'd been away for so long? No doubt Fox and Vix would let their annoyance over that be known the moment they saw her.

"It feels weird being here tonight, actually…" Juli quietly confessed to Alezi.

"Why? You've done this a thousand times."

"Yeah, but I've never had a boyfriend before."

"You've been with plenty of guys, Ju."

Juli's face was stricken with deep offence at the implication. "Thanks!"

"You know what I mean. What's so special about this

one?"

"He listens to me. Whenever I've had a bad day and I just need to vent, he just sits beside me and listens."

"Does he ever say anything back?"

She shrugged, "Sometimes."

"How do you know he isn't just zoning out?"

"I guess I don't, but does that matter?"

"I guess not. I can't wait to meet this guy. Anyone that can put a dopey smile like *that* on your face has got to be special."

Juli blushed. She cleared her mind and adopted her stage persona, 'Crystal', following Alezi out onto the floor. She heard a few regulars call out "Welcome back, Crystal!" and "We missed you!"

Juli took up position on her regular stage and began dancing seductively, performing a handstand before wrapping her legs around the cold pole, pulling herself upwards, towards a particularly eager fan who suddenly made a grab for her protruding chest. Despite her being a semi-regular, this was the first time this had happened to Juli. She reactively pulled back and smacked his hand, far harder than she'd meant to, and he jumped up and grabbed her right wrist firmly, leering at her menacingly. Somehow she managed not to lose her grip as she dispassionately regarded his vile leer upside down, the blood slowly rushing to her head.

"You owe me a lap dance, or I'll sue!"

The bar didn't have security in those days, Fox and Vix not yet having established a working relationship with the bikers, relying instead on the kindness of regulars to break up any trouble. Luckily for Juli, a few sprang into action, dragging this man away from her before making sure she was okay.

Juli stood up, feeling woozy. She apologised to Fox and said she didn't feel well and wanted to leave early. Fox nodded and said "See you next time," to which Juli replied, "I'm not sure there'll be a next time."

Vix overheard this and stepped over. "Hey, don't

sweat it, hon, we all get a scare once in a while. Just take a few nights to get over it. We need you for the nine-day night lineup… it just hasn't been the same without you. They missed you, you know," she said of the crowd. "They kept asking for you by name."

"I'm sorry, I don't think I can," Juli replied, tears welling in her eyes.

Alezi came over and said, "Crystal here has a boyfriend."

Fox and Vix exchanged knowing glances. What were they thinking, Jerin wondered? That it wasn't like her? That they all felt that way at first? That it wouldn't last? It didn't matter; they clearly didn't like it. Jerin expected one of them to remark that she hadn't been there for almost two months, then she ups and quits. Perhaps it was Juli's expectation that was going through his mind.

It was Alezi who said, "Whatever you decide, Ju, we're behind you."

Juli nodded weakly. "Thanks."

"Come on, let's get you home." Alezi finished early to walk with her. Jerin understood why Juli put up with her now.

But upon exiting the bar, they found that creep was waiting for them with two friends. "Oi, you an' me got unfinished business," he growled.

Alezi reached for her pepper spray, getting one of the lackeys in the eyes. He screamed in pain, covering his face with both hands as he fell sideways onto the floor of the dirt alley.

But the other creep sent Alezi flying with a backhand strike and the big one grabbed Juli while she was calling to Alezi to check if she was okay.

He took a large serrated knife out and held it to her throat, unzipping his trousers and pulling out his erect penis, demanding she suck him dry.

She sobbed as the other lackey held a knife to Alezi's throat. What choice did she have?

She did as bade, hating every excruciating second of

it. She'd never forget the disgusting way he grunted with pleasure. She keeled over and vomited afterwards as him and his friends walked away, laughing. She sat down and cried on the cold concrete while Alezi sat beside her, stroking her hair.

"It's okay, Ju… it's over now."

Jerin wondered where he'd been during all of this, then remembered he'd been working late that night. He'd wondered why Juli hadn't answered her phone when he'd finished. She always waited up to speak to him. Getting angry over that had led to their first fight, and he'd quickly bought her flowers as an apology afterwards. If only she'd spoken up… he guessed he was the comfort she needed to get over it, and he was glad to have been there for her, but he still wished she'd told him. Somewhere in the back of his mind, he thought he may have known all along… maybe that was the true reason he never wanted her to go back to that lurid, vile bar.

*

"I'll drive if you like," Alezi insisted as Juli unlocked the car.

After discovering the ring, Juli didn't think anything else could surprise her, yet this succeeded. "What?"

"You're not exactly in a fit state to drive at the moment."

"I didn't mean that. I was wondering when exactly you learned to drive?"

"When I was sixteen. I used to have a car, you know."

"You had it for what, a year? And when was the last time you even drove?"

Alezi considered this. "Uhm, eight or nine years ago?"

"That doesn't exactly leave me brimming with confidence!"

"Hey, the roads between here and the hospital are pretty quiet this time of day. Have some faith, okay?"

Juli hesitated for a moment. It *was* the best option, though she still had reservations. "Alright. I hereby give you the benefit of the doubt. But if I think you're unsafe, we stop and switch."

"Deal."

Juli put the holdall in the back, sat in the passenger seat and handed Alezi the key. "Press the round black button, wait for the red light to go out, then press the red button."

Alezi did as instructed, starting the car successfully first time, complete with its familiar violent judder and cloud of smoke. As they slowly set off, Alezi did her best to quickly familiarise herself with the positioning of the various levers, buttons and switches, none of which were in the same position as in the vehicle she briefly owned. She was having particular trouble with the old-fashioned manual gearbox, a true relic of bygone times.

During the long journey, Alezi felt the tension growing, and needed to say something to take their minds off of what lay ahead of them.

"Juli, do you remember when we first met?" Alezi rhetoricked, just to get Juli's mind in the right place: not necessarily a great idea considering it took her back to *Sirens*.

Juli simply made an "mm-hm" acknowledgement, thinking to herself about how ditzy Alezi had been back then, how it was a miracle they'd become friends at all, but aside from Vix and Fox, Alezi had been the only friendly girl in the bar.

"Well, back then, my mum thought I was some sort of secret genius," Alezi continued. This was the first time she had ever told anyone this little gem.

Alezi caught Juli's wrinkled brow of incredulity in the periphery of her vision as she barked a single "Ha!"

"Really," Alezi insisted. "I was going to university when we first met, at her insistence, studying advanced Darinian and math."

"I can't imagine you studying anything that taxing!"

"Yeah, well needless to say, I dropped out pretty sharpish. It took me ages to work up the courage to tell her. She deluded herself into believing I could become a bank director or a doctor overnight. Who knows, maybe I could have done more, but back then I was so sure of my looks that I never even tried."

"Were you really that naïve?"

"I guess I bought into the media lie that we can all grow up to be stars, just because one person says we can become whatever we want to be if we just believe. During my short stint at uni, I worked in a little corner café at weekends. I always wore short skirts, left the top few buttons of my shirt undone... amorous men were forever giving me generous tips and telling me I could be a model, so I blew my pitiful wages on photo sessions to build up a portfolio. I never saved a penny."

"But you were forever going to the most prestigious districts of Solaria for photo shoots..." Juli trailed off in bewildered astonishment.

"They were hell. Half a dozen catty women trapped in a tiny room together, squeezing into the most outlandishly flamboyant outfits imaginable... it doesn't exactly inspire confidence when your legs are being held up by a bitch who'd happily drop you on your face while you pose like a wheelbarrow for a ridiculous fetish website... it was bizarre and horrible all at once. Maybe if I'd hung in there I could have done okay, built up that portfolio, but I messed it up. I *always* mess it up."

"At least I'm not alone in that respect," Juli remarked, stunned. "I guess this explains why I've never seen any of your pictures!"

Alezi laughed. "I was always too afraid of what you might say if I told you! Most of my clothes and accessories were bought secondhand. Most models are too stuck-up to wear the same thing twice, and they don't really need the money, so I took advantage of that. I soon worked out which shops had the best stuff."

"I guess it's true that you never really know anyone." She realised something. "So when you said you got rid of your car because you didn't use it...?"

"I couldn't afford it," Alezi confessed. "Fuel, tax,

upkeep… travelling by tram is way cheaper. I was so stupid… all that money I wasted… I just didn't want to admit I was a failure."

"So you were just keeping up appearances?"

"Yeah, I guess. I know, I'm dumb…"

"Alezi, I never cared about any of that stuff. I'm not your friend because you wear flashy clothes. Actually, to be completely honest, I always kind of hated that about you. That and your damned fake posh accent."

"I know. I guess the reason I like you is that I don't feel I have to be the persona around you. I can relax, let my guard down. I can just be *me*. I almost forgot what that feels like."

"So that's why you were never a bitch around me the way you were around most of the other girls at Sirens."

"Yeah. I hated acting that way, but if you don't fight back those bitches will happily tear you apart. Believe me when I say you don't want to get to know them. After a while that abhorrent behaviour becomes second nature, and you're doing it without even trying."

"Unless, alone, they're not too bad… like they're putting on a persona to protect themselves," Juli suggested.

"Good point," Alezi conceded.

"That's it for the confessions though, right? You're not going to tell me that you used to be a man or anything, are you?"

Alezi burst out laughing. She'd once heard that comedy often blossomed during tragic moments, but never would have believed it had she not witnessed it herself.

Juli laughed at the sheer absurdity of it all. Alezi was many things, but more often than not she knew exactly what to say to lift Juli from a dour mood.

"I'm glad you're my friend," Juli told Alezi.

"Really?" Alezi sounded astonished, as though someone had just convinced her that cats were made of chocolate.

"Right now, I honestly don't know what I'd do without you."

"Thanks, Juli… that's the first time anyone's ever said that to me."

They pulled up outside the hospital. Alezi cut the engine, still gripping the wheel firmly, the pair of them staring up at the imposing building's many windows, gleaming brightly beneath the harsh barrier-shine.

Alezi looked at Juli, who smiled wanly before unclipping her seatbelt. Alezi did the same, watching Juli all the time, afraid her friend might pass out. They exited the car and approached the hospital's main entrance slowly in dread-filled silence.

*

For their one-year anniversary, Jerin and Juli went to their then-favourite restaurant, Katana. It wasn't too expensive or flashy, the food was always good, and the waiters and waitresses were always attentive and courteous.

Jerin watched as he and Juli sat on opposite sides of the table as the waiter placed their dishes before them — teriyaki-marinated phesan with noodles for Jerin, caman curry with rice for Juli. The waiter nodded, they thanked him, and he left them to tuck in.

As Jerin wound noodles around his fork, he spotted Juli looking at him with adoration. He stopped, loose noodles dangling from his fork. "What?"

"Nothing. I was just thinking about how much I love you. Is that a crime?"

"Maybe."

"Then perhaps you should lock me up?"

"…Maybe."

"And punish me for being a bad girl!"

"…"

She laughed at him; in the past year, this was the first time she had ever rendered him speechless.

"I've got a little bit of money saved," she deviated. "I've always dreamed of owning a house… once I found the right person to share it with…"

He quickly ate the noodles before they became cold; she had planted her fork into her mound of stodgy rice to break it up, but had yet to take a single bite. She was looking at him expectantly, and he had no idea what to say. She was smiling so beautifully.

It would mean he could finally move all of his old junk out of his mum's basement, but weren't houses extortionately expensive?

"Can we afford it?" he asked skeptically.

Her smile slowly melted away. "Why not? We easily earn enough…" her voice dropped very low, little more than a whisper, as she said, "unless you don't want to."

He reached over, placing his left hand on her right, hoping to reassure her. "I want to. I just want to be sure we can afford it before we blindly rush in and realise we've bitten off more than we can chew. Maybe we should take a little longer to save first?"

He knew he spent far too much and had become accustomed to it… but surely he could change his reckless spending habits for her? He needed to run the figures to be sure, but he knew it would be well worth it. He wanted it too, and why waste money on rent if they didn't need to?

"We'll sit down tomorrow and work it all out," he suggested.

She smiled weakly before looking down at her plate, eating in silence. She sniffed back a tear. He hated seeing her upset, but hated more that he was to blame. He wanted to say something to comfort her, but wasn't prepared to make promises he might not be able to keep.

He wished he could have lied to her just that once, just to see her smile.

As he looked at her forlorn face, everything faded to black.

*

Their footfalls echoed every step of the way along the endless cold corridors as they marched towards Jerin's room. Juli's grip on Alezi's hand tightened.

"Whatever happens, I'm here for you," Alezi

reminded her.

As they reached the door to the isolation ward, Juli was unable to catch her breath, beginning to hyperventilate.

Alezi rested her hands on her friend's shoulders and looked into her eyes. "Relax. Take deep breaths."

Alezi began to breathe with Juli synchronously, slowing down to coax her friend back to a normal rhythm. A tinge of a smile tugged at the corner of Juli's upper lip.

"What?" Alezi asked.

"You sound like you're in labour!"

Alezi allowed herself to laugh at this remark, then recomposed herself. "Are you sure you can do this?"

Juli looked over at the heavy windowless double doors, and drew several slow, deep breaths, holding them before slowly exhaling. She nodded. "I need to."

They held hands and slowly walked forwards in silence, their feet glided smoothly over the spotlessly clean floor which reflected the ceiling's fluorescent lights too effectively for Juli's liking, the oscillating pulses making her eyes hurt.

The silence was the worst part. It was unbearable. The doors whooshed open and they stepped inside, Juli once more drawn straight to Jerin's room.

The bandage had been replaced by a small patch of gauze, but he looked like he was being prepared for the morgue. His eyes had become dark, sunken sockets, and his hair was turning grey. He had become so emaciated in such a short time, and he looked impossibly old, like he was already dead. *Just like dad.* All of the equipment was gone, except the life-support machine.

Inside the room, Mr Venura was suited up all alone, administering a syringe of what was probably some kind of painkiller. He glanced up. "You made it just in time."

Alezi looked at Juli. "Do you want me to come in with you?"

Juli nodded. Tears welled in her eyes. Alezi took her hand and helped her suit up.

They entered the sterilisation chamber together, bearing the torturous wait with great difficulty.

Alezi glanced at Juli and saw she was beginning to sob already. She realised she was crying too.

She couldn't believe this was happening.

The inner door hissed open, but Juli couldn't move, all strength evaporating in an instant as the full impact of what was happening hit her.

This was it.

The end.

Nothing would ever be the same again.

Alezi looked at her through her own veil of tears and they hugged, crying on one another's shoulders while Mr Venura stood respectively silent, clasped hands hanging before him, head bowed.

Juli summoned what little strength she had, and they stepped into Jerin's room together for the last time.

"Jerin, I'm here," Juli said softly.

In his dark isolation, he heard her. He tried to speak, but his throat was too hoarse for the words to come out.

The world around him was growing ever more dark and cold, fading away.

He dropped to his knees and concentrated, summoning what little strength was left in him, reaching out to her.

She appeared before him in his room, but he could see her clearly this time. There were ill-defined shadows that he had no doubt were Alezi and Mr Venura, but all of his attention was on her. His mind's gaze penetrated the suit she wore and saw only her saddened beauty and the ring adorning her finger. He smiled as well as he could.

He felt her soft touch as she took his hand. She looked down at him forlornly. Mr Venura's countenance matched hers, tears rolling down his cheeks. He made no effort to reach under the mask to wipe them away.

"I love you, Jerin Endersul," she whispered, struggling to hold back the tears long enough to speak. "I should have listened to you more. Before we met, it was as if I'd never lived. I don't know what I'll do without you. Thank you for the time you gave me. I know now that you never stopped loving me." She paused for a moment to regain her composure. "I'll never forget you."

Part of him heard *I'll never forgive you.* If those words had crossed her mind, he wouldn't blame her one little bit. He loved her more than words could convey, and he had let her down.

With a final effort, he sent one last instruction through his withered body.

"He squeezed my hand!" Juli sobbed.

"His mind is riddled with tumours, I'm afraid that's just a reflex action," Mr Venura replied solemnly.

Juli nodded, still holding his hand as she spoke softly to Alezi.

"It was never about the finances," Juli said. "He didn't care about that. He cared about *me*. He only wished he could have spared me this pain... and I was too short-sighted to see it."

"I saw the photos from the park on his phone. He really did love you, Juli."

"I know."

Mr Venura looked down at Jerin's weary, wrinkled face, then looked up at Juli and Alezi. "It's time. He's suffered enough."

Juli nodded silently, staring at Jerin's closed eyes.

Mr Venura flicked the switch on the life-support machine, and Jerin's chest stopped rising, falling flat for the last time.

Juli gripped his hand tightly, tears flowing free as his face turned an ashen grey.

She turned to Alezi, throwing her arms around her, sobbing uncontrollably. Alezi held her tight, comforting her as well as she could, her own heart feeling every bit of Juli's unbearable pain.

Juli took off her helmet without a word of protest from Mr Venura, and leaned forwards, kissing Jerin on the lips, then the forehead. She stroked his hair.

"Your pain is over now. Sleep well."

With a glum look on his face, Mr Venura spoke quietly to one of the nurses outside, "Time of death… nine eighty-two, the thirty-third of the seventh."

Juli and Alezi exited the isolation room, took off their coveralls, and wandered in silence down the cold corridors together, never looking back.

*

Jerin felt the world darken and cool as all strength and life left him at last.

He felt her kiss him for the last time, and then she was gone. And he was alone. The room faded to black, and all that remained was that vivid image of the city falling from the sky. Flames licked at it, slowly consuming everything. He could have sworn he heard screaming. Then it crashed into a valley, and there was only silence.

After that, there were no more visions.

No more memories.

No more dreams.

No more pain.

-Epilogue-

Horran Venura waited while the phone rang and rang. His hands were shaking, his cheeks damp with tears.

Eventually, there was a *click* as it was answered. "Yes?"

"The results are in," Horran said as dispassionately as he could, which wasn't easy. Detachment had never been his forte.

"And?"

"The formula needs refining, but it is capable of what you said and more... much more than I'd anticipated. I'll send the full results over in the morning."

"Fantastic! And what of our little lab rat?"

That Vince would refer to Jerin in such a callous manner made Horran's hands shake with rage. "He passed away a few hours ago. Brain tumours."

"Pity. We can't have that. Begin running the simulations. Perhaps we'll be lucky enough to come across a few more test subjects soon. Good work, Horran. You'll go far."

Horran hung up, throwing the handset across the room in rage, watching it explode into a shower of plastarch shards, leaving a dent in the plaster of his office wall.

"Damn you, Vince," he cursed under his breath. "I'll see you burn for this."